Karen Preusse

ALL THE WAY HOME

ALL THE WAY HOME

Wendy Corsi Staub

PINNACLE BOOKS
KENSINGTON PUBLISHING CORP.
http://www.pinnaclebooks.com

PINNACLE BOOKS are published by

Kensington Publishing Corp.
850 Third Avenue
New York, NY 10022

Copyright © 1999 by Wendy Corsi Staub

Pinnacle and the P logo Reg. U.S. Pat. & TM Off.

Printed in the United States of America

ISBN 0-7394-1006-7

For my cherished new baby son,
Brody Alexander Staub

and, of course, for Mark-Daddy and big brother Morgan James,
with all my love

And heartfelt gratitude to my dear father-in-law, Leonard Staub,
for his incredibly generous gift:
a new computer that made researching and writing this book a pleasure!

PROLOGUE

Carleen Connolly is the third to disappear.

Rory realizes, after it has happened, that she has somehow, somewhere in the back of her mind, been expecting it all along—that perhaps she's always understood that one day she would wake up to find her older sister gone forever.

The thing is, she had pretty much figured on Carleen—reckless, impulsive Carleen—getting into a terrible accident with the Chevy, which she has been sneaking out of the garage at night for years, long before she actually turned sixteen and got her license. Whenever Rory heard the ominous wail of ambulance sirens from her bed at night, she would brace herself for a ringing phone or a knock on the door—for the imminent news that her sister was dead, that she'd gone and wrapped the Chevy around a pole or missed a curve out on winding Lakeshore Road.

Or maybe she had believed Carleen would run off with one of the older boys she was always seeing—elope to Maryland the way Mrs. Shilling's daughter, Diana, had a few years back.

Then again, Carleen might just leave home alone, on her own, headed for New York City a few hours south. How many times, after a screaming battle with their parents, had Carleen threatened to do just that? "I'm going to run away! You wait and see. I'm out of here!"

And Daddy would shout back, "You want to leave? Go ahead. See how far you get with no money and no high school diploma."

And Rory, when she had been young enough to think her sister was serious about leaving, would cry and beg Carleen not to run away. Because, even though there always seemed to be some kind of trouble when Carleen was around, the thought of life without her was depressing.

Well, now Carleen is gone.

And Rory's life isn't just depressing; it has turned into a nightmare.

Because her sister hasn't had an accident.

And she hasn't eloped, or run away.

Carleen has simply disappeared.

Just like the two teenaged girls before her.

Nice, wholesome girls who grew up here in Lake Charlotte, New York, a sleepy village in the foothills of the Adirondack Mountains, where people chat with each other from front porches and keep an eye on each other's children and leave their doors unlocked at night . . .

Until this summer.

Everything changed when the first girl vanished. Kirstin Stafford. Age thirteen. Never came home from an after-dinner bike ride around the lake on a hot June evening.

Then, a few weeks later, it was Allison Myers, a fifteen-year-old who disappeared from a Fourth of July picnic out at Point Cedar Park.

No trace of either girl was ever found.

Now there is Carleen Connolly, seventeen, whose mother found her canopy bed empty one morning in late July in the third-story bedroom of the big old house at 52 Hayes Street.

For years after, Rory Connolly will do a double take every time she sees a girl with long, straight black hair, or catches a whiff of Poison perfume, or hears a piercing, high-pitched whistle, the kind you make by sticking two fingers into your mouth.

Carleen had long, straight black hair.

Carleen wore Poison perfume.

Carleen used to whistle like that.

But Carleen is gone.

"She probably just ran away," Rory's next-door neighbor, Emily Anghardt, keeps saying reassuringly, her big brown eyes solemn and her voice, still retaining a hint of a southern accent, low and soothing. "You know how Carleen is."

Yes, Rory knows how Carleen is. Everyone in Lake Charlotte knows how Carleen Connolly is.

How she seemed like such a nice girl until she became a teenager, when she started smoking and drinking and got caught shoplifting beer at the A&P. How she disrespectfully calls her parents by their first names behind their backs and sometimes even to their faces, and how she brags about stealing money from her mother's purse, and how she curses and cuts classes and cheats her way through school.

What most people don't remember, though, is that Carleen has another side—a vulnerable side.

Carleen once came sobbing out of the woods carrying a rabbit whose leg had been bloodied and broken in a hunter's trap, and she insisted on paying for the veterinarian bill out of her allowance, then held the suffering animal in her lap while the vet put it out of its misery, stroking its matted fur as it heaved its last shuddering breath.

Carleen used to go over and play the piano for old Miss Prendergrast next door, and shovel her walk when it snowed, and of all the neighborhood children, only Carleen was allowed to pick the raspberries from the briars that grew along Mrs. Prendergrast's back fence.

And sometimes—long after Carleen had outgrown the Barbie dolls she and Rory had always shared and she had taken to making fun of her little sister's "babyish games" whenever anyone else was in earshot—she would pop into Rory's bedroom and play Barbies with her, making her swear not to tell a soul.

Rory never had.

Rory knows something else about her big sister that she wouldn't dare tell anyone, not even Emily, even though they've been best friends ever since Emily's family moved into Mrs. Prendergrast's house almost two years ago.

Rory must keep her sister's deepest, darkest secret, even now that Carleen is gone. After all, she promised.

"Don't worry, Rory," Emily says daily. "Carleen'll be back sooner or later."

And Rory wants to scream at her to stop saying it, to just shut up, even though she knows Emily is only trying to make her feel better. After all, what else can one friend say to another under circumstances like these? Emily can hardly voice what's on everyone's mind as the grim, steamy August days drift by with no evidence, no leads, no word.

No, Emily can hardly say to Rory, "Carleen has obviously been kidnapped and probably murdered by some psycho child molester, and it's only a matter of time before he strikes again."

So Rory mutely lets Emily reassure her, and she constantly looks over her shoulder, and there never seems to be a moment during that endless, humid summer when she isn't wondering about Carleen, and what has happened to her.

And when it happens again—when her best friend Emily Anghardt disappears just before Labor Day weekend—Rory realizes that no matter where her life takes her, no matter what happens to her from now until the day she dies, she will never feel safe again.

CHAPTER ONE

"So, Rory . . . thanks. For coming," Kevin says gruffly, his eyes focused on the Departures screen above their heads, as if he's looking for his commuter flight to JFK in New York, which he's checked and double-checked countless times already.

Gate four, On Time, 4:35 P.M.

It's only three-thirty now.

Rory watches the earnest expression on her younger brother's face, wondering when he turned into a man. It's as though she hasn't looked at him, *really* looked, on the few occasions she's seen him since she left home.

Last night, she hadn't gotten in until late, and she was so exhausted from the long hours of driving that she hadn't stayed up to socialize. Today there was a flurry of activity as she settled in and Kevin prepared to leave.

And then she was driving him to the airport, and here they are, and she's noticing for the first time that there's a shadow of a beard covering Kevin's jaw and that his always lanky frame has picked up some bulk, filling out the thin cotton shirt and snug faded jeans he's wearing. He's grown up, and for the first time, he's striking out on his own.

She realizes he's talking to her, thanking her.

"You're welcome," she tells him, reaching up to brush a clump of sandy hair out of his eyes.

"Tell Mom . . ." He trails off, shrugging. "Never mind. I guess it doesn't matter what you tell her. She won't understand. She doesn't understand anything, except that I'm leaving. She can't figure out why, or that I'll be back, even though I've told her . . ."

"She'll be all right," Rory assures him, noting the worry in his green eyes, trying to push back a wave of guilt that sweeps over her.

He's old beyond his years, her kid brother.

Thanks to her.

He's the one who was at home to pick up the pieces when Daddy dropped dead of a brain aneurysm a year and a half after that terrible summer.

That was what had done their mother in. Becoming a widow. No longer having a husband there to take care of her, the way Daddy had in the twenty years they were married.

Maura Connolly had always been fragile, always nervous, always unstable.

After Kevin's birth, she had gone into a deep depression that lasted almost a year, Rory remembered. She locked herself away in her room, not even emerging to attend daily mass, as she always had, and Daddy hired a nanny to take care of the baby and Rory and Carleen, and he finally forced Mom to go see a doctor. Nobody ever said psychiatrist, but that must have been it, Rory later realized. The doctor had put her on some kind of medication, and eventually, she had come back to life. She was never quite the same, but at least she could function as a normal human being.

But when she lost first Carleen, and then Daddy, she went off the deep end again, this time for good. Her eyes had gradually grown vacant; her body weak and frail; her voice listless; her mind, apparently, ultimately retreating to some distant place.

Rory had realized it was happening, of course. She would have to be blind not to notice her mother's withdrawal from the world.

But she was away at college by then—way out in California, as far from Lake Charlotte as she could get. And she rarely came home once she left, unable—or maybe just unwilling—to face the echoing emptiness in the big old house on Hayes Street, and the three people who lived there still, amidst the memories.

Just Mom, and Kevin, and Molly, who had just turned three when Carleen vanished, and who couldn't possibly remember her sister very well, or Daddy, either, even though she liked to claim that she could.

There had been a time when Molly, as a preschooler, had

insisted on calling Kevin "Daddy." She wouldn't stop for a year or two, though he corrected her repeatedly.

Well, Kevin *has* been a father to Molly, Rory reminds herself. The only real parent Molly has known, with Mom the way she is.

And now Kevin, who has just graduated from the Albany college he attended as a commuter student, is leaving to spend the summer in Europe.

Which is why Rory has come home at last.

Because Molly, at thirteen, is too young to take care of herself full time.

And Mom . . .

Well, Mom needs to be taken care of, too.

"She leaves the stove burners on, Rory," Kevin is saying, as he toys with the strap of his conspicuously new carry-on duffel bag. "So be sure that you check the stove every night before you go to bed. She makes tea, and then she forgets."

"I'll check them." She doesn't mention that this is the third time he warned her about Mom and the burners.

"And she'll want to wear a sweater every day, even when it's ninety degrees out. Don't let her. She'll pass out from heat exhaustion, like last summer. I put most of her sweaters—"

"I know. In the black trunk in the attic."

"But she might find them. She's always up there lately, poking around. God knows why. Anyway, the trunk is locked. The key is—"

"In the drawer above the bread bin in the pantry."

"Sorry." He flashes a tight smile. "I can't remember what I've told you and what I haven't. There's so much you have to worry about, between Mom and Molly . . ."

Rory nods. Molly, with her dark curls and flashing blue eyes, has reportedly been a handful lately.

"I just worry, Rory," Kevin says, inhaling deeply, then puffing his cheeks and letting the air out audibly, rocking back on his heels.

"Don't worry. I'll take care of everything. Please don't worry."

It's my turn, Rory adds silently, as guilt once again creeps over her. How could she have turned her back on the three of them for so many years? How could she have left Kevin, barely an adult even now, to cope alone?

Simple.

She just hasn't allowed herself to look back. Hasn't allowed the painful memories to haunt her. And the more time that passed, the easier it was to forget about the sister and father and best friend she had lost—and the family she'd basically abandoned.

Meanwhile, she had gotten her art degree from Berkeley, then wandered the country for a couple of years, footloose and unfettered, as though she hadn't a care in the world. She worked as a ski instructor in Colorado one winter and sold insurance in Texas the following spring. She wandered north to New York and was a temp secretary on Wall Street until she grew tired of the corporate world and urban life and returned to the West Coast, becoming an artist's model in Santa Cruz.

She never cut herself off completely from her family, of course. She called home every couple of weeks or sometimes every other month, checking in, telling them where she could be reached—just in case.

What?

In case something happened to Mom? Or Molly? Or Kevin?

In case one of them fell off the face of the earth, the way Carleen and Emily had, or dropped dead, as Daddy had?

She had been living in Miami this winter when Kevin tracked her down, told her about the summer trip he wanted to take.

"I've been seeing this girl, Katherine, all year," he told Rory, "and she's spending the summer backpacking across Europe. She wants me to come with her—"

"Oh, wow, you've *got* to go!" Rory burst out enthusiastically. "I did that between my junior and senior years, remember? I almost didn't come back to the States. It was incredible. You'd better be going, Kev."

Silence.

And then it had dawned on her, *why* he was calling her.

Because he wouldn't be able to go if she didn't come home to take care of Mom and Molly.

And so, here she is.

She's home for the summer.

In Lake Charlotte, where people still talk about the long-ago summer when four teenaged girls mysteriously vanished and were never heard from again.

"You grew your hair."

Rory looks up at her mother, who's sitting across the table, watching her.

Unnerved by the sudden steady gaze from those familiar green eyes the exact shade of her own, Rory isn't sure what to say. Her shoulder-length auburn hair is shorter, actually, than she'd worn it all winter in Miami, when she would pull it into a thick braid and let it dangle down her back. Then again, it's longer than the boyish bob she'd worn for a year or so a while back, which, come to think of it, might very well have been the last time she had seen her mother.

Maura is toying with the heavy silver cross hanging from a chain around her neck as she watches Rory. She's always worn that cross, Rory recalls. She once said it was a confirmation gift from her own mother. When Carleen, and then Rory, made their confirmations, Maura had bought them similar crosses. Rory remembers wearing it just once, until someone said, "Hey, what're you, a nun all of a sudden?" After that, Rory had put it away in the bottom drawer of her dresser and hoped her mother would never mention it.

She hadn't.

"Why did you grow it?" her mother wants to know, still looking at her head.

"I just . . . I like long hair."

Her mother's hand flies to her own shorn gray locks. Kevin said he takes her to the beautician every six weeks to have it trimmed in this easy-care style, reminding Rory not to miss the next appointment.

When Rory was growing up, Maura Connolly's thick, glossy black hair had hung down to her waist. Most of the time she wore it loose, but sometimes, on hot summer days, she coiled it at the back of her neck in some intricate twist that deceptively required only a few pins. Rory would sit on the big queen-sized bed upstairs and watch her, marveling at her mother's expert movements at the back of her head that didn't allow a single tuft of hair to escape, even though she couldn't see what she was doing.

"Do mine now, Mommy," she would beg, and her mother would smile and pretend to tame her daughter's wild, flaming locks into some semblance of her own hairstyle.

And though Daddy would make a point of commenting on her "grown-up 'do," Rory would know she looked nothing like her mother, or Carleen. They both had that exquisite ebony-and-ivory coloring; dark, dark hair and pale, flawless skin.

But Rory had inherited her father's red hair and freckles. Not even silky, soft red hair, but wiry, unruly curls that tangled past her neck and refused to lie flat against her scalp.

"Molly?" her mother suddenly says, turning her head and looking over her shoulder, toward the screen door at the other end of the kitchen. "Where's Molly?"

"She's babysitting next door, Mom. Remember?"

"Kevin?"

"He's not here, Mom," she says patiently.

She thinks about how she'd hugged her kid brother that last time at the airport, wishing they'd had more time together, thinking that maybe she'll stick around a while after he comes home in September.

"Go ahead, Rory," he'd said gruffly, squirming as though he wasn't used to hugs. "Get out of here. Your parking meter is going to expire."

"Don't you want me to wait until you get on the plane so I can see you off?" she'd asked, only half teasingly.

"Nah," he'd said with a casual wave of his hand, and she wondered whether he was worried she'd make some big emotional scene telling him good-bye, or whether he was afraid he'd change his own mind about leaving.

"Kevin's in Europe for the summer, Mom," Rory says now. "Remember?"

Her mother nods, but her eyes are blank.

Rory takes a bite of the salad she made for their dinner, noticing her mother's still-heaping plate.

"Eat, Mom," she says.

"It's too hot to eat." The words are expressionless.

"That's why I made just a salad. It's light, and it's healthy. You love salad," Rory adds, then wonders why on earth she would say such a thing. She has no idea whether her mother loves salad; has no idea what her mother likes to eat.

Maura never was much of a cook. Occasionally, she'd surprise the rest of them and whip up something that actually looked and tasted good. Like the loaf of Irish soda bread she made one St. Patrick's Day, or the pots of vegetable soup she'd concoct when the summer garden yielded more tomatoes and beans and zucchini than they knew what to do with.

But most of the time, she boiled hot dogs and served spaghetti made with sauce from a jar and, when all else failed, which was several times a week, ordered pizza.

No one seemed to mind.

"So, Mom," Rory says brightly, looking around the kitchen so she won't have to gaze into that disconcerting emptiness any longer. "I was thinking that we should fix the house up a little while I'm here."

No reply.

But her mother does take a bite of her salad, putting it gingerly into her mouth and setting her fork down again while she chews. Her movements are slow, mechanical.

"We can take down that wallpaper," Rory goes on, gesturing at the faded ivy pattern covering the kitchen walls, "and put up something new. Or maybe just paint everything white. Brighten it up a little. What do you think?"

No reply.

Rory points to the window above the scarred old porcelain sink. "We can get some pretty curtains to hang there," she suggests, wondering what ever happened to the white priscillas with red rickrack trim that used to be there. "And the cabinets are so dark—maybe we can strip that stain, or paint them. The pantry cupboards, too."

She glances at the narrow galley space adjoining the kitchen, its three walls lined with glass-fronted storage space above rows of drawers below. It would be nice, she thinks, if the cupboards were painted white and if, beyond the glass, you saw pretty china or sparkling glassware instead of the jumble of canned goods and cereal boxes stored there now.

This place has so much potential, Rory thinks wistfully, noting the elaborate crown moldings and hardwood floors and high ceilings.

But no one has ever bothered to do anything with the sprawling Victorian. Not the previous owners, and certainly not Daddy and Mom. He was the *least* handy person on the planet, and Mom was the least creative. They had simply bought the place when Mom was pregnant with Rory, realizing they'd outgrown their one-bedroom apartment over Talucci's Pizza Parlor, and they'd moved in.

And that was that.

Growing up here, Rory had never appreciated the house as anything more than a roof over her head, a place where she had her own room, a big yard to play in, and, at the back of the property, the vast bank of woods that eventually led down to the lake.

Only now does she realize that this must once have been a grand home, set far back on a sloping, shady, brick-paved street above the downtown district. These days, the more upscale citizens of Lake Charlotte live in the new network of cul-de-sacs west of town, a development called Green Haven Glen. But before the turn of the century, Hayes Street had been one of the most fashionable addresses in town.

The other houses on the block are similar to this one—gingerbread monstrosities displaying architectural quirks typical of the previous century: turrets and cupolas and wraparound verandas. Most of them, like this one, are surrounded by tall black iron fences and shaded by vast, spreading trees, their stone foundations and latticework obscured by old-fashioned blooming shrubs and perennials—lilacs, hydrangeas, peonies, lilies, irises.

And most of them, *unlike* this one, have been painstakingly restored in the years since Rory left home. Now that nearby Saratoga Springs has once again become a popular resort town, the once-depressed local economy has slowly bounced back, and it shows.

When she drove into town last night, Rory had noticed that the streetlamps on Main Street are bedecked with hanging pots trailing colorful petunias and impatiens, and that the 1950's-era aluminum façades and neon signs of the commercial buildings seem to have been replaced by charming, old-fashioned wooden storefronts, some with a hand-painted shingle dangling above the entrance. There's a bagel shop now, and several conspicuously trendy cafes, and right here on Hayes Street, the Shillings' old house is now a bed and breakfast.

The Connollys' rattletrap home stands out more than ever. Even the place next door, once occupied by Miss Prendergrast, and after that, by Emily's family, is sporting new coats of paint: contrasting shades of rose and plum, which, Molly informed Rory this afternoon, were the original colors of the house a hundred years ago.

"How do you know that?" Rory had asked, amused by her sister's authoritarian air.

"I'm friends with the couple that lives there. The Randalls. I babysit for their little boy."

That's where she is now. Rory can hear her voice drifting in the open windows as she pushes the toddler in a tire swing in the backyard next door.

Rory supposes it's good that the old house is finally lived in after all these years. Not long after Emily vanished, her family picked up and moved away, and as far as Rory knows, the house, already in disrepair, had stood empty ever since.

She tries to tear her thoughts away from that depressing subject. She rarely allows herself to think of the friend she had lost a decade ago. Or of her sister.

But now that she's back in Lake Charlotte, the topic isn't going to be easy to avoid, even if it happened . . . nine years ago? No, ten.

Ten years ago this week, the first girl had disappeared.

How could it be that four girls could simply evaporate into thin air, leaving not a single clue?

In the back of her mind, Rory had assumed for a long time that someday one or more of the bodies would be found. If you follow this type of thing on the evening news, it seems as though missing persons always turn up dead sooner or later, and the cases are solved, or at least put to rest.

The Lake Charlotte Police Department had worked around the clock trying to come up with some evidence that would at least reveal what might have happened. But there was nothing.

Various theories had been discussed on playgrounds and at lunch counters and over back fences. Some people thought the girls had been kidnapped, drugged and taken out of the country, where they were sold into white slavery. Others—mostly middle school boys—guessed that they had been abducted by aliens. And then there was the grisly speculation that they had simply been butchered by some serial killer, their bodies burned or buried or weighted and dumped in the lake.

Of course, no one ever voiced those theories to Rory's face. She still recalls how many conversations drew to an awkward, abrupt halt when she would appear. As the sister of one victim and closest friend of another, she had become something of a celebrity. And despite her typical middle-child hunger for attention, this was the last kind of notoriety she—

"Where's Kevin?"

Her mother's words snap her back to the present, and she sighs softly. "He's not here, Mom. We just talked about it a few minutes ago. Remember?"

"Is he upstairs?"

"No."

Across the ocean. And you won't see him for months.

"He's on vacation," Rory says gently. "But I'm here now. And I'm going to take care of you and Molly. If there's anything you need, you just tell me and I'll get it for you. Okay?"

Her mother's eyes are aimed toward her face, but they're eerily unfocused, as though she isn't really seeing anything. She's faded again, retreating to that distant place where no one can reach her . . . and, perhaps, where nothing can hurt her.

Rory goes back to her own salad, forcing herself to eat, though she suddenly has no appetite.

CHAPTER TWO

Molly carries little Ozzie into the house and sets him on the floor in the kitchen.

She stoops beside him and brushes dirt off his little khaki shorts. It lands on the worn green linoleum, but she figures it doesn't matter. The entire house is under do-it-yourself construction; there's plaster dust and dirt and clutter everywhere. And it's only going to get worse when they rip off most of the back wall of the house to add the big family room Michelle has been talking about.

"Look at you, you're filthy," she tells Ozzie, picking dandelion fluff out of his curly white-blond hair.

"Fil-see," Ozzie echoes, grinning.

"Yup, filthy. You need a bath before bed—"

At the mention of the word *bed,* the two-year-old opens his mouth and lets out a piercing screech.

"No, you don't have to go to bed yet," Molly hastily assures him.

"No bed!" he bellows. "No bed!"

"No bed," Molly agrees. "First a bath. You want a bath? It'll cool you off. It's so sticky out tonight. Come on, let's go right up the back stairs."

He allows her to pick him up and carry him across the kitchen, where she tugs on a wooden door until it opens to reveal a steep flight to the second floor.

The treads creak as she ventures up through the shadows, and she keeps up a steady stream of cheerful conversation with Ozzie to keep herself from being spooked.

There's something about this old house that makes her uneasy, but she doesn't like to dwell on it, because if she lets it bother her, she won't be able to babysit for Ozzie anymore, or come visit Lou and Michelle and the new baby, who is due in August.

Until the Randalls moved in here last year, this place was known to Molly and her friends—in fact, to every kid in Lake Charlotte—as the "haunted house." Everyone knows what happened to the last kid who lived here, Emily Anghardt.

Well, actually, no one knows what happened to her, but that's the scary thing.

Emily—and Molly's older sister Carleen—and two other girls fell off the face of the earth ten years ago.

Molly remembers Carleen, even though everyone says she couldn't possibly. She remembers Carleen giving her a present, a doll with black curls so like Molly's, and that Carleen kept an eye on her while she played on the playground at Point Cedar Park. She remembers Carleen getting her undressed for her bath, touching each of her bare toes gently as she recited the nursery rhyme Molly loved:

This little piggy went to market
This little piggy stayed home
This little piggy had roast beef
This little piggy had none
And this little piggy cried "wee wee wee wee"
All the way home.

She remembers how Carleen would then tickle her feet as Molly screamed in delight, begging her sister to recite the rhyme again. And again.

And she remembers that Carleen always would.

She doesn't remember anything about Carleen's disappearance, which is strange, if you think about it, because you'd think a kid would be aware of something that traumatic happening in household.

She does remember Daddy dying—how Mom had started screaming from the bedroom one night and how Kevin, who had been reading her a story, had dashed down the hall, and then the sirens had wailed up to the front door and men came pounding up the stairs. Mom screamed through it all, nonstop screeching at the top of her lungs.

And after that, she never screamed again, or even raised her voice. From that day on, she has spoken in a soft monotone, and she never smiles, or cries. Never betrays any hint of emotion.

Kevin says she's depressed, but Molly doesn't know about that. Molly's been depressed before, plenty of times—most recently, when she found out last month that her current crush, Ryan Baker, likes Jessica Thomerson. But when she feels bad about something, she doesn't act like Mom.

Mom's basically just . . .

Well, crazy.

It's not something Molly has ever acknowledged to anyone, not even her friend Rebecca Wasner, who lives two doors down and must have a pretty good idea. But who wants to go around admitting their mother's crazy?

Still, there's no other word for it. Mom's pretty much always spaced out, and she asks questions that make no sense, and half the time she's talking to people that aren't there.

"Bath?" Ozzie says, as they walk down the second-floor hall past the open bathroom door.

"Oh, right. Bath," Molly agrees. "I almost forgot what we were doing up here."

She makes a detour into the bathroom and starts the water running into the old claw-foot tub, plugging the drain with the rubber stopper attached to a silver, beaded chain.

Then she carries Ozzie down the narrow, dark hall with its peeling wallpaper, going into his room at the far end, at the head of the wide, graceful, open front staircase.

The little boy's room is one of the few areas in the house that isn't being renovated. Lou and Michelle fixed it up right after they moved in, patching the walls and painting them white and refinishing the hardwood floor so that it's shiny and smooth, so different from the floors in the rest of the house.

A bright pink cast-iron doorstop shaped like a pig keeps the door to the hallway from swinging closed; Michelle had mentioned that her husband keeps saying he'll fix the hinges, but he hasn't gotten a chance yet, so she bought this doorstop at a craft fair recently. "They had all kinds of different animals," she'd told

Molly, "but Ozzie chose the pig, because he loves when you do 'This Little Piggy,' Molly."

There's a built-in bookcase on the wall to the right of the door, jammed with children's books. And a colorful mural is painted on one wall, courtesy of Michelle, an artist. A plump, bespectacled Mother Goose is surrounded by characters from her nursery rhymes: Humpty-Dumpty and Little Jack Homer and Mary, Mary, Quite Contrary, and others Molly doesn't recognize.

Probably because after Carleen disappeared, they weren't very big on nursery rhymes in the Connolly household. She remembers Kevin reading to her now and then, usually from books that had no pictures and were adventure or science fiction stories about boys his age.

Nobody else ever bothered to read to her, although Kevin claims Daddy used to tell her stories before tucking her into bed at night.

She wishes she could remember that. She wishes she could remember more of *him*, more things they did together, so at least she'd have that. A solid memory of his face and his voice and his love.

But there's so little left of him in her mind, just snatches of songs he would sing to her and fragments of scenes where he would be kissing or hugging her.

She can't remember Mom ever being affectionate.

Rory, either, although when she came yesterday, she had folded Molly into her arms in a stiff hug.

Molly sets Ozzie on his changing table and begins absently stripping off his clothes.

Well, she amends, maybe it's half *my* fault that the hug was so stiff. After all, she's hardly feeling warm-hearted toward her sister.

How can she, when Rory's stayed as far away as possible for most of Molly's life? Kevin says it's Rory's way of dealing with what happened to Carleen and Emily, and to Dad.

As far as Molly's concerned, it's a lousy way of dealing. She barely knows her one remaining older sister, a sister Kevin claims loves and cares about her, about all of them.

"Doesn't she always remember your birthday, and send you Christmas presents?" he points out whenever Molly grumbles about Rory's absence. As if a few presents—most of them inappropriate, like a Barbie doll, when Molly has never played with dolls in her life—can make up for the fact that Rory never bothers with any of them.

And now here she is, home for the summer, acting as though she and Molly are going to become all chummy while Kevin's away.

The thought of her older brother brings a sharp pang in the vicinity of Molly's heart. She frowns, missing him desperately even though he just left this afternoon.

How could you leave me? she demands silently, thinking that by now, he must have boarded the jet at JFK Airport and is about to take off for London.

Either that, or he's changed his mind about going and hopped the next commuter flight back to Albany. And any second now, she'll hear his voice in the driveway next door, calling her, saying he couldn't leave her for the whole summer.

"Molly got a boo boo?"

She realizes that Ozzie's watching her face, his big brown eyes wide with concern.

"A boo boo? Oh, you mean because I look sad? Yes, Molly has a boo boo, sweetie," she says wistfully. *A big, hollow boo boo right in her heart.*

"I will kiss it for you," Ozzie declares. "Where the boo boo is?"

She smiles and ruffles his big blond corkscrew curls. "I'll tell you what, Ozzie. A great big hug will help the boo boo heal. Okay?"

She pulls him into her arms and squeezes him tight, feeling his small heart thumping against her own.

He's so sweet, this child. And his affection is so . . . *needed.*

Especially now that Kevin's gone and she has no one else.

Tears spring to her eyes and she holds Ozzie close until he squirms and demands to be put into his bath.

She leaves his little sandals on, knowing he'll insist that he be allowed to walk down the hall. The floors are a mess, and she hasn't let him go barefoot since he got a splinter several weeks ago.

"I walk," Ozzie says eagerly, bolting for the door the moment she sets him on his feet. "I walk."

"No, you *run*, little guy," Molly says with a laugh.

She hurriedly follows him back down to the bathroom, flicking the light switch outside his door as she goes, so that the naked bulb in the ceiling high above illuminates the long hallway.

She knows Ozzie likes to linger in his bath, and once or twice before, she's found herself having to make her way along the darkened hallway back to his room.

Being in the dark in a haunted house isn't a prospect she would like to repeat.

And even though she's never actually seen a ghost here, or heard so much as a strange creak, she's certain the place is haunted. So is Rebecca, who lives on the other side of the Randalls and refuses to babysit here. If Molly didn't love Ozzie and his parents so much, she wouldn't be willing to set foot inside, either.

She can't help thinking of the girl who used to live here. Emily Anghardt.

She doesn't remember her at all. But there are times, when she's alone downstairs at night after Ozzie's asleep, that she feels connected to Emily in some inexplicable way.

After all, this was her house. She lived here, slept here, played here. And one day, she walked—or, perhaps, was carried—out the double front doors with the leaded glass panes, and she never came back.

The very thought of what might have happened to Emily, and to Carleen, and the others, sends a chill down Molly's back despite the muggy summer night. So does the local legend that Emily Anghardt's spirit haunts the house.

"C'mon, Ozzie," she says brightly. "Let's take off your sandals now."

"Do 'wee wee wee,' " he responds, wiggling his toes expectantly as she unfastens the buckles of his sandals. "Do 'wee wee wee,' Molly."

"Sure," she tells him, and begins, "This little piggy went to market . . ."

It's dusk, and lamplight spills from the windows of the once-grand old houses looming along Hayes Street. There's no breeze to stir the heavy, still air. He can hear crickets, and the faint sounds of a baseball game coming from a television set or radio, and, farther off, the steady drone of a lawn mower.

He's the only one walking along this street right now, looking for all the world like he's taking a casual stroll after dinner on a warm summer night.

He slows his steps as he nears number 52, a shabby three-story house set back behind a cagelike wrought-iron fence. The gate stands half open, as though beckoning a visitor—or perhaps, he notes as an afterthought, as though providing a potential escape route, should an occupant be startled into having to flee.

He studies the house as he passes, noting the lopsided front steps and the gaping holes in the porch railing where spindles are missing. The place is badly in need of a paint job, having faded to a peeling, nondescript neutral shade with a muddy-colored trim. The shrubbery is unkempt, though the patchy grass is at least mowed, and the bright pink dianthus in full bloom by the front steps seem conspicuously out of place in the drab landscape.

So this is where Carleen Connolly lived, he muses, and moves on, glancing up at the next house on the block.

Number 54.

And this is where Emily Anghardt lived.

This place is just as run down as number 52, but it shows subtle signs that somebody intends to do something about it. There are paint cans stacked on the front porch, and a ladder is propped against the side steps. A big Dumpster, the kind you can rent when you're working on renovations, can be seen at the back of the long, straight driveway that runs along the far side of the house.

The first floor is dark, but there are lights on upstairs. He knows that a young family lives there now, with a new baby on the way. He wonders if they know the history of the place, or if they care.

And he thinks about the Connollys, still living at number 52, even though the place must hold memories of the daughter they lost.

He walks on up the straight, sloping sidewalk toward the corner, leaving the two big houses behind, not wanting to be so bold as to stop right here and stare, and risk bumping into one of the occupants.

He doesn't need to know them yet. There will be plenty of time for that later.

After all, he'll be here all summer.

Just as he was ten years ago.

Rory hesitates outside the closed door in the third-floor hallway, her hand on the knob and her heart pounding.

Then, after closing her eyes briefly, she turns the knob and pushes the door open.

Nothing but blackness.

She reaches out, feels along the wall to her right, just inside the doorway, until she finds the light switch. She flicks it and blinks at the burst of brightness overhead, then finds herself looking around at her sister's old bedroom.

A wave of emotion surges over her and she reaches out to grab the nearby desk for support.

Oh, God, Carleen, she thinks, desperately missing the sister she has tried so hard to forget.

She takes a deep breath to steady her emotions and notices that the air is hot and musty-smelling. She forces herself to look around.

There, on the cluttered desk, is a Stephen King novel with a bookmark in place—*The Shining*. Carleen had been reading it that summer, Rory recalls. She was always reading something.

The bookcase on the far wall of the room is packed with double rows of books, and more are stacked on the floor beside it. Some are mainstream fiction, and there are a few cherished classics and hardcovers among them; others are dog-eared young-adult paperbacks—mostly "sophisticated" books by authors like Avi and Richard Peck and Paul Zindel, rather than the Sweet Valley High series that takes up most of the shelf space in Rory's room across the hall.

Above the bookcase hangs a wooden crucifix, identical to those in every other bedroom in the house, placed there, of course, by Maura. Rory remembers being frightened, as a child, of the gory image of the blood-encrusted gaping wounds in Christ's feet and hands. She swiftly moves her gaze past the crucifix even now, focusing on the wide dresser beside the bookcase.

One drawer is ajar, as though someone has just grabbed something out of it and not bothered to close it all the way. Rory notes the dresser top is cluttered with cosmetics and hair clips and lotions, and she can see a round purple glass bottle that she recognizes as Carleen's favorite perfume. Christian Dior's Poison. Some boy had given it to her for her seventeenth birthday, and Carleen had bragged about how expensive it was. She used to douse herself in it, ignoring everyone's wrinkled noses and comments that she was wearing too much.

Over there on the bedside table is Carleen's senior yearbook, and, tossed haphazardly on the floor, a familiar-looking maroon leather-bound document binder that Rory recognizes as her sister's high school diploma. She herself got one just like it from Lake Charlotte High School the following year.

There's Carleen's canopy bed, the one Mom and Daddy had bought her for her thirteenth birthday after she'd begged them. Rory, who had always believed her sister was Mom's favorite anyway, had, of course, been jealous. But Carleen had generously allowed her to spend a few nights in the bed when she was away on a Girl Scout camping trip.

That was back when Carleen was still herself, before . . .

Well, before everything changed.

Rory takes a few cautious steps into the room, noting that it's just the way her sister left it ten years ago. Mom wouldn't let anyone touch it after Carleen vanished, saying she wanted her room to be waiting the day she came back.

And Daddy hadn't argued.

Maybe he, too, thought Carleen was coming back.

Or maybe he knew how traumatic it would be for Mom to give up hoping.

During the first few weeks and months after Carleen disappeared, there had occasionally been reason to think that maybe she was out there somewhere, alive; that maybe she had simply run away. Doug McShane, the detective in charge of the police investigation, said they had received tips from people who claimed to have seen her—but then, nothing ever came of any of the information.

And, as Daddy said, the world is full of crackpots and sickos.

Rory remembers the night she had answered the phone to hear a girl's voice, a girl claiming to be Carleen. And her heart had leapt into her throat even though it didn't sound like her sister's voice, and she was momentarily fooled until the girl burst into a fit of giggles, and she realized it was just some kids playing a prank.

Another time a psychic showed up at the door and told Mom she had a message from Carleen. She said Carleen was alive and being held in an underground dungeon by a stranger. For two hundred dollars, she would describe the stranger and provide his initials.

Mom, the devout Catholic who should have known better than to believe in occult mumbo jumbo, would have given her the two hundred dollars if Daddy hadn't come home right then and thrown the so-called psychic out.

Rory still remembers how the woman had scurried to her car parked out at the curb as Mom wailed helplessly and Daddy yelled.

"Don't you think I want to believe she's alive someplace?" he had hollered at Mom after the psychic had driven away. "Don't you think that my heart jumps every time Doug McShane calls and says he's got another tip from someone who says they saw her?"

And that was when Rory, who was crouched at the top of the stairs listening, had realized her father thought Carleen was dead.

That was when she allowed herself to believe it, too.

And after that, she had never set foot inside Carleen's room again. She knew it would be too painful to see everything waiting for her, as if she were coming back.

Now, after ten years, the pain has dulled somewhat to a hollow ache. Now she's an adult. Now she can stand here and look at her sister's room and mourn the loss of someone she had once loved, but she isn't paralyzed with grief the way she once might have been.

Now there's only this deep-seated sadness.

And, of course, the mystery.

What happened to you, Carleen?
And to you, Emily?

She reaches into the neck of her T-shirt and pulls out a locket on a chain, fingering it absently as she thinks about her sister. Then, realizing the room is unbearably warm, she steps over to the window and tugs on it. After a few tries, it begins to raise with the reluctant, squeaky groan of wood scraping along wood.

The air outside is hardly cool, but not nearly as stifling as it is in here. Rory inhales the sweet scent of honeysuckle blossoms from the sprawling hedge two stories below.

She stands looking down at the side yard, remembering how she and Carleen used to spread their Barbie dolls in the shade of the big oak tree just inside the fence. They would play there for hours, trading clothes and setting up elaborate Barbie houses among the gnarled roots jutting out from the base of the tree.

Carleen had the best ideas, Rory remembers, smiling faintly. *She was always staging a Barbie wedding or sending her Ken off to war. And I would forget to play with my own dolls. I would end up sitting there, watching the scenes she created with hers, like the audience at a show.*

If her sister had lived, Rory thinks wistfully, she might have become an actress. Or maybe an interior decorator—she was a genius at designing her Barbie houses, turning postage stamps into framed "prints" for the walls and propping plastic coffee can lids on spools to create tables.

A sudden, involuntary shudder takes Rory by surprise.

She stares out into the twilight below, feeling as if something startled her, when there's nothing to see but a deserted yard.

Then she catches a glimpse of movement out of the corner of her eye. Turning her head, she sees the dark silhouette of a person moving along the sidewalk beyond the black iron fence.

It appears to be a man, and he's walking slowly, his head turned in Rory's direction, almost as if he sees her standing up here in the window.

He might, she realizes, remembering that the light is on behind her.

She steps back automatically, instinctively wanting to conceal herself, and then wonders why.

It's probably just one of the neighbors, she tells herself. Everyone on the block must know that this was Carleen's old room. That's the kind of detail that's become legendary in Lake Charlotte—at least it was in the year Rory lived at home, after her sister vanished.

She remembers the way cars would slow in front of their house as curious onlookers stared, and how kids would gather on their bikes outside the iron fence, peering at the house as though they expected to see Carleen's ghost.

Rory sighs and moves to the light switch, turning it off and plunging the room into darkness once more. She pulls the door closed behind her and goes slowly down the stairs to the second floor, passing her mother's closed door.

She hesitates for a moment, considering knocking and asking if her mother is all right.

But that seems too invasive somehow. Kevin told her that their mother spends a lot of time in bed, sometimes watching her portable television and sometimes just staring at the ceiling or out the window. The only time she leaves the house on her own is to walk to morning mass at Holy Father Church two blocks away.

Rory vowed, when she came here this summer, to make an effort to turn her mother around—to get her out of bed and back out into the world.

But tonight, she's too exhausted to make the effort.

She passes the closed door to the master bedroom and continues to the guest room down the hall. This is where she's staying for the summer, instead of in her old room upstairs, across the hall from Carleen's.

She's been telling herself that she's chosen to stay down here because it's cooler, and because she wants to be near her mother and Molly.

But the truth is that her childhood bedroom, like her sister's, simply holds too many haunting memories. And though she now realizes that it's going to be impossible to spend the summer here avoiding any thought or discussion of the past, the last thing she wants is to immerse herself in it.

She goes into the guest room, leaves the door open behind her so that light spills in from the hall, and turns on the big, ancient box fan propped in the window. As the motor hums to life, she sits on the edge of the twin bed and looks out the window, facing the same view as she had from Carleen's room directly overhead.

There's no sign of the man she had seen on the sidewalk.

Yet for some reason she finds herself shivering again, hugging herself as she stares out into the still, steamy summer night.

CHAPTER THREE

"Cap'n Crunch? I used to love that stuff." Rory peers over Molly's shoulder into the bowl of cereal in front of her on the table.

Her sister glances up and narrows her eyes. "Do you mind? I'm trying to eat."

"Just checking to see if it's the kind with crunch-berries," Rory says.

Silence.

"So, is it?"

"No," Molly tells her. "It isn't."

"The peanut butter kind?"

"No. Okay?"

Rory shrugs, refusing to take her sister's hint. Maybe, she tells herself, Molly just isn't a morning person. Carleen never was. She would growl at anyone who tried to talk to her before noon.

Or maybe Molly just can't stand me, Rory thought ruefully, going over to the counter and looking around for a coffee maker. *I guess I can't blame her for that. She thinks I took off and left everyone behind without a second thought while I gallivanted around the country these past ten years.*

Which is basically what I did.

Rory sighs, opens a cupboard in search of the Mr. Coffee machine she vaguely remembers from years ago. Yesterday morning, there hadn't been time to make coffee. She'd forgotten all about it in the flurry to get acclimated and see Kevin off. Now she has a pounding headache from not feeding her three-cup-a-day caffeine habit, and if she doesn't find that Mr. Coffee machine . . .

But the cupboard is filled with stacked glass mixing bowls, all of them faded pastel colors and most of them chipped, and an unfamiliar Corning Ware casserole set that looks as though it's never been used.

She tries another one. No coffee maker, although there's a china teapot with the spout broken off and a bunch of mugs her father used to collect from places he visited. They're the souvenir kind, imprinted with cheesy slogans and mottos. Rory moves them around, looking at the names of places. There are a few from Albany. One from Niagara Falls. One from the Catskills.

You never went far from home, did you, Daddy? Rory thinks wistfully. She considers the places she's been since she left Lake Charlotte; thinks about how she's skied in the Rockies and sailed in the Florida Keys; camped in the Black Hills and braved a Minnesota winter.

Patrick Connolly would have loved it, all of it. He had taught American history and geography at the local community college. When Rory was young, she used to sit on his lap and turn the pages of his big atlas while he told her about faraway places, told her stories of what had happened there in the "olden days," as she used to call them. He could go on for hours, and she would feign fascination long after she had lost interest, because nobody else ever listened to him, and because she felt safe, curled up there on her father's lap, his strong arms draped around her shoulders and his deep voice rumbling in her ears.

Oh, Daddy, Rory thinks, her eyes suddenly stinging with tears. *I got my wanderlust from you, didn't I? You never wanted to live your whole life in this little town, in this run-down house, saddled with a teaching job and bills and a wife who was too emotionally fragile to go farther than the A&P a few blocks away.*

Only now does Rory grasp the extent of her father's longing. Back then, he acted as though it didn't matter that he never went anywhere, that they never did anything. He used to tell Rory that someday he was going to retire and buy one of those big old RVs and see the country.

Who knew then that he wasn't going to live to see forty?

So he'd never seen any of the places he dreamed of and read

about. Never went more than a few hundred miles from Lake Charlotte, except for the year they had spent in California while he was on sabbatical.

Rory tries to push that out of her mind.

That was different, she reminds herself. That was a terrible time. So many years of Daddy wistfully talking about how he'd love to take a sabbatical, and Mom flatly refusing to leave Lake Charlotte—and then, boom. Trouble struck, and they saw their only chance to escape. A hollow victory for Daddy. The year in California was more like an exile than a vacation.

Rory hurriedly closes the cupboard and turns away, anxious to forget the period in her life when everything fell apart, setting into motion a chain of events that had ultimately destroyed her family.

Her gaze falls on Molly, still sitting at the table with her back to Rory, crunching her cereal and flipping the pages of *Seventeen* magazine.

Rory contemplates telling her sister that she used to read that magazine, too, when she was Molly's age. She and Carleen used to bring it into the upstairs bathroom they shared and try to duplicate the models' hairstyles and makeup on each other.

Carleen.

Everywhere Rory turns, there are ghosts.

I should never have come back here. Why did I come back here?

Because you had no choice, she reminds herself. *Because you couldn't run away forever. Deal with it. Get past it. It's time to start forgetting.*

Apparently, learning to forget means first allowing the memories back in.

She clears her throat and blurts, "Is there a coffee maker?"

Molly jumps, clearly startled, then shakes her head without turning it around. "Uh-uh."

"No coffee maker?" Rory asks incredulously.

"Mom drinks tea," Molly says in a voice that lets Rory know that if she had been around all these years, as she should have been, she would have known that.

As if she could forget the perpetual sight of Maura, hunched at the table in the very spot where Molly is now sitting, clutching a steaming mug of the strong Irish brew.

"I know Mom drinks tea," Rory replies in an I've-known-Mom-longer-than-you-have tone.

She instantly regrets it. She's the adult here. Not a jealous kid sister. Not anymore.

But for a moment there, Molly had sounded eerily like Carleen. And Rory had been a child again, trying not to let her big sister's superior attitude get to her.

"Carleen's acting big again, Daddy. Tell her to stop."

"You can act big, too, Rory . . . just climb up on a chair and act big."

"Daddy! That's not what I mean. It's not fair that she always acts like she knows more than me and it's not fair that she can do more stuff than I can."

"That's because she's the oldest, Rory."

"But that's not fair. I wish I could be the oldest . . . Someday, will I get a turn to be the oldest?"

"Don't be silly, Rory. That's impossible. Carleen is the oldest. That's just how it works."

You were wrong, Daddy. My wish came true, Rory thinks grimly now. *I'm the oldest. I have a responsibility to this family. Mostly to Molly. She needs me whether she knows it or not.*

"So there's no coffee maker anymore," Rory says thoughtfully, looking around the kitchen.

"There's never been a coffee maker. I told you, Mom doesn't drink it."

But Daddy did, Rory tells her silently. *You don't remember that.*

Aloud, she says, "I guess I'll have to buy one, then. I can do that in town. Do they still sell stuff like that at McShane's?"

Molly looks at her blankly.

"The hardware store," Rory says. "McShane's."

"There's a Home Depot on High Ridge Road."

"McShane's is gone?"

Then Rory realizes. Of course it must be gone. The owner, Hank McShane, had been an old man when she was a kid, and his only son, Doug, hadn't wanted to take over the family business. He had become a cop instead. He was the detective who had worked on Carleen's case.

There it was again.

"Where's that Home Depot?" Rory asks, even though she heard Molly the first time.

Her sister rolls her eyes as she repeats herself, and Rory says, "I don't know if they sell small appliances, but they'll have paint, and I needed to get some today anyway."

"Why?" Now Molly turns to look at her.

"Because I'm going to paint the kitchen cupboards and trim."

"Why?"

"Because . . . I mean, look around. It needs it."

"You can't just show up here and take over. You can't just go around painting stuff," Molly tells her.

"Somebody has to. This place is a wreck."

Molly says nothing, just turns back to her cereal and her magazine.

"Want to come with me?" Rory asks, though she already knows the answer. "We can stop at that new little cafe on the way—the one where the Rainbow Palace used to be—"

"Rainbow Palace?"

"That's probably before your time. It was a Chinese restaurant on Front Street, but it closed before I left for college."

"Well, the cafe's not new. It's been there, like, forever."

Not *forever*, Rory wants to say, but thinks better of quibbling. She recognizes Molly's need to remind her that she hasn't spent much time in Lake Charlotte these past few years.

She goes on. "Anyway, I can get an espresso, and—"

"Nope."

Just when Rory thinks her sister is going to leave her answer at that curt, single word, Molly adds grudgingly, "I have to meet someone."

"Oh."

Anyone I know? Rory almost asks. But she stops herself just in time. She doesn't know Molly's friends. She doesn't know anything about her life.

Silence falls between them.

Molly's spoon clinks against her bowl.

She turns a page of her magazine so forcefully that it rips.

Rory sighs. "Okay," she says. "I'll be back in a few hours. Tell Mom."

"Tell her yourself." Molly pushes her chair back. "I'm outta here."

"When will you be back?"

"Later" is Molly's sullen reply as the screen door bangs shut behind her.

Rory stands in the middle of the kitchen for a moment. Then she gets her sister's bowl from the table and puts it into the sink, absently running water into it long after the milk has swirled down the drain.

Hearing a screen door slam next door, Michelle Randall glances out the open window next to the bathroom sink.

A pretty redhead with long, untamed curls is striding quickly toward the detached garage, and Michelle can hear the impatient jingling of the car keys in her hand even from up here.

That has to be Molly's older sister, Rory. Michelle decides that now isn't the time to catch her and introduce herself in a neighborly fashion.

Even if the woman wasn't clearly in such a hurry, it would take Michelle forever to lug her enormous body—not to mention Ozzie—down the steep flight of stairs in this heat. Besides, her stomach is still roiling from being sick in the toilet a few moments ago.

"Are you done frowing up, Mommy?" Ozzie asks from the floor at her feet.

She glances down and sees that he's playing with the long-handled brush she uses to clean the toilet.

"Ozzie, no!" she shrieks, grabbing it and prying it from his chubby fingers.

He promptly bursts into tears.

"That's yucky, sweetheart," she says, shoving the brush back into the plastic holder behind the tank and scooping her toddler into her arms. "Come on, let's scrub your hands."

"No! No scrub!"

"Ozzie, stop squirming," Michelle says sharply, struggling to keep her grasp on the little boy despite her enormous, protruding tummy.

She hoists him toward the sink, turns on the water, and reaches for the antibacterial soap. They go through a lot of that these days. Ozzie gets into everything.

Oh, Lord, what am I going to do when I have a baby to take care of, too? she wonders, exhausted already though it's barely nine A.M. She didn't sleep more than a few hours total last night, thanks to indigestion and the baby pressing on her bladder, which meant countless trips down the hall to the bathroom.

Maybe it's a mistake to have another one right now, she thinks wearily. She shouldn't have let Lou talk her into it. They have their hands full with Ozzie, who's in the throes of the Terrible Twos, not to mention this big old house that's under renovation and will be for what's bound to feel like forever.

We never should have bought this place, she tells herself. *I knew it from the start.*

Lou was the one who had stumbled across the For Sale sign one day, and insisted that they look at it even though it was obviously falling apart. He was the one who had talked her into buying this place, calling it a steal. It *was* surprisingly inexpensive for a house this size—due, no doubt, to the fact that it had stood vacant for years, and was rumored to be haunted. Aside from all that, she had thought they were taking on more house than they needed or could afford.

The renovation is going to be a slow process; they don't have the money for most of what they want to do, even with Lou's recent promotion at the law firm to junior partner.

Before he left for the office this morning, Lou had reminded Michelle to call John Kline, her second cousin and the architect they're working with, and set up an appointment to discuss the family-room addition.

When Michelle suggested that they hold off until they have some money in the bank, Lou argued that they'll need the extra space as soon as possible, with a baby on the way.

"But we can use the extra money, too," Michelle had pointed out. Until she got pregnant, she had been planning to go back to work this fall at the elementary school where she had taught art until Ozzie was born.

But now she's expecting the baby in late July or August, and it will be at least another year before she'll feel like she can leave Ozzie and the new little guy in day care or with a full-time sitter.

There are too many crazies out there; it's just too hard to find someone you can trust with your children these days.

Michelle feels a pang of loss, thinking about her mother, who died only months before Ozzie was born. Mom had lived right here in town, and she would have loved spending her retirement years taking care of her grandchildren.

Lou's mother, on the other hand, isn't the grandmotherly type. Iris is too busy with her garden club and bridge club and God knows what else, and, besides, her winters in Clearwater Beach keep getting longer and longer.

No, Michelle can't count on her to help out.

Of course, there's Molly. She's terrific with Ozzie. But she's just a kid herself. Michelle doesn't like to leave her alone with Ozzie at night if she can help it. The few times she has, Molly has seemed nervous about it. And just the other night, she asked Michelle if she thought the house was really haunted.

Michelle would rather not think about that possibility. She's a grown woman, and when they bought the place, she and Lou laughed off the rumors that the house was haunted by the ghost of Emily Anghardt, the young girl who disappeared from here and presumably was murdered. But the past few nights, with Lou working late at the office, she's found herself spooked about being alone here.

Must be the pregnancy. She's feeling vulnerable in a lot of ways lately.

Drying Ozzie's hands, she says, "How about if we go downstairs for a snack?"

"Snack? Yes, snack. Yummy!" he replies eagerly, and makes a beeline for the door.

"Wait for Mommy," she calls, hurrying to catch up. She presses one hand into her aching lower back and uses the other to wipe a trickle of sweat from her forehead. The temperature is already steamy, and the sun has only been up a few hours. Weather like this is unusual in the foothills of the Adirondacks, even in late June.

"What should we have, Ozzie?" Michelle asks her son in the kitchen, surveying the contents of the cupboard. She really needs to get to the supermarket later. Things are looking pretty bare, and she just got groceries a few days ago.

"Ice cream," Ozzie says firmly, his eyes lighting up at the prospect of his favorite treat.

"It's too early for ice cream," Michelle tells him. "How about a couple of crackers and peanut butter?"

She takes out a box of saltines, thinking they'll settle her stomach. Nothing like having morning sickness the whole nine months, she thinks grimly. She reaches into the nearly empty inner waxed paper bag and pulls out a couple of crackers.

"No. Ice cream," Ozzie insists.

The saltines taste unpleasantly dry in this heat and Michelle eats only one, putting the rest back into the bag.

"Okay," she says, returning the box to the cupboard. "It's got to be ninety degrees out. Ice cream it is, Ozzie."

Molly nudges Rebecca's arm and tilts her head in the direction of two boys coming out of the bait and tackle shop across from the park bench where they're sitting.

"Look. There's Ryan Baker," she says.

"Oh, gee, Molly, is *he* why we're sitting here instead of at the library?" Rebecca's serious gray eyes look dismayed behind her owlish glasses, and she flips her long, slightly frizzy dark hair over her shoulders impatiently.

"Relax. The library doesn't open until ten."

"It's ten-fifteen."

"Oh. Well, don't be ridiculous. How would I know he was go to be here?" Molly asks, watching as Ryan and his friend Andy Chase get on their bikes, balancing fishing poles over their shoulders.

"Maybe you overheard Jessica telling Amanda yesterday that Ryan couldn't go with her to the mall today because he and Andy were going fishing at the park after they finish their paper routes," Rebecca says pointedly. "I know *I* heard her. Everyone at Carvel heard her. She wants the world to know that she and Ryan are going out."

"Oh, really? I didn't hear her say that," Molly lies, intent on Ryan, who's skillfully peddling across the street in their direction.

She admires the way he wears his Yankees cap backward. That must be why his face is ruddy from the sun. The other day, when she bumped into him at the gas station where they were both getting air in their bike tires, she noticed that he has a sprinkling of freckles across the bridge of his nose, and that the tip of it is peeling from a recent sunburn.

Lately, she notices everything about Ryan Baker.

Too bad he doesn't notice her.

Except . . .

Did he just glance in her direction as he rode his bike up over the curb onto the sidewalk a few yards away?

"Hi, Ryan!" she calls impulsively, then just as impulsively wants to crawl under the bench and hide.

Maybe he'll think Rebecca said it, she thinks hopefully, and glances at her friend, whose nose is buried in some dumb library book she's about to return. It's about cats. Rebecca loves cats. She's wearing a pink T-shirt with a kitten's face appliquéd below her shoulder. Molly gave it to her for birthday last month, but now she wishes she hadn't. It looks so juvenile.

"Hey, Molly. Hi, Rebecca," Ryan says, slowing his bike in front of them.

Molly realizes he's only waiting for Andy, who's stuck on the other side of the street, waiting for traffic. Still, Ryan didn't have to stop in front of her. He didn't have to say hi.

No, *hey*. He'd said *hey*, in that casual way of his, around a piece of gum he's chewing.

"Hey, Ryan," Molly says.

"Yeah?" He back-pedals, balancing his bike somehow without falling over.

She feels herself blush under his glance. "Oh . . . I just meant, hey. You know, as in 'hi.' " *Which you already said, you idiot.*

He treats her to a good-natured grin. "Hi. What are you guys doing?"

"Going to the library," Rebecca informs him, looking up from her book.

"Yeah? That's cool."

Yeah, right. Molly wants to smack Rebecca for speaking up. She had planned to tell Ryan they were going to walk down to the lake, and then Ryan would tell her that was some coincidence because he and Andy were on their way to the lake, too, to go fishing, and she would look stunned, and then he would say, "Why don't you come along?"

And then Andy and Rebecca would vanish conveniently the way things seem to happen in fantasies, and Molly would be alone with Ryan, and he would kiss her passionately and ask her to marry him.

Or something like that.

"So what's been going on with you this past week?" she asks lamely, praying that the traffic will keep whizzing by, tons of traffic, and Andy will be stuck across the street for at least another hour.

"You mean since school got out? Nothing," Ryan says. "This town is beat."

At least he didn't mention dating Jessica.

"Yeah," Molly agrees. "This town is beat."

"You guys going to that party out at the Curl?"

"Party?" Molly echoes. "When?"

"Friday night."

"At the Curl?" she echoes, just to make sure.

Ryan nods and says, "Where else?"

The Curl, Molly knows, is the crescent-shaped stretch of beach that dips out into Lake Charlotte. During the day, it's filled with people—mostly little kids splashing in the almost landlocked shallow water between there and the shore. But at night, all the cool kids hang out on the stretch of beach, drinking beer around bonfires and doing who knows what else.

Molly was at the Curl a week ago, with Ozzie and his mother, but she has never been out there after dark.

"Yeah, we'll be there," she tells Ryan, who nods, then rides off with a wave as Andy catches up with him.

"Molly! We can't go to a party at the Curl," Rebecca says.

"Why not?"

"My parents won't let me, for one thing."

"So sleep over at my house. Kevin's gone, and my mother probably won't even ask where we're going." This is the first time, Molly realizes, that it'll come in handy to have a mother who's always so out of it.

Most of the time, it's just embarrassing, especially with Rebecca, whose mother is, like, a total Martha Stewart, always baking cookies and doing crafts and gardening, making the Wasners' house as homey as the Connollys' is neglected.

"What about your sister?" Rebecca asks pointedly.

And for a moment, Molly thinks she's talking about Carleen. She thinks Rebecca means, Won't your mother be worried about you after what happened to your sister, even if it was ten years ago?

But then she realizes that Rebecca isn't talking about Carleen at all. That the shadow of what happened to her oldest sister doesn't necessarily loom over everyone else in town the way it's hung over Molly's family these past ten years.

No, Rebecca's talking about her other sister. About Rory.

"Oh, please," Molly says, curling her mouth in disdain. "*She* has no say in what I do."

"I thought she was here to take care of you."

"Take care of me? Her? No way. She has no right to tell me anything. She's never even been around. I don't have to listen to anything she says."

Rebecca watches her, but says nothing.

Molly squirms under her friend's knowing gaze. "Come on," she says, rising abruptly. "Let's go to the library."

Rory steers Kevin's car, which he's loaned her for the summer, out of the Home Depot parking lot onto High Ridge Road, then slams on her brakes, realizing she was just about to go through a red light.

That light was never here.

Hell, the vast shopping center was never here. It used to be just acres and acres of fields, dotted with an occasional tree or one of those high tension towers, the kind everyone is saying causes cancer.

Now there's a Home Depot and a Wal-Mart—where she'd had at least a dozen different coffee makers to choose from—*and* a huge grocery superstore, the kind that sells everything. *Everything.* Rory found herself buying imported coffee and fresh bagels and firm pink lox and even one of those exotic horned melons. As she glances over her shoulder at the bags of groceries on the seat behind her, she wonders who's going to eat all this stuff when the house is so empty these days.

Me, she thinks resolutely. *I'll eat it. And so will Mom. And Molly.*

She had gone into the store because of Molly in the first place, to buy more Cap'n Crunch. *With* crunch-berries. She'd also bought brownies and some of those cookies with the M&Ms from the store's bakery department, thinking Molly would probably like that kind of stuff.

Thinking she could win her sister's stony heart with baked goods.

You're a fool, Rory tells herself. *Molly's going to see right through you.*

Oh, well. Rory likes brownies and cookies, herself. She'll eat them.

Right after she paints the entire first floor of the house.

I guess I got a little carried away, she tells herself ruefully, thinking of the cans and cans of white paint she just bought at Home Depot. All she could think was that she had to do something to make the house less run-down, less gloomy.

White paint will make it sparkle, she thinks as she heads back toward town. *Besides, painting will keep me busy.*

And if she's busy, she won't be able to brood. About Molly. About Carleen. About Daddy. And about Mom.

Mom, who, when Rory had gone up to tell her she was going shopping, had been in the middle of an animated conversation.

With Daddy.

"No, Patrick, you're wrong about that," Rory had heard her say in the split second before she knocked on the master bedroom door. "It wasn't on the dresser; it was under the bed. See? I told you I dropped it last night."

Even after Rory's knock, Mom had continued talking to her dead husband. Arguing with him, actually.

And for just a split second, hearing her mother's voice, Rory had somehow managed to forget that her father has been dead for almost ten years. And when reality rushed back, she found herself remembering suddenly how, in the dark months after Daddy's death, she had occasionally convinced herself that he wasn't dead after all—that it was all merely a horrible nightmare.

Amazing how easy it was for her to cling to that childish denial at times when grief would have otherwise overwhelmed her.

Then again, she hadn't gone to his wake or funeral; actually, none of them had. Mom was unable to get out of bed, sedated by her doctor. And there was no extended family to come to the rescue. No aunts and uncles—Rory's father had been an only child, and her mother's one brother had been killed in Vietnam.

Rory had never known her paternal grandparents; both had died before she was born. Her mother's father had also died young, and though Grandmother Mary had still been alive at that point, she was senile, living in an Albany nursing home.

So Mom's friend Sister Theodosia had been summoned to Lake Charlotte to take care of Rory and Kevin and Molly, just as she had when Carleen disappeared. Of course, that summer, she was around all the time anyway. She had just returned from Mexico that spring, where she'd done some kind of missionary work, and was temporarily assigned to a church in nearby Saratoga Springs. She was always showing up in the Connolly house that summer, spending her days off with Mom, and generally making Rory and Carleen's lives miserable with her dour presence. It wasn't long afterward—in fact, it was that September, a month after Carleen vanished—that the nun was transferred to the Buffalo area. And after that, they seldom saw her.

Still, when Daddy died, Sister Theodosia was the first person Mom called. She was the one who had made the funeral arrangements for Patrick at Holy Father, and she was the one who had forbidden the children to attend, saying it would be too traumatic.

Rory has never forgiven the nun for that.

I should have been there. I never got to say good-bye to him.

And she had never even glimpsed her beloved father's lifeless body, which would undoubtedly have made his death real to her and banished fantasies that he was still alive.

As it happened, for all she knew it was just an elaborate prank Daddy was playing on all of them. He hadn't really died; no, he had simply gotten fed up with all of them and gone off to see the world the way he'd always wanted to do. And someday he would come back.

Yeah. Sure.

Denial.

And Mom's still doing it.

Chills had run down Rory's spine as she stood outside the master-bedroom door listening to that one-sided conversation, and she had walked away without telling Mom she was going out.

It had sounded so real. It sounded like the way Mom used to talk to Daddy, back when he was here and she wasn't so . . .

Crazy.

Mom's crazy, Rory tells herself again now, as she has ever since she left the house in a hurry, as if she could somehow flee the startling knowledge.

Mom's bonkers. She's totally gone off the deep end.

And what's Rory supposed to do about it? Does Kevin realize how nutty their mother has become? Does anyone?

Rory thinks of Sister Theodosia, her mother's one friend in the entire world. Last she knew, the Catholic nun was still up in Buffalo, living at the rectory of some church there. Maybe Molly will know how to get in touch with her.

Much as Rory dreads the thought of contacting Sister Theodosia, she realizes she has to do it. If anyone knows Mom, it's the woman who has been her closest friend since childhood, when they grew up next door to each other in an Albany suburb.

Rory has never liked the stern-faced nun, and not just because she forbade her to attend her father's funeral. Sister Theodosia has a way of making you feel as though you've done something wrong, even when you haven't.

"Sister Teddy," Carleen used to call her. Behind her back, of course. And behind Mom's. Mom doesn't believe in saying anything negative about a religious person.

But Carleen did. In the months before she vanished, when the nun was spending so much time in Lake Charlotte, Carleen would perfectly mimic Sister Teddy's deep, monotone voice and her flinty stare. She used to say that Sister Teddy looked as if she had a giant cross stuck up her behind.

"I really miss you, Carleen," Rory says aloud softly, with a chuckle.

Then her smile fades as she finds herself wondering if she'll ever know what happened to her sister—and if she'll ever stop caring.

Tonight, when he walks slowly past 52 Hayes Street, he sees that there's someone standing on the driveway.

A twenty-something redhead, clad in cut-off shorts and a black tank top. She's winding the garden hose around the reel attached to the house, and the lawn looks freshly watered.

Hmm.

He tries not to turn his head as he passes, resisting the urge to stare at her. Not just because he's curious, but because the shorts and shirt are somewhat skimpy and she's barefoot and tanned and toned, and her hair is a glorious tumble of curls.

Rory Connolly.

Carleen's younger sister.

She's come back to stay for the summer while her brother, Kevin, goes off to Europe.

He knows this because Betty Shilling, the old lady who runs the bed and breakfast where he's staying, told him. She's lived on this block almost her whole life and she knows everyone and everything that's going on.

She comes in handy, Betty Shilling, with her neighborhood gossip.

He reaches the end of the street and thinks about turning and walking back instead of going around the block as he had planned. But he decides he shouldn't. Not with Rory Connolly out there on the driveway. She might notice him, and then what?

He isn't ready to approach her.

Not yet.

But soon.

Nodding to himself, he continues walking.

Lou is snoring.

Lou snores every night. Lou has snored nightly ever since he broke his nose playing football as a child; he has snored nightly despite the operation two years ago to correct the deviated septum that was supposedly causing him to snore.

Michelle has never had a problem sleeping through the racket until now. Now, at 3:33 on a steamy June night, with her belly swollen with an almost-term baby and her chest and throat burning with indigestion and her bladder needing to be emptied yet again, Michelle is restless. She lies on her side with two pillows beneath her head, another propped against the small of her back, and a fourth tucked between her knees, listening to Lou snore and feeling the baby pitch and roll inside her. A tiny foot must be jabbing into her ribs, and there's a triangular bump protruding to the left of her navel that has to be an elbow.

She sighs heavily as the digital clock on the nightstand flicks to 3:34, and over the baby monitor plugged in beside the clock, she thinks she hears Ozzie stirring in his crib.

She swings her legs over the edge of the mattress and hoists herself to a standing position, waiting a moment until the light-headed feeling subsides.

Then she makes her way down the hallway, which is lit only by a nightlight plugged in near the baseboard at the top of the front stairs, the only working outlet in the hall.

In Ozzie's room, she finds him sound asleep, his mouth slightly open and both arms thrown up over his head, in the exact position he was in the last time she checked, less than forty-five minutes ago.

He hasn't moved.

But she thought she heard something—a rustling whisper of a sound—and she thought it had come over the baby monitor.

Absently rubbing her belly, she stares down at her sleeping child uneasily, not certain what's bothering her but knowing that something isn't right.

It's the pregnancy, she tells herself finally, tiptoeing out of Ozzie's room. *God knows none of my senses are working properly these days.*

For one thing, her ability to smell seems to be in overdrive. She can pick up the aroma of frying meat wafting from a block away, and it's always enough to send her gagging and lurching for the toilet.

And nothing tastes right anymore, either. She used to love chocolate; now she can't stomach it. And she's never liked lemons, but lately all she craves is lemonade.

So now my ears are out of whack. Now I'm hearing things. Great. Pretty soon, I'll be seeing things, too.

She huffs a little as she trudges to the bathroom, wiping a trickle of sweat from her hairline. The night is hot and still, and she can smell honeysuckle blossoms from the hedge next door drifting through the open bathroom window.

After washing her hands and splashing cool water on her face, she realizes that she's feeling queasy again. The nausea comes and goes at all hours of the day with this pregnancy. Not like with Ozzie. When she was expecting Ozzie, she felt great.

The ultrasound in the second trimester indicated that she's most likely carrying another boy, but Michelle isn't convinced. Maybe this baby will be a girl, she thinks idly, walking back out into the hallway. Didn't she read something someplace about female hormones causing increased morning sickness in pregnant women?

Wearily, she heads downstairs to find something to settle her stomach before she goes back to bed. Just a handful of cereal or a couple of saltines; suddenly, she's feeling sleepy again.

She turns on lights as she moves through the quiet house, though there's enough moonlight filtering in the windows to see her way to the kitchen. There's something spooky about the darkened rooms, and it isn't so hard to believe that there are ghosts lurking in the shadows.

In the kitchen, Michelle crosses to the cupboard and takes out the box of saltines from this morning. It feels lighter than it should.

Frowning, she opens the flaps and looks inside to see that there are only two saltines left in the bottom of the waxed paper bag, along with some small broken pieces and crumbs.

There were more than this earlier today—weren't there?

At least a dozen crackers, maybe more. She remembers how she ate only one from the handful she took out and put the rest back into the bag.

Where did they go?

Lou didn't eat them. He worked late tonight, and came straight to bed when he got home.

And Molly didn't babysit today. There's been no one in the house but Michelle and Ozzie.

Could Ozzie have . . . ?

No, she thinks, shaking her head firmly. Ozzie can't reach this cupboard. Even if she *had* taken her eyes off him long enough for him to sneak alone into the kitchen.

But she hadn't. He was under her constant supervision after the toilet brush incident this morning.

Okay. If Lou hadn't eaten the crackers and Ozzie hadn't eaten the crackers . . .

I must have done it, Michelle tells herself dubiously. *I must have done it, and forgotten all about it.*

She's momentarily shaken by the thought that she could actually have done something and not remember.

Am I losing my mind? she wonders.

No. Of course not.

After all, isn't forgetfulness a symptom of pregnancy? Just last week, she'd spent a good hour searching the house for her library books before she'd given up and gone in to say she'd lost them. The librarian had given her an odd look and told her that she'd dropped them off the day before, and she'd instantly remembered that yes, of course she had. She'd somehow forgotten.

And she still hasn't managed to call her cousin John, the architect, even though Lou reminds her constantly to take care of it. It keeps slipping her mind, the way everything else seems to lately.

Mulling that over, she methodically chews and swallows the last two crackers and tosses the empty box into the trash.

Then, slowly, she makes her way back through the house up to bed, turning off the lights again and trying not to be spooked by the path of darkness behind her.

When she's back in bed beside Lou, with the pillows once again strategically placed and her bladder empty and her stomach settled, she can't fall asleep, even though she was yawning only minutes ago.

For some reason, she keeps thinking about those stupid crackers.

Keeps wondering why, if she really did eat them, she hadn't just finished them, instead of leaving two measly crackers and some crumbs in the bottom of the bag. Lord knows, she's eaten everything else in sight lately.

Okay, if you didn't eat them, she asks herself reluctantly, *then who did?*

CHAPTER FOUR

"What are you doing?"

Rory jumps at the sound of a voice behind her and turns to see her mother standing in the doorway of the kitchen. Her hair is disheveled and she's wearing a faded floral sundress Rory remembers from her childhood, which means it must be at least ten years old, probably more. Her feet are clad in heavy burgundy pumps and she's clutching a black faux leather handbag, neither of which go with the summer dress. Despite the June heat, there's a white sweater over her shoulders, the long sleeves hanging empty and the top button fastened at her throat.

"Good morning, Mom. Are you going out?" *Like that?* But she doesn't say the last part. She's not a teenaged girl anymore, worried about what her friends will think of her crazy mother in her crazy get-up. She has her own life, far from here, and she could care less if people talk about Maura.

"I just came back from church."

"Oh, right." Rory hadn't realized she was gone. But she should have known. Maura never misses daily mass. "Can I make you something for breakfast? There are bagels and lox and—"

"What are you doing, Rory?"

Mom is staring at the open paint can on the newspaper-lined linoleum; at the dripping white-coated brush in Rory's hand.

"I'm painting the woodwork," she says in a small voice, feeling suddenly like a little girl.

She braces herself for her mother's reaction.

There's no raised voice. No *how dare you?*

Her mother's eyes move to the frame around the window over

the sink. There's a vivid line between the bright new white paint and the dingy old part.

"Good" is all Maura says, with a shrug.

She moves to the stove, sets the beige tea kettle on the burner, lights the flame.

Rory goes back to her painting, trying to think of something to say as her mother measures imported tea leaves from a metal canister. Mom has always been frugal, but she orders the tea directly from Dublin, her one indulgence.

Finally, her mother seats herself at the kitchen table with her steaming mug—liberally sweetened as always, Rory notices as she counts the heaping spoonfuls of sugar Maura dumps in.

"Where's Molly?" she asks; there has been no sign of her sister yet this morning.

"In bed, I guess."

"Does she always sleep this late?"

"It's only nine o'clock."

Rory, who has been known to sleep until noon if undisturbed, has no response to that.

There's silence in the kitchen for a while, broken only by the soft, swishing sounds of Rory's paintbrush and her mother's occasional sips and swallows.

Finally, Rory says impulsively, "I know the stereo in the den is broken"—she had already tried that, earlier—"but is there a radio around someplace, Mom?"

There's a pause. "I don't know."

"I just thought it would be nice to listen to music while I work. There used to be that transistor radio of Dad's in the hall bathroom upstairs, but it's gone."

"Mmm."

"And I know Molly has a boom box in her room, but I can't ask her to borrow that. I know how teenaged girls are about loaning their stuff to . . ."

She trails off. She was about to say, *To a sister.*

Once again, Carleen's ghost seems to have seeped into the room. Rory wonders if her mother is remembering, as she is, the battles she and her sister used to wage over clothes, record albums, books.

She used to sneak into Carleen's room to borrow things, and

would promptly put them back in perfect condition, yet, somehow, Carleen always knew. Sometimes, she would let Rory slide, only later making a catty comment like "I hope you enjoyed wearing my jean jacket last weekend." But most of the time, Carleen would throw a fit.

As if she never borrowed my black velvet headband or my one perfect pink frost lipstick that didn't clash with my hair.

Rory realizes that she's thinking like a fifteen-year-old again. That, in her mind, Carleen will be forever seventeen.

We never got the chance to get past all that sibling rivalry stuff, she thinks with a pang of loss. *We never got the chance to grow past it, to become friends.*

She glances over her shoulder and sees her mother just sitting at the table, her hands cupped around the half-empty mug of tea in front of her, a faraway expression in her eyes.

"I thought I'd take a ride over to Saratoga Springs one of these days," Rory says, after more uncomfortable silence.

There's no reply.

"Would you like to come with me, Mom? We could go to lunch at Hattie's Chicken Shack, and maybe do some shopping. There are some nice stores on Broadway and I'd like to get—"

"I can't."

That's all Maura says, in a clipped tone. Just *I can't.* No reason. No excuse.

Why can't you? Rory wants to ask. But she doesn't dare. She knows the reason. Which reminds her . . .

"So, Mom," she says conversationally, "what's up with Sister Theodosia these days?"

Her mother blinks. "What do you mean?"

"Is she still in Buffalo? What church was she at? Wasn't it Our Lady of . . . something-or-other?"

"No. No, it was St. Lucretia's."

"Is she still there?"

Her mother nods.

"Do you see her often?"

"Not often."

When was the last time? And does she realize you've gone crazy?

Rory dips her brush and slaps more paint onto the woodwork; too much. It spatters and starts to run down and she quickly catches the drips with her brush, smoothing the excess paint over the edge of the frame. She concentrates on getting it into the cracks at the corner, making sure there are no bare patches.

"It would be nice to talk to Sister Theodosia after all these years," she says after a few minutes, when the painting is under control again.

Will her mother know she's lying? Of course she will. Surely Maura can't think Rory was actually fond of the dour-faced nun. But then, Carleen was the only one brazen enough to vocalize her dislike for Sister Theodosia.

"Mom?"

Rory turns to see that the chair at the table is vacant; even the mug of tea is gone.

She hears footsteps slowly ascending the creaky hall stairs.

With a sigh, she dips the brush into the paint again.

"No, Ozzie, on the paper. On the *paper!*" Michelle grabs her son's chubby hand, which is dripping with red goo, just as it's about to come down on the top of the picnic table. She guides it to the shiny white paper, already covered in smears of green and blue.

"That's right, sweetie," she says, watching him spread streaks of red over the page. "See? Isn't finger painting fun?"

"Fun," agrees Ozzie. "More paint."

She catches his hand before he can tip over the shallow foil dish of red paint, and helps him coat his fingers with more.

With a sigh, she watches him go to work again, an expression of pure bliss on his chubby features. After a moment, she grabs a blank sheet of paper for herself and dabs her forefinger into the red paint.

"Mommy paint, too?" Ozzie asks, delighted.

"Sure, why not?" She drags her finger over the page, creating intricate swirls of red.

Gee, haven't you come a long way? she asks herself sardonically, thinking about the long-ago summer she spent in Paris, seated before an easel on the Seine. It was ten years ago this year, she realizes. She'd been a college student then, an art major at Buff State, and dazzled over the opportunity to study watercolor technique with Marcel du Bois, one of the world's greatest living painters. When she'd left Lake Charlotte in May, she'd been reluctant to go so far from home—from her mother and Lou, whom she'd been dating for a few years by then. But how could an aspiring artist stay homesick for very long in Paris?

August had arrived much too soon, and her instructor had encouraged her to stay, telling her she had a rare talent and he'd like to keep working with her. Praise from the great du Bois never came easily, and Michelle had actually hesitated, albeit briefly, before telling him that she had to get home. Back to Lake Charlotte and Lou, for a brief week together before she went back to Buffalo and he left for Long Island, where he would enter his first year law school.

Now she remembers how much they'd argued during those fleeting days together. Lou seemed to have changed over the summer; he was no longer his happy-go-lucky self. Part of that might have been due to the summer job he'd taken to pay his law school tuition—working on the new sewer line the town was building out on High Ridge Road. Great money, but who would be thrilled with the long, grueling hours in the heat of summer? Certainly not Lou, who had been a lifeguard out at the Curl beach every summer since he was sixteen.

But Michelle had known the job wasn't the only miserable thing about Lou's summer. He resented her for leaving for three months; he'd even tried to talk her out of going to Paris before she left. And once she was back, it seemed as though all he did was gripe about all the great times they *could have* had together, making her feel guilty for ruining his summer. She had half expected Lou to break up with her that fall, but when they saw each other again at Thanksgiving, he was his old self again.

A month later, he gave her an engagement ring for Christmas. In January, she transferred to a state school on Long Island and finished her degree there. Lou talked her into changing her major to elementary education so that she could teach art, pointing out that she could hardly expect to build a career as a painter. Lou had always been practical. And she was always a dreamer.

Still am, she tells herself now with a faint smile as she spirals a bit more red paint onto her paper. She watches Ozzie mix a splotch of red with blue to make purple, and wonders whether he inherited her artistic talent. Too early to tell.

"Good, Ozzie," she tells him. "That's purple. See? Red and blue make purple."

"Purple. Like Barney."

"Like Barney," she echoes, smiling.

She and Ozzie work quietly, she with careful strokes and he in slapdash toddler style, and she's lost in her memories of the past. She remembers the crummy one-bedroom apartment she and Lou rented in Smithtown after they were married, and how she worked two waitressing jobs to support them as Lou struggled through law school. He had terrible study habits—he liked to be active, out playing sports or hanging around with friends, rather than sitting in a chair poring over texts and notes.

Still, he graduated and managed to pass the bar—on the third try—then landed a job with a small practice in their hometown. He had hoped to settle in New York City with a high-profile firm, but Michelle refused, wanting to be near her widowed mother. As an only child, she felt obligated.

Thank God Lou finally gave in on that one. At least I had a few years with Mom before she died. And if we hadn't lived with her and saved money, we would never have been able to afford this place, she thinks, looking up at the back of the big house.

Pretty soon, the shady spot where she and Ozzie are sitting at the picnic table will be encompassed by the new family room. The yard will still be a good size, though, she concludes, glancing around. It stretches quite a distance back, with raspberry bushes rambling along the property line.

Michelle and Ozzie had inspected the briars this morning before settling down to paint. There's going to be a large, early crop this year. Another day or so, and the berries will be ready to pick.

Maybe I'll make a berry pie, she decides. *Or preserves, even.*

Her mother had always put up jars of homemade jam in midsummer.

Then again, the thought of slaving in a hot kitchen isn't entirely appealing. Especially with Ozzie getting underfoot, and her belly growing more enormous with every passing day.

"Mommy paint," Ozzie commands, realizing she's stopped and jabbing her in the arm with a purple finger.

"Careful, Ozzie!"

Michelle grabs one of the damp paper towels she had the

foresight to bring outside, and wipes at the streak of paint. It's the washable kind, but she doesn't want to get any on her one decent pair of maternity shorts.

"I think we're done painting for this morning," Michelle tells her son, who promptly lets out a shriek of protest. She wipes both of his hands, and then her own, on the paper towels. Then she wearily grabs him by the arm, careful not to brush his paint-smeared hand against her clothes, and starts pulling him toward the house as he continues to bellow.

"Quiet, Ozzie," she says firmly, glancing over at the Connollys' house on one side, then the Wasners' on the other. "The neighbors don't want to hear you screaming."

"Don't worry about it," a voice says.

Michelle gasps and spins around.

"Sorry . . . didn't mean to scare you."

A face peeks through the honeysuckle hedge on the property line, and Michelle recognizes Rory Connolly. She's never met Molly's older sister, though she vaguely remembers seeing her around town years ago, when Michelle was in high school and Rory just a freckled little kid with that distinct mop of red hair.

In fact, Michelle's friend Sarah had babysat for the Connolly brood a couple of times, before declaring them too wild. Especially Carleen, the oldest—the one who had later disappeared, that same summer Michelle was in Paris. She had returned home to find Lake Charlotte in turmoil over the four missing girls.

Now Michelle looks at the middle Connolly sister and decides she looks nothing like Carleen or Molly, both of them dark-haired and blue-eyed. Rory's auburn curls fall in a glorious mass to her shoulders, and Michelle's artist's eye notes the intense, varied shades of red glinting in the sunlight.

"I'm Rory Connolly," the woman says in a likable, straightforward way. "I don't think we've ever met."

"Michelle Randall. I don't think so, either, although I do remember you when you were a little girl."

"Really? You're from Lake Charlotte, then?"

"Yup. I used to be Michelle Panati."

"Shelley Panati?"

"That's me. At least, it *was*." Michelle smiles at the old nickname, the one she'd had her whole life, until she met Lou. He was the first one who had ever called her Michelle. *"Michelle, ma belle . . ."* He used to sing the old Beatles song in her ear when they slow-danced. He hasn't sung it in a while. Years, probably.

But then, when was the last time they slow-danced? At their wedding? And if they tried now, he wouldn't be able to get closer than a few feet away, Michelle notes ruefully, glancing down at her protruding belly.

"I remember you," Rory is saying. "You hung around with Sarah Carter, our old babysitter."

"That's right."

"She stopped coming after that night Carleen locked her in the linen closet. God, she was always such a terror when we had sitters . . ."

Rory trails off and her green eyes cloud over.

Michelle realizes she's thinking about her sister. Nobody ever did find out what had happened to her or the other girls.

It's bad enough when someone close dies, Michelle thinks, an image of her mother popping into her head. But it must be even more horrible to live your life wondering whether someone you love is dead or alive, the way Rory Connolly has.

Michelle can't think of a thing to say. For a moment, the only sound is chirping birds and a lawn mower rumbling in the distance.

Luckily, Ozzie fills the gap by announcing, "Paint."

"No, Ozzie, we're through," Michelle tells him, then sees that he's pointing to Rory. She realizes her neighbor is dressed in a dark T-shirt and shorts that are covered in white spatters, as are her arms and legs.

"That's right, little guy," Rory says with a wry grin. "I'm covered in paint. Just like you."

"Luckily, his is the washable kind," Michelle says.

"Unfortunately, mine isn't. I never should have started this project. I've only been at it a few hours and I'm already sick of it—not to mention a mess."

"What are you painting?"

"The trim in the kitchen. I thought I'd perk the place up a bit. It's so damn dreary. Oops, sorry." She belatedly covers her mouth with a hand and glances down at Ozzie. "I'm not used to watching my tongue."

"It's okay."

"Anyway, I had planned to do some painting when I decided to come home for the summer, but I was thinking more along the lines of oils and watercolors than latex semigloss."

"You paint, then? I mean—"

"I majored in art in college. Berkeley."

"Me, too. Buff State. Then I switched."

"Majors?"

"And colleges. I ended up majoring in education and teaching art—but I'm not even doing that anymore. This is about as artistic as I get these days," Michelle says ruefully, gesturing toward the picnic table, where the finger paints are still spread out.

"Hey, don't knock it. Looks like you have a Picasso in the making. Huh, little guy?" Rory reaches down and ruffles Ozzie's hair. "Molly babysits for you, doesn't she?"

"Molly? Where's Molly?" Ozzie brightens and looks around.

"He loves your sister," Michelle tells Rory. "She's terrific with him."

"She is?" Rory looks incredulous. "I mean, I don't know her all that well these days. She's just kind of quiet when she's around here. Your typical sullen teen. But then, she's a thirteen-year-old girl. I guess we all go through that stage—miserable at home, and all sweetness and light everywhere else."

"The old adolescent angst," Michelle says, nodding. "I should probably be happy with two boys. At least they don't seem as moody as teenaged girls."

"So you know what you're having, then?" Rory asks with a gesture at Michelle's stomach. "Another boy?"

"That's what the doctor says."

"When are you due?"

"Not soon enough. Early August, supposedly." Michelle pushes a damp strand of hair out of her face. "But then, we've got a lot to do before the baby comes, so I guess I should hope the baby takes his time."

"You've done a lot of work on the house," Rory notes, bobbing her head toward the construction Dumpster near the garage. "Is it almost done?"

"Actually, no. I don't think it's ever going to be done. And now we're going to rip off the back wall and add on a family room. Which reminds me ... I have to call the architect. My husband'll flip if I forget to do it again today."

"Well, it was nice talking to you. Maybe you and Ozzie can come over to visit someday. It would be nice to have some company, especially a little kid. The place is too quiet."

"Maybe we will," Michelle says politely, though she can't quite imagine dropping by the Connolly house.

Molly, Rory, and Kevin are all pleassant enough, but their mother is a different story. From what Michelle has seen, the woman is just plain weird. She scurries to and from church every morning with her head bent as if against a strong wind, and she never answers Michelle's greetings or bothers to look up. Aside from those early-morning walks to Holy Father a few blocks away, she hardly sets foot outside of the house.

But sometimes at night, Michelle sees Maura Connolly standing in a second-floor window overlooking the Randalls' house, just staring vacantly for hours. It's eerie, though Lou insists Michelle shouldn't worry about it.

"She's just a harmless nutcase," he's always saying. "Who knows? Maybe you'd be nutty, too, if your kid vanished off the face of the earth."

Maybe I would, Michelle thinks now, instinctively tightening her grip on Ozzie's arm.

"Well, I guess I'll see you around," Rory says.

"Sure," Michelle replies, and starts to turn toward home.

Rory gasps, causing her to spin around again to see her neighbor gaping at her bare legs, pointing.

Michelle looks down to see bright red blood streaked all over her thighs. "No! Oh, no! My baby!"

Startled by her outburst, Ozzie immediately starts crying.

"It's okay, it's okay, Ozzie. Don't panic, Michelle." Rory holds her steady, rubbing her arm.

Trembling, Michelle reaches down to touch the sticky blood—then nearly sobs in relief.

"It's paint," she says, shaken. "It's only paint. Ozzie must have gotten it on me when I wasn't looking."

"Thank God." Rory releases her arm and shakes her head. "I thought it was blood. I thought something had happened with the baby ..."

"So did I. I . . . God. I'd better go in and get cleaned up."

Her heart still pounding, Michelle walks slowly toward home, holding Ozzie's hand tightly.

Just a false alarm, she tells herself up in the bathroom as she washes the red paint off her legs with a cool wet washcloth. *Everything is fine.*

But for some reason, she can't quite shake the distinct feeling that something isn't right.

"I met the little boy you babysit for when I was outside a little while ago."

Molly looks up from the peanut butter sandwich she's making. "Ozzie?"

"Yup. He's cute," Rory says, pausing with her paintbrush poised over the can. "And he really likes you."

"Uh-huh." Molly dips the knife into the almost-empty jar, spreads another glob on her bread, and then licks the knife. She's about to scrape some more peanut butter from inside the rim of the jar when Rory stops her.

"Don't do that, Molly."

"Why not?"

"It's gross, that's why not. You get your spit into the peanut butter."

Irritated, Molly tilts the jar and says, with exaggerated patience, "It's almost empty. I'm just going to throw it away, not put it back into the cupboard. So don't stress about it, okay?"

Rory shrugs and goes back to her painting.

Molly slaps the two pieces of bread together with one hand, still holding the knife with the other. She deliberately licks it again, slowly, and considers closing the jar and putting it back into the cupboard just to irk Rory.

Ooops, she'll say. *There's more in here than I thought. I'll just save it for later.*

After all, what difference does it make if her spit gets into the peanut butter jar? Like she really cares. Besides, Mom doesn't eat it. Kevin used to, but he's gone. And it's not as if Rory has any claim to anything in this house.

"Listen, Molly?"

"What?" Warily, she turns toward her sister, who's perched on a chair, straining to reach the trim above the back door.

Rory says in a low voice, "I wanted to talk to you about Mom."

"What about her?" Molly tosses the knife into the sink and the jar into the trash, half expecting Rory to remind her she's supposed to wash it out and recycle it. What a pain *that* is—scrubbing out every trace of icky, gooey peanut butter just because there's a new law in Lake Charlotte, thanks to a bunch of environmentalists. Rory's probably one of those save-the-planet, granola-head types, Molly speculates.

Her sister carefully balances her paintbrush on the rim of the open can and climbs down from the chair to come face-to-face with Molly. "I'm worried about her."

"About Mom? Why?" Molly's stomach turns over. First Kevin leaves, now something's wrong with her mother? "What happened to her?"

"She's just . . . so out of it."

"Well, *duh!*" Relieved, Molly picks up her sandwich and the glass of milk she'd poured for herself, and starts for the door.

"Where are you going?"

"Outside. To eat my lunch. On the back steps."

"Can't you eat it in here?"

Molly blinks. "Why would I? It smells like disgusting paint fumes in here."

"It does not. The windows are open and, anyway, this kind of paint has no fumes."

"It does, too."

"Well, I'm not done talking to you yet."

"What, you thought it was up to you to tell me that Mom's off her rocker? It might be news to you, but I've been living here my whole life, helping Kevin take care of her," she says pointedly.

Where have you been? she wants to add. *Why haven't you been with us? Why did you get to leave, to go out into the world and do whatever you feel like doing? And now Kevin's gone, too. And pretty soon it's just going to be me taking care of Mom for the rest of my life, because God knows you won't stick around long.*

She doesn't say any of it, but she's pretty certain Rory knows what she's thinking. How could she not?

Her sister doesn't quite meet her gaze when she says, "It's

much worse than it's ever been. She's having imaginary conversations with Daddy."

"She always does that. Carleen, too."

"Oh." Rory seems to be pondering that.

Molly shifts her weight. Rory's standing in front of the chair, which is blocking the door. Molly can't get out unless she asks her sister to move, and for some reason, she doesn't do that. She just stands, holding her sandwich and milk, waiting.

"What about Sister Theodosia?" Rory asks after a moment.

"What about her?"

"Does she know what's going on with Mom?"

"I have no idea. She visits her once in a great while; they go to church, whatever."

"When was the last time she was here?"

Molly thinks about that. She never pays much attention to the dour nun's visits, preferring to make herself scarce whenever Sister Theodosia is around. There's something unpleasant about the woman. For someone who's supposed to be spending her life helping people, she has a pretty lousy attitude. She's not *mean*, exactly, but she never smiles, and she always looks as though she's put out by something.

"I guess she was last here during Lent," Molly says. "Like, in March. Because I remember that she caught Rebecca and me sitting here eating a can of Beefaroni by accident and she freaked."

"By accident? You mean on a Friday?" A smile quirks Rory's lips.

"Yeah. No meat on Fridays during Lent."

"Right. Carleen once made a big point about eating a hot dog in front of Sister Theodosia on Good Friday. When she started freaking out, Carleen pulled out the package and waved it in her face. They were tofu wieners."

Molly grins. "What'd she do?"

"Sister Theodosia? Oh, you know, probably sighed deeply and told Carleen she'd pray for her soul. She was always saying stuff like that about her."

"About Carleen?"

"Yeah." Rory's smile fades.

Molly knows what she's thinking. That all those prayers for

Carleen's soul didn't do much good, because something awful happened to her.

"Anyway," Rory says, all business again, "I thought I might call Sister Theodosia and talk to her. Maybe ask her to come for a visit."

"What? A visit? *Why?*"

"So that she can give us some insight into Mom's problems. She's losing touch with reality, Molly. We can't just sit here and do nothing."

"Well, what's Sister Theodosia supposed to do about it? Pray for *Mom's* soul?"

"She knows Mom better than anyone. Mom trusts her. Maybe she can help."

"That's crazy. All you're going to do is upset everyone. Why did you have to come back and start stirring things up, Rory? God, you have no right to go around starting trouble."

"I'm trying to *fix* things, not start trouble!" Rory shot back. "And I have every right. She's my *mother.*"

"So? She's *my* mother, too."

Rory's mouth tightens into a straight line, and Molly waits for her to say something else, but for some reason she doesn't. She just abruptly moves the chair out of the doorway, opening the escape route.

Molly takes it, making a beeline for the back steps and letting the screen door bang closed behind her.

"Here, kitty, kitty." Rebecca Wasner stands on the back porch, surveying the yard for Sebastian, the kitten she'd convinced her mother to let her keep from Ralphi's latest litter.

"Here, kitty, kitty."

No sign of a scampering ball of peach-colored fur. At Rebecca's feet, sunning herself on the top step, Ralphi lifts her head lazily, as if to search for her errant offspring.

"Don't worry, I'll find him," Rebecca tells the cat, a fat tabby her parents had once thought was a boy, and thus named Ralph. When Ralph got pregnant the first time, his name was altered accordingly.

"Here, kitty, kitty. Come on, where are you?"

Rebecca walks down the steps and into the yard, careful not

to brush against the lilies in bloom along the stone garden path. She knows from experience that their stamens leave ugly, permanent yellow stains on clothing, and she won't have time to change before going babysitting.

Today she's sitting for the Willeski family over on Lincoln Street, while their harried mother runs errands. Between the twin two-year-olds and a newborn, Rebecca figures she won't have time to even open the library book she's packed in her knapsack. It's a new biography of the author Laura Ingalls Wilder, who wrote all the Little House books.

Molly had teased Rebecca when she selected that book from the shelf, saying, "Haven't you outgrown all that 'Little House on the Prairie' stuff by now?"

And Rebecca, who cherishes her complete boxed set of pale-yellow paperbacks and still rereads them on occasion, had blushed and mumbled some inane reply.

Luckily, Molly had swiftly dropped the subject, either because she knew she'd embarrassed Rebecca, or because she was preoccupied with the encounter she'd just had with Ryan Baker.

That's all she talks about lately. Ryan.

Rebecca loves her best friend, but they seem to have little in common lately. It started last year, actually, when Molly first stopped collecting Beanie Babies, then decided she wasn't a Spice Girls fan anymore.

Although Rebecca can live with that. She's not into Beanie Babies or the Spice Girls this year, either.

But now Molly's no longer interested in making braided bead bracelets or clipping Matt Damon's picture out of magazines, pastimes that had kept them both happily occupied on gray Saturday afternoons all winter and spring.

Meanwhile, Rebecca has absolutely no desire to stake out Ryan Baker's house, which is Molly's current idea of fun.

At this rate, Rebecca is starting to wonder whether their lifelong friendship will survive the summer. Especially with Molly wanting to go to that stupid party out at the Curl tomorrow night.

"You *have* to go with me," she'd told Rebecca.

"How would we even get there? It's not like I can ask my mom to drop us off."

"I have it all figured out."

"What, ride our bikes?"

"No!" Molly had looked horrified. "That would be so cheesy. No, we'd just hike down through the woods—"

"No way. At night? I don't even like the woods during the day."

"Oh, please, Rebecca. It would be so easy. You know that path behind the Randalls' house? It comes out on Lakeshore Road, like right near the Curl."

"Hike through the woods at night? With all those bugs and wild animals?" Rebecca had shuddered.

"Wild animals? Like, chipmunks?" Molly's voice had been filled with disdain."

"Like coyotes. And wolves. And bears. No way."

"Oh, come on, Rebecca. I can't show up alone."

"Why not? Ryan will be there. You can talk to him."

"What if he's with Jessica?"

"Then you can leave," Rebecca had pointed out, with what she thought was the utmost logic.

Molly didn't see it that way. "I can't *leave*. I have to be there, no matter who he's with. How else am I going to make him fall in love with me?"

"If he's with Jessica or some other girl, how's he supposed to fall in love with you?" Rebecca had asked, perplexed.

"God, you just don't *get* it" was Molly's eye-rolling reply.

Rebecca knows she's right.

She just *doesn't* get it. Maybe she never will. Maybe she'll still be playing with her cats and babysitting and rereading *The Long Winter* while Molly and everyone else she's known since kindergarten have a blast in high school.

"Doomed to be a goober," Rebecca murmurs softly, walking across the yard, her eyes peeled for some sign of Sebastian. She sees something moving in a thatch of pachysandra near the Randalls' yard, but it turns out to be a chipmunk.

"Hi, Rebecca!"

She looks up to see little Ozzie Randall waving from a screened window on the second floor.

"Hi, Ozzie."

Michelle appears behind him, saying, "Careful, Ozzie, there's no guard on that window. Oh, hi, Rebecca."

"Hi, Mrs. Randall."

"You can call me Michelle, remember?" she says casually, as she has ever since they moved in next door to the Wasners.

But Rebecca feels funny doing that. Her parents always taught her to address adults as Mr. or Mrs. And even though Michelle seems young and laid back, she's still an adult. So most of the time, Rebecca doesn't call her neighbor anything at all. Molly, meanwhile, cheerfully calls Michelle and Lou by their first names, as though she's known them her whole life.

Rebecca wonders if Michelle thinks she's not as friendly and nice as Molly is. After all, she refused whenever Michelle asked her to babysit those first few months after they moved in. She always made some feeble excuse, and sensed that Michelle saw right through her.

But how could she come right out and say she couldn't babysit next door because she's terrified to be alone in that house?

Granted, it looks immensely better than it did before the Randalls moved in, when it was standing vacant and abandoned, as if in memorial to Emily Anghardt, who had lived there with her father until she disappeared ten years ago.

Rebecca was only three that summer, but she has vague memories of the unrest that had gripped the neighborhood after first Carleen Connolly, and then Emily, had vanished from their homes. She remembers that her mother, who used to let her play alone in the screened porch while she was busy in the kitchen, had suddenly refused to let her out there by herself. And she remembers lying in her bed at night hearing the squawk of a two-way radio through her open window, and seeing the revolving red pattern on the ceiling of her room, reflected from the dome light of a police car parked out front.

The experience left her perpetually haunted by the sense that she's never quite safe, no matter how secure things seem. She can be sitting in the living room in front of a crackling fire, Christmas tree lights sparkling in one corner, cozily watching television with her parents and her younger brother, Casey, on one of those clear winter nights when the ground is blanketed in fresh snow, and still she'll feel as though all isn't right with the world. As though something dark and scary is looming.

And the feeling has always intensified whenever she glances

out her bedroom window to see the house next door. The house where Emily Anghardt lived.

"Looking for Sebastian again?" Michelle calls down from the window.

"Yup. Have you seen him?"

"No, but we've been inside since lunch. I'll keep an eye out and let you know if he wanders onto our porch again."

Sebastian apparently doesn't share Rebecca's wariness of the Randalls' house. He's been known to show up on their doorstep, mewing, until Michelle puts out a saucer of milk.

"I love cats," she once told Rebecca. "But Lou's allergic."

Rebecca has already decided that when and if she ever gets married, it will have to be to someone who's not allergic to cats. She would never part with Sebastian or Ralphi for anything or anyone. They love her unconditionally.

"How are you feeling?" Rebecca remembers to ask Michelle, who is expecting a baby later this summer.

"You really want to know?"

Rebecca smiles. "Sure."

"Fat. Tired. Sick. Impatient. Aren't you glad you asked?" Michelle grins and keeps a grip on a squirming Ozzie's shoulders. "Oh, well. I'm almost there. Just a few more weeks. Then I'll *really* have my hands full."

"I guess so." Rebecca wants to say that she'll be glad to come over and help out after the baby comes, but she just can't do it. She knows she'll never bring herself to set foot in that house, no matter what.

She can't believe Molly isn't terrified of the place, though she suspects that her friend's bravery is, at times, an act. Molly's always been the kind of person who can't stand to let people see her weakness. Not even her best friend.

How many times in all the years they've known each other has Rebecca asked Molly how her mother's doing, only to be told, tersely, "She's fine"?

Meanwhile, everyone in town knows that Mrs. Connolly is far from fine. She went off the deep end years ago, when Molly's sister disappeared and then Mr. Connolly died.

Molly doesn't like to talk about her mother, or what happened to her sister or her father. And she rarely mentions Rory, even now that she's back in town. The only family member Molly has ever talked freely about is Kevin. She adores her older brother, and Rebecca is certain the sentiment is mutual. Kevin has never minded carting Molly and Rebecca around town, taking them to the mall and out for ice cream—stuff most older brothers would balk at doing.

"Isn't he great?" Molly is always asking Rebecca. "Isn't he the best?"

Then Kevin decided to go off to Europe, and Molly clammed up about him, too. Rebecca knows her friend is feeling abandoned in her brother's absence, but Molly won't talk about that.

No, these days Ryan Baker is the topic of all her conversations. For her friend's sake, Rebecca hopes he really will fall in love with her. But in her opinion, Molly's building him up to be some kind of god, when he's merely a thirteen-year-old boy with freckles and a sunburned nose.

"It's time for Ozzie's nap, Rebecca. We'll see you later," Michelle calls down.

"See you later." Rebecca waves, then scans the yards one more time for a sign of Sebastian.

Nothing.

With a sigh, she goes inside to get her knapsack and head over to the Willeski house, telling herself the kitten is just out hunting mice in the woods, and will surely turn up by nightfall.

A thumping sound startles Rory as she's wearily dabbing the bristles of her paintbrush into the final hard-to-reach corner of the crown molding above the refrigerator.

She pauses and listens, at first thinking it's coming from upstairs. Mom is hidden away in her room as usual, having refused to emerge even for the simple stir fry Rory went out of her way to prepare amidst the paint mess. At least, Rory assumes she's in her room—there was no reply when she knocked at the door to summon her mother to supper.

Molly wasn't around, either, leaving Rory to scoop the mountain of rice and vegetables—minus her own small serving—into an old, warped Tupperware container and wedge it into the refrigerator that's still crammed full from her shopping trip yesterday. Apparently, nobody eats much around here. Or talks much.

The only time Rory has spoken a word to anyone since early afternoon was when she called St. Lucretia's in Buffalo to ask for Sister Theodosia. She had been told that her mother's friend was out of town for a few days. Rather than leave a message, Rory had said she'd call back.

There's another thumping sound, and this time, Rory realizes that it's coming from the front hallway. Still grasping her paintbrush, she makes her way down from the counter she was standing on, nearly losing her balance in the process. To stop herself from toppling to the floor, she instinctively uses the hand clutching the paintbrush, leaving a long smear of white paint on the side of the refrigerator.

"Great," she mutters, jutting her lower lip to blow the mass of damp bangs away from her forehead. "What a mess."

Another thump from the front hallway sends her hurrying to see what's going on. She almost stops short when she sees the outline of a person standing on the other side of the screen door and realizes what she heard was someone knocking. It's a man, tall and broad-shouldered, his face obscured by the shadows of dusk.

In any of the places Rory has lived since leaving Lake Charlotte, an unexpected visitor wouldn't faze her in the least. She's always made friends quickly, the kind of friends who drop by and call at all hours.

But in the few days since she's been home, she's begun to grow accustomed to the silent, lonely house. Molly seems to have friends, but they don't come over. And her mother, of course, is as isolated as ever.

Must be some kind of delivery, Rory tells herself as she walks more slowly toward the door. Maybe Federal Express or UPS. But she sees, glancing at the grandfather clock as she passes it, that it's nearly nine o'clock at night, making that scenario unlikely.

She reaches the door. "Yes?" she asks, reaching for the old-fashioned switch on the wall. She presses the antique button and the porch is flooded with light.

"Hi," says the man, and she sees that he's a stranger.

A walking cliché—Tall, Dark, and Handsome. He's got the required square jaw, full lips, long lashes fringing eyes whose color she can't discern—and a nose that's slightly on the big side, saving his face from male-model perfection.

"Hi," she responds, suddenly conscious of her paint-covered clothes.

"Are you Rory Connolly?"

"Who wants to know?" she asks flippantly, feeling for all the world like she's suddenly Molly's age.

"I'm Barrett Maitland. I'm staying at the bed and breakfast down the street."

"Mrs. Shilling's?"

"That's the one."

"God, how is she? I keep meaning to get over there and say hello, but I haven't had a chance. I've kind of been . . . busy." She gestures at her clothes and the still-glistening, white-coated paintbrush in her hand.

"I'll give her your regards," says Barrett Maitland, whoever he is.

"Uh, can I help you with something?" Rory asks, eyeing him with interest that she hopes comes across as mild suspicion. No need to let him think she's checking him out or anything.

"I'm a writer . . ."

"Uh-huh," she prods, when he seems to hesitate.

She keeps her hand on the knob and glances down to see that the screen door's latch is in place. Her mother must have done that when she came home from church this morning, since no one else has used the front door all day.

Good thing, Rory thinks. *It wouldn't be a good idea to leave the door open so that any handsome, bed-and-breakfast-dwelling writer can just walk in off the street. He seems harmless enough, but . . . you never know.*

"I'm working on a book, and I was wondering if I could talk to you." Barrett Maitland speaks in a slow but straightforward manner, as though he's rehearsed what he's going to say.

"Talk to me?" Rory frowns. "Why do you need to talk to me?"

"I'm a true-crime writer, and—"

"Oh," she says flatly.

Now I get it. You're one of those ghouls wanting to rehash what happened to Carleen. What a waste of Tall, Dark, and Handsome.

"Look," he says quickly, "I know what you're thinking."

"You do?" She looks him in the eye. "What am I thinking?"

"Okay, maybe I don't," he concedes with candor, throwing his hands up in a gesture she can't help but find appealing. "But let me say that I'm writing a book a about what happened here ten years ago, and it's not going to be one of those sensationalized, tabloid-style pieces of trash that make a ton of money and become a Movie of the Week."

"Really? Then why are you writing it?"

"Because it's been ten years since those four girls disappeared, and the crime hasn't been solved. Maybe some new evidence will come to light that'll—"

"So you're not just a true-crime writer, you're an amateur detective?"

He shrugs. "Listen, I know where you're coming from, Rory."

She's taken aback—not just by his use of her first name, but by the apparently genuine expression of sympathy in his eyes. Hazel eyes, she notes, staring into them.

And yes, it's sympathy there. Not pity.

She learned a decade ago that there's a big difference between the two.

Still, he's the enemy. Here to dredge up the horrors of the past. As if it isn't hard enough to forget, without people like him meddling where they don't belong.

"I'd rather not talk to you," Rory says, her hand still on the knob.

"I know. And I don't blame you. But what if there's a chance that talking to me will trigger some crazy chain of events that will ultimately lead to solving the mystery?"

"You've obviously read too many detective novels."

"Probably. Written a few, too. Horrible ones."

Intrigued, she asks, "Were they published?"

"Nope. They're under my bed back home."

"Where's that?" she asks, suddenly curious.

"What?"

"Your bed. Home."

"New York City."

Is it her imagination, or did he hesitate slightly before answering? She finds herself wondering if he's telling the truth. Wondering if he has arbitrarily plucked New York City out of thin air.

But why would he lie about something like that? she asks herself. *What difference does it make to me where he's from? None. I'm not going to talk to him if he's from New York City, and I'm not going to talk to him if he's from Dubuque, Iowa.*

And anyway, hesitating before answering a question like that means nothing. I would hesitate, too, if someone asked where I'm from. Lake Charlotte? It's my hometown, but I haven't lived here in years. Miami? It's the last place I lived, but it's not home.

Where is home?

Uncomfortable with the direction her thoughts are taking, Rory forces her attention back to Barrett Maitland. "So, you're here in town just to write your book?" She notes that he looks like a tourist, in his white polo shirt, khaki shorts, and docksiders without socks.

"That's right. It's a great little town. I'm staying the summer, just like you."

Her head snaps up. "How did you know I'm here for the summer?"

"Mrs. Shilling told me."

"Oh." Rory wonders what else her neighbor has told him. He certainly picked the right place to stay if he wants a direct line on the neighborhood gossip.

"So, I was wondering if we could talk."

"About my sister?" she asks directly, clenching one hand on the knob and the other around the handle of her paintbrush.

"Does it bother you to discuss Carleen?"

"What do *you* think?"

"I think it must be painful. Especially after being away for so long. Coming back here must be extremely difficult. Everywhere you turn, there must be memories, especially in this old house. You must be torn between needing to remember the sister you loved and trying to forget what happened to her."

"Eloquently stated," she says tartly, needing to mask her surprise that this stranger has so aptly managed to put her muddled emotions into words. "You must be a good writer."

"I am." He rocks back on his heels, his hands in the pockets of his shorts. "Can I come in? I won't stay long. I promise."

"You can't. I'm busy." She waves the paintbrush at him, and for some reason, glances down to make sure the door is still locked. As if he's going to force his way in.

Huh. As if.

There's nothing threatening about this man. Still, she can't help but feel apprehensive.

"What are you painting?" he asks.

"The kitchen. And, look, I've been at it all day and I just made a huge mess that I have to clean up," she remembers, thinking of the brush mark on the refrigerator. "So I'm afraid I can't help you."

"If you won't talk to me, maybe your mother will?"

She gives a curt laugh. "My mother? No way."

Obviously, Mrs. Shilling hasn't told Barrett Maitland *everything* about the Connolly family.

"How about your brother? I know he's away for the summer, but if you could give me a number where I could reach him . . ."

"Sorry." She starts to turn away from the door.

"Come on, Rory, can't you cut me a break? My publisher is expecting a completed manuscript by Labor Day."

"That's not really my problem, is it?"

"Okay, look, if you won't talk to me tonight, how about tomorrow?"

"I'm busy tomorrow," she lies.

"Saturday, then? We can go out for an espresso."

"Espresso?" She turns back to him.

What are you doing, Rory? You can't be considering meeting this man, no matter how much you crave an espresso.

"There's this little cafe on Front Street where that Chinese restaurant used to be."

"I know. I saw it."

"We can sit for an hour and talk. And if it makes you uncomfortable, you don't have to stay."

"I don't know . . ."

Are you out of your mind? You can't do this.

"Seven-thirty? Saturday night?"

"Okay," she hears herself say.

I can't help it. There's no one to talk to around here. Nothing to do. I can't spend the entire summer painting woodwork, humming to myself. I'll end up like Mom.

"Great." Relief is evident in his voice. "I'll come by for you. We can walk over if it's nice out."

"No," she says abruptly. There's something too intimate—too datelike—about the thought of walking over to the cafe together on a nice summer night. "I'll meet you there. I have . . . errands I have to run before that."

"Whatever," he says easily. "I'll see you then."

"Fine."

She turns and walks back down the hall toward the kitchen, listening to his steps retreating down the wooden front steps. She finds herself wanting to turn and make sure he's walking away—that he isn't lingering to watch her through the windows.

Which is an odd thought. Why would he do that?

Because there's something strange about him. Something I can't put my finger on.

She should never have agreed to meet him Saturday night. She'd done it out of loneliness. Boredom.

And, hell, the man is great-looking.

Her lips curve into a smile.

What's wrong with being attracted to someone like him? Who wouldn't be?

You shouldn't be.

He's a true-crime writer. He wants to know about Carleen.

So? She doesn't have to tell him anything. She can say she's changed her mind. That she can't talk about that after all.

She starts scrubbing the paint mark off the side of the refrigerator, thinking about how long it's been since she had a date. Almost a month. Josh, the guy she'd been seeing in Miami, had left to sail his boat to Nantucket for the summer. She would probably have gone with him if Kevin hadn't called and asked her to come home.

So much for Josh. She hasn't heard from him since, though he'd promised to write.

Not that she's pining away. He was fun, but not someone she'd ever settle down with for the long haul. He lives on his boat, spends his life aimlessly drifting from one place to another.

Are you so different? Rory suddenly realizes. *Since when do you want to drop anchor and settle down?*

And where would she even do it? Not here. Not in Lake Charlotte. This isn't home.

An image of her father pops into her head.

Poor Daddy, with his atlases and globes and dreams of getting out of this tiny town. He never had.

Except that once. In California for that year on sabbatical. What a nightmare *that* had been.

Don't think about that, Rory commands herself. *It was long ago. It doesn't matter anymore.*

Think about something else.

She does. She thinks about Lake Charlotte, wondering if she could ever really stay put in a place like this.

True, it isn't exactly the dinky little burg it once was. There's all that new shopping out on High Ridge Road, and the upscale houses going up over in Green Haven Glen. Even the downtown area has been revitalized, with those boutiques and cafes.

There's this little cafe on Front Street where that Chinese restaurant used to be.

"That's it!" Rory says aloud, stopping in midscrubbing motion.

That's what's bothering her about Barrett Maitland.

How would he know that the cafe used to be the Rainbow Palace? Molly doesn't even remember that. The restaurant has been closed down for years.

So? Maybe he's been in Lake Charlotte before. He didn't come right out and say he's new here, did he?

No, but he definitely gave that impression . . . didn't he?

Confused, Rory analyzes her conversation with Barrett Maitland. Why wouldn't he have mentioned coming to Lake Charlotte in the past?

Oh, come on. Why would he?

Part of her wants to think that she's being way too suspicious of the guy. But it's not the common-sense-driven part of her.

No, it's the lust-driven, bored, lonely part, the part that wants him to be just a nice, regular guy who is who he says he is.

Not that that's so great, either.

I mean, a true-crime writer doing a book about the four girls who vanished from Lake Charlotte?

Hardly Mr. Perfect for you, Rory.

But at least it's a better alternative to . . .

Something else. Something too scary to even consider.

Still, the common-sense-driven part of Rory is leaning toward thinking Barrett Maitland isn't who he claims to be.

Because he was obviously in Lake Charlotte years ago. How else would he know that the little cafe used to be the Rainbow Palace?

Well, maybe someone told him. Maybe Mrs. Shilling mentioned it. After all, she's the type of person who goes on and on about everything.

That must be it, Rory concludes.

Then argues with herself, *But that's a stretch. It was just the way he said it—as if he knew. As if he remembered the Chinese restaurant.*

Okay, this has got to stop.

She's making herself crazy, overanalyzing some inane comment, being ridiculously suspicious of the man.

Besides, what's to stop her from coming right out and asking him when she sees him Saturday night? She can say, *"Barrett, have you ever been in Lake Charlotte before?"*

That's what I'll do. I'll ask him. And I'll take it from there.

The mosquitoes are biting like crazy tonight, buzzing around the warm, humid air trapped in the overgrown mock-orange hedges beneath the kitchen window at 52 Hayes Street.

A few more minutes, and then I'll have to get out of here before I'm eaten alive.

But it's so tempting to just stay, despite the mosquitoes, and watch Rory. To smile as she grunts in frustration, trying to scrub the white splotch on the side of the refrigerator.

She's not doing a very good job. She keeps stopping, staring off into space, as though something's bothering her, distracting her.

Once, she said something aloud, but it was hard to hear what it was, even with the screen conveniently open.

You'd think she'd lower the blinds.

You'd think she'd be worried that someone might be hiding, watching her.

You'd think she'd be more cautious . . .

Especially after what happened to her own sister.

But that was a long time ago.

Maybe Rory feels safe, now.

Foolish Rory . . .

She's always been a little reckless.

A mosquito buzzes loudly, seeking a patch of exposed flesh that will make a tender landing site.

Careful not to rustle the bushes when you move your hand.

Okay, good, now wait until it lands on your arm.

Slap!

There. The mosquito has been satisfyingly annihilated, leaving behind a barely perceptible smear of blood.

But it's there.

Blood.

The slightest sight of it, the faintest smell of it, brings back memories that won't stay buried forever. Memories of what happened here in Lake Charlotte ten years ago.

No! No! Please, I don't want to think about that again—

But it's too late.

The gory images come rushing back, along with the ghastly stench of rotting flesh and the hideous screams of tortured girls who should have known better.

They just should have known better.

And now, with the memories, come a flash of rage.

It was their fault. All of them. Not mine.

They ruined everything.

I only did what I had to do.

And I'll do it again if I have to.

In the kitchen, Rory suddenly turns on the faucet. The rush of water spills out the open window as she starts scrubbing her hands, standing at the sink, scrubbing, scrubbing . . .

Yes, keep at it, Rory. Dried paint isn't easy to get off your hands.

Neither is dried blood.

And believe me, Rory—I know.

CHAPTER FIVE

"Please come with me, Rebecca. I mean, I'm totally begging you."

"I told you, I can't, Molly." Rebecca folds her arms across her chest and tries not to meet her best friend's gaze. But Molly's in her face, standing less than a foot away on the other side of the Wasners' screen door.

"Why can't you?"

"Because . . . I'm busy," Rebecca lies. "I have to help my mother with some things around the house."

"Your mother isn't even home. She goes to Bingo at Holy Father every Friday night and you know it, Rebecca."

"Well, I told her I'd do some stuff while she's gone."

"Come on, Rebecca," Molly pleads, reaching out to open the screen door. She tugs on it. "Why's the door locked?"

Because I'm in the house alone and I'm afraid, as usual.

Aloud, Rebecca says, "I don't know. I guess I must have locked it without thinking." She slides the hook out of its loop and steps back as Molly pushes the door open and crosses the threshold.

"You've got to come with me, Rebecca," she says, putting a hand on Rebecca's forearm. "I really need you with me."

"No, you don't. You're going to that party to see Ryan, not to hang around with me."

"But I told you, I need someone to be with while I scope out the Ryan situation," Molly says patiently. "I mean, I can't just show up alone like some friendless geek. What's Ryan going to think?"

Rebecca sighs. "Why do you care so much what he thinks, Molly? You barely know him."

"I'm in *love* with him, Rebecca. Totally in love."

Rebecca stares at Molly, feeling like her best friend has become a stranger. She has the familiar blue eyes and curly dark hair, but she's no longer the comfortable, reliable person Rebecca has known her whole life.

Rebecca hears a soft meow and looks down to see Sebastian circling her feet. He brushes cozily against her bare ankle, and she bends to scoop him into her arms, resting her cheek against his soft, furry head. He purrs and nuzzles her with his wet, velvet nose.

Feeling fortified, somehow, by her kitten's affection, Rebecca says firmly, "I'm not coming to that party, Molly, and you can't change my mind about it. My parents would kill me—"

"I told you to say you're sleeping at my house—"

"And besides that, I don't want to stand around alone like some dork while you chase after Ryan."

"I won't leave you alone. I swear."

"Oh, yeah? What if Ryan asks you to . . . I don't know, go on some moonlit walk on the beach, just the two of you?"

Molly's face lights up. "Do you think he will?"

"No," Rebecca says flatly, hating herself for feeling a prickle of satisfaction when Molly's hopeful expression instantly evaporates. She holds tight to Sebastian, who's started squirming in her arms, and goes on, "But that's not the point. The point is, you only want me to go because you want to use me. You don't want to be with me."

"Well, why *would* I?" Molly asks, her blue eyes flashing with sudden anger. "You're about as much fun to be with as Sister Theodosia lately."

Rebecca scowls at the comparison to the sour-tempered nun who occasionally visits Molly's mother.

"You don't know how to have fun anymore, Rebecca," Molly goes on. "All you want to do is go to the library and play with your stupid cats."

As if on cue, Sebastian writhes his way out of Rebecca's grasp and leaps to the floor, landing gracefully on his feet. He meows loudly, looking meaningfully at the door.

"No, you can't go out," Rebecca tells him absently, and tries to think of something to say to Molly.

This is awful. They've had maybe three fights in the whole history of their friendship, and none were as serious as this. This time, Rebecca's feeling as though they're about to turn an important corner.

She knows that if she gives in and goes to the party with Molly, their friendship will be saved.

If she doesn't, it might not be.

"My cats aren't stupid," she says lamely, still smarting from Molly's comment.

"Yes, they are. And they smell, too."

"They do not! Cats are the cleanest animals around."

"No they aren't. Pee-eeuuh." Molly looks down at Sebastian and wrinkles her nose.

That does it.

"Get out of here," Rebecca says, hands on her hips. "Just go to your stupid party and stop bugging me."

"Gladly. It wouldn't be any fun with you around whining, anyway."

Molly tosses her dark curls, shoves open the door and stomps out onto the porch.

Naturally, Sebastian seizes the opportunity to dart out of the house.

"No . . . come back here!" Rebecca calls in frustration.

Molly pauses and turns around.

Rebecca sees a glimmer of hope in her eyes—along with a smug expression that says, *I knew you'd change your mind.*

Rebecca's temper ignites once again.

"Not *you*," she says coldly to Molly. "I was talking to the cat."

She watches Molly march down the steps and along the walk, turning along the street toward home without a backward glance.

Sebastian, meanwhile, has disappeared into the bushes.

"Sebastian!" Rebecca calls, irritated. "Get back here, kitty. Come on, it's almost dark out."

Of course, the kitten doesn't heed her warning. Why should Sebastian care if it's almost dark?

Rebecca's the one who minds that. She's the one who doesn't

want to be alone in the house at night. Somehow, things seem a little less scary with the kitten scampering around.

After a few moments of waiting on the porch, she gives up on Sebastian and returns to the living room just as the mantel clock finishes striking the hour. The television set is on. When Molly showed up at the door, Rebecca had been watching the tail end of that *Parent Trap* remake on cable. Now it's over, and the opening credits for some other movie are on the screen.

She watches for a minute, before she realizes it's a sequel to that horror movie, *Scream*. She quickly moves toward the set to turn it off. Molly made her watch *Scream* last year when she was sleeping over one night, and Rebecca had had nightmares about a stalking serial killer for months afterward.

Now, she stands in the suddenly silent living room, aware of the long shadows cast by the twilight falling outside. The only sound is the clock's steady ticking on the mantel and the faint breathing of Ralphi, who is asleep on one end of the sofa.

Relax, Rebecca tells herself. *Dad and Casey will be home any minute.*

But she knows that isn't necessarily true. Her brother had had a seven-thirty Little League game that won't be over yet, and, afterward, her father, who coaches the team, often takes everyone out to Talucci's for pizza.

Maybe I should have gone with Molly, Rebecca tells herself, walking across the living room and stopping in front of the lace-curtained bay window that overlooks the side yard and the Randalls' house.

No, she shouldn't have gone to the party. She can't let Molly talk her into doing something she isn't comfortable doing.

But now Molly's mad at you, Rebecca thinks. *You might have lost your best friend.*

She stares morosely into the shadowy yard, noticing that light spills reassuringly from most of the windows of the house next door.

The Randalls are obviously home. If Rebecca needs anything, she can just run over to get Michelle.

That scenario is so ridiculous that she frowns. What would possibly send her running *toward* the creepy house next door? If it weren't for that place looming ominously nearby her whole life, she probably wouldn't be such a nervous wreck all the time.

Has it always been this bad? Or is it just lately that she seems to have gotten more apprehensive?

Hard to tell.

With a sigh, Rebecca turns away from the window, grabs her library book about Laura Ingalls Wilder from the end table, and sits down next to the slumbering Ralphi.

"Lou? Is that you?" Michelle calls, looking up from her copy of *Child* magazine, her heart lurching into a race as a footstep creaks in the hall outside the living room.

"Who else would it be?"

Michelle sighs with relief as her husband appears in the doorway. She's been so jumpy all day for some reason. Now, when she should be relaxing, with Ozzie safely tucked into bed and the house silent and empty, she has found herself poised, listening, as though waiting for something to happen. For something to strike.

"What are you reading?" Lou asks, glancing at the magazine.

"An article about toilet training," Michelle replies.

"What does it say?"

Actually, she has no idea. She's read the opening paragraph over and over again ever since she sat down almost a half hour ago.

"Nothing I didn't already know," she tells Lou briefly. "How was your day?"

"Long. Exhausting." His suit coat is slung over one arm, his navy-and-red striped tie loosened at the neck of his rumpled dress shirt. He looks weary, but handsome as always.

There are times when Michelle takes his looks for granted, other times when she glances up at her husband and finds herself captured not by his gorgeous face, but by the fact that he chose *her*.

Not that she's so horrible-looking, when she isn't bloated with nearly nine months worth of baby. Back when she and Lou were dating, or newly married, she had always been casual about her looks. She was naturally slender, with long, naturally wavy brown hair and pretty features that didn't demand much makeup.

But once she'd had Ozzie, she'd been conscious of the fact that her figure was padded in places that had always been effortlessly lean, and there were circles under her eyes that didn't seem to fade, even on the few nights when she got a full eight hours' sleep.

And now, pregnant again, and more exhausted than ever, and feeling frumpy in her maternity wardrobe, she's acutely aware that she and her husband appear woefully mismatched. Lou might be tired and rumpled, but there's still something sharp and professional and put-together about him. There always has been.

Meanwhile, she's sitting here with her painfully swollen ankles propped on a footstool, wearing this huge pink nightshirt with a dumb floppy bow at the neck in that cutesy maternity style.

"Is Ozzie asleep?" Lou asks, tossing his jacket over the back of a chair and jerking at the knot on his tie, pulling it off.

"Maybe not asleep—he wasn't the last time I checked—but he's in bed." She glances at the baby monitor on the table beside her. "And if he's not sleeping, at least he's been quiet. Thank God."

"Was he a handful again today?"

"Of course. Knocked over a huge display of cereal at Wegman's, and he must have reached out of his seat and tossed all kinds of things into the cart when I wasn't looking. I didn't realize it until I got to the checkout, and then it was too late to put everything back. So I ended up buying stuff we'll never eat."

"Like what?"

"Those fake bacon bits. Not one, but *three* cans of cream of potato soup. And corn nuts."

"Corn nuts? I happen to like corn nuts."

"You do?"

"Sure. My mother used to buy them for me when we took long car trips."

"*Iris* bought you corn nuts?"

Lou smiles. "My mother wasn't always a prudish snob, Michelle."

"Iris and corn nuts, huh? Why do I find that hard to believe?"

"She was once as human as you and me. Husband number three corrupted her."

"Good old Murray, huh?" Michelle barely knew him. He had

died of a sudden heart attack shortly after she and Lou began dating, the summer she graduated from high school. She remembered wondering, at the time, why Lou seemed so detached from his stepfather's death. Only when she knew him better did she realize Lou had never let himself get attached to Murray. He'd made that mistake with his mother's second husband, Frank, who had been the only father figure Lou had ever known, since his own dad walked out on Iris before he was born. He had been devastated, at ten, when his mother and Frank were abruptly divorced.

And when Murray came along, Lou didn't bother to bond with him. It was his way of shrewdly protecting himself from getting hurt again.

As it turned out, he'd been wise to do so, given Murray's untimely death. The man had been wealthier than anyone realized—and not just from his thriving dental practice. He turned out to have been a successful high roller—which explained all those weekends in Atlantic City and vacations in Vegas—and, ultimately, the widowed Iris had wound up living the high life.

You'd think she would have offered to help us out through the years, Michelle thinks bitterly, not for the first time. But her mother-in-law seems oblivious to the fact that her son and daughter-in-law are perpetually in a financial struggle. Lou has never asked her for help, and Michelle has never felt comfortable suggesting that he do so. He's not particularly close to her; never has been.

Not the way Michelle was close to her mother. Joy Panati had been forced to make ends meet on Social Security and her meager secretary's pension. Still, she had always been generous with Michelle and Lou. That was just her way. She was so big-hearted.

Michelle swallows hard over the lump that always readily forms in her throat when she thinks about her mother.

I miss you so much, Mommy . . .

"Anyway," Lou is asking, "where are those corn nuts? I'm starving. I haven't eaten since breakfast."

"There's some left-over tuna salad in the fridge."

Lou makes a face. "No, thanks. I feel like something crunchy. I need junk."

"They're in the cupboard. Next to the can of peanuts. Also crunchy, and a more healthy kind of junk."

"I'll be right back. You want anything?"

"I'd love a cherry Popsicle."

"Do we have any?"

"I bought some today. I was craving them. Ate almost the whole box, but there should be one or two left."

Lou heads into the kitchen and Michelle turns back to her magazine, feeling at ease now that her husband is home.

She manages to get through the first few paragraphs of the article before Lou calls to her from the kitchen. His words are muffled.

"What?" she asks, sticking her finger in the magazine page and sitting up straighter. He does this all the time—goes into another room, then talks to her so that she can't hear what he's saying. She always ends up frustrated, getting up and going to him. And right now, with her swollen feet, she doesn't want to move.

"Where did you say you put them?" he calls loudly enough for her to hear.

"The cherry Popsicles?"

"I know where *those* are," he says sarcastically, loud and clear. "I meant the corn nuts."

"In the cupboard."

"Which cupboard?"

"The one above the microwave."

"What?"

She sighs and raises her voice. "The one where we keep the snacks."

"Where the peanuts are?"

"That's the one."

"They're not there."

"Yes, they are." Michelle waits, not wanting to get up, listening as he searches the cupboard, rustling cellophane packages and clattering cans against the countertop.

"They're not here, Michelle," Lou says again a few minutes later.

"Great," she mutters, putting her magazine aside without remembering to save her place, and hoisting herself to her feet. "The man can never find anything."

"I'm coming," she calls to him, and makes her way to the back of the house.

In the kitchen, she finds him holding her cherry Popsicle in one hand and putting things back into the cupboard above the microwave with the other.

"They were right next to the can of peanuts," she tells him.

"No, they weren't. But I found these," he replies, holding up a package of Fritos. "They'll do the trick."

"But I bought corn nuts."

"You must have put them back."

"I did not," she says, irritated.

"You must have. Here, take this, it's dripping," and he hands her the cherry Popsicle.

She licks it quickly, then says, "I know I bought the corn nuts. I remember putting them away."

"Well, they aren't here. Maybe you ate them."

"The whole bag?"

"There was only one Popsicle left," Lou points out with a shrug.

"Are you implying that I do nothing but stuff my face?"

"Of course I'm not implying that. All I said was, maybe you ate the corn nuts."

"And I said I didn't. I don't like corn nuts, and I wouldn't eat an entire bag of them, let alone not remember doing it."

"Did you call your cousin about the plans for the family room?" Lou asks, as if poised to point out, once again, that her memory is going.

"Yes, I called him. He says he'll come over some night next week to go over things with us."

"Which night?"

"He wasn't sure. He'll let us know."

"I hope he gives us enough advance notice. I'm really tied up at work these days." Lou shoves a handful of corn chips into his mouth and says, crunching, "In fact, I'm going to have to go in to the office over the weekend."

"Not Sunday."

"Why not Sunday?"

"Because we're taking that childbirth refresher course Sunday night at the hospital. Remember?"

"No."

"And you think *I'm* forgetful?" Michelle shakes her head.

"I thought we agreed that those breathing exercises were useless the first time around," Lou said. "Remember? You told me they were bullshit."

"That was when I was in the middle of hard labor. We have to go to this class, Lou. I signed us up, and I've got Molly lined up to babysit."

He sighs and reaches into the bag of Fritos again. "Fine. Whatever. I'll work tomorrow."

"Not all day?" Is it her imagination, or is he suddenly spending nearly every waking hour at work?

"I hope not all day. Look, I don't want to put in all these hours, Michelle, but I just got promoted. It goes with the territory."

"I know." She sighs. "I just feel like we hardly see each other these days. And things are going to get so crazy once the baby is here . . ."

"It'll be okay. At least then you'll be back to normal."

She bristles. "What's that supposed to mean?"

"Nothing. Just that you're kind of nutty when you're pregnant," he says, apparently oblivious to the warning tone in her voice. "You know, you're so moody, going around complaining all the time, forgetting things—"

"I *didn't* eat those corn nuts!"

"Okay, I believe you. Calm down, Michelle."

"You think I'm nutty? Like Mrs. Connolly next door?"

"Of course I don't think that. It's just your hormones. After you have the baby, you'll be back to normal."

She glares at him, then tosses her half-eaten Popsicle into the sink and stomps out of the room, muttering, "I don't care what you think . . . I didn't eat the corn nuts. I bought them, and I put them away next to the peanuts."

And then what?

And then they vanished into thin air, just like the crackers did the other day, Michelle thinks uneasily as she picks up her magazine again and stares blankly at the page.

It's almost midnight.

Rory paces to the window of her room and looks down at the

silent, empty street below, as if expecting to see Molly coming in the gate.

Where *is* she?

She left hours ago, saying over her shoulder, when Rory asked, that she was going down the street to Rebecca's. But Rory just called over there to check on her, and a sleepy-sounding Mr. Wasner had said Rebecca was in bed and, as far as he knew, Molly hadn't been there.

Rory shakes her head grimly as she stares out into the darkness, telling herself that Molly's just testing her authority. She thinks she can do whatever she wants now that Kevin's gone.

Well, she's wrong.

Rory is in charge here, and she's not about to let her sister run around at all hours of the night, the way Carleen had.

Her jaw tightens as she thinks that she's not about to let anything happen to Molly. No way.

A sudden footstep in the hallway sends her flying to the door. She jerks it open, expecting to see Molly sneaking in.

Instead, there, at the foot of the stairs leading down from the third floor, is her mother.

"Mom! My God, what are you doing?"

Maura Connolly, caught in the light spilling out of Rory's room, blinks and says, "I've got to get to the church. I'm late. Patrick is waiting."

"Mom . . . no."

Rory can only stare at the grotesque sight before her.

Her mother is wearing her wedding gown. Rory recognizes it from the old black-and-white framed photo on the mantel in the living room. There are streaks of dirt, probably from the attic floor, on the skirt, and the bodice is torn where Maura apparently tried to wedge her size twelve self into the size eight dress. A pillbox hat sits askew on top of her mother's gray hair, with a pouffy veil spilling past her shoulders.

"I'm late," Maura says again. "Patrick is waiting."

"Mom, where did you find that dress? In the attic?"

Maura's voice is reasonable, but her eyes are vacant. "This is my wedding dress."

"I know, but . . . why are you wearing it?"

A tinkle of laughter spills from her mother's lips. "Oh, Rory, did you forget? This is my wedding day!"

"Mom . . ." Rory doesn't know what to say. Gently, she puts a hand on her mother's white-glove-covered wrist. "Come on, Mom. Let's get you ready for bed."

"Bed? But it isn't time for bed."

"Yes, it is. Look—" Rory gestures at the small round window at the far end of the hall. "It's dark outside. See?"

"It's night?" Maura frowns, confused. "But it can't be. It's my wedding day."

"No, Mom, your wedding day was long ago."

"I missed it? But where's Patrick? Is he still at the church? He must be so angry."

"He's not angry, Mom."

"How do you know? Where is he?"

He's dead.

And you're crazy.

And I've got my hands full.

Why did I ever come home? Rory finds herself wondering. And then, *Why did I wait so long?*

Everything is falling apart. She's got to make things right again, somehow. She's got to save Mom from completely losing touch with reality, and she's got to get Molly under control.

Wearily, Rory guides her mother into the master bedroom and begins unfastening the row of tiny pearl buttons up the back of the dress.

"Hey, Molly, you want a beer or something?" Ryan Baker asks.

"Sure," she says happily, though she's never had a beer in her life. "I'd love one."

"Hey, you're not cold, are you?"

"Cold?" How can she tell him she wasn't shivering; she was quivering from pure joy. She doesn't dare. It didn't take long to figure out that the way to fit in at this party is to act unfazed by everything.

No, she can't admit she's so excited to be here—surrounded by the coolest kids in Lake Charlotte, in the midst of their beer drinking and their hip music—that she's actually quivering with joy.

Then again, she can't very well claim to be cold on a night like this, either. It's warm and humid and still, with no breeze to stir the water gently lapping at the sandy shore. She can hardly believe that if she hadn't taken a chance and hiked down here alone through the woods behind the Randalls' house—which she had to admit *was* pretty scary—she would be lying in her bed at home, staring at the ceiling, letting such a glorious summer night go to waste.

She's saved from replying to Ryan's question by Amanda Falk, who pops up and says, "Hey, Ryan, have you seen Jessica?"

"Nah," he says vaguely, to Molly's delight.

"Didn't she come here with you?"

"Nope. I came with Andy."

"Oh." Amanda's ice-blue eyes flick over Molly. "So Jessica isn't here?"

"Not that I know of."

"Good." Amanda breaks into a smile. "She's really getting on my nerves lately. All she talks about is herself."

"Tell me about it," Ryan says, rolling his eyes.

Molly makes a mental note never to talk about herself to Ryan, no matter what.

"I'll be right back," he says to Molly, and makes his way toward the cooler over by the bonfire someone lit on the beach.

She watches him go, admiring the fit of his Levi's from behind, and the way they bag around his ankles, above his white sneakers.

"So what's going on?" Amanda asks, startling her.

"Huh?" Molly turns her attention back to Jessica's *friend—former* friend, from the sounds of things.

"I never see you at parties."

It takes a moment for Molly to realize that Amanda's just making conversation, not being critical. With her perfect dark pageboy and impeccable wardrobe, Amanda is the kind of girl who intimidates Molly.

"Oh, I go to them sometimes," Molly says, trying to sound airy and nonchalant.

"Which ones?"

"Usually high school ones," Molly tells her on a whim. "That's probably why I never see you."

"Probably," Amanda says, looking impressed. "Are you hanging with Ryan tonight?"

Molly hesitates before nodding.

"Are you two going out or something?"

"Oh . . . well, no." *Not yet*, Molly adds to herself.

"I think he likes you, though."

Her heart soars. "You do?"

"Yeah. I can tell. He used to look at Jessica that way."

"What way?"

"You know how he does that thing where he ducks his head and kind of raises his eyes to see you?"

"I know exactly what you mean."

"Well, like that. He only does that when he likes someone."

"Really?"

"Totally." Amanda grins. "Jessica is going to be so pissed when she finds out Ryan's going out with someone else."

"But . . . we're not going out."

"You will be."

"You think?"

"Definitely. I'll even put in a good word for you. Ryan and I are old friends. He listens to me. Our mothers are in the same garden club."

Molly smiles, wondering why she never noticed before how nice Amanda is. For some reason, she always assumed she was snotty and stuck-up, like Jessica.

Wait till I tell Rebecca about this, Molly thinks, then catches herself, remembering the fight she and Rebecca had.

She wonders if their friendship is over.

Well, so what if it is? she thinks stubbornly. Rebecca's been such a bore lately, it'll be no great loss.

Besides, Molly can always make new friends.

"So, who did you come with?" she asks Amanda, banishing her thoughts of Rebecca.

"Dana and Noelle and Lisa. They're over there. Want to come and say hi?"

"I don't know." Molly scans the beach over by the campfire, looking for Ryan.

Amanda laughs and grabs her arm. "Don't worry, he'll find you. Come on."

"Okay," Molly says, and allows herself to be pulled over to the most popular girls in her class.

"Here, kitty, kitty," Rebecca calls softly, standing in the middle of the deserted backyard. "Here, kitty, kitty."

Where on earth is Sebastian? She hasn't been able to sleep all night, knowing her kitten is outside wandering around. It wouldn't be so bad if her mother hadn't insisted that they have his claws removed so he wouldn't shred the furniture. That left him virtually defenseless against whatever predators roam the woods.

Rebecca can't stand thinking about what could happen to poor Sebastian out here alone. Now, it's past one in the morning and she finally snuck downstairs to see if she can find him.

"Sebastian!" she hisses into the still night air. "Where are you?"

No telltale rustling in the woods.

This is all Molly's fault, Rebecca thinks bitterly, creeping along the row of blooming peonies toward the dense patch of pachysandra near the Randalls' yard, where Sebastian sometimes likes to hide.

If she didn't make me so angry when she was here earlier, I never would have told her to get out. I would have been paying more attention to Sebastian, and he never would have gotten away when Molly opened the door.

She knows Molly's sister Rory called earlier, looking for her. She heard her father answer the phone, and figured out what was going on by eavesdropping on his end of the conversation. She wanted to feel glad that Molly was going to find herself in trouble with her sister, but, instead, she was plagued by guilt, adding to her difficulty in falling asleep.

If she couldn't go to the party with Molly, the least she could have done was offer to cover for her.

Then again, why should she?

What's Molly done for me lately? Absolutely nothing, that's what, she thinks churlishly now. *And I've lost poor Sebastian because of her.*

"Here, kitty, kitty . . ."

She prowls along at the edge of the pachysandra, listening for the kitten. Not a sound to stir the still night air.

It's almost eerily quiet, Rebecca notices. There's not even a slight breeze.

The calm before the storm, she finds herself thinking, though she's pretty sure there's no rain in the forecast.

"Here, kitty, kitty . . . Here, Sebastian . . ."

She stops at the rusted post marking the property line between the Wasners' house and the Randalls'. Does she dare cross into the yard next door?

She glances up at the house; sees that it's looming above her, dark and silent. Not that it would matter if the lights were on and Michelle or Lou were awake. They wouldn't mind if she went into their yard looking for her cat.

But I mind, Rebecca thinks nervously. *I'm too spooked to go over there in broad daylight, let alone in the dead of night.*

Dead of night.

Now there's a comforting phrase, she tells herself, standing with her forefinger in her mouth, mindlessly chewing on her fingernail.

Don't be such a wimp. You have to go over there. What if Sebastian is there? What if he's in trouble? What if he got into a fight with a coyote and dragged himself, bleeding, to the Randalls' back porch?

Rebecca glances up again at the foreboding house, then takes a deep breath and lifts her bare foot to step forward.

A sudden burst of light stops her in her tracks.

"Rebecca? What are you doing out here?"

She spins around and sees her father standing on the back steps in his T-shirt and boxers, in the glow of the floodlight that now illuminates the yard.

"I'm looking for Sebastian, Daddy. I told you, he got outside before, and I'm worried about him."

"He'll come back in the morning." Her father rubs his eyes sleepily. "Now get inside."

"But he doesn't have any claws—"

"He'll be fine. Come on, before Casey and your mother wake up, too."

"All right." With an odd mixture of reluctance and relief, Rebecca turns away from the Randalls' yard and walks briskly toward home.

* * *

The front door quietly clicks shut, an almost imperceptible sound, but one that causes Rory to sit up straight on her father's old easy chair in the darkened front parlor.

She strains, listening. Quiet footsteps move toward the staircase.

"Molly?" she calls, standing and heading toward the archway leading to the hall.

There's no reply, and for a moment, she hesitates, filled with doubt, the goose bumps prickling on the base of her neck. What if it isn't Molly? What if it's some dark intruder?

"What?"

At the sound of her sister's voice, Rory expels the breath she hadn't realized she was holding.

She looks into the hallway and sees Molly paused with one foot on the bottom step, gingerly placed as though in an effort to avoid creaking.

"What do you think you're doing?"

Molly turns to face her, blue eyes flashing. Rory notices that she's lined them with dark pencil, and her lashes are thicker than usual. Mascara. And she's wearing lipstick. A cranberry color that's too dark for her Irish-cream complexion.

"What does it look like I'm doing? I'm going up to bed."

"Really? It looks an awful lot like you're sneaking into the house in the middle of the night."

"I'm not sneaking in. Why would I have to sneak in?"

"Maybe so that I won't hear you?"

"Why would I care about that?" Molly tosses her head defiantly. "What would it matter to you when I come and go?"

"It would matter," Rory says evenly, "because I'm in charge here."

"You are not."

"Oh, yes I am . . . Molly." It takes every ounce of Rory's willpower to use her name, not to call her *young lady* instead.

The stern phrase would come so naturally.

She's transported back over the years, back to so many other hot, still summer nights, to another dark-haired, blue-eyed teenaged girl standing on these very steps, poised to sneak up the stairs to her room.

"Just what do you think you're doing, young lady?"

Daddy's voice would carry all the way up to Rory's bed on the third floor, where she lay awake, wondering where on earth Carleen had been, what she could possibly have been up to, out at this hour.

"I don't have to listen to you."

Rory blinks, realizing the words have come from Molly, not Carleen. But it could have been her older sister speaking. Molly sounds like her, looks like her, acts like her.

"Look, you just can't do things like this, Molly," Rory says, trying to be reasonable. "You can't stay out by yourself in the wee hours—"

"I wasn't by myself."

"Great," Rory says flatly. "Who were you with?"

"Just . . . someone."

"A boy," Rory says, shaking her head. "You were with a boy, weren't you? Molly, you're going to get yourself into trouble just like— God, why don't you stop to look at yourself, to think about what you're doing?"

"What makes you think I don't know what I'm doing? You have no right to—"

"I have *every* right!"

"You're not my mother."

"No, but you need one desperately," Rory retorts, then bites down on her tongue.

Don't lose your cool. Don't fly off the handle. Don't say anything you'll regret. You can't slip. You can't let her know. You promised.

"Molly," she says after a moment, keeping her voice level, "why don't we talk about it? Why don't you tell me where you were, what you were doing? I can give you advice—"

Molly rolls her eyes. "I don't need your advice. I can take care of myself."

"No, you can't. You're too young to run around with boys, letting them take advantage of you. You need to be careful!"

"That's bullshit."

"Watch your mouth!"

"Why should I? I can say whatever I want. I can do whatever I want, and you can't stop me."

"God, Molly, what are you trying to do to yourself? You're going to ruin your life the way your mother ruined hers!"

The moment the words spill from her mouth, Rory realizes what she's done. Oh, Christ. She gasps and claps a hand over her lips, hoping Molly didn't catch what she said.

But her sister is staring at her through those eyes that are clumsily rimmed with too much makeup. "*My* mother?" Molly echoes.

"Mom," Rory says quickly. "I'm talking about Mom."

"No, you aren't."

"Of course I am."

"No. Oh, my God." Molly's voice is an octave higher, a little-girl wail that makes Rory cringe, makes her sick with regret.

"Molly—"

"You're not my sister, are you?"

"Molly—"

"And *she* wasn't, either." She flings a careless hand at the framed photo of Carleen that hangs above the stairway landing. "She was my mother, wasn't she? And you're my aunt."

Rory can't swallow over the miserable lump in her throat, can't speak, can't even meet Molly's questioning gaze. All she can do is nod.

I'm sorry, Carleen. God, I'm so sorry. I promised you I'd never tell a soul. I promised Daddy, and Mom.

"Why didn't anyone ever tell me?" Molly's voice is barely a whisper. "Why didn't Kevin tell me? He could have—he should have—if anyone would, Kevin should have."

"He couldn't," Rory manages to say. "We both promised."

"You promised who?"

"Mom and Daddy. And Carleen. We swore we would never say a word."

Molly is silent, one fist clutched against her mouth. Rory can see that she's trembling all over.

I should go to her. I should put my arms around her.

But she intuitively knows that if she does, Molly will freeze up or flee. Right now, she's talking; she's listening.

I have to keep her here. I can't let her take off without knowing the truth. I owe her an explanation, Rory tells herself. *She needs to know what happened, and why.*

"Carleen was so young when she got pregnant," she says softly, watching Molly. "Only thirteen. As old as you are now. But she was already so wild. Running around with kids who were much older, getting into trouble. She never told Mom and Daddy, but somebody—I guess it was Daddy—found a pregnancy kit in the trash. Carleen admitted it. She said she wanted an abortion, but Mom—well, you know. Mom's so religious."

She hears a strangled sound—a sob wrenched from Molly's throat.

"She didn't even want to *have* me?" Molly asks, her head bent, shoulders quaking.

"She was only thirteen, Molly," Rory says, wanting her to understand, somehow—to forgive Carleen.

Even though I never did, Rory realizes with sudden clarity. *I never forgave her for getting pregnant, for what it did to Mom, and Daddy—to all of us. We all suffered. We were all burdened with this horrible sense of shame, this dirty secret.*

And maybe I blame Molly for being born, for destroying our family. Maybe I didn't slip when I told her the truth just now. Maybe I subconsciously wanted to do it on purpose, to hurt her.

Oh, my God, what kind of person am I?

"Tell me," Molly prods, refusing to look at Rory.

So she does, carefully keeping the bitterness from her voice as she says, "Carleen was always Mom's favorite."

No need to drag her own age-old resentment into this. No need to let Molly know how much it had always stung, knowing her mother loved her sister so much more. Or how she'd maybe felt a slight, fleeting satisfaction that Carleen had screwed up so royally. That was when she'd naively harbored a secret hope that she could replace her sister in her mother's affections. Too soon, she'd realized that Mom would be even more distant, and not just from her. From all of them.

One more thing to blame on Carleen.

And Molly.

Oh, God. What have I done? She's just a kid. She doesn't deserve this. And it's not her fault.

"Rory!" Molly prods.

"Sorry. I'll tell you. It's just . . . hard."

Molly just looks at her.

Rory clears her throat. "When Mom found out what Carleen had done, she was devastated. She took it personally, like Carleen deliberately betrayed her morals to hurt Mom. She insisted that Carleen go through with it and have the baby—"

"Me."

"Right," Rory says reluctantly.

The baby is so much more impersonal. As if it will allow Molly to somehow separate her very existence from what had ultimately been such a devastating tragedy for their family.

"Mom and Daddy agreed that no one could know about it. This is such a small, gossipy town—they were so worried about what people would say—well, mostly Mom. *She* was worried. Daddy didn't really give a damn about things like that. But he wanted to get the hell out of here, and if you ask me, Carleen's pregnancy was the one chance he ever had to make Mom leave. So he took a sabbatical, like he always wanted to do. Mom didn't argue. How could she? We went to California."

"I was born there."

Rory nods. "You knew that, didn't you?"

"Of course I knew that. I just never knew Mom wasn't the one who gave birth to me."

"Molly, I know this is all so overwhelming—but try to understand that we all did what we had to do. Mom and Daddy, and Carleen—even me and Kevin. We all did what we thought was best. Mom and Daddy figured that if they pretended you were theirs, it would make life more bearable for everyone involved."

She pauses, fully expecting another outburst from Molly, but there's only silence.

She sees that her sister is still shaking, though—shaking all over, as though struggling to maintain her composure.

Fighting against the urge to touch her, knowing it will only alienate her, Rory takes a deep breath and goes on. "It was so awful in California. Carleen was sick the whole time, and miserable, and she wasn't herself. She totally withdrew from the rest of us, and she didn't make friends. Mom spent all her time in church, or praying. And Daddy was busy with his teaching position. Once in a while, he'd take me and Kevin someplace—we went to Disneyland, and we used to go to the beach sometimes."

She thinks back on those hazy, long-ago California days, remembering how uncharacteristically subdued her father had been. He was finally out in the world, finally able to see some of the places he'd researched and taught, and he couldn't enjoy it. He was burdened with a pregnant thirteen-year-old and a wife who was rapidly lapsing into the mental illness she'd always managed to hold at bay.

That, for Rory, had always been one of the most lamentable aspects of the whole damn tragedy. That her father's fate was sealed in those grim months on the West Coast. He was so obviously trapped, destined to live the rest of his life fulfilling his obligation to his wife, to his children.

She closes her eyes briefly and sees him standing absolutely still on some Pacific beach, at the very edge of the water, looking out at the horizon.

Did he sense, even then, that he would die young? Did he realize that he would never be free, that his dreams would never come true?

"What about my father?" Molly asks.

And for a moment, Rory almost thinks Molly's reading her thoughts. That she's asking about Patrick Connolly, and his shattered life.

Then she realizes what her sister is asking, and she's forced to burden her with yet another bleak reality of the past.

"We never knew who he was," Rory says quietly. "Carleen wouldn't tell us. Mom never pushed her to—she never wanted to know. But Daddy—he was furious about it for a long time. He used to demand the guy's name, saying he was going to beat the hell out of him. As if that would make Carleen want to tell," she adds with an acrid laugh.

"So nobody knows who my father is, then?" Molly asks in a small voice. "And there's . . . there's no way to find out?"

Rory shakes her head. "We never even knew whether he knew she was pregnant. Probably not. I wonder sometimes if Carleen would have told us about him eventually, if she hadn't . . . disappeared."

How close she had been to saying *died*.

But she never voices that likelihood to anyone, and she's not going to start now. As long as what happened to Carleen remains a mystery, there's hope, however slim, that she's still alive someplace.

And that's why I can't talk to Barrett Maitland, Rory reminds herself. *Because if he starts prying into the mystery after all these years, he might solve it. He might find out that Carleen and the others were murdered.*

But isn't it better to know?

No, she answers her own question. *It isn't better. How can it be better to find out someone you loved so much is dead?*

She realizes tears are trickling from her eyes, and she wipes at her cheeks with the back of her hand.

Molly is staring off into space, that fist still pressed against her mouth, her skinny legs and arms still visibly trembling.

"Are you all right, Molly?" Instinctively, she reaches out and touches her sister's shoulder, knowing even as she does that it's a mistake.

Molly shrinks back under her touch, flinching as though Rory's hand is a hot brand.

"Just . . . leave me alone!" she bites out, and then she's on her way up the stairs, hurling herself toward the second floor so quickly, so blindly that she nearly crashes into the figure standing on the landing.

Rory gasps.

Her mother is standing there, wearing the flannel nightgown she insisted Rory put on her earlier. Her gray hair is disheveled, but for once, she doesn't appear the least disoriented. She steps back slightly as Molly pushes by her and disappears around the corner.

"Mom?"

Rory's gaze locks on her mother's as Molly's bedroom door bangs shut above. Maybe she just came down now. Maybe she didn't hear a word of what she and Molly were talking about, or if she did, maybe she didn't comprehend.

But those bottle-green eyes aren't blank, as they had been when she'd caught Maura earlier in her wedding gown. Now they're piercing and angry, boring into Rory's consciousness and filling her with the sick, guilty awareness that she has broken a sacred promise made so many years ago.

"I'm sorry, Mom," Rory says, putting a foot on the stairs, prepared to go to her mother, to explain what happened. "I didn't mean to tell her, but—"

Without a word, her mother turns and swiftly goes back upstairs, her door echoing Molly's moments earlier.

Wearily, Rory sinks down on the bottom step and buries her head in her hands, longing for someone to share this oppressive burden.

If only Kevin were here.

If only Daddy had lived . . .

I'm so alone. So totally alone.

As the stark truth settles over Rory, she fights the almost overpowering urge to just get up and walk away. Leave, like she had before, when she was younger and filled with restless longing, and didn't give a damn about anything but herself.

How many times did Daddy feel this way? she wonders desolately. *How many times was he tempted to turn his back on this whole messed-up family and just get the hell out of here?*

But he never did.

And I can't, either.

She takes a deep breath, lets it out slowly, and gingerly rises to her feet, making her way slowly up the stairs to bed.

CHAPTER SIX

Seated in a lawn chair in a skimpy patch of shade beneath a tall lilac shrub, Michelle carefully tears out the magazine page containing the potty-training article, which she's finally just finished reading. One of the author's tips is not to start training a toddler just before or after a new sibling's birth.

"Guess what? You get to keep wearing those diapers a while longer, kiddo," she says to Ozzie as she begins folding the page accordion-style.

"Diapers?" Ozzie looks up from the patch of dirt where he's busily digging with his little plastic shovel, in search of pirate treasure, just like the little boy in the bedtime story she'd read him a few nights ago.

She'd planned to take him out to the beach at the Curl this afternoon since Lou is working, but she just doesn't have the energy. Of course, once Ozzie found out he wouldn't be able to dig in the sand as she'd promised, he'd thrown a major tantrum.

Which is why he's now happily engaged in excavating what should have been a flower garden in full bloom. Last fall, she'd dug up this wide patch of earth at the back of the yard, planning to fill it with snapdragons and cosmos and petunias, like her mother had always done. But by the time spring arrived and the annuals would have been ready to put in, she'd thought better of gardening.

Her doctor had warned that it was possible to pick up the disease toxoplasmosis from soil that's frequented by cats. It isn't usually serious unless someone is pregnant, since it can cause birth defects in infants. Knowing that the Wasners' cats are always using her yard as a litter box, Michelle had decided not to take chances.

When she'd mentioned it to Lou, he'd told her she should start chasing Ralphi and Sebastian away from their yard, anyway. "I can't stand those damn animals always coming around here," he'd said, and added, as if she didn't know, "After all, I'm allergic."

"Treasure, Mommy!" Ozzie says, jabbing his little orange shovel into the surprisingly deep hole he's managed to create.

"That's right, Ozzie, you're digging for treasure." She finishes folding the magazine page and uses it as a makeshift fan, waving it in front of her sweat-dampened face.

Later, she'll take Ozzie over to Carvel for ice cream. The place is air-conditioned, and she wouldn't mind a hot fudge sundae.

Might as well take advantage of this pregnancy while it lasts, she tells herself, knowing she'll have to diet like crazy to get all this weight off once the baby's born.

It seems like all she's done these past few days is sit around and eat everything in sight—except, of course, those corn nuts, no matter what Lou thinks.

As far as Michelle is concerned, they just vanished from the cupboard, a thought that is so troubling it kept her awake most of the night while Lou snored peacefully beside her.

Could someone possibly have broken into their house, not once, but twice, and stolen food from the kitchen cupboards?

Bizarre as it seems, Michelle is really starting to believe it—in part because the only other remotely plausible explanation for the missing corn nuts and crackers is that she's losing her mind.

She turns her attention back to her magazine, flipping through to see if there are any other articles she wants to read before she tosses it into the recycling bin. Nope, not really. The only other piece pertaining to the mother of a two-year-old is one entitled, "How to Tame Your Toddler's Temper," by Dr. Electra Van Dyke, presumably a child psychologist.

"Treasure, Mommy!" Ozzie says excitedly, pounding his shovel into the dirt. It makes a dull sound, scraping against a rock or something.

"Mmm hmm." She closes the magazine again and absently brushes her bangs away from her damp forehead, wondering when this heat wave is ever going to break. She caught this morning's weather forecast on television, and temperatures are supposed to stay in the high nineties over the weekend, though there's a chance of a thunderstorm tonight that might cool things down.

"Help, Mommy," Ozzie says urgently, tossing his shovel aside and digging in the dirt with his chubby bare hands.

"No, don't do that, Ozzie. You're going to get filthy," Michelle says wearily, getting out of her lawn chair and bending to pull him back from the dirt. "Come on, let's go get cleaned up and I go to Carvel."

"No!" He stomps his little blue sandals and screws up his face in fury, brewing another tantrum. "Treasure, Mommy! Treasure there!"

"We'll dig for treasure again tomorrow," she quickly promises, knowing that of course he'll hold her to it. For a two-year-old, he has an amazing memory.

Unlike his mom, she thinks as she makes her way toward the house, pulling a protesting Ozzie along.

Did I eat those damn corn nuts and forget? Did I eat the crackers and forget? Am I going to open the freezer tomorrow and find an entire roasting chicken or a half-gallon of ice cream missing, too?

She sighs and drags Ozzie to the kitchen sink to scrub the dirt from his hands, taking Dr. Electra Van Dyke's advice and pointedly ignoring his ear-splitting wails about the buried treasure in the backyard.

Rory hears Ozzie Randall's angry screams coming through the screens for the second time this morning. She smiles faintly. He must be a handful, that kid. You've got to hand it to Michelle, dealing with him when she's so hugely pregnant and the weather is sticky enough to make anyone cranky. And her husband never seems to be around. Rory glimpsed him leaving earlier, apparently headed for his office, since he had a briefcase in one hand and a commuter mug of coffee in the other.

Michelle's husband is handsome in a cute businessman kind of way—a look that has never particularly appealed to Rory. She doesn't remember Lou Randall from her childhood, since he's got to be about ten years older than she is, and was an only child. She knows that his family, like Michelle's, is from Lake Charlotte. She vaguely remembers that Lou's mother was married to the

Connollys' dentist, Dr. Murray Overman, who died not long after recommending that an adolescent Rory get braces.

She never did. Her parents couldn't afford it, a fact that really bothered her father, who kept promising her that someday they'd have enough money to get her to an orthodontist.

"Don't worry, Daddy, I'm fine," she used to tell him. Sometimes it did bother her when Carleen teased her about her teeth, but she told herself she really didn't want a mouthful of metal, anyway.

To this day, every time she looks in the mirror, her gaze zeroes in on the slight gap between her front teeth. She kind of likes the way it looks now. It gives her face character.

See, Daddy? It turned out okay.

Setting her empty coffee cup in the sink, Rory walks into the hallway and stands at the foot of the stairs, listening.

No sound from above.

Molly is, if not sound asleep, still shut in her room.

And Mom left for morning mass a little while ago, right on time and betraying not a hint of the tumultuous drama that had taken place in the wee hours.

Rory wonders if Maura even remembers what happened. Maybe she's managed to shut it out, somehow.

She needs help, Rory thinks, returning to the kitchen and picking up the telephone. *She needs help, and I've got to get it for her.*

She reaches into the pockets of her cut-off jean shorts and pulls out the scrap of paper with the phone number of St. Lucretia's Rectory in Buffalo. Swiftly, she dials the number, keeping one eye on the hallway in case Molly or her mother should suddenly appear.

"Good morning. St. Lucretia's."

"Good morning. I'd like to speak to Sister Theodosia, please."

"Whom may I ask is calling?"

That's a good sign. The other day when Rory asked for the nun, the receptionist had immediately said she wasn't there.

"This is Rory Connolly. I'm . . . an old friend."

"Just a moment."

A click, and Rory is on hold.

She rinses out her coffee cup while she waits, then wanders

nervously around the kitchen, anxiously picking things up, examining them absently, and putting them down.

A chipped crock full of wooden spoons.

A vaguely familiar, clumsily woven potholder she or Carleen must have made in elementary school.

A dusty bud vase that's most likely never held a cut flower.

Another click, and then a clipped voice is saying, "Hello?"

"Sister Theodosia?"

"Yes?"

"It's me—Rory. I tried to reach you the other day—"

"I was away. How are you, Rory?" There's no warmth in her tone, not the slightest hint of genuine curiosity behind the perfunctory inquiry.

"I'm fine," Rory replies, trying to think of the best way to bring up the subject of her mother. Whatever she had planned to say has left her, and she finds herself fumbling for the right words.

"You're home in Lake Charlotte, then?"

Startled, Rory asks, "How did you know that?"

"Your mother and I do keep in touch. She must have mentioned that you were coming."

For some reason, Rory can't imagine her mother and Sister Theodosia having a normal, old-fashioned chat. She has no idea what they've ever spoken about when they're alone together, but she realizes now that she must have assumed theirs isn't an ordinary friendship. What had she been thinking? That they merely recited prayers together? Of course they would catch up on each other's lives. That's what old friends do.

"Speaking of my mother," Rory turns her attention back to the matter at hand, "I'm worried about her, Sister."

"Why?"

Again, the question is cursory. Not a hint of concern or emotion.

"Mom is acting very strangely, Sister. I think she's lost touch with reality."

"In what way?"

Taken aback, Rory fumbles. "She's just . . . odd. It's like she's not all there, most of the time. She's lost in her thoughts—"

"Introspection is hardly a sin, Rory. And perhaps she's lost in prayer."

"But—I think she's seeing things. Hearing things. She keeps

talking to my father—it's like she thinks he's actually here with her."

"Some would say that our faith is built on mysticism, Rory. Our Bible is filled with scripture about men and women who were considered crazed by those who didn't believe."

Rory blinks. "But—this has nothing to do with religion, Sister."

"For a woman as pure of conviction as your mother is, everything has to do with religion."

Frustrated, Rory bursts out, "Mom just isn't *right*, Sister. She's lost her mind. I know you've seen her recently. You must have noticed."

There's silence, and then Sister Theodosia asks, with that same irritating composure, "What is it that you'd like me to do, Rory?"

"I don't know," Rory says, realizing it was a mistake to have called.

She's about to tell the nun to forget about it when she says, "I can come to see her, if that's what you'd like."

"You don't have to do that. I know you're busy—"

"I'm in the middle of a two-week vacation. I'm free to travel if I wish."

It figures that she's spending the time right there in the rectory, Rory thinks grumpily. She can't quite imagine the nun embarking on a vacation.

An image pops into her head.

Sister Theodosia on water skis, wearing her habit and that perpetual prune-faced expression.

Rory finds herself grinning.

"Lake Charlotte is less than five hours from here. I can be there late tonight."

"You don't have to come, Sister," Rory says again, wondering what she's gone and started.

"No, you wouldn't have called unless you needed me. I've always been there for your family, Rory. Always."

"Thank you, Sister. I knew I could count on you," Rory says without a trace of sincerity.

"Good-bye."

There's a click in her ear, and she realizes the nun has abruptly hung up.

What a character, she thinks, replacing the phone and sighing.

But at least I won't have to deal with Mom alone. At least someone else can see how crazy she is.

And as for Molly . . .

With a sigh, Rory heads for the stairs to deal with Problem Number Two.

The mail has arrived earlier than usual today, he realizes, stopping at the box in front of the townhouse on his way out for his ritual Saturday-morning stroll through the quiet, upscale Back Bay neighborhood. Usually the mail doesn't get here until early afternoon on Saturdays.

He pauses to flip with patient disinterest through the stack of bills, catalogues, and grocery store circulars. On the bottom of the pile is a plain manilla envelope, addressed to him.

There's no return address, but his gut twists when he glances at the postmark.

Lake Charlotte, New York.

With suddenly trembling hands, he tears open the envelope, barely registering the scrawled note on the letterhead of an Albany detective agency.

Here are the latest, taken just this week—an interesting development is all it says.

He moves the letter aside, along with the agency's enclosed monthly bill, and focuses his gaze on the photos.

They're slightly blurry and taken from a distance, and it's clear the subjects were utterly unaware of the cameraman's presence.

The first shows a familiar, dark-haired adolescent sitting on a bench with another girl, chatting with a grinning boy on a bike.

Molly.

She has a crush on the boy. That's obvious from the nervous smile on her face, from the *please-like-me* plea in her eyes, which is plainly evident even from the photographer's distance. The other girl, he recognizes as Rebecca, her best friend from a few doors down Hayes Street.

The next picture shows a pretty redhead standing in the side yard of a house he knows too well. She's covered in paint, engaged in what appears to be an animated conversation with a pregnant woman and toddler on the other side of the honeysuckle hedge.

Rory.

She's come home.

He lets out a shaky sigh and tucks the pictures back into the envelope before returning to the townhouse, his morning walk forgotten.

"Molly?"

Rory's voice drifts through the bedroom door, accompanied by a staccato knock.

"Are you all right in there?"

Molly, lying on her bed staring at the ceiling, fully clothed in the shorts and T-shirt she'd worn to the party last night, doesn't reply.

"Molly? Are you asleep?"

"Yes." She turns her head toward the wall and closes her eyes. "Go away," she orders, thinking that if her sister dares to open her door, she'll . . .

She doesn't know what she'll do, but she sure as hell won't allow Rory to just barge in on her like that.

"Are you all right?"

"I *said,* I'm sleeping!" she calls through clenched teeth.

"Okay."

Rory's footsteps retreat back down the hall, and a moment later, she hears her sister going downstairs.

No.

Not her sister.

Her *aunt.*

This whole thing is so sick, Molly thinks, rolling onto her stomach and holding tightly to her damp pillow. She sees that the pink-checkered pillowcase is smeared with black, and for a moment she's bewildered. Then she remembers the eye makeup, and how she spent the entire night sobbing uncontrollably, holding the pillow against her face so that no one would hear.

She has never been so miserable in her entire life.

Never been so alone.

And just last night, she had thought she had never been happier. After they'd both pretended to drink their beers—she had never tasted anything so bitter and disgusting in her life, and was pretty certain Ryan found it equally loathsome—Ryan had asked her to go for a walk on the beach. He'd held her hand, and he probably would have kissed her if Andy Chase didn't pop up to ask if he was ready to leave yet.

"Not yet," Ryan had said, then asked Molly, "Can you stay out a while longer?"

"Sure," she'd naturally replied, not caring that it was well past midnight.

"Good. My parents are out of town and my brother's supposed to be watching me but he's got his girlfriend over and he doesn't care when I get home. As far as he's concerned, the later I stay out, the better."

Molly thought she would die from pure bliss when he asked her if she had a boyfriend, and he said, "That's great" when she told him she didn't. He gave her a ride home on the handlebars of his bike, pedaling with expert balance and ease through the deserted streets of Lake Charlotte. And when he waved to her from the glow of the streetlight, she heard him call softly, "I'll see you real soon, okay, Molly?"

The sound of her name on his lips had been dreamily echoing in her mind when she slipped into the house and started to steal upstairs.

Then Rory had crashed into her reverie, effectively shattering her joyous mood even before she'd dropped that bombshell.

Molly was still reeling from Rory's revelation, knowing that as long as she lives, she'll never fully recover from the shock.

Her whole life has been a lie.

She flips onto her back again, her eyes settling on the intricate network of cracks and water stains on the ceiling, patterns she now knows by heart. She had, after all, watched each line become visible as the dawn light crept slowly in earlier, as the sound of a car moving slowly along Hayes Street drifted up through the screen. She had realized it was the newspaper delivery van, tossing editions of the *Foothill Gazette* onto every porch on the block, except the Connollys'. They've never bothered to subscribe to the local daily paper.

Why does my family have to be so weird? Molly wonders miserably now. *It isn't fair.*

There's no one I can even confide in, she thinks miserably, realizing the burden of the news might be a little less devastating if she could at least share it.

But Kevin is gone, and Rebecca isn't speaking to her, and that about covers the people she trusts in this world.

Everyone leaves, she thinks morosely, swallowing hard around a lump in her throat.

Carleen.

Daddy.

Kevin.

Even Mom—she might be here physically, but she's totally escaped into another world, and that might be worse than actually taking off, the way Kevin did.

Of course, Daddy couldn't help leaving. He's dead.

And Carleen—well, who knows what happened to her?

Not that it matters, Molly thinks bitterly. *Carleen was never there for me, even when she was around. Rory came right out and said she didn't want me—that she wanted to have an abortion.*

God, I wish she had. I wish I'd never been born. My own mother didn't want me.

Her sister's face flashes in her mind, clear as that photo of her on the wall above the stairs.

Carleen is getting her undressed for her bath, smiling, patiently touching each of Molly's bare toes.

"This little piggy went to market . . . This little piggy stayed home . . . This little piggy had roast beef . . . This little piggy had none . . . And this little piggy cried 'wee wee wee wee,' all the way home."

"Do it again, Carleen! Please, please, do it again!"

"All right, you little munchkin. Just one more time, though. This little piggy . . ."

Tears sting Molly's raw, burning eyelids and she swipes at them with her pillowcase, not caring that another smudge of black makeup appears along the ruffled edge.

I have no one.

Not a single soul in this world who's there for me.

Her thoughts drift to Ryan, and for a crazy moment, she wonders if she can confide in him.

She quickly dismisses the notion.

After all, what's she supposed to do? Call him and say, *"Remember me from last night? Well, I just found out my whole family has lied to me all my life, and my missing sister is really my mother, and nobody has a clue who my father is, and can you please help me sort out this mess, because I have nobody else to turn to?"*

They've all left, she thinks again, images of her family running through her mind.

Kevin.

Carleen.

Daddy.

Mom.

Rory's face sticks there, though.

Yeah, she left, too, Molly reminds herself stubbornly. *Just like the rest of them.*

But she came back.

She's here now.

She's worried about you.

So what? She's the one who ruined my whole life by telling me all this. Why didn't she just leave it buried, where it belongs? Why did she have to throw it in my face? I didn't need to know. I didn't want to know.

She hides her face in the pink-checkered pillowcase again, clinging to it as though it's a life raft, soaking it once again with a torrent of bitter tears.

Barrett Maitland stands at the edge of Lake Charlotte, eyes fastened on the narrow, paved bike path several yards away, separating the beach from winding Lakeshore Road, which traces the shore.

So. A decade ago this very day, according to local legend, Kristin Stafford rode her bike along that very path . . . and vanished.

Barrett would have known the particulars by heart even if they hadn't been neatly laid out in this morning's edition of the local paper, the *Foothill Gazette.*

TEN YEARS SINCE FIRST DISAPPEARANCE screams the front-page headline, accompanied four grainy photos of smiling, unsuspecting teenaged girls.

It's all there, in a detailed chronicle that takes up a good part of the front page, sharing space with the latest White House scandal. The story is continued on page two, where the enterprising reporter tells precisely how Kirsten Stafford got on her bike as she often did after supper, apparently unworried about tires that her father later said had needed air.

How several reliable witnesses had seen her riding along the path as the sun set on the horizon.

How she had waved cheerfully at those she knew, and reportedly even at those she didn't, with characteristic breezy friendliness that might have somehow led her into trouble.

Because Kristin Stafford never came home.

Not a trace of her was ever found.

Not even her pretty lavender bicycle with the personalized license plate, Barrett mentally echoes the last line of the article that is, in his opinion, on the melodramatic side.

I could have done much better, he thinks somewhat smugly, walking slowly along the beach, sidestepping a pair of sun-suited towheads busily digging in the sand.

But you aren't in Lake Charlotte to write articles for the Foothill Gazette, *are you?*

He makes his way up to the bike path, then crosses it. He glances up and down winding Lakeshore Road; sees that it's momentarily devoid of any traffic. Despite the humidity and blazing sun, it's still a little early for the locals to head for the beach. Most Lake Charlotte residents hardly seem to be early risers like the New Englanders he'd encountered while in college up in Vermont. This is your classic sleepy little town, he reminds himself, knowing from experience that by midafternoon, the sand and water would undoubtedly be dotted with sunbathers and swimmers—

That is, if that thunderstorm they're predicting doesn't hit sooner than expected.

Barrett crosses the road and stands on the narrow patch of grass on the opposite side. In front of him is a bank of woods that rises fairly steeply, obscuring any view of the town nestled above. There's a faint trail leading upward.

After glancing over his shoulder to see that the few people dotting the beach aren't even facing in his direction, Barrett steps into the woods. He expertly makes his way along the overgrown trail, skirting fallen logs and large boulders, hearing birds chirping overhead and small animals darting away in the underbrush as he passes.

It's peaceful, here. The foliage is so dense that it absorbs any sound from the beach below and the town above.

Finally, Barrett reaches the top of the incline and the trees give way to a tangled hedge of briars that stops him from going any farther. He peers past them, past the patch of dirt and an orange plastic shovel, past the large yard with its tire swing and picnic table, narrowing his eyes thoughtfully at the big, familiar rose-and-plum house looming beyond.

"Mom? Have you seen Sebastian?"

Cheryl Wasner looks up from the petunia plant she's busily dead-heading in a container on the brick patio. "No, not this morning."

Rebecca's heart sinks. She stands on the back porch, absently watching her mother. She'd been so certain poor Sebastian would have made his way home by now.

But when she'd awakened, much later than usual thanks to a mostly sleepless night, he hadn't been in the space where he usually sleeps at the foot of her bed. Her father and Casey, engrossed in a computer game in the den, said they hadn't seen him.

"Did you eat breakfast yet?" her mother asks, straightening and tossing a handful of faded petunia blossoms into a wheelbarrow full of weeds.

"No. I'm not hungry," Rebecca says glumly.

"Worried about your kitten?"

She nods.

"Don't worry, 'Bec—cats always take off gallivanting at this time of year."

"Ralphi never did."

"Ralphi is an exception. She's the laziest animal on the face of the earth. Besides, she's a female."

"But we had Sebastian fixed, Mom."

Her mother smiles faintly. "That doesn't mean he's lost all his instincts to roam and mate."

"But he doesn't have any claws. He'll get slaughtered out in the woods."

"He'll be okay," her mother says, running a hand through her short, colored blond hair with maddening assurance. "Come on, let's go in and have some cinnamon toast before I start the weeding. I wanted to talk to you about Molly."

Rebecca shoots a glance at her mother. "What about her?"

"Her sister called here late last night, looking for her. She seemed to think she was with you."

"Well, she wasn't."

"Obviously. Do you know where she was?"

"No." Rebecca hates lying. She's terrible at it.

"Where was she, Rebecca?"

"I told you, I don't know." She averts her eyes from her mother's probing gaze, staring intently at a pot full of geraniums as though they're the most fascinating thing she's ever seen.

"Rebecca," her mother says after a moment, "I know Molly is your friend. But it's not a good idea to lie for her. If she's doing something or going someplace she shouldn't be, her family needs to know."

"Her mother doesn't even care where she goes."

"I don't think that's the case. That poor woman has been through a lot. And anyway, her sister obviously cares and is worried about her."

"I'm sure Molly's fine. She knows how to take care of herself."

"Not necessarily. Terrible things can happen to young girls if they aren't careful."

Her mother's words send a chill down Rebecca's spine, but she merely shrugs and says, "Don't worry about Molly, Mom."

Mentally, she adds, *What she does is none of my business anymore.*

CHAPTER SEVEN

The cafe on Front Street is no Starbucks, but clearly Lake Charlotte has come a long way since Rory left town.

She's pleased to see that the cafe offers a number of hot and cold espresso drinks, along with a glass case filled with pastries, bagels, and rolls. The place is pleasantly crowded with fairly well-dressed, youngish people, none of them recognizable. Rory figures they must be mostly summer people, though it strikes her that they *could* be locals. After all, she doesn't know everyone in town the way she once did, and Lake Charlotte is apparently becoming a little more upscale.

She self-consciously tucks her sleeveless coral turtleneck into her white denim shorts, feeling underdressed. She's glad she took the time to put on makeup and paint her toenails, bared in white leather sandals, a matching shade of coral. She had considered putting on a madras plaid sundress, but deliberately decided against anything so formal. She doesn't want Barrett Maitland to think she got all dressed up for him, since this is hardly a date.

I should never have agreed to meet him, she tells herself as she waits at the counter for her iced cappuccino and chocolate biscotti, which she couldn't resist. She didn't eat supper. It's just too damn hot, and besides, she's getting tired of eating alone. She's used to meeting a date or a group of friends for dinner, or cooking for a bunch of people at whatever apartment she's currently calling home.

Now, after nearly a week with her family in Lake Charlotte, she knows that she's going to lose it if she doesn't start getting out and doing something, or at least having a decent conversation once in a while.

No chance of that at home, she thinks grimly. Her mother and Molly don't exactly qualify as good company.

"Rory?"

A hand on her bare elbow.

She turns to see Barrett Maitland standing behind her.

"Oh, hi." She's glad to see he's wearing jeans, a plain navy polo shirt, and those same docksiders, again without socks. He looks as casual as she does.

Damn good-looking, too, she can't help thinking, noticing that he's picked up a ruddy suntan since she saw him last.

"Did you go to the beach today?" she asks, on a hunch.

He hesitates. "Yeah, for a while."

Why does he always do that? she wonders. Why does he seem to carefully measure his responses to the most inane questions, as though he has something to hide?

Because he must, she concludes. *And that's why I can't trust him, even for a second.*

"Am I late? Have you been here long?" he asks, checking his watch.

"No, I just got here a few minutes ago. And you're not late."

"Good. I thought I was early."

Actually, he is. She had intentionally arrived before Barrett, needing to be used to the territory and settled in before he showed up and churned up all her emotions with his probe into her sister's disappearance.

Not that she plans to tell him anything about that.

"Did you already order?"

Rory nods.

"But I wanted to treat you."

"It's no big deal." Besides, she thinks, if she pays her own way, this isn't a date.

Not that he ever called it one. They're simply meeting so that she can ostensibly help him with his research for his book. The fact that she's attracted to him doesn't automatically transform it into a date.

"Grande skim iced cappuccino, no cinnamon?"

"Right here," Rory tells the *barista*, grabbing the tall cup from her outstretched hand.

"I take it you're a woman who knows exactly what she wants, and likes things a certain way," Barrett comments.

"Why is that?" She knows what he's getting at, and she doesn't intend to flirt with him. This isn't a date.

"Your drink sounds pretty complicated."

She shrugs, telling herself it's corny of him to use her beverage order to interpret her personality. "Aren't you going to order?"

"Sure." He turns to the girl waiting behind the register. "I'll have a coffee."

"What kind?"

"Just plain old coffee."

"Iced?"

"Nope."

"What size?"

"Regular."

"You mean tall?"

"Whatever." He grins and turns to Rory, saying in a low voice, "I think she's thrown by that. Maybe I should have made it a skim decaf with extra cinnamon."

She can't help smiling. He's so laid-back, it's hard not to let go of some of her tension around him. Still, she can't help wondering if his relaxed demeanor is just an act—if he's acting so easygoing in an attempt to get her to put her guard down, so she'll spill some family dirt he can use for his book.

"I thought you were going to have an espresso," she tells him while they wait.

"Why is that?"

"When you asked if I wanted to meet you here, that's what you said."

"That's because I figured you for an espresso-type woman and I wanted to lure you here. Me, I happen to be a plain old coffee kind of guy."

She bristles at his blatant use of the word "lure," though he used it in a teasing tone. She isn't the kind of woman who allows herself to be *lured* by anyone, particularly a nosy true-crime writer.

The tables are all filled when they turn to find a place to sit. The only available spot appears to be an overstuffed maroon velvet couch in a nook by the plate-glass window overlooking the street. It's too intimate as far as Rory is concerned, but what can she do except follow Barrett over and sit beside him?

"So what have you been doing with yourself since you got to town?" Barrett asks after dumping three packages of sugar into his cup and stirring it. "Besides painting the kitchen, I mean."

"Not a whole lot. Mostly just catching up on family stuff."

Where did that come from? she wonders. It sounds so *normal* . . . and what she's been going through with her family is anything but.

"Your mother must be glad to have you home."

"Mmm," Rory says noncommittally, wondering how much he knows about her mother.

"What about your sister? Molly, isn't it?"

"Right." She volunteers nothing more.

"How old is she?"

"Thirteen."

Under any other circumstances, she'd find his questions harmless. They could be likened to the usual first-date chitchat, getting to know someone. But Rory can't help but balk when it's this particular man asking these particular questions.

"Look," she says directly, "I shouldn't have come here tonight."

He raises an eyebrow. "Why not?"

"Because I'm just not comfortable with some . . . stranger prying into my family. We've been through enough already. All we want is to be left alone." She plunks her untouched foamy drink onto the low, magazine-covered coffee table in front of them and starts to rise.

"Wait, Rory, please. We don't have to talk about what happened to Carleen if you don't want to."

She stops, surprised. "We don't?"

"Not if it bothers you."

"But . . . I thought that's why we were here."

"It was supposed to be. But after a week with no one to keep me company but Mrs. Shilling, I'm glad just to be here with someone like you."

"I know what you mean," she hears herself say.

"Family stuff getting to you?"

"Not really." She knows she shouldn't tell him anything. *Anything.* She should stand up and walk out, as she'd been about to do.

Instead, she finds herself saying, "It's only been a week since I've been here, too, but I really miss . . . doing things. Talking to people who aren't . . . related to me."

There, that's harmless enough, she tells herself, realizing she's been clenching her jaw, and letting it relax. *You can chat a little with him, and it doesn't have to be disastrous. Just because you blurted the truth to Molly last night doesn't mean you're going to get yourself into trouble talking to this man for a short while.*

"Where do you live . . . when you're not here, I mean?" Barrett asks.

"Miami. I mean, that's where all my stuff is."

"But it isn't home?"

"Nah. Too hot and humid."

"Just like here," he says, with a nod at the sunny sidewalk beyond the comfortable air-conditioned climate of the cafe.

"Yeah, but this weather is unusual for Lake Charlotte. In Miami it's steamy all the time."

"So you're planning to move back up North?"

"Maybe," she surprises herself by saying. Until this moment, she didn't realize she'd ever consider it, but now that she's said it, she realizes she kind of likes the idea.

"Where? Here?"

"No," she says quickly. "Not here."

"Too small-town?"

"I don't mind small towns. I grew up here, remember? And I like small towns." That, too, is news to her. But as she hears herself talking, she realizes that there's something to it. She just never stopped to think about it before. About finding a place to belong. "I like the laid-back people in small towns," she muses. "I like the slow pace."

"So do I."

She glances at him. "You do? Then why do you live in New York City?"

"I'm a writer," he says, as though that explains everything.

"And . . .?" Rory prods. "I mean, you can write anywhere."

"Nah. Writers belong in New York. That's what I always

thought, anyway. I figured, if I wanted to make it big in this business, I should move to the place that's the center of the publishing industry. I came to the city ten years ago this fall, when I graduated from college—"

"Where'd you go?"

"Bennington. You?"

"Berkeley."

"Actually, I already knew that," Barrett tells her. "Mrs. Shilling mentioned it. She said you're an artist."

"I wanted to be. But it's not like I'm doing masterpieces or having gallery showings or anything like that. When it comes to a career, I'm still trying to get my act together, I guess."

Let's face it. I have no ambition. I've spent my whole life doing my best not to settle down.

"So am I."

"You? Trying to get your act together? But you write books."

"I've published exactly two. This will be my third."

"What were the others about?"

"Remember that prostitute in Philadelphia who was killing johns and stuffing their bodies into Dumpsters a few summers ago?"

Rory nods. That case was all over the papers. "The Spanish Rose?"

"That was her street name. She was the subject of my first book, *Deadly Spanish Rose*. I know, I know—cheesy title."

She laughs. "I didn't say that. How did you happen to write about her?"

"I don't know . . . it hit the papers right around the time I got interested in doing a true-crime novel. Plus, my college roommate happens to live in Philly, so I had a free place to stay while I was doing research."

That makes sense, Rory thinks. Everyone knows writers are always broke. Although now that Barrett Maitland has had some success, he clearly isn't having money problems. That shirt he has on looks pretty basic, but she knows it must have cost at least a hundred bucks.

"What was your second book?" she asks him.

"It was called *Devil and the Deep Blue Sea*."

"Catchy title."

"Especially since it was about that cult of Satanists on Fire Island—the ones who were making human sacrifices on the beach and letting the tide wash the body parts away."

"Nice. Very uplifting." Rory shakes her head, sipping her drink through the straw and adding, "How can you write about such gory stuff?"

"Hey, don't blame me. I'm not responsible. I mean, I don't dream this stuff up, or participate. I just tell what happened."

"Both of those cases were solved," Rory points out, putting down her cup and looking him in the eye. "Why do you want to write about what happened in Lake Charlotte? That's still a mystery."

"Maybe that's why," he says, not wavering under her gaze, though she senses that he wants to look away. "I've always been drawn to mysteries. I'm a big Amelia Earhart buff, you know? Maybe I'll write about her next. About how she started out to fly around the globe and vanished off the face of the earth."

"Just like my sister did," Rory comments flatly.

Now he does break the eye contact, lowering his gaze to the almost-empty cup of coffee in his hand.

"Why did you choose this particular case? Why Lake Charlotte?" Rory asks, deliberately adding, "I mean . . . have you ever been here before? Did you want to come back? Is that it?"

"No, that's not it. I told you, I'm always intrigued by mysteries. And this was a mystery. My editor suggested it, so I followed up."

"Oh." She notices that he managed to sidestep her question about whether he's been here before.

There's definitely something suspicious about Barrett Maitland.

"Listen," she says, standing and facing him. "I have to go now. It was nice talking with you—"

"Rory—"

"I really have to get home. My mother—"

She breaks off, realizes there's nothing she can say about her mother without giving away that Maura Connolly isn't exactly *normal.*

"Your mother . . .?" he prods, when she doesn't finish the sentence.

"She's expecting company. An old family friend. And I promised I'd be there to say hello."

"Okay," he says, not bothering to keep the disappointment from his voice. "Maybe we can get together again?"

"I told you, I'd really rather not discuss my sister with you."

"And that's okay with me ... although, I'm hoping you'll change your mind about that. What I mean, though, is maybe we can get together again just to ... hang out."

"I don't think that's a good idea."

"Why not?"

"Because I don't trust you," she says evenly. "You might say you want to see me just for casual conversation, but you have a job to do. You're here to snoop into the past, and that's someplace I just don't want to go, ever again."

"I guess I can't say I blame you," he says after a moment, regret plain on his features. "Okay, Rory. Maybe I'll see you around the neighborhood."

"Maybe."

I hope not, she thinks as she walks out onto the sidewalk, the heat wrapping around her like a wet, hot towel.

She turns toward the back parking lot where she left Kevin's beat-up Honda, wondering, as she walks through the narrow, shadowy alley, whether Sister Theodosia is going to show up tonight, and what she's going to do with her now that she's summoned her.

There's no way she's going to be able to help with any of this mess, Rory thinks, fumbling in her pocket for the keys and unlocking the door.

She finds herself wondering if Sister Theodosia knows the truth about Molly—that she's Carleen's illegitimate daughter. Is that the kind of thing her mother would confide in a nun, even if she *is* her closest friend?

With a sigh, she gets into the car and turns on the engine just as thunder rumbles faintly in the distance.

A storm is supposed to roll in later tonight, she remembers, rolling down the window with one hand as she shifts into gear with the other. Good. The air is terribly oppressive tonight. Maybe some rain will cool things off.

* * *

Molly sits at the kitchen table, clenching the phone so hard her fingers ache, bracing herself as it rings once . . . twice . . .

"Hello?"

"Hello, is Ryan there?"

"This is."

"Oh. Hi, Ryan, it's me. Um, Molly. From last night?" she adds, feeling like an idiot the moment that part comes out. Of course he remembers her.

"From last night? Molly? I'm sorry . . . *who* is this?"

Her empty stomach roils. This was a bad idea. A terrible idea. What had she been thinking, calling him?

"Molly . . . Connolly," she says haltingly. "I . . . we go to school together, and last night—"

A burst of laughter cuts her off.

"I know who you are, Molly. I was just busting your chops."

"Oh."

A twinge of anger makes its way in. He thinks it's funny to tease her? Does he have any idea what kind of nerve it took for her to pick up the phone and call him? Does he care?

"So what's up?" Ryan asks easily.

"Not much." She's about to say *I should go,* but he cuts her off.

"Want to come over or something?"

"Come over?"

"Sure."

She hears a protest in the background, an indignant, "Hey, what about me?"

"Hang on a second," Ryan says, and she can tell he's covering the phone with his hand as he holds a muffled conversation with someone.

"Who was that?" she asks when he comes back on the line.

"Oh, that? Andy. He and I were hanging out, but he was just leaving."

"Are you sure you want me to come over? I mean . . . it's kind of late." She glances at the stove clock and sees that it's past nine.

"It's not that late," Ryan replies. "Besides, my parents are away, remember?"

"What about your brother?"

"Oh, please. He's up in his room with his girlfriend. They never come out."

"Oh." Molly ponders that. Is it a good idea to go over to a boy's house alone at night, with no adults around?

Who's going to stop me?

"Okay," she tells Ryan abruptly. "I'll be there in a little while. See—"

"Hang on, don't you want to know where I live?"

"Oh . . . sure."

She knows exactly where he lives. Over in Green Haven Glen, on a quiet cul-de-sac called Marsha Court. She's worked up the courage to ride by on her bike once or twice, sneaking furtive glances at the big blue Colonial sitting on a neatly landscaped yard—so modern and upscale and well maintained, his house. So different from her own.

The last thing she wants is for him to realize she's made it her hobby to know every detail about his life, so she says, in what she hopes is a convincing tone, "Wait, I'll grab a pen and paper out of this drawer and you can tell me your address."

She leans over to open the silverware drawer and close it audibly, then says, "Okay, go ahead."

"It's in Green Haven Glen. Twelve Marsha Court. Third house on the right. Blue with white shutters and a basketball hoop over the garage."

"Okay. I'll find it. I'll be there in . . . forty-five minutes?"

"That long?"

"Well, it's not like I can just drive over. There's no one here to give me a ride." *Except my crazy mother, and she doesn't drive, anyway.* "I'll have to walk."

"Don't you have a bike?"

"Yeah."

"So ride it. I'm only, like, a mile away. You'll be here a lot faster."

She can't help but feel flattered that Ryan's so eager to see her. She hadn't wanted to go riding her bike to that party last night at the Curl because, as she had told Rebecca, there was something vaguely uncool about that. But Ryan had ridden *his* bike—how well she recalls that moonlit ride home on his handlebars—so obviously, that particular mode of transportation wasn't as cheesy and immature as she'd thought.

"Okay, I'll ride my bike," she tells him. "I'll be there in a half hour." That'll barely give her time to change her clothes and put on some makeup.

As she hangs up, Molly hears the sound of a car in the driveway. Rory?

Damn.

Looking out the window, she sees not Kevin's little red car, but a big black monster with chrome trim. For a moment, she's perplexed. Then she recognizes the car.

"Sister Theodosia?" she whispers incredulously. "What's *she* doing here?"

But she knows. Rory summoned her. Great.

She watches as the door on the driver's side opens and the familiar figure of a woman steps out. The nun is tall and angular, clad in a severe black habit that flaps around her head and her spindly, black-stockinged legs. Molly has never seen her wear anything else, though the nuns at Holy Father here in Lake Charlotte dress like regular people when they're not in church. Sister Carlotta, her CCD teacher, even wears jeans sometimes.

Molly can't imagine Sister Theodosia in jeans. Not in a million, trillion years.

I'm outta here, Molly thinks, scurrying toward the stairs before the nun can come in and waylay her. *I'll just run up and get ready to go to Ryan's and I'll sneak out without anyone realizing it. Mom's here. She can deal with Sister Theodosia.*

"Mommy! Funda!"

Michelle jumps at the shriek coming over the baby monitor. Ozzie was sound asleep when she left him in his room less than fifteen minutes ago.

"Funda!" he screams again as she heads up the stairs as fast as she can in her bulky condition.

Funda, she knows, is toddler-speak for *thunder.* The distant rumbling must have awakened him. Ozzie's terrified of thunderstorms, and Michelle knows there's a big one on the way. She peeked out at the twilight sky just before sitting down and saw massive dark clouds on the gray horizon.

In Ozzie's room, in the soft violet glow of the Barney nightlight, she finds her little boy cowering with his blanket over his head.

"Don't worry, Ozzie. Thunder can't hurt you," she says, pulling the blanket off and patting his sweat-soaked hair.

"No! No *funda!*"

"Let me show you something," she says, lifting him out of his crib and carrying him to the window. "See those clouds in the sky? They're filled with rain. They're going to open up and let the rain fall down and wash the whole world clean."

"No!"

She sighs. "Ozzie, it's so hot. The rain will help cool things off so that we can all get some sleep tonight."

For a change.

"Where's Daddy?" Ozzie asks abruptly, looking around.

I wish I knew.

"Daddy's at work," she tells Ozzie.

Or so he says.

She just tried calling the office, and there was no answer. Granted, there's probably a good explanation. He might have stepped out to get something.

When he called home earlier and he said his research was taking longer than he expected, she told him to make sure he got something to eat for supper.

"You can't keep skipping meals, Lou," she said. "You're going to get too run-down."

"I'll get something from Talucci's later. You want me to bring anything home for you?"

In this heat, Italian takeout wasn't particularly appealing, so she told him not to worry about her. "Just come home," she'd told him. "I miss you."

"I miss you, too, babe. I'll be home as soon as I can."

Now, as she stands in the window holding her sleepy two-year-old awkwardly against her ungainly belly and looking out at the summer storm building, she allows herself to wonder, for the first time, if her husband is having an affair.

"Sebastian!" Rebecca hisses into the darkness. "God, where are you, kitty?"

Rebecca glances up at the foreboding sky, knowing the heavens are going to open up any second. The storm has been building for some time, now. She cringes, seeing a flash of lightning out in the direction of the lake.

If Mom and Dad knew she was out here again, they'd be angry. She snuck down from her room and tiptoed past the living room, where they were sitting in front of the television, sipping iced tea and engrossed in some video they rented from Blockbuster.

It amazes her that nobody seems worried about Sebastian but her. Everyone acts as though it's perfectly normal for him to have taken off for two whole days.

But Rebecca simply *has* to find her kitten. She can't let poor little Sebastian stay outside, especially with the storm coming. He might get struck by lightning, or hit by a falling tree if it's one of those fierce storms that blows in off the lake with high, gusting winds.

"Sebastian!" she calls out loud in frustration, not caring that it's late and people might be sleeping, or that her parents might hear.

Where can he be?

Out gallivanting, without a care for his worried mistress?

Lost in the woods?

Or somewhere nearby, crouched, watching her, thinking this is a game, like when he hides behind the potted fichus tree and she throws his catnip mouse into the center of the floor for him to stalk and then pounce.

Maybe that's it.

She moves toward the Randalls' yard without thinking, deciding it would be just like playful little Sebastian to lie in wait, perhaps in the tangle of trees and bushes at the back of their property, watching her frantic search. Any second now, he's going to jump out at her, meowing happily, purring and rubbing against her legs.

"Come on, kitty ... let's get inside before we both get drenched," Rebecca coaxes, crossing into the next yard, forgetting to be afraid of the haunted house, almost certain now that she feels her cat watching her.

But where is he?

Maybe the woodpile by the berry bushes. It's probably filled with mice and spiders. She shudders at the thought, but moves toward it, knowing Sebastian would find those things palatable.

"Come on, kitty."

Nothing.

"Come on, Sebastian, there's a storm coming."

She glances up at the sky. The clouds are closing in fast and the air is hushed and expectant. She steps around a big patch of dirt next to the woodpile and hears the leaves on a nearby lilac tree rustling, signaling that a storm is approaching.

Then Rebecca realizes there's not a breath of wind to stir the dense green foliage. No, the night is absolutely still.

"Sebastian?" she calls expectantly, slowly turning in the direction of the rustling sound.

It takes her a moment for her eyes to adjust so that she realizes a face is looking back at her from amidst the foliage.

An oddly familiar face, and it's wearing an expression that fills her with panic.

Panic, and utter shock, as she recognizes those features, and the evil intent in the piercing eyes.

She opens her mouth and screams just as a deafening clap of thunder booms overhead, drowning her out. The figure pounces, clapping a hand over her mouth to curtain the scream, and simultaneously bringing a chunk of firewood down on her head.

With that, a smothering shroud of silent darkness swoops in to claim Rebecca Wasner.

CHAPTER EIGHT

Rory sits straight up in bed with a gasp and looks frantically around the room, disoriented, searching for Carleen.

There's nothing but darkness.

Trembling, she slowly comes back to reality.

It was nothing but a dream.

A dream in which her sister was hiding in the shadows, taunting her, calling, "Here I am, Rory . . . here I am. See?"

But Rory didn't see. She kept looking desperately toward the disembodied voice, searching for Carleen, but there was nobody there. Nothing but Carleen's laughter, as though she'd played a wonderfully dirty trick on her kid sister once again.

"Just a dream," Rory says again, leaning slowly back against the pillow.

But it was so damn realistic.

Probably because she's once again sleeping in her girlhood bedroom, right across the hall from Carleen's old room.

She came home from the cafe to find an unfamiliar but unmistakable black car in the driveway, and realized Sister Theodosia had arrived. Sure enough, she found the woman busily making up the bed in the guest room, and greeting Rory with a terse, "Please keep your voice down; your mother just went to sleep. I moved your things upstairs so that I could be in here. I always am, when I come to stay."

"That's fine," Rory had answered, though it was far from fine.

She doesn't want to be *here*, in the room that holds so many memories of the past.

Like Carleen's room, everything is pretty much the way she'd left it. Bookcase filled with childhood paperbacks, bureau stuffed with outdated clothes, old snapshots taped to the mirror, bloody crucifix hanging above the bed.

Rory's room, however, hasn't remained the same as a shrine to her memory.

It's simply that nobody has bothered to clean it or sort through her things in the years since she left. There was a thick layer of dust on every surface when she first came up here earlier, and it took her nearly an hour to get rid of it. As she worked her way through the room with a damp dustcloth, she came across one memento after another, and found herself repeatedly transported back over time. Some things, like the miniature plastic compass her father had given her, triggered fond, if wistful, recollections—others, like the Barbie dolls she had shared with Carleen, filled her with remorse.

And the whole time, she was conscious of Sister Theodosia in the guest room downstairs, wondering what the nun had told her mother when she arrived. They must have spoken to each other. Rory had found two still-wet mugs in the drying rack beside the kitchen sink.

She tried to imagine her mother and Sister Theodosia sitting at the table, chatting over a cup of tea. What on earth would they talk about? Had Sister told her mother that Rory had summoned her because she thought she was losing her mind?

And where in the hell was Molly? Rory had checked her sister's room upon returning home and found it empty.

What if she was so upset about what I told her last night that she ran away?

There was no way to tell, and, Rory reminded herself, nothing she could do about it until morning, except call the police. And she didn't want to do anything that extreme. Not yet. For all she know, Molly was staying out late again with her friends, to prove a point.

Let her! she thought stubbornly. *She'll have no one to blame but herself when she gets into trouble. I just can't let myself care what she does.*

But as Rory got the third-floor bedroom into livable condition, she kept her ears strained in vain for the sound of a slamming door below, or footsteps on the stairs.

Finally, exhausted, she had climbed into bed. But sleep wouldn't come.

Instead, she had noticed a cloying scent in the air. It was barely there, so faint she had, when she first noticed it as she walked up the stairs earlier, assumed it was her imagination.

But as she lay awake into the wee hours, listening to the thunderstorm raging outside her window, waiting for Molly to come home, she became certain it was really there.

The scent of Carleen's perfume.

Poison.

Was Carleen's ghost there in the room, haunting her?

Rory didn't want to believe in ghosts. And she didn't want to think about Carleen.

Still, she was tormented by images that persisted in drifting back over the years . . .

Carleen suggesting that they do crayon murals inside Rory's closet, saying their parents would never notice . . .

Carleen laughing as Rory was punished for that, and for so many other pranks she dreamed up and blamed on her kid sister.

You were such a brat, Rory thinks now, staring into the empty darkness as rain beats relentlessly against the roof above her head. *But, God, I loved you. Why did I love you?*

Who knows?

I just did.

She realizes a tear is trickling down her cheek. Then another. She doesn't bother to wipe them away.

She just lies there in her old room, still smelling a hint of that familiar perfume, crying softly, desperately missing her lost big sister as the rain pours down outside.

"What time did you get home last night?" Michelle asks Lou when he steps out of the shower.

He grabs a towel and buries his face in it, drying himself vigorously and making a muffled reply to her question.

"What?" she asks, watching him carefully.

"Read, Mommy," Ozzie commands from his perch on the cushioned plastic ring positioned over the toilet.

"I said, it had to be after midnight." Lou wraps the towel around his waist. "You were sound asleep."

No, I wasn't, Michelle thinks, remembering how she'd lain awake for hours last night, listening to the deafening storm and waiting for Lou. When he'd finally come home and crawled into bed, she remained absolutely still on her side of the bed, her enormous stomach and swollen legs propped in a nest of pillows. She wanted to confront him, to ask if he was really at the office, but by the time she finally worked up her nerve, he was snoring peacefully beside her.

She watches him now, noticing the way the water droplets glisten on his lean torso, remembering how, when they made love, she used to drive him crazy by nuzzling the hollow above his belly button. It's been a long time since they've made love. She wonders now whether that's just because of her pregnancy and his stress at the office. She wonders, with a sickening feeling, if some other woman has been nuzzling her husband's bare skin.

"Read, Mommy." Ozzie points to the *Once Upon A Potty* book she's holding open in front of him.

"Just a second, Ozzie. Did you eat supper?" Michelle asks Lou.

"If you can call a slice of pizza supper, then, yeah, I guess I did." He ruffles Ozzie's hair. "How's it going, sport?"

"I go potty," Ozzie says proudly, swinging his little legs back and forth.

"I can see that." He turns to Michelle. "I thought you said when I called yesterday that you weren't going to start training him until after the baby comes."

"I changed my mind," Michelle says, surprised. She hadn't thought Lou was listening to that part of the conversation. He'd seemed so distracted. "I figured I might as well get him used to the potty seat as soon as possible."

"That makes sense. That was some storm last night, wasn't it?" He looks out the window. "Looks like some branches came down in the yard. I'll have to get out there later and clean up."

"Don't forget, we have that childbirth class."

"How could I forget? I can hardly wait to hold your head and shoulders in my lap and practice yelling, 'Breathe!' 'Breathe!'— what fun."

"Stay, Daddy," Ozzie protests as Lou starts out of the bathroom.

"I'm just going into the bedroom to get dressed, Ozzie. Then you and I will go downstairs and have breakfast together, okay? How does that sound?"

"Mommy, too?"

"Mommy, too," Lou agrees, before walking down the hall, whistling.

Michelle wants to run after him, to ask whether everything's as all right as it suddenly seems. Whether he still loves her.

Of course he does. You're just pregnant, and hormonal, and insecure.

Lou's the same as he's always been. Wrapped up in his work, and distracted. He's never been particularly affectionate, and he's always had that biting streak of sarcasm. None of that has ever particularly bothered her until lately.

And that's because you're an emotional wreck lately. You're imagining all sorts of things, from food-stealing thieves to a cheating husband.

"Read, Mommy! Read now!"

She sighs and turns back to *Once Upon A Potty*, then thinks better of it. "Listen, Ozzie, you don't give Mommy orders. That's not polite. How do you ask Mommy nicely if you need something done?"

Her son appears to be pondering that, his elbow resting on his bare knees, his chin in his small hand.

Then he breaks into a smile. *"Pwease*, Mommy? Pwease read?"

She smiles back. "Okay, sweetie. I'll read."

Barrett Maitland hears the sirens just as he's finishing raking the last bite of Mrs. Shilling's cinnamon French toast through the pool of maple syrup and melted butter on his bone china plate.

He pauses, listening to the wail outside the open dining-room window, his head tilted as the sirens seem to be coming closer.

"I wonder what's going on?" Mrs. Shilling emerges from the kitchen and bustles through the room, heading toward the front parlor and wiping her hands on a dish towel as she goes.

Barrett waits, the piece of French toast poised in front of his mouth.

"It's the police. They're turning onto this street!" Mrs. Shilling calls from the front room.

The dark-haired, middle-aged woman seated across the table from Barrett catches his eye. Her name, he recalls, is Beth something-or-other, and she mentioned that she's from Brooklyn. She raises her eyebrows, as if to say, *what a busybody.*

He wants to point out that police sirens aren't as common in a small town as they are in New York. That to the residents of a place like Lake Charlotte, police sirens mean that something bad has happened to somebody who is, most likely, an acquaintance.

He knows all too well that on this particular day, in this particular town, wailing sirens are likely to stir memories of another day, a terrible day, a decade ago . . .

When it all began.

He realizes he's been holding his breath. He lets it out slowly, still poised, listening.

"They're pulling up in front of the Connollys' house," Mrs. Shilling calls. "Oh, my goodness, I wonder what's happened over there this time? That poor family."

Barrett thinks of Rory Connolly, of the stubborn expression she'd been wearing when she left him the night before.

He sets down his fork with a clatter as Beth from Brooklyn says in a stage whisper, "She acts as if we know these people. As if we care."

Barrett doesn't look at her.

Mrs. Shilling says, "No, they're not stopping at the Connollys'. They've gone past it. They're at the Randalls'—no, the Wasners'. Yes, that's where they're stopping. At the Wasners' house."

Barrett is conscious of the woman across the table wanting him to look up, so she can catch his eye and make another disdainful comment about small-town nosiness.

He took an instant dislike to her when their hostess introduced them yesterday. She's one of those know-it-all city types, in town for her college roommate's second wedding and making a point of letting people know she's not the least bit happy about it.

"I should be in the Hamptons this weekend. I have a full share in a beach house. What a waste. Anyway, I don't believe in second-time brides going to all the fuss of a white dress and walking down the aisle. I wouldn't be here if she didn't beg me to be the maid of honor," she had confided in Barrett when they bumped into each other outside the hall bathroom late last night. "What do you think?"

"About what?" he'd asked, preoccupied.

"Second weddings. Have you ever been married?"

"No."

"Neither have I. But if I was ever going to get married, and then married again, I wouldn't have a bridal party. Not at my age. Not for a second wedding. It's just tacky."

The woman talks too much. And Barrett is hardly in the mood.

Mrs. Shilling bustles back into the room, all aflutter, untying the old-fashioned apron she wears over her pink polyester shorts set. "I'm going down there," she announces to her guests. "I'll be back shortly. I just want to make sure everything is all right. After all, I *am* a neighbor."

Barrett pushes back his chair and says, without glancing at the woman across the table, "I'll go with you."

Molly pulls the pillow over her head to drown out the sound of sirens. All she wants to do is sleep.

And go back to her dream about Ryan.

Where was I? He was kissing me passionately . . .

But was that the dream, or a sweet memory of what had happened between them the night before, on his parents' chintz living room couch?

She smiles faintly, burrowing into her thin summer quilt and waiting to drift away again.

But the sirens are still at it. Louder than before. And they're not going by.

They're groaning to a lower octave, as though they're stopping right out in front.

Molly's heart begins to pound.

No, please, let me get back to my dream.

The squawk of a police radio reaches her ears.

She squeezes her eyes closed in a futile effort to escape the sudden certainty that something has happened. Something awful.

"What is it?" Sister Theodosia asks Rory.

She turns away from the front door to find the nun walking down the stairs, her spine held perfectly erect, as always, beneath her somber black habit.

"The police," Rory says briefly, biting her lower lip as she looks out at the street again, at the three patrol cars that make up the entire local police force. They're pulling up at the curb two doors down, on the other side of the Randalls' house.

"What's going on?"

"I'm not sure."

Several officers emerge from the cars and move swiftly across the neatly clipped lawn toward the house, disappearing from Rory's view.

"Your mother and I are going to morning mass," Sister Theodosia says, effectively pulling Rory's attention away from the scene outside.

"Where *is* Mom?"

"In her room, getting ready for church."

"Did you talk to her last night?"

"We spoke, yes."

"Did you notice that she's . . . having problems?"

"We prayed together" is the nun's cryptic answer.

Rory studies the woman's angular face, searching for some hint of warmth in her bottomless black eyes. There is none.

"Are you coming to mass with us, Rory?"

She hesitates only briefly before lying, "I went yesterday."

Lying to a nun about going to church?

Jeez, Rory, how low can you go?

She glances back at the police cars on the street, an unsettled feeling stealing over her. If Molly wasn't safely asleep in her bed, she might have a reason to be worried. But she peeked in on her sister on the way downstairs just ten minutes ago, and was relieved to see a familiar tangle of dark hair on the pink-and-white checkered pillow.

Still, the police seem to be parked in front of Molly's friend Rebecca Wasner's house. Rory remembers Rebecca, who had always been a pudgy, serious-faced little girl, wearing glasses even as a toddler, and following sunny Molly around like a devoted puppy.

"I'm going to go down there and see what's going on," Rory decides aloud, turning back to Sister Theodosia.

The nun has vanished.

After a moment, Rory hears the clatter of the tea kettle being set on the stove in the kitchen.

Sister Theodosia always did have a way of coming and going

in absolute silence. How many times, in Rory's childhood, did she seem to sneak up on Rory and Carleen, startling them?

It's like she doesn't walk around the way a regular person does, Carleen had once commented. *She just seeps in and out, like a creepy ghost. How does she manage to not make a sound in those big clunky shoes of hers, anyway?*

It's just too eerie. Sister Theodosia being here, the scent of Carleen's perfume last night . . .

Shoving those disconcerting thoughts from her mind, Rory heads quickly up the stairs to get dressed. She sees her mother just coming out of her room, clad in a dark winter dress and a heavy cardigan sweater.

"Mom, you're going to be too warm in those clothes," Rory tells her wearily. "Come on, I'll help you change."

Her mother frowns. "Rory, I thought I told you to go outside and play. Stop bothering me. Can't you see I'm busy?"

Oh, God. How many times has she heard those words in her lifetime?

Go outside and play . . . Can't you see I'm busy?

Busy.

Uh-huh. Her mother would invariably be sitting in a chair, staring out the window when she'd say it. Just sitting and staring, as though expecting to see Daddy or Carleen lurking out there among the trees.

"Mom, I can't go outside and play. I'm a grown woman. Remember?"

"Emily is out there looking for you. Go play with her."

"Emily?" Rory's stomach turns over at the sound of that name. The name of her best friend in the world, who, like her sister, had simply disappeared.

"She's waiting in her yard. Go ahead."

"Mom, that was years ago. Emily's gone. She's been . . . gone for a long time. Remember, Mom?"

Just like Carleen.

Rory's mother's eyes drift past her.

"Mom, please change your clothes."

"I'm cold."

"It isn't cold out." The rain has cooled things down and broken the unbearable humidity of the day before, but it's hardly cool enough for a jacket, and certainly not a woolen dress and sweater.

"I'm cold," her mother says again.

Rory contemplates arguing, then thinks better.

"Fine," she says shortly, continuing to the staircase leading up to the third floor.

If her mother thinks she's cold, let her wear whatever she has to. Those sirens are still audible in front of the Wasners' house, and Rory is anxious to find out what's going on.

"What is it, Lou?" Michelle gets up the minute her husband comes back inside, shoving her hefty body out of the easy chair so quickly, she feels distinctly dizzy once she's on her feet.

"It's their daughter. Rebecca."

Michelle holds on to the back of the chair to steady herself. "What happened to her?"

"Are you all right, Michelle?"

"I just stood up too fast. I'm fine."

"I told you to take it easy." He crosses over to her, puts a hand on her arm, and with a gentle push, forces her to sit again.

He's been all concerned ever since she had a contraction during breakfast. False labor, she's certain—it's too early.

But Lou was so worried about her, insisting that she rest with her feet up while he settled Ozzie in front of a video, that she decided not to tell him it's probably nothing.

When those sirens raced up to the house next door a few minutes ago, Lou wouldn't hear of her coming with him to investigate. "Just stay here and keep an eye on Ozzie," he'd said firmly.

Now he's wearing a grim expression.

Michelle asks, again, filled with dread, "What happened to Rebecca?"

"She's gone."

"*Gone?*"

"Vanished from her bed sometime last night. Her parents are frantic."

"Oh, my God." Michelle glances at Ozzie, who's oblivious, sitting cross-legged on the floor, engrossed in a Barney tape he's watched hundreds of times. "How could she vanish from her bed? You mean someone broke into their house and kidnapped her?"

"That's what it looks like. I don't know the details. The police just got there."

"I just saw her." Michelle thinks of her last encounter with the slightly gawky, soft-spoken neighbor girl. "She was looking for her kitten. She was so worried, poor thing. She just dotes on those cats of hers."

"I know."

For once there's no trace of Lou's usual derision for anything feline. He appears to be as distraught over the disappearance as Michelle is.

"Maybe there's been some mistake," she suggests hopefully. "Maybe she was sleeping over a friend's house and forgot to tell them."

"Maybe," Lou says. "But her parents are hysterical."

"Oh, God. Oh, my God. Did you see the local paper yesterday?" Michelle asks, remembering. "This is just like—"

"I know. I thought the same thing. It was ten years ago last night that the first girl disappeared. Kristin Stafford. You weren't around here that summer, Michelle. You don't know what it was like."

"I remember what it was like when I came back," she points out. "Everyone on edge. People suspicious of their own friends and neighbors . . . And they never caught whoever did it."

"No," Lou says, shaking his head. "They never did."

"Lou, I'm scared. The Wasners live right next door. What if something happens to Ozzie—"

"He'll be fine, Michelle. Relax. Nobody's going to kidnap Ozzie. Anyway, you were probably right. There's probably a logical explanation. The girl probably ran away."

She knows he's just pacifying her, but she sees that Ozzie has glanced up at them, having heard his name mentioned. She doesn't want to scare him. "Right. She probably ran away," she says to Lou.

"And she'll turn up sooner or later."

"Maybe." Ozzie has gone back to his video. Michelle adds, in a low voice, "It's just . . . she's not the type to run away, Lou. I know her—maybe not all that well, but still, I get the sense that she's the responsible type."

"Even responsible kids find ways to rebel at some point, Michelle. When my senior class in high school voted on superlatives, I was elected Mr. Straightlace. Little did anyone know I had spent that Halloween setting mailbox fires."

"That's terrible!"

"I know. Don't ask what got into me. I surprised myself."

"Yeah, well, by the time I met you, you weren't all that straight-laced."

"I changed in college. The dorm was one big party—there was no escape. I learned how to have fun." Lou walks back over to the picture window facing the porch, parts the sheer drapes, and looks out. "The police are still there. And now a bunch of people are standing on the curb. Mrs. Shilling is front and center, of course."

"Of course." Michelle knows the woman is the neighborhood gossip. "Then again, Lou, here we are, peeking out the windows to see what's going on."

He drops the curtains and turns away from the window. "I'm going to go finish my coffee."

"Okay. I'll be here." She props her swollen legs onto the foot-stool again.

"Any more contractions."

"Nope."

But she's still feeling a little woozy, even though she's sitting down. Must be her nerves.

Poor Rebecca Wasner. What on earth could have happened?

Michelle focuses her gaze on the back of her son's head.

If anything ever happened to Ozzie, I would die. I would just curl up and die, she thinks grimly.

Then doubles over as another contraction clenches her belly.

Molly is filled with an acute sensation of dread as she makes her way toward the knot of people gathered in front of the Wasners' house. Most are familiar faces from the street.

She spots Rory right away. She's talking to Mrs. Shilling and a dark-haired guy Molly doesn't know. All of them are wearing serious expressions, talking in low voices.

Molly slows her pace, needing to put off knowing.

Because it's Rebecca.

She's certain about that.

And it's something awful. And if nobody says it out loud, it won't become real.

She concentrates on other things. On the way everything seems to sparkle after last night's downpour. On the fresh, damp, grassy scent in the air, and the tiny droplets of water still clinging to the leaves of the hedge separating the Randalls' front yard from the sidewalk.

She thinks about the Randalls, about how she's supposed to babysit there this afternoon while they go to a childbirth preparation class at the hospital.

The baby will be here soon.

That'll be nice.

Babies are sweet.

Molly stops several paces away from the crowd and the police cars and the Wasners' house. She glances up. The house looks deceptively the same as always.

Neatly clipped shrubs.

American flag.

Wicker furniture on the porch.

See? Everything's fine. You can go back home and—

Rory turns her head suddenly, as though sensing Molly's presence. Their eyes meet, and Molly recognizes the mixture of distress and sympathy in her sister's gaze. She's seen it before. Years before, in other peoples' eyes, when she was too young to understand what it meant. When she couldn't grasp the enormity of losing Daddy, and Carleen, too, and how it made people feel sorry for her, poor little girl, having lost both her father and sister in so short a time.

And now . . .

"Molly," Rory says, breaking away from the crowd and coming toward her.

"No." Molly shakes her head, taking a step backward.

Don't you dare tell me, Rory.

Don't you dare make this real.

"Molly," Rory says again.

Molly backs away, then turns and begins running toward home.

She runs as fast as she can, and it feels good, her sneakers slapping against the concrete and her hair streaming out behind her.

All too soon, though, she's home. She takes the steps two at a time, conscious of the pounding footsteps behind her, and throws the door open.

Rory grabs her from behind, catching her on the shoulders, saying, "Molly, Molly, don't run away. It's okay. It's going to be okay."

"No it isn't!" Molly hollers, spinning to face her sister.

Tell me I'm wrong, Rory. Tell me again that everything really is going to be okay. Please.

"It's Rebecca" is all Rory says at last, her gaze fastened on Molly's.

"No."

"She's gone, Molly. Nobody knows where she is." She pauses to heave a deep breath, then adds, "Her parents found her bed empty this morning."

"No!"

"Molly . . ." Rory folds her into her arms and Molly lets her. She allows her head to fall on her sister's shoulder and she allows her tears to soak Rory's T-shirt and she allows Rory to croon her name and whisper, "Shhh . . . shhh" as she strokes Molly's hair.

The way a mother would comfort her hurting child.

Mom has never comforted Molly this way.

But Mom isn't my mother.

Renewed pain surges through her gut.

It's too much. It's all too much.

"I can't take it anymore," she says, pulling back from Rory and looking up at her face.

Rory's eyes are still sympathetic. She understands. She knows what Molly means For some reason, that helps.

So does the fact that she doesn't tell Molly again that it's going to be okay.

She says only, "I know. You've been through hell."

"I want it to stop. God . . . I want it all to go away."

"I know."

She closes her eyes and sees her best friend's face.

"What happened to Rebecca?" she asks Rory. "Where is she?"

"Nobody knows. You don't have any idea, do you, Molly? You're her friend. You two must nave been together."

"No. We haven't. We had an argument. God, it was so stupid. Friday night. I haven't talked to her since then. I haven't seen her." Her voice breaks and tears rush in.

"Shhh," Rory says again.

"Why did I give her such a hard time about that stupid party? I knew she didn't want to go. Why did I start a fight over it? If I hadn't, we would have been together yesterday and she wouldn't be missing."

"No, Molly. Don't blame yourself. You have nothing to do with this."

And she knows Rory's right. But still a sick feeling comes over her as she thinks of Rebecca.

Poor Rebecca.

What could have happened?

Pounding feet on the porch steps catch Molly's attention. She turns to see Lou Randall standing on the other side of the screen door.

"Molly, thank God," he says, slightly breathless, his eyes flicking briefly to Rory, then back to her. "I was hoping you'd be here. I know this is a terrible time—" He breaks off awkwardly, adding, reluctantly and belatedly, as though he isn't sure if she's aware of it, "Rebecca . . ."

"She knows," Rory tells him.

"I'm sorry," he says simply, to Molly, and repeats, "It's a terrible time, but . . . we need you. It's an emergency."

It's Rory who responds first, as Molly's head reels. "What is it?"

"My wife is having pains in her stomach. She's pregnant—we think they're contractions. They're pretty strong. I called the doctor and he said he'll meet us at the hospital. But Ozzie—"

"It's okay," Molly speaks up, finding her voice. "I'll watch him."

"Molly, are you sure?"

"I'm positive. I'll come with you," she says, making a move toward the door.

"Molly, wait . . ." Rory puts a hand on her arm. "I don't think this is a good time to—"

"It's okay, Rory."

And strangely, it is.

Not just because there's nothing else she can do—how can she tell Lou that she can't help him under circumstances like this?

Besides, watching Ozzie will get her out of here.

Away from Rory's sympathetic eyes.

Away from Sister Theodosia and Mom.

What about Rebecca? You can't escape that.

But I can't deal with it now. I just have to get out of here. If I don't I'll go crazy.

"I'll come with you," Rory offers. "Just let me grab my keys and—"

"No," Molly quickly cuts her off. Lou is already down the steps, striding swiftly toward home. "I'll be fine alone, Rory."

"Molly, this isn't a good time to—"

"I know, but Ozzie—he doesn't like strangers," she lies. "It will just upset him if you come, too. I'll be fine. I'll be right next door. If I need anything, I'll yell."

"Molly—"

"See you," she calls over her shoulder, dashing through the door, down the steps, and onto the sidewalk to follow Lou. She nearly smashes into a stranger who's just turning in their gate.

"Sorry!" he says, and she looks up to see the dark-haired man Rory had been talking to earlier.

"It's okay," Molly mutters, hurriedly pushing past him.

"Are you all right, Molly?" he calls after her.

"Fine," she flings back, wondering how he knows her name. Rory must have told him.

It isn't until she's dashing up the Randalls' front steps that it strikes her that she's heard that deep voice before.

But where? When?

A long time ago.

She briefly turns her head to look back toward home. The man isn't visible from here, but she doesn't have to see him again to know that he doesn't look familiar.

No. Not at all. I must be mistaken about knowing him, she tells herself, following Lou into the house.

* * *

"Rory?" Barrett calls through the screen, looking into the front hall. "Are you here?"

She sticks her head out of a nearby doorway. "Barrett?"

"Hi. I just . . . I wanted to make sure everything's okay."

Rory sighs and walks toward the door, running a distracted hand through her red curls. Her hair flops stubbornly back into its wayward shape, as though she hasn't yet washed or brushed it this morning. "Things could be better."

"Is Molly okay? I saw her running away."

"She's just going next door to babysit."

"Now?"

"It's an emergency. The woman went into labor."

"Oh. Busy morning on Hayes Street, huh?" he asks humorlessly.

"Looks that way. Listen, I was just going to grab a cup of coffee and then go up to take a shower, so—"

"Mind if I join you? Just for the coffee part, of course," he adds quickly, offering her a faint grin.

She hesitates, then returns it. "If you want to, I guess it's okay."

"I just thought maybe you could use some company, with all hell breaking loose around here. It must bring back memories," he adds cautiously, as she unlatches the screen door and holds it open for him.

"It does."

"It was like this when Carleen disappeared, wasn't it." It's a statement, not a question.

She nods. "And Emily, too."

"Your next-door neighbor."

"And best friend. Just like Rebecca is Molly's best friend. God, Barrett, I hope nothing terrible has happened to her, but all I can think is that this is no accident. It's just like before. It's starting again." Her green eyes bore into his, as though she's asking him to tell her that it's not true, that this is different.

"I don't know," he answers instead. "There's no way to know, is there?"

"No. Not yet. Not until it happens again."

She turns away from him.

He doesn't know what to say.

Abruptly, she offers, "Come on into the kitchen if you want some coffee."

"Sure." He follows her down the hall.

As he does, he sees the framed childhood photos carefully arranged on the wall above the stairs rising along one side of the hall, none appearing more recent than a decade ago.

He notes the faded floral paper, some edges curling along the baseboards and around the doorways, and the threadbare green runner stretched beneath his feet, hiding most of the scarred, dull hardwood floor.

He glances at the small round pie-crust-edged table in the corner beside the archway leading into the kitchen, at the porcelain vase of artificial flowers sitting, precisely centered, on top of an Irish lace doily.

It's exactly the same, he thinks incredulously. *All of it. Exactly the same as it looked ten years ago.*

CHAPTER NINE

"How are you feeling now, Michelle?"

She looks up to see the familiar face of her doctor poking through the curtain separating her bed from the one near the window.

"Better, thanks, Doctor Kabir."

He gives a reassuring smile, but his black eyes are concerned. "I'll be in to check on you again in a moment."

She nods and turns her head on the pillow to look at Lou, who's sitting in the single chair beside the bed, his eyes focused on the computer screen showing the progress of the fetal monitor strapped to her stomach.

"What's going on?" she asks him.

"Nothing. No contractions for a long time, now. I guess it isn't labor."

"I guess not." She shakes her head. "They were coming fast and furious at home, though. After the first one at breakfast I thought it was just Braxton-Hicks, but—"

"Braxton-Hicks?"

"You know, false labor. But then it really kicked in. And I thought, I'm going to have this baby more than a month early."

"I hope not."

"So do I. It's too soon. I just want the baby to be all right, Lou," she says, and her voice cracks. She swallows hard, adds, "I've had this feeling lately, like something bad is going to happen."

"That's just because you're pregnant. It's your hormones."

"No, I don't think so. I really feel like something's going to go wrong." She finds herself bursting into tears.

"Michelle, come on." Lou stands and looks down at her, after a moment, reaching down to briefly pat her arm. "It's going to be okay."

"Are you sure?"

He nods, but she notices his expression isn't exactly comforting. Well, he hasn't ever had the best bedside manner. Probably thanks to Iris, who isn't the most nurturing person in the world.

"I'm sorry for falling apart," Michelle says, sniffling.

"Don't worry about it." He looks edgy even as he says calmly, "After what happened this morning at the Wasners', you're just emotional."

"I know. Maybe that whole thing brought on the stronger contractions, Lou."

"Maybe. You were upset, and the stress might have triggered false labor."

"Right."

They're silent for a moment.

He sits again, looking at the monitor. "The baby's heart rate is staying in the range the nurse said is safe," he comments. "So that's good."

"Yeah. That's good."

"All right, Michelle," Dr. Kabir says, stepping abruptly back through the curtain and flashing his white, white teeth at her. "Let's have a look."

"Is everything okay?" she asks, nervously watching him lift and examine the long strip of paper printing out from the monitoring device.

"The contractions have stopped," he says, nodding. "But then, you probably were aware of that. No more pain?"

"None. I feel completely normal . . . well, as normal as a person can feel in this condition," she adds, glancing at her mountain of a belly sticking up from beneath the white sheet.

"It was probably just Braxton-Hicks," the doctor says, glancing at the clipboard in his hand. "Even so, I want to do a level two ultrasound to check the baby's condition, and I want to keep you here for a while, under observation."

"For a while?" She thinks of Ozzie, back home with Molly. "How long?"

He shrugs. "At least a few hours. If the sonogram is normal and there are no more contractions, we'll let you go."

"So I don't have to stay overnight?"

"Not unless the baby is in distress or there's reason to think you're going into active labor."

"Good." She glances at Lou. "If I have to stay overnight I don't know what we'll do with Ozzie."

"Don't worry. Molly is there. She's a responsible kid."

She's a responsible kid.

She'd said almost the exact same thing about Rebecca just a few hours ago. The connection sends a chill down her spine.

"I know she's responsible, Lou," she almost snaps, "but after what's happened next door, I don't want her alone with Ozzie at night."

"Calm down, Michelle. Nothing's going to happen to Ozzie. Or Molly, for that matter. Stop worrying and focus on the baby."

"Is something wrong at home?" Dr. Kabir glances from Michelle to Lou.

"It's our next-door neighbor," Lou answers before Michelle can open her mouth. "A teenaged girl. Her parents think she's missing and—"

"They don't think she's missing," Michelle cuts in. "Don't downplay this, Lou. She was kidnapped from her bed last night, Doctor."

His thick, dark eyebrows shoot up. "Kidnapped?"

"Possibly," Lou says, shooting a look at Michelle, "but there's a chance it could just be a misunderstanding between her and her parents. Or she might have run away—it's still too early to tell. The police are looking into it."

"I see. Well, that's certainly a distressing situation, Michelle, but try not to fret about it," the doctor says.

Lou promptly flashes her an *I told you so* look, which she ignores, feeling inexplicably irritated with him.

"The main thing for us to focus on now is making sure that this baby is in good condition. I'm going to order the sonogram for you. Someone will come up to get you and bring you downstairs for that shortly. Okay?"

Michelle nods and watches him slip back out through the curtain.

She turns to Lou. "Call home and check on Ozzie, will you, Lou?"

"You heard what the doctor said. I'm sure everything is—"

"Call home, Lou," she repeats, urgently. She tries not to let a sense of panic move in, but she can tell her pulse is racing. "What if something's wrong with the baby?"

"Then the doctor will fix it."

"What if I go into labor?"

"Then you'll have the baby. It's early, but he'll be fine, I'm sure."

"But that means I'll have to stay overnight," she protests, feeling frantic despite her efforts. "Ozzie—"

"If you have to stay overnight, we'll get a hold of my mother and she'll come to stay with Ozzie."

"Yeah, sure." Michelle shakes her head. "We'll never get a hold of Iris on a weekend. She's probably out of town."

"You're getting all worked up for nothing, Michelle. Calm down," Lou says in a stern tone he reserves for when Ozzie is doing something he shouldn't.

"Don't talk to me that way."

Lou seems poised to snap back, but apparently thinks better. He sighs and says, "Okay. I won't talk to you that way. I'm sorry."

"Please call home, Lou."

He throws up his hands. "Fine." He looks around the curtained area. "There's no phone."

"I think I saw a pay phone down the hall when we were coming in. Out by the nurses' station."

"Right. I'll find it." With that, he disappears through the curtain.

While he's gone, Michelle watches the computer screen beside the bed, reassured by the sound of the regular, rapid-fire staccato rhythm of the baby's heart.

"You've got to be okay," she whispers to her unborn child. "I need you to be okay And Ozzie, too."

Long minutes pass.

Michelle taps her fingers nervously on the bed rail. How long can it take to make a simple phone call? Something is wrong at home. She's certain of it.

Relax. He probably stopped to use the bathroom after he called Molly. Or maybe they're still talking.

Lou and Molly engaged in a long conversation?

That's hard to imagine. Her husband isn't the type to pay much attention to a teenaged babysitter. He usually offers little more than a nod and a gruff "hi" when he sees Molly, or Rebecca.

Rebecca.

Michelle battles a renewed surge of panic.

After several more agonizing minutes, she hears footsteps. She wonders if it's just the orderly coming to take her downstairs for the sonogram. Can she persuade him to wait until Lou gets back? How can she focus on one baby when her other baby might be in trouble?

But it isn't an orderly who parts the curtain, it's Lou.

"No answer," he says abruptly. "That's what took me so long. I tried a few times."

"No answer?!"

"Relax, Michelle. They're probably just playing outside."

Her heart is throbbing. "Lou, you have to go home to check on them."

"Go home? But you're having a sonogram in—"

"I don't need you here for that. I'll be fine. Just go home and check on Ozzie, Lou. Please?"

He stares at her for a long time, and she realizes that his features betray some of the tension she feels.

"Okay, I'll go," he finally says. "But I'll come straight back here. And don't worry, Michelle, I'm sure everything is fine."

"With the baby, you mean?"

"With Ozzie. The baby, too," he adds. "All of it. Everything's going to be okay. You'll see."

Really? Then why don't you sound convinced? she asks herself, watching him retreat out of sight.

On this last Sunday afternoon in June, despite the overcast skies, the path through the Public Garden is predictably crowded with strolling couples, college students, and tourists.

He weaves his way among them, careful not to splash anyone

as his jogging shoes land in pools of water left over from the earlier thunderstorm. He crosses the bridge spanning the pond bordered by sweeping weeping willows and dotted with the famous swan boats, and makes his way toward the Arlington Street Gate, wiping trickles of sweat from his forehead.

The weather is clearing now, and he knows, having heard this morning's forecast, that the sun is supposed to poke through by midafternoon.

He emerges onto Arlington Street, crossing it just as the light turns green, and covers another block, then turns the corner. Newbury Street, in the heart of the Back Bay, is Boston's quintessential upscale thoroughfare. He doesn't bother to glance at the majestic Ritz-Carlton Hotel on the corner, nor, as he passes them, at the row of fine boutiques including Giorgio Armani, Burberry, Brooks Brothers, Cartier, nor the sprawling NIKE TOWN superstore, part of a new wave of businesses that are popping up here to challenge the Back Bay's old-money atmosphere.

There was a time when all of it had taken his breath away, when he'd been dazzled by the glamour and excitement of the city. A time when he couldn't imagine ever fitting in here on Newbury Street, ever setting foot inside of the upscale Louis, Boston, a palace of a men's clothing store on the corner of Berkeley Street, or dining at one of the pricey cafes with their intimidating wine lists and exotic daily specials.

But that was when he had newly arrived, a shell-shocked small-town transplant needing desperately to make a fresh start in a place that felt a world away from his tiny hometown—even though Lake Charlotte was merely a short drive away, less than three hours.

Lake Charlotte.

Molly.

Rory.

Carleen.

He tries desperately to shove the intruding image from his mind, but it persists. Carleen, with her long, glossy dark hair, her infectious laugh, her biting sense of humor.

You were years ahead of yourself, honey, he tells the image. *Trying to be a woman before you'd finished being a kid. I tried to warn you.*

You wouldn't listen.

"Hey, watch it!"

Startled, he glances up just in time to avoid crashing into a waiter at a sidewalk cafe, carrying a tray of drinks.

"Sorry," he calls over his shoulder, noting that he's almost home. He slows his pace, breathing hard, cooling down, doing his best not to think about the past.

About a beautiful, rebellious girl named Carleen Connolly.

About the tragic mistakes they'd both made.

"Treasure, Molly!"

"Good, Ozzie. Treasure." She widens her eyes, smiles, and nods at him in that condescending way you do with small children, as though you're as fascinated as they are about some trivial thing like digging in a pile of dirt.

She hadn't wanted to trek out here to the backyard, but Ozzie insisted, crying and pointing to the dirt pile and managing to convey to her, in his limited toddler vocabulary, that his mommy had promised he could dig for treasure today.

So here she is, sitting in a lawn chair in a patch of shade beneath the lilac tree, in full view of the police investigation taking place at the house next door. Ozzie seems happily oblivious to the uniformed detectives combing the Wasner house, inside and out, for some clue to what happened to Rebecca. No, Ozzie lives the blessedly insulated life of a two-year-old, in which the worst thing that can happen is for someone to take your shovel away from you.

Molly tried, a few minutes ago, only to inspire a blood-curdling scream that caused several police officers to look up from dusting the Wasners' back door for fingerprints.

So she let Ozzie keep digging, even though she's tired and hungry and ready to get inside, away from the blatant reminder that her best friend is gone, and nobody knows what happened to her.

"Treasure! Treasure!"

Ozzie's shovel has struck something buried in the dirt.

"Molly help!" he cries excitedly, hurrying over to her and pulling her up from her chair.

"No, Ozzie, Molly doesn't want to get all dirty."

"Help, Molly. *Pwease?*"

Charmed by his polite request and his big brown eyes, she relents. "Okay, I'll help. It's probably a rock. I'll get it out of the way so you can keep digging."

"Dig," Ozzie agrees, and hands her the orange plastic shovel.

Molly crouches at the edge of the grass, surprised at how deep a hole he's managed to dig. "Not bad for a little guy," she tells him, poking his shovel into the hole, keeping an eye out for worms and bugs.

The plastic strikes something hard, and she tries to pry it loose.

If it's a rock, it's not just some small pebble, she realizes, scraping some dirt away with the shovel and seeing that the object extends beyond the hole Ozzie dug.

"I can't get it out, Ozzie," she says, offering him the shovel. "Just dig someplace else, okay?"

He scrunches his features like he's going to burst into another scream, and she says, with a quick glance toward the cops still working on the doorknob of the Wasners' house, "Okay, Ozzie, just calm down. I'll move the rock, or whatever it is, so you can keep digging."

With a sigh, she steps gingerly with her sandaled feet from the grass into the dirt, positioning herself directly over the hole. She scrapes away more dirt, widening the hole so that she can get to whatever it is that's stuck in here.

Ozzie is crouched next to her as she works, silently engrossed in her progress. She hears one of the detectives next door call to another, "Hey, Bob, was that blood on the front sidewalk?"

Blood?

Oh, God.

Molly feels like she's going to throw up.

"Nah," replies the other cop. "Turned out to be a spot of paint from when they did the trim last fall."

"Treasure, Molly?"

"Ozzie, I think we need to go inside," she says, swallowing hard.

"No! Treasure."

"Okay, I'll do this for one more . . . what *is* this?"

She peers into the hole, having uncovered the edge of the buried object. Now she can see that it's curved and somewhat pliable, like some kind of tire. That's what it is, she realizes, brushing more dirt away with her hands to reveal spokes.

Just an old bike tire.

"Molly?"

She glances up at the sound of a male voice calling her name and sees Lou Randall on the driveway.

"Daddy!" Ozzie shouts, running toward him. "Buried treasure!"

"Mr. Randall? Is everything okay?" Molly asks, standing and dusting herself off before following Ozzie.

"Everything's fine. I *figured* you guys were just playing outside."

"Ozzie told me his mommy promised he could play with his shovel in the dirt this afternoon."

"She probably did."

"Buried treasure," Ozzie says again, as Lou scoops him into his arms and gives him a quick peck on the cheek.

"How's Michelle?" Molly looks past him, expecting to see his pregnant wife getting out of the Ford Explorer.

"She's still at the hospital, actually."

"Is she in labor?"

"They don't think so. She's about to have some tests to check on the baby. I tried to call home to check on you guys, but when I couldn't get through, she got worried and sent me home to check."

"God, I'm sorry. I didn't hear the phone ringing. We shouldn't have come outside," Molly says.

"It's okay. But do me a favor and stay in now, so I can reach you if I need to. I've got to dash back to the hospital," he adds, checking his watch as he sets Ozzie back on his feet. "Be a good boy for Molly, sport."

"Tell Michelle I hope everything's okay."

"Thanks, Molly, I will," he calls, already striding back to the car. The Explorer's motor is still running. He starts to get in, and then, as an afterthought, glances at the house next door and calls, "Any news about your friend?"

Molly swallows hard, afraid to try to speak, and shakes her head.

"Are you okay, Molly?"

"I'm fine," she manages to answer. "Don't worry about me and Ozzie. I'll take good care of him."

"Bye bye, Daddy," Ozzie calls, waving as his father pulls out of the driveway.

"Come on, Ozzie," Molly says, grabbing his grubby hand in her own. "Let's go in and wash up."

"No! Dig!"

"You heard your dad. He wants us to stay inside. I'll read you a story and we'll have some ice cream or something, okay?" she asks as they step through the back door into the kitchen.

"Ice cream!" Ozzie echoes with his usual enthusiasm.

She stops short.

Something just creaked overhead.

"Ice cream!" Ozzie shouts again.

"Shh, Ozzie," Molly says, grabbing him by the shoulders to keep him still. "What was that?"

"Ice cream!"

"Ozzie, be quiet!" She cocks her head, listening.

She hears it again.

A faint creak.

Like a footstep on a loose floorboard.

Paralyzed with fear, Molly listens, and even Ozzie is motionless, as though he, too, senses that something is wrong.

Several moments pass.

There's nothing but silence.

Calm down. Don't panic. This is an old house, Molly tells herself. Old houses are always creaking, making settling noises.

Settling noises that sound like footsteps?

Don't jump to conclusions. Or, if you're that freaked out, call Rory. She said she'll come over if you need her.

You don't need her, of all people.

You can take care of yourself, and Ozzie, too.

Besides, what is there to worry about? There's a bunch of police officers right outside.

Right. Police officers who are investigating what happened to Rebecca—who vanished off the face of the earth last night. Just like Carleen.

What if the same person who abducted all those girls years

ago is back? What if he's the one who took Rebecca? What if the kidnapper is hiding here, in this house, right now?

Molly swallows.

"Ice cream, Molly?" Ozzie asks in a small, hopeful voice.

"In a minute, Ozzie," she says absently, turning to glance out the kitchen window toward her own house next door. Should she bring Ozzie right over there?

No. She can't. She just promised his father she'd stay here, inside, in case he tries to call again from the hospital.

Besides, Mom and Sister Theodosia are home. She saw the big black car pull into the driveway next door earlier. She doesn't want to drag them into this.

No, she'll have to call Rory and ask her to come over here.

To do what? Save you from the kidnapper?

Molly hesitates, not wanting to call.

Not wanting to admit to anyone, least of all Rory, how scared and vulnerable she is.

But she thinks again of Rebecca, and of the sound she thought she heard overhead, and a chill slips down her spine.

Setting her jaw resolutely, Molly moves toward the phone, picks up the receiver in a trembling hand, and begins to dial.

The phone rings just as Rory, her mother, and Sister Theodosia are finishing their mostly silent lunch around the kitchen table. Sister Theodosia made watery scrambled eggs when they returned from mass, and Rory was so starved she agreed to join them when she came downstairs after her shower.

Big mistake.

The eggs are disgusting, and the tension at the table is palpable. She can't think of a solitary thing to say.

She can hardly confide in them about her earlier conversation with Barrett Maitland, who is turning out to be a nice guy, after all. So nice that she agreed to meet him again tonight for coffee, against her better judgment. But maybe she was being too hard on him earlier, too suspicious for no good reason . . .

Nor can she bring up the topic of her mother's problems so that the three of them can have a nice little chat and fix everything. No, she never should have asked Sister Theodosia for help.

The only person who can help her mother, she now realizes,

is a psychiatrist. She'll just have to convince her to see one. And she's not about to do that in front of Sister Theodosia, who made it clear that she thinks prayer is the answer.

So Rory sits silently at the kitchen table and pokes at her eggs with her fork, and when the phone rings, she leaps up to answer it, grabbing it gratefully, like it's a rope and she's struggling in a riptide.

"Hello?"

"Rory?"

"*Molly?*"

"Can you come over?"

"What's wrong?"

"Nothing, just . . . can you come?"

"I'll be right there." Rory hangs up and turns to see both her mother and Sister Theodosia watching her expectantly.

"That was Molly—"

"Where is she?" her mother asks, knitting her brows in obvious confusion.

"Babysitting. Next door. Remember? I mentioned that earlier, when you asked me about her when you got home from church," Rory says, darting a *See? I told you* glance at Sister Theodosia.

"What's wrong over there?" the nun asks.

"Nothing. She just wants me to come over. I think she just wants someone to keep her company," Rory says, heading for the door. "I'll be back in a little while."

She steps outside and looks toward the house next door, realizing she hasn't set foot inside the place in years. Not since Emily . . .

Shoving that unsettling thought out of her mind, Rory quickly crosses the yard to the honeysuckle hedge, glancing toward the street as she emerges from the well-worn path between the branches. From here she can glimpse police cars still parked at the curb of the Wasners' house next door.

Did they find something? Is that why Molly's upset?

Please, don't let it be that, Rory prays as she hurries toward the back door.

Molly's waiting behind the screen, holding a squirming, protesting Ozzie.

"What's wrong?" Rory asks, alarmed, seeing that her sister's face is even paler than usual.

"Nothing. I—"

"Ice cream, Molly! *Pwease!*" Ozzie hollers.

"He wants ice cream," Molly says wanly. "I told him he could have some, and . . ."

"I'll get it for him." Rory steps inside, past her sister, and looks around. "Tell me what's going on, Molly."

"It's nothing, really. I shouldn't have called."

Rory crosses the familiar kitchen to the freezer, trying not to notice that the place is laid out exactly as it was when the Anghardts lived here. Everything looks the same, right down to the worn linoleum. The appliances and furniture are different, but in the same spots: stove and refrigerator opposite the back door, table in the nook by the window.

Emily and her father had never used their table. It was always piled with clutter, Rory recalls. She had once asked Emily where they sat when they ate their meals, and Emily had shrugged and replied, "Wherever. In front of the television, or sometimes I just stand at the counter. It's not like we have these real sit-down meals with just the two of us."

Shutting out the memory of her lost friend, Rory opens the freezer and spots a carton of fudge ripple. Ozzie breaks into an excited dance at her feet as she removes it.

"Something must be happening for you to have called me over here," Rory says quietly to Molly, who just shrugs.

She opens and closes cupboard doors and drawers until she locates a spoon and a small plastic bowl. She scoops out a small portion of ice cream for Ozzie, sets it in front of the booster chair at the table, and lifts him into it. He grabs his spoon and digs in with gusto.

"It's just . . . I thought I heard this noise, and I guess I panicked," Molly says when Rory turns back to her.

"What kind of noise?"

"A footstep. Actually, two footsteps. Coming from upstairs."

Rory stares at her. "Are you sure?"

"No. In fact, I'm pretty positive now that it was just my imagination. I'm just freaked out by this whole thing with Rebecca. I guess my mind is getting carried away. Like there's some crazed kidnapper on the loose in the house," she says with a forced, derisive laugh that comes out sounding hollow.

"That's understandable, Molly. You've been through so much these last few days. But still . . . did you look upstairs so you can put your mind at ease?"

"No way!" her sister replies promptly.

"Do you want me to?"

"No . . . Yes. If you wouldn't mind."

"I don't mind."

Yes, I do.

And not because I think there's some psycho kidnapper lurking in a closet up there, either.

I mind because I don't want to walk up those stairs and down that hall. I don't want to look into Emily's old bedroom, and I don't want to remember her, and I don't want to wonder what happened to her.

"Do you . . . do you want me to come with you?" Molly asks, watching her, as though she senses Rory's reluctance.

"No. Just stay here with Ozzie. I'll be right back."

"Rory, be careful, okay?" Molly calls after her.

"Molly, don't worry."

At least the rest of the first floor looks different from when the Anghardts lived here. Now, despite the obvious signs that it's undergoing renovation—like the half-stripped wallpaper in the front foyer and the rough, patched living-room walls where dark paneling had been ripped away—it's more homey. The dining room has been painted a soft raspberry color framed by white crown molding, and there are soft floral balloon curtains framing the bay windows. The living-room furniture is oversized and upholstered in a comfortable-looking chintz with contrasting throw pillows, and there's a row of children's videos in the glass-fronted cupboard by the fireplace, where Emily's father had kept his hunting rifles.

It's clear that a family lives here now.

The Anghardts' home had lacked any hint of coziness. Their furniture was boxy and functional, and the windows had been covered by ugly Venetian blinds. What the place had lacked, Rory realizes now, was a woman's touch. Emily didn't have a mother; she'd mentioned once that her mom had died giving birth to her, and that the loss had shattered her father.

Rory barely remembers him; he was a quiet, brooding type, usually clad in a plaid flannel shirt or a T-shirt, jeans, work boots, and, in colder weather, one of those tweedy caps with a visor and ear flaps. He wasn't home a whole lot. He worked the night shift at some plant and spent his days sleeping, which was why Rory and Emily spent most of their days playing in the yard, or over at Rory's house, and evenings at Emily's, where there was no one home to care whether they watched R-rated movies on HBO or made a mess of the kitchen baking cookies or brownies.

There were times when Rory felt sorry for Emily, living alone with her father in that big, quiet, shabby old house, and other times when she envied her for the peace and quiet and privacy. Mr. Anghardt never bothered them when they were playing in Emily's room, the way Rory's family was always barging in when they played in hers.

Patrick Connolly, with his flaming hair and an Irish temper to match, had been the kind of father who was known to fly off the handle, yelling and throwing things around once in a while, but he would also grab you unexpectedly and give you a bear hug.

Meanwhile, Mr. Anghardt never yelled, but he never seemed to show any warmth toward his daughter, either—at least, not when Rory was around. Once in a while, Emily would show Rory a pretty bracelet or ring, or a new stuffed animal for her collection, saying proudly, "See what Daddy gave me?" She would cling to those tokens of her father's affection, as though they proved that he loved her—that he didn't resent her for being born, and killing her mother in the process.

You were so lonely, so desperate to be loved, Emily, Rory thinks now, looking back with a new perspective on her friend's unconventional home life. *Just like Molly is now.*

She sighs and hesitates only briefly at the foot of the steps before starting up, dragging her fingers slowly along the polished wooden railing she and Emily used to slide down when her father wasn't home.

I've never had another friend like Emily, she thinks wistfully, stopping on the landing to look out the small round leaded window that overlooks the well-worn path through the honeysuckle hedge. *I've never let another person get that close to me. It would hurt too much to lose anyone else.*

She reaches the upstairs hall dim and high-ceilinged and tunnel-like as she remembers, and she walks slowly to the doorway of

Emily's old room. A fresh, fierce wave of pain unexpectedly sweeps over her and she presses a tightly clenched fist against her trembling mouth as she looks around at the crib and the colorful nursery rhyme mural and the basket of toy trucks and cars.

The only thing that is remotely the same about the room is a pile of stuffed animals on the window-seat alcove where Emily used to keep her collection, and the built-in bookshelf beside the closet door, which now holds copies of *Pat the Cat* and *Goodnight Moon* and what looks like the complete works of Beatrix Potter, instead of those Sweet Valley High books Rory and Emily would trade back and forth.

For the first time, Rory allows herself to absorb a profound loss that had somehow gotten swept up into the one that had preceded it and the one that had followed it. Sandwiched between the trauma of Carleen vanishing and the devastation of Daddy's death, Emily's disappearance had somehow never hit her with full force . . .

Until now.

Now, she stands sobbing in the doorway of what had once been her best friend's room. She sees Emily curled up there on the cushioned window seat; Emily, with her sweet, smiling face and her clear, sky-colored eyes and the long, silky blond hair Rory had always coveted.

She hears Emily's voice saying, "Come on, Rory, let's play Monopoly—you can be the banker this time," or, "Look, Rory, see the new ring Daddy bought for me? It's jade. That's my birthstone."

Poor Mr. Anghardt, losing first his wife, then his daughter. He'd been so overwhelmed by his grief that he'd packed up and moved away not long after that horrible summer. Rory thinks about him now; hopes he's found happiness, wherever he is.

But you haven't, she reminds herself. *You never got over losing so many people who were close to you. Why would he? Why would anyone?*

Maybe if there were some sense of closure, she realizes suddenly. Maybe if she had gone to Daddy's funeral, or if Carleen and Emily's bodies had been found, maybe then she would have been able to finish grieving, put it to rest, and go on.

As it is, it's as though everything's hanging in limbo—no sense of whether people she loved are alive or dead.

But of course they're dead, she tells herself. *Certainly Daddy is, and after all these years with no sign of them, Carleen and Emily must be, too.*

Then again . . .

What if they're not?

What if Daddy faked his death so he could escape his miserable life here?

What if Carleen ran away?

What if Emily . . .

Well, there's no plausible explanation for what had happened to Emily, or the other two girls who had vanished in Lake Charlotte that summer.

And, Rory tells herself, it's completely irrational and childish to even go around pretending, for one second, that Carleen or Daddy or Emily might still be alive somewhere.

With a sigh, she turns away from her best friend's former bedroom, remembering, as she does, what she's supposed to be doing up here. Looking for a hidden intruder.

That's about as likely as Daddy walking through the door someday, she tells herself, but for Molly's sake, she makes her way down the hall and starts opening doors, giving each room a cursory inspection before moving on.

She can only hope that Rebecca Wasner will turn up safe and sound, so Molly won't spend a lifetime not knowing what happened to her best friend.

That doesn't change the fact that Molly already lost Carleen and Daddy, just like I did. Or that Molly just discovered—thanks to my big mouth—that Carleen wasn't her sister and Daddy wasn't her father.

Now there's something that'll screw a person up royally.

Molly, she thinks desolately, doesn't have a chance.

"Owww!" Michelle winces at the pressure on her belly as the ultrasound technician presses the transducer down hard beneath her navel.

"Sorry . . . I just need to get a better look at the placenta before we call it quits," the woman says, her eyes intently focused on the screen beside the table where Michelle is lying, uncomfortably flat on her back, with her stomach sticking out and slicked with a film of gel.

In the darkness of the small room, the screen glows with the image of the fetus curled up inside her womb. Moments ago, the technician had showed Michelle the reassuring sight of the baby's small heart beating rapidly, and the dark blob that she's fairly sure is the baby's testicles, which means the first test was right and it's going to be another boy.

"Does the placenta look all right?' Michelle asks the woman anxiously, as the transducer glides across her belly, then probes again.

"Mmm" is all the woman says.

She already told Michelle she can only perform the test, not discuss the results. That's for the doctor to do. But every time the woman rapidly presses the buttons on her keyboard to freeze the image on the screen and zero in on some part of the baby, Michelle wonders what she's doing, what she's found; whether anything is terribly wrong.

And the whole time, her worry about the baby mingles with her fear over Ozzie's safety. They came to get her for the test moments after Lou left.

"Can you please have my husband meet me downstairs?" she called to the woman at the nurses' station, who had promised to send Lou right down.

But he still hasn't arrived.

The ultrasound technician freezes the screen, zooms in, and prints another image.

Was that the baby's brain?
What's wrong with the baby?
Where's Lou?
Is Ozzie all right?

Just when Michelle thinks *I can't stand another second of this,* there's a knock on the door.

"Yes?" calls the woman, looking up expectantly from her keyboard.

The door opens and Lou's face appears in the shaft of light from the corridor. "I'm her husband," he says.

Michelle struggles to raise herself on her elbows. "Lou! Is Ozzie—"

"He's fine," Lou says. "They were playing outside."

"Lie back," the technician says.

Lou comes to stand beside the table, peering at the screen. "Is the baby—"

"I don't know," Michelle tells him, torn between relief that one son is safe and fear that the other is in trouble. She reaches up to find Lou's hand and squeezes it.

"Well, what does the test show?" Lou asks, looking from her to the technician.

"The doctor will discuss the results with you upstairs."

"Can't you just tell us what you see?"

"I'm afraid I can't," the woman says, not unkindly, but in a tone that suggests she'd rather they didn't pursue the matter.

Michelle knows that it's her job, that she must have done hundreds, thousands, of these exams, and that it's against the rules for her to reveal the results and she's not going to start now. Still, she finds herself suddenly filled with loathing for the ultrasound technician, with her perfect pageboy and her flawless makeup and her slender build and her manicured, polished nails tapping on the keyboard.

"Please lie back," she tells Michelle again, this time more firmly than before.

I hate you, Michelle thinks irrationally in response.

But she lowers her head and shoulders onto the table again.

As the transducer moves once more over her belly, Lou squeezes her hand and his eyes meet hers.

He offers what Michelle knows is supposed to be a reassuring smile and comes across as anything but.

Michelle squeezes her eyes shut.

CHAPTER TEN

"Do This Little Piggy, Molly!" Ozzie commands, waving his bare toes in her face as she bends past him to turn off the water pouring into the tub.

"Not tonight, Ozzie."

"Pwease, Molly?"

"Not tonight."

She wearily braces herself for a tantrum, but, surprisingly, he cooperates as she lifts his naked, chubby little body into the bath and hands him his *Sesame Street* tugboat.

"Good boy, Ozzie," she says, patting his head, then reaching for the washcloth.

Good girl, Molly!

Carleen's voice unexpectedly echoes back through the years.

"You didn't even cry when that shampoo got into your eyes. You're so brave! Now turn around so I can finish washing your legs and feet."

Carleen used to give her baths. She used to do This Little Piggy, and read stories to her, and take her to the playground at Point Cedar Park down the street . . .

The playground?

A thought rushes into Molly's head, then flits right out again before she can grasp it.

There's something about being at the playground with Carleen. Something she should be aware of.

She closes her eyes, probing her distant memory, but whatever it is that she should remember is as elusive as a fleck of shell in a pool of slippery egg white.

Frustrated, she begins to dunk the washcloth into the water and wet Ozzie's hair.

Carleen used to use a cup to wet mine, she remembers suddenly. *You have so much hair, Molly . . . it takes forever to get it all wet.*

Her hair is thick and curly, like Rory's. But it's dark, like Carleen's.

Well, she was my mother.

My mother.

My mommy, giving her baby a bath.

Ozzie blinks and rubs his eyes as she grows careless with the washcloth and water splashes into his face.

"Oh, I'm sorry, sweetie," Molly says. "Are you all right?"

"Yup. Water in Molly's eyes, too," Ozzie observers, pointing.

"Right. That's just water."

She wipes at the tears spilling over, wondering if there's ever going to be another day in her life that she won't spend fighting off sobs.

Ozzie goes on playing with his boat, undaunted.

Did she love me? she wonders, pouring a dollop of orangey-pink baby shampoo into the palm of her hand. *Is that why she spent time with me? Why she would do This Little Piggy as many times as I asked?*

Of course she didn't love you.

She didn't even want you.

That's what Rory said, anyway.

Well, what does Rory know?

She was always jealous of Carleen.

That's what Kevin had told Molly. He'd said they were always fighting—that, Molly remembers—and Daddy would tell them to stop. Rory would tattle on Carleen, and Carleen would call her a little brat, and Daddy would say they were sisters and sisters should love each other. He even gave them those heart-shaped lockets that time.

Rory still wears hers. Molly glimpsed it inside the collar of the button-down shirt she'd been wearing the first day she arrived. She wouldn't have known the significance of the lockets Daddy had given Rory and Carleen; Kevin is the one who explained it to her years later. He said that in Rory's locket, Daddy had put a tiny picture of Carleen, and in Carleen's locket, a tiny picture of Rory.

"Never take them off," he'd ordered. "They will remind you that you're sisters, a part of each other forever. Someday, you'll be best friends. You're lucky to have each other."

Molly knew Daddy was an only child, that he always wished for a sibling. That was why it bothered him so much when Carleen and Rory argued so bitterly.

Kevin told Molly he was pretty sure Rory had worn her locket, but he wasn't sure about Carleen. "Probably not," he had said. "She was the one who was always starting most of their fights. I really don't think she could stand Rory. She thought she was a spoiled brat. She used to do really mean things to her. But I guess that's what big sisters do. Rory wasn't always so great with me, either."

Molly doesn't remember Carleen being mean. At least, not to her. When she was with Molly, as long as nobody else was around, she was always gentle and patient.

Not like a big sister at all.

And that's because she wasn't. She was my mother.

Molly scrubs Ozzie's hair into a foamy white cap as he splashes with his boat.

She thinks about how Rory acted when she was here this afternoon. *She* was gentle. And patient. When she came back downstairs after a long time, which must have meant she searched thoroughly, she told Molly, "There's no one there. You were right. It must have been your imagination."

Relieved, Molly had thanked Rory, then impulsively asked her if she wanted to stay for a while, maybe have some ice cream.

To her surprise, Rory said yes.

As they sat eating ice cream with a sticky Ozzie, they talked. Not about Rebecca, or Mom, or the secret Rory had inadvertently revealed to Molly.

Just about . . .

Stuff. The kinds of things Molly and Kevin talk about. Wondering whether ice cream tastes better with hot fudge or plain old chocolate syrup, discussing the "new evidence" that Princess Di's death was a conspiracy, and speculating about what was going to happen when *Friends* resumes in September.

Mundane, everyday stuff that Molly desperately needs to focus on after the traumas of the past two days. Molly had realized, as she and Rory talked, how much she misses Kevin, and how nice it would be if Rory were always around.

Then she reminded herself that she doesn't want that. No, she hasn't forgiven Rory for telling her about Carleen being her mother, and she certainly hasn't forgiven her for leaving years ago and never bothering to look back.

You don't forgive a person for something like that. Ever.

She hears a car door slam someplace out the open window. Are Michelle and Lou home? They'd called from the hospital a while ago to say that the ultrasound results appeared to be okay, but the doctor wanted to keep Michelle a few more hours for observation.

"Just a second, Ozzie," Molly says, standing and peeking out the window.

There's no sign of the Randalls' Ford Explorer. Their driveway is empty. But, Molly sees, Kevin's red Honda is backing out carefully past Sister Theodosia's car next door.

Rory had mentioned she was going out for coffee later, with a friend.

What friend? Molly had wanted to ask, curious, but she didn't, because by then she was back to sulking about Rory's abandoning the family.

Now she thinks about the handsome guy who had been talking to Rory out in front of Rebecca's house, and who had later shown up at their house. Is he the friend Rory is meeting tonight?

Who the heck is he, and why did Molly think she knew his voice for a moment there?

He must be an old friend of Rory's, from high school or something, she decides. That would explain why he seemed familiar.

She turns back to Ozzie in the tub. "Come on, kiddo," she says, crouching and picking up the washcloth again. "Let's clean your hands. There's dirt under your fingernails."

"Dirt," Ozzie agrees. "Dig again later?"

"No, not tonight," Molly tells him, quickly adding, "Maybe tomorrow, though. But I won't be here to help with the buried treasure. Your mommy will be here with you."

She'll have to remember to tell Michelle about that old bike tire buried in the yard, she thinks, scrubbing Ozzie's hands.

"Rough day, huh?"

Rory glances up at Barrett Maitland, watching her from across the small round table. "Why do you ask?"

"You just sighed. And you look exhausted."

"I *am* exhausted." She realizes her thoughts must have drifted from their conversation, which hadn't been about much of any-thing—just pleasant small talk, really.

"How's your sister handling this thing with her friend?"

"You mean Rebecca's disappearance?"

He nods.

"Molly's pretty shaken up by it, but she's a tough kid. She's babysitting for the people next door. I should call over there in a little while and make sure she's okay," she adds, checking her watch. It's past eight-thirty.

Outside, shadows are beginning to lengthen on the street as dusk sets in once again. Rory wonders if Molly's okay in that big old house now that night is falling. While she and Rory were eating ice cream and chattering at the table, she seemed to have forgotten all about the footsteps she'd thought she heard. But then her mood had suddenly shifted again, and she withdrew, and there was no trace of the sisterly camaraderie they'd shared for the first time.

"I hope Rebecca turns up alive," Barrett says.

"Do you think she will?" Rory looks up from her espresso to see a solemn expression in his dark eyes.

"I don't know." He fiddles with a wooden coffee stirrer, using the tip to trace a drop of moisture along the edge of the table.

"Do you think this is connected to what happened in Lake Charlotte ten years ago?"

His gaze shifts up to meet hers. "Do you?"

She shrugs. "All I know is that I don't want my kid sister to lose her best friend. Like I did," she adds, suddenly wanting to tell him—tell anyone, really—about Emily.

I need closure, she thinks, just as she did back in the hallway of the old Anghardt house. If Barrett Maitland's book can somehow solve the mystery of what happened a decade ago, then maybe she should help him with his research.

It might be painful to talk about Carleen and Emily, but is it any less painful to live with not knowing?

"Emily Anghardt," he says, watching her intently.

She nods. "She was my best friend. You knew that," she realizes.

"Mrs. Shilling told me the two of you were inseparable. Do you . . . want to talk about her?"

"Sure . . . about Mrs. Shilling?" she asks, and grins at the look of dismay that flashes over his face. "I'm just kidding," she says. "I'll talk about Emily. If I have to. If it'll help you with your book."

"Carleen, too?" he asks cautiously.

She hesitates, then nods. "But not right now. Okay? Not yet. I can talk about Emily. Not . . . Carleen."

"Why did you suddenly change your mind about helping me?"

"Because of what you said about the book maybe bringing some new detail to light—something that will help to solve the mystery. I just want to know what happened," she says, her voice raw with emotion.

"I understand."

There's a pause.

She looks up at him. "So, do you want to . . . I mean, do you need to ask me questions and take notes or something?"

"Why don't we just talk about Emily? If there's anything I need to write down, I will later."

She nods. "What do you want to know about her?"

"When did you meet her?"

"The day she moved in. I remember seeing the moving van pull up, and then I noticed her sitting on the front steps. She had her chin on her hands, you know, looking kind of sad and so alone—"

"The lonely new kid on the block."

"Exactly. A total cliché. I went right over and introduced myself to her."

He smiles. "So you weren't the shy type even then."

She feels her face grow warm under his gaze "No, I was never shy."

"Were you instant friends?"

"Pretty much. I helped her unpack the stuff for her room. She had this big stuffed animal collection And she loved books. She had so many books. And trinkets and things like that—she was a pack rat. And she loved jewelry."

"So it makes sense," he murmurs thoughtfully.

"What does?"

He looks her in the eye. "Did you know that Emily once tried to shoplift a ring from Chance's Department Store on Main Street?"

She blinks. "What are you talking about?"

"Mr. Chance didn't press charges. She was only twelve at the time. Her records were sealed."

"How do you know all this?"

"Mrs. Shilling told me."

"How does *she* know?"

"Apparently her son was a Lake Charlotte cop."

"Bucky Shilling?" She remembers him, a beefy guy with a wicked overbite. "Is he still around here? Did you talk to him?"

"No, he moved away. But apparently, back when he was on the force, he knew about your friend being arrested, and he didn't keep it to himself."

"God . . . I can't believe it," Rory says, shaking her head. "Emily shoplifting. That just doesn't go with my memory of her. If you had said Carleen did something like that, I would believe it. But Emily . . . she wasn't the rebellious type."

"Maybe you didn't know her as well as you thought."

"I guess not. But when you're a girl that age—twelve, thirteen—you tell your friends pretty much everything. I can't believe she never told me. You said it was a ring?"

He nods. "And when you said she loved jewelry, I figured that was why she took it. I know her father didn't have much money."

"No, he didn't. That was part of the reason she made such a big deal every time he gave her something." Rory pauses. "On the other hand, I wonder if it was her father giving her those things at all. Maybe she was shoplifting them for herself. Maybe she lied to me."

"Why would she do that?"

"Who knows?"

Oh, Emily, she thinks. *Were you trying to convince me that your father loved you? Or were you trying to convince yourself?*

"What was he like?"

"Her father? You know ... removed. He wasn't around that much, and when he was, he was sleeping. He worked nights. I hardly ever saw him."

"What about her brother?"

"What brother?" She takes a sip of her espresso, sets the cup down, tells him, "Emily didn't have a brother."

Barrett frowns. "Yes, she did."

"No, she didn't. I'm sure about that, at least. It was just her and her father."

"She never mentioned a brother?"

"Nope. You must be thinking of somebody else."

"No. I'm positive about this ... So you never knew?"

"What are you talking about?" Her heart is starting to pound.

"Emily did have a brother, Rory. I was looking into their family's past as part of the research for my book and I came across her mother's obituary. It listed a twin son and daughter as surviving children. He was Emily's twin. His name was David."

"There's no way. How could I not have known about something like that? She was my best friend. I was in her house all the time. Believe me, there was no twin brother there!"

"That's because he didn't live there," Barrett says with maddening certainty. "David was mentally retarded, Rory. I did some checking and I found out that when Emily and her father moved to Lake Charlotte, he was placed in St. Malachy's home for special-needs children and adults, down in Poughkeepsie. He's still there."

"All right, Michelle, I'm going to release you," Dr. Kabir says, looking up from his clipboard with a smile "Everything looks good."

"What about the baby being breech?" she asks, wondering, as she has repeatedly in the past few hours, how she could not have noticed that obvious detail when the ultrasound was being performed. She had just been so distracted—and of course the woman doing the test hadn't said anything about it.

"The breech position is something we need to keep checking,

but at this point, there is still the possibility that he'll turn again before you deliver. That's been known to happen, although it isn't necessarily common in the last few weeks of a pregnancy. If he remains breech, we'll talk about your options."

"But his position has nothing to do with the cramps I was having?"

Dr. Kabir shakes his head. "As far as I can tell, those were just some very strong Braxton-Hicks contractions, Michelle—maybe compounded by the tension in your body. Your cervix hasn't begun to dilate yet."

She nods and glances at Lou, who has risen from his seat by the bed and looks anxious to get out of here.

"I'll see you in my office for our regular appointment this week, and we'll see if the little guy has done a somersault yet," the doctor says with a smile, shaking Lou's hand and giving Michelle a pat on her arm. "But in the meantime, you need to reduce the level of stress in your life. Take plenty of time to relax—starting now. Go home and get some sleep. You both look exhausted."

Sleep.

Suddenly, Michelle can't wait to crawl between the sheets at home, close her eyes, and allow sleep to give her a reprieve from this horrible day.

"I honestly can't wait to go home to bed," she tells Lou as the doctor leaves the room and Lou begins gathering her clothes from the cupboard where the nurse stored them earlier.

"Bed? You've been in bed all day."

She scowls. "Well, I've hardly been resting. I'm hooked up to this machine, and I'm completely stressed out about the baby—"

"Yeah, but at least you haven't been sitting on that hard chair for the past eight hours. My back is killing me."

She glares at him, wondering how he can be so insensitive. "I'll trade places with you in a minute," she snaps. "You see how it feels to have this giant baby wedged inside you, and how it feels to know you're going to have to get him out somehow even though his legs are down and his head is up—"

"The doctor said before that if he doesn't turn, a C-section is an option."

"That's major surgery! I don't want a C-section. How am I

going to take care of a new baby, and Ozzie, if I have to recuperate from surgery?"

Lou rubs his eyes. "Michelle, don't worry about it until you have to, okay? Now let's get going."

"I have to wait for the nurse to unhook me from this machine," she says irritably, gesturing at the fetal monitor still strapped to her stomach. She adds sarcastically, "But if you want to go on without me, I can always walk home."

"Don't be bitchy, Michelle."

"Me? Bitchy? You're the one who—"

"Let's not argue again. Please. I'm so tired of arguing."

"Is that why you spend so much time at work, Lou?"

He stares at her. "Is that what you think?"

"What should I think?"

"Try thinking that I have to work as hard as I can to earn the promotion they just handed me. Try thinking that I have to keep my job so that we'll have health benefits to pay for this baby, and your doctor bills, and Ozzie's . . . try thinking that I have to come up with enough money to pay the mortgage every month and put food on the table and—"

"I'm not the one who thought we should go into so much debt to buy such a huge house, remember?"

He sighs. "Now we're on the house again? What is it that you don't like about it, Michelle? What is it that you want to do? Move? Will that make you happy?"

"Yes!" she blurts out.

They're silent for a moment. Out in the hallway, a cart clatters by, a reminder that people are around. Nurses and orderlies and other patients can undoubtedly hear them shouting, at each other.

She shakes her head, realizing she's gotten carried away. "I mean, no. No, I don't want to move, Lou," she says, utterly exhausted. "I Just—I'm just so stressed out. And you're never home. And everything seems to be too much to handle, all of a sudden."

He watches her.

She wonders if he's going to reach out and touch her, stroke her arm, tell her that everything's going to be okay.

She wants him to do that.

He doesn't.

And when he doesn't, she wonders again if he's having an affair. All this tension between them can't just be due to her hormones and their financial troubles and their worries about the baby . . . can it?

Helen, the pleasant, chatty nurse who's been taking care of her, bustles into the room, drawing the curtain all the way back with a smile as though she hasn't heard the bitter argument spilling out into the hallway. "Okay, Mrs. Randall, I hear we're going to spring you from this joint. Let me get you unhooked from these machines and you can be on your way home to little Oscar."

"Ozzie," Michelle corrects her.

"Oh, that's right. Ozzie! How could I forget? Like the Wizard of Oz."

Earlier, when she had first arrived and was making small talk to put her patient at ease, the nurse had asked Michelle how they had happened to choose such an unusual name for their little boy. So Michelle had told her the story about how she and Lou had always loved the classic Judy Garland film, and how Lou wanted to name the baby Glinda, after the Good Witch, if they had a girl. And they spent her whole pregnancy teasing each other with possible boys' names connected to the movie—Toto, and Munchkin, and Brick. And then, when she was in the long stage of early labor at home and they still hadn't come up with a boy's name, Lou popped the video into the VCR to take her mind off the pain. And at some point, they just looked at each other and simultaneously blurted it out—*Ozzie*—stunned that they hadn't thought of that before.

"And what are you going to name this baby?" the nurse had asked with a smile.

"I'm not sure," Michelle had said, realizing they really should sit down with the baby-name books and come up with a list of names. They haven't really even discussed it yet. Is it just that the novelty has worn off by the second pregnancy? Or is it that there's something wrong between them, generating tension instead of anticipation about the upcoming birth?

"Anyway," the nurse says now, busily unhooking the wide elastic belt from around her stomach, "I'm so glad everything turned out to be okay."

"So am I," Michelle says tightly

She glances at Lou, who is brooding in the doorway, his arms folded across his chest.

But it's not okay, Nurse. The baby is breech, and all my husband and I do is argue, and there's a kidnapper on the loose in our neighborhood. Everything is falling apart, and I've never been more frightened in my life. And I have this feeling, this horrible feeling, that the worst is yet to come.

"So you're sure Emily never mentioned her brother?" Barrett asks, watching Rory closely. She looks pale beneath her freckles.

"No, she never did. I'm positive. It's just so strange, Barrett. Why wouldn't she tell me? The shoplifting thing, I can understand. She was embarrassed or ashamed or whatever. But why not tell me about her brother?"

"Maybe for the same reasons," Barrett suggested.

"You mean, because he was mentally retarded? But that wouldn't have mattered to me. I would never have a problem with something like that."

"Apparently, Emily did. Maybe her father did, too. I've called St. Malachy's a few times to check into it. They didn't want to tell me much, but one time I reached an aide there who gave me some interesting information. She hasn't been working there long, but she heard from someone who knew them that Emily and her father used to come to see David often, and even took the brother home with them for visits up until ten years ago—"

"Visits? At home?"

"Did you see him there, then?"

There's a faraway look on Rory's face. "No. No, but I remember a few times," she says slowly, "when Emily mentioned that some relative was coming to stay with them. One time it was during Christmas, and another time in the summer—she didn't want to talk much about it, she only said that we wouldn't be able to see each other while the visitor was around because her father made her spend time showing him around, that kind of thing. The first time he came, I suggested that I could come along, but she said her father wouldn't like that, because he thought it should be just the family, or whatever. I never thought . . . it must have been her brother. He must have been the visitor. I never saw him—but then, I didn't pay much attention. The first time it happened was during Christmas, and I was busy with my own family, the holidays, whatever. And the second time he came—I remember now that it was right around the time that Carleen disappeared. So I was distracted. I didn't pay much attention."

"It makes sense that she didn't want you to meet him because she was afraid of what you might think. I understand that he's profoundly retarded. And she was what, twelve? Thirteen? The age when all girls care about is fitting in, seeming normal to their friends."

"But that's so incredibly sad."

Barrett nods. "Even sadder—after Emily disappeared and Mr. Anghardt moved away from here, he never bothered with David again."

"Is he still alive?"

"Nobody even knows. Maybe not. And David had no one else. His mother—Mrs. Anghardt died giving birth to the twins. But you knew that, didn't you?"

"I didn't know there were twins, obviously, but I did know she died in childbirth. I just—my head is spinning. I suddenly feel like I never knew Emily at all."

"I'm sorry. I didn't mean to spring all this on you unexpectedly."

"It's okay. It happens." She smiles ruefully, as though her comment has a private meaning. He doesn't press her about it.

Instead, he asks, "Do you remember any details about the day Emily disappeared?"

"That's the thing . . . I really don't. I was in such a fog. My sister had vanished right before that. I remember Emily telling me that she was sure Carleen would turn up alive. She was always there for me, trying to comfort me. And then she—she was gone, too." She shakes her head, staring off into space, then says abruptly, "You know what, Barrett, I actually don't feel like talking about this anymore. Is that all right? Can we just talk about something else?"

"Sure." He tries to cover his acute disappointment. "What do you want to talk about?"

"I don't know . . . maybe I should just go home and—"

"Don't," he says, reaching across the table and touching the hand clasped around her cup. "Don't go home. Not yet."

She looks up, surprised.

He looks into those green eyes of hers.

Don't go home, Rory. Stay here, with me.

Trust me . . . even though you don't want to.

Even though you have every reason not to.

"Do you want to go for a walk down to the lake?" he asks, holding his breath for her reply.

It's a long time in coming.

Then she shrugs and says, "Why not?"

Several hours later, the streets of Lake Charlotte are quiet, deserted. Most houses are dark.

Not 52 Hayes Street

A female figure is silhouetted in a lit second-floor window, looking out over the yard of the house next door. It's impossible to tell from here who it is.

No matter.

Though she's looking in this direction, she can't possibly see that there's someone standing here in the honeysuckle hedge, watching, listening . . .

Waiting.

Waiting for a chance to do what must urgently be done.

I have to get that damn bicycle out of the dirt pile before that little brat digs the whole thing out and somebody realizes what it is.

For all I know, that "Kristin" license plate is still attached to the back of the seat. I have to get it. I have to destroy it.

I would have done it last night, if that stupid Wasner girl hadn't come barging out here, looking for her lost kitty cat.

If only I hadn't wrung the stupid animal's neck when it came sniffing around me in the bushes while I was watching Rory the other night. But I had no choice. It was about to open its mouth and let out a big old meow, and then Rory would have turned and looked out the window, and she would have seen me here.

And I can't let her see me.

Not yet.

There's a flash in the window overhead. The light has gone out. The second floor of the Connolly house is completely dark.

But is somebody still there, looking out?

Will she see the dark-clothed figure walking back toward the woodpile?

I can't take any chances.

No. It wouldn't be worth it.

I'd better wait.

CHAPTER
ELEVEN

On Monday morning, a uniformed police detective shows up at the Connollys' front door shortly after Maura and Sister Theodosia have left for daily mass.

It's Rory who opens it to see him standing there, and the first thought that runs through her mind is that something has happened to someone. Mom was in an accident on the way to church, or Kevin has been injured in Europe—

"Are you Molly Connolly?" the officer asks doubtfully.

She shakes her head, careful not to slosh the coffee in the full, steaming mug she'd just poured herself in the kitchen. "I'm Rory. Her older sister."

"I'm Detective Mullen from the Lake Charlotte police. I need to ask your sister some questions. Is she here?"

This is about Rebecca's disappearance. They want to ask if Molly knows anything. God, I hate to put her through that.

She remembers the hot summer morning ten years ago when she was questioned by Detective Doug McShane about her sister's disappearance.

"Did Carleen mention anything to you about running away, Rory?"

Of course she did, Rory had thought. Carleen told anyone who would listen that she was dying to get out of here. But she didn't run away. I know she didn't.

To Doug McShane, she'd simply said, *"No, she didn't."*

"Do you know if your sister had any enemies. Rory? Anyone she mentioned having problems with recently?"

Definitely. My father. And Sister Theodosia, this nun friend of my mother's who's been underfoot all summer. And me. My sister can't stand me.

"No. Officer McShane she didn't have any enemies that I know of."

"Rory, did your sister ever mention dating anyone special? Did she have any boyfriends that your parents might not have known about?"

You'd better believe she did. She had tons of boyfriends. She liked older guys. And she sure as hell wouldn't have told my parents about any of them. She was always sneaking around with guys she shouldn't be with.

"My sister had boyfriends. Officer McShane, but I didn't know their names."

Then, a few weeks later, Doug McShane was back, asking Rory whether Emily Anghardt had mentioned running away, or had any enemies, or had a boyfriend . . .

Endless questions, and Rory had known somehow that they weren't going to lead anywhere, known that there was no way she had information that was going to solve the mystery. She was as mystified as anyone else about what had happened to her sister and her best friend and those other girls.

But as Doug McShane questioned her, she found herself feeling guilty, and filled with renewed anguish, as though there was something she should have known so that she could have stopped these horrible things from happening to her sister and Emily; as though there was something she should be able to tell the police so they could march right out and know where to find them.

She doesn't want Molly to go through that. God, no. She doesn't want Molly to suffer any more emotional trauma than she already has.

Rory looks at Detective Mullen standing on her front porch, at his crisp uniform and his gun holster and his no-nonsense expression, and she says firmly, "Molly is here, but she's still upstairs sleeping."

"Would you mind waking her?" the officer asks, and it's more of a command than a request.

Rory had checked on her sister on her way downstairs a short time ago. She'd knocked on Molly's closed door but there was no answer, and after a moment's panic, remembering that Rebecca had vanished from her bedroom, just as Carleen had, Rory had opened the door and peeked in.

Thankfully, Molly was there, sound asleep, looking so peaceful that for a moment Rory had stood there remembering what she was like as a tiny girl—so sweet, so helpless, an innocent victim of the dark secret they had all been forced to keep.

"Actually, I would mind," Rory says, folding her arms across her chest and looking him in the eye. "My sister had an exhausting day yesterday, and she needs to rest."

"Listen, Ms. Connolly, I'm sure you know what this is about. And I don't need to tell you that your neighbors, the Wasners, are beside themselves over the disappearance of Rebecca. They've told us that Molly was her best friend. She might know something that can help us to find her."

"I doubt that," Rory mutters. "When she wakes up, I'll have her—"

"Please wake her up, Ms. Connolly."

She stares at the man for a long moment, and then, realizing he's not going to budge, sighs and says, "Fine. I'll wake her up. But I can guarantee that when I tell her why, it's going to be a while before she pulls herself together and comes down to talk to you."

"I'll wait."

"I figured." She turns away from the door and starts up the stairs.

"Dig, Mommy? Dig in dirt?"

Michelle glances at Ozzie, notices that his Winnie the Pooh video has ended and automatically started rewinding. She shifts her feet on the padded footstool, trying to find a comfortable position, and takes another sip of her decaffeinated tea before saying, "Ozzie, we're not going to go outside and dig this morning. Mommy needs to rest."

"But Mommy, you already rested."

No kidding. Any more rest and I'm going to go stir crazy, Michelle thinks grumpily.

Still, she had promised Lou, before he left for the office, that she would try her best to do nothing but take it easy all day.

"Just turn on the TV for Ozzie and let him watch videos all day," he'd said when she pointed out that caring for a toddler isn't very restful. "Or get Molly to come over and help you for a few hours."

But Molly had looked so wan and exhausted when they arrived home last night that Michelle hated to do that to her. Poor kid just found out her best friend is missing, and she was nice enough to bail Michelle and Lou out yesterday so they could go to the hospital. No, Michelle can't ask her to come over and babysit again so soon.

Besides, she doesn't feel like resting, no matter what Lou and the doctor say. After all, she slept ten hours last night, waking only to scurry to the bathroom every hour or so, and, for a change, falling immediately back into a deep sleep whenever she climbed back into bed. When she got up this morning, she was surprised to feel more energetic than she had in days.

In fact, she actually wouldn't mind getting outside with Ozzie for some fresh air this morning. It would do them both some good. She hates to plunk him in front of the television for hours on end. She'll be doing enough of that when the baby comes, especially if she has to have a C-section.

The baby's breech position and the prospect of facing major surgery are thoughts she doesn't particularly want to entertain right now. Nor does she want to brood about the state of her marriage. Things seemed better this morning, after she and Lou had both gotten a good night's sleep, but their relationship is far from rosy. Either the stress is getting to them both, or he really is having an affair.

Or, she amends, maybe keeping some equally devastating secret that's putting distance between them. She remembers what he said about the financial pressure and how he's being forced to work such long hours. She actually finds herself wondering if it's possible that Lou has some secret vice that's been eating away at their money—maybe a drug problem, or maybe he's a compulsive gambler like his stepfather Murray was.

Right. That's totally realistic. He's shooting up or flying to Atlantic City when I'm not looking.

She shakes her head, deciding she has way too much time to sit around and think crazy thoughts. Besides, if she hadn't long ago left all their finances up to him, she would know exactly what's going on.

But no, she was always content to let him balance the checkbook and pay the bills and make investments. She never bothered herself with details like that, not having the slightest interest in anything remotely mathematical. Even in school, she'd always gotten As in art and music and English, and Ds in math and science, figuring she'd never need to know that stuff anyway, since she was going to be a famous artist.

And now look at me.

No wonder Lou's been impatient.

"Come on, Ozzie. Let's go outside and dig," she says abruptly, reaching for the remote control and clicking the television off.

"Yay!" Ozzie claps his hands together and races out of the room.

She hoists herself out of the chair, jams her swollen feet into a pair of sandals—open-toed shoes are the only ones that fit—and shuffles to the kitchen. She finds Ozzie waiting impatiently by the back door, holding his little orange shovel.

"Know what?" she asks him, seized by a sudden impulse. "Those berries must be perfect by now. I'm going to pick a huge batch of them and make a raspberry pie. That'll be a nice surprise for Daddy when he comes home tonight."

"Pie," Ozzie echoes agreeably.

Lou had always loved her mother's raspberry pie, invariably served warm, with vanilla Häagen-Dazs He had loved the way Joy Panati pampered him while they were living with her, taking care of him in a way his own mother never had. Michelle remembers how she had promised herself back then, sitting at her mother's kitchen table watching Lou heap praise on Joy's cooking, that she would always remember to do nice little things for her husband, to compensate for his rough childhood and Iris's lack of maternal nurturing.

When's the last time you did anything for him? she asks herself guiltily, as she rummages through the cupboard for a bowl big enough to hold a few quarts of raspberries. *You never cook dinner anymore. He eats takeout, if he gets to eat at all.*

Her defenses kick in.

It's summertime. It's hot out. I'm huge and pregnant. And anyway, he's never home for dinner.

Still, you should at least try. Try and pamper him a little. Maybe he really misses that. Maybe he needs it. Maybe it'll get things back to normal between the two of you.

She finds a big stainless-steel bowl in the cupboard and tucks it under her arm, saying to Ozzie, who's doing an impatient jitterbug by the back door, "Okay, okay, sweetie, Mommy's ready now. Let's go."

They step out into the glorious morning and Michelle feels better instantly. The sky is the purest of blues, with a few fluffy clouds sailing high. The sun is dazzling, warm on her bare arms, but not uncomfortably hot as it was a few days ago. The air is almost crisp by comparison to the humidity that vanished with Saturday evening's storm.

Ozzie races toward the dirt pile at the back of the yard, and Michelle follows as fast as she can, realizing she's moving more quickly than she has in weeks. Is it the lack of humidity, or is she simply energized by the thought of making a pie for Lou, making things right between them?

Her son settles himself in the dirt, plopping right down with a toddler's lack of concern for the little white denim shorts she thoughtlessly threw on him this morning.

"So I'll use Shout on them," she says aloud to herself, not willing to let anything stress her in the least.

Michelle goes past him to the tangle of berry shrubs climbing along the back of the property, separating their yard from the woods. She holds her bowl in one hand and lifts the nearest vine, careful not to let the thorns pinch her fingers as she inspects it for ripened berries. Remembering the abundant pale-pink buds she had noticed the other day, she knows that by now most of them will be a lush, deep red color, so ripe they'll easily slip into her hands as she picks them.

What's going on?

Michelle stares at the clumps of stark yellowish nubs that had only days before been dotted with raspberries. She moves on to another branch, and then another. All that's left are the bare stems, and a few hard greenish-pink berries that have yet to ripen.

Must be birds, she tells herself. *Or deer. Or bugs.*

But she knows that's not the case. Birds peck at the fruits, fully ripe or not, leaving some half eaten, and deer devour the whole thing, stems and all. Bugs eat only the fleshy part, and chew holes in the leaves as well.

But birds or deer or bugs wouldn't manage to eat every single ripe berry in the entire crop and leave the ones that aren't yet fit for human consumption.

These briars have been picked clean with methodical precision. Somebody has obviously been back here, eating them.

So?

It could have been Lou.

But he hasn't been home to do it, unless he came out here in the dark late Saturday night, after he got home, without her noticing, and that's highly improbable. No, it must have been Molly and Ozzie yesterday. Lou said they were outside.

"Ozzie," she says, turning to him, "did you and Molly pick raspberries yesterday?"

He glances up, then responds with a disinterested, "Nope."

"Are you sure? Did Molly eat them while you were busy digging?"

"Molly digged, too. Molly found treasure, Mommy! Buried treasure. See? In here . . . Help me find it, Mommy." He's furiously scooping dirt from the hole.

She notices that it's grown considerably. In fact, a huge patch of soil seems to have been freshly turned over.

"Wow, Ozzie," she says mildly, "you and Molly really spent a lot of time digging for buried treasure yesterday, didn't you?"

"Yup. Mommy dig, too?"

"Not right now." She walks away from the berry bushes, sitting in her lawn chair that's still positioned under the spreading lilac branches and holding the empty stainless-steel bowl in her lap. "I'll just watch you, sweetie."

So much for the berry pie for Lou.

Oh, well. She can do something else. Make him a meatloaf, or something.

But the thing is . . .

What happened to all those raspberries? Did Molly eat them when Ozzie wasn't paying attention?

Maybe.

And if she did, so what? Michelle certainly could care less about the babysitter helping herself to some fruit from the yard.

Besides, it might not have been Molly. Michelle knows that their backyard is occasionally used by neighborhood kids as a cut-through to the path through the woods that leads down to Lakeshore Road. When they first moved in, Lou was always hollering at teenaged trespassers, telling Michelle, when she protested that they weren't doing any harm, that it was just asking for trouble, letting kids cut through their yard.

"If any of them ever tripped and fell while they're climbing over that woodpile and got hurt, Michelle, we'd be looking at a personal injury lawsuit."

"You're just paranoid, Lou."

"I'm an attorney, Michelle," he'd pointed out. "I know about these things."

It's been a while since Michelle has seen anyone venture across their yard to the woods. Lou must have scared them all off. But maybe some brave kids had been here recently and eaten the berries.

A perfectly logical explanation, but it doesn't explain why food seems to keep disappearing around the house, too.

Do ghosts eat? she finds herself wondering.

And then, with a brisk shake of her head, she tells herself she really is losing it.

There's no such thing as ghosts, and if there were, they certainly wouldn't be required to do anything as mundanely human as eat. They'd be too busy ... haunting. Or whatever it is ghosts do.

She glances idly over at the Wasner house next door. It's quiet today. She saw a police car pull up out front earlier, but the place isn't crawling with cops the way it was yesterday. She wonders whether they've found any clue as to what happened to Rebecca. The whole thing is so unsettling.

"No treasure, Mommy."

"Hmm?" She looks up to see Ozzie tossing his shovel aside, apparently dejected that he hasn't come across pirate gold the way Barney did in that video he loves so much.

"No treasure," he repeats. "Let's go." He toddles off toward the house, having lost interest in the dirt, at least for the time being.

Grateful for the diversion, Michelle follows him.

* * *

Molly closes the front door behind Detective Mullen and turns abruptly to go back upstairs to her room.

"Are you okay?"

Rory is standing there.

"I'm fine." Molly starts up the stairs, thinking, *Please, can't you just leave me alone? Why can't everyone just leave me alone!*

"Are you sure? Because I went through this. I know what it's like, Molly."

She pauses on the stairs, asks, "You went through *what*? What did you go through, Rory?"

"I was questioned by the cops after Carleen disappeared. And again after Emily did. I know what it's like, Molly—"

"You do not."

"Yes, I do. You sit there with some cop staring at you and asking you all kinds of nosy questions, and I know how it is— how you try to think of something—anything, any little thing— to tell him so you can feel like at least you're doing your best to help, when you know the whole time that there's nothing—you don't know anything, and you can't tell him anything meaningful; you can't do a damn thing. You're completely helpless. And you just want them to leave you alone."

Yes.

That's exactly how it is.

Molly closes her eyes, standing there, her hand on the railing.

Rory's right. She *has* been there. She *does* know.

But she doesn't want to give this to Rory.

Why should she let Rory know that she's reached her, that she's nailed it right on the head?

Rory obviously needs to feel like an understanding big sister; she needs to make up for all the hurt she caused when she left Lake Charlotte and didn't look back, for all the pain she caused Molly just the other night when she told her that shocking, devastating secret Molly would have rather not known, should never have known.

Molly's not going to forgive her for that. She's not going to let her sister ease her guilty conscience. She doesn't owe Rory that. She doesn't owe Rory anything.

"Oh," she says, as though she's surprised, "is that what it was like for you, Rory? That's too bad. It wasn't like that for me at all. I just told the detective what I know. And that's *nothing*. I know *nothing*. Why should I feel the least bit guilty and helpless over that?"

"You shouldn't," Rory says quickly. "I didn't mean it like—"

"I'm going back to bed," Molly says, continuing up the stairs, going into her room, slamming the door shut behind her to discourage any notion Rory might get of coming after her to pelt her with more nuggets of big sisterly understanding.

She sits on the edge of her rumpled unmade bed, trembling, struggling not to cry. God, she's so weary of all the crying. She managed to hold her tears back the whole time the detective sat across from her at the kitchen table, scribbling notes on his pad and watching her so closely, as though he expected her to reveal some tidbit of a clue.

Now she lets out a shaky breath and glances at her desk, at the framed photograph sitting beside the stacks of books she'd cleaned out of her locker, and notebooks from the school year, and other clutter she really should put away. The rest of it. Not the photo.

Rebecca gave her the photo for Christmas. It shows the two of them, arms around each other, laughing about something. Rebecca is wearing her old Leonardo DiCaprio T-shirt leftover from her *Titanic* phase, and Molly is in one of Kevin's huge flannel shirts with the sleeves rolled up, and they both look casual, and comfortable, and happy just to be together.

Rebecca's gone.

Until now, she has managed to hold her grief at bay, but it hits her all at once and she finds herself shaking, sobbing, nauseated.

I need help with this, she thinks plaintively, the ache in her heart so intense that it scares her. *I can't handle this alone. It's just too huge and horrible.*

But there's no one.

No one to help her.

No one to turn to.

Nothing to do but pull herself together and go on.

Downstairs, she hears the phone ring once . . . twice . . .

Rory must have answered it.

Maybe it's Kevin, Molly thinks hopefully. *Maybe he's calling to check in on me. After all, he's been gone a whole week already. You'd think he'd want to know how things are back home. You'd think he'd at least want to call and say hi. He promised he would.*

She wonders if he's going to end up doing what Rory did. Just turning his back on the family, on her, while he goes off to see the world. After all, he's just about the same age Rory was when she left. It would be so easy for him to just get rid of the responsibility he's had weighing him down for so long. She can almost understand how he might—

There are footsteps on the stairs, then a knock on Molly's door. "It's for you, Molly."

Rory would have said immediately if it was Kevin.

"I don't want to talk to anyone." She pauses. Then, thinking of Ryan, asks Rory, "Who is it?"

"A friend of yours . . . Amanda Falk?" Rory replies in a *do you know her?* tone. "Should I tell her you—"

"I'll take it," Molly says, quickly wiping her tears and stepping out into the hall. She brushes past Rory, hurrying down to the kitchen, wondering why Amanda is suddenly calling her.

She's Jessica's friend, after all, and even though she was all friendly at that party the other night, Molly knows better than to think she wants to be pals. Girls like Amanda and Jessica—girls who live in Green Haven Glen and wear designer clothes and are effortlessly pretty—don't seek out girls like Molly. No, obviously Amanda and Jessica were temporarily on the outs, and Amanda wanted to see Ryan cheat on Jessica with anyone, anyone at all, even a nobody like Molly Connolly.

Still, in response to Molly's cautious "Hello?" Amanda sounds breezy and enthusiastic, asking, "What's up, Molly? How's everything going?"

"Okay, I guess."

"I heard about your friend. God, are you all right?"

"I'm okay," Molly repeats, touched that Amanda would call to check on her. "I mean, it's so awful, but I'm hanging in there."

"What's going on? Do they know what happened to her?"

"No. The police came to talk to me a little while ago and—"

"They did?" She hears Amanda say to someone in the background, "You guys, the police actually questioned her!" Then, to

Molly, "That's just Dana and Lisa. They're over here. We were all just kind of wondering what was up, you know, 'cause it's so scary. The whole thing with Rebecca, I mean."

"I know."

"Listen, we were just thinking about going out on Lisa's boat this afternoon. Are you into it?"

Molly hesitates.

"Molly, you shouldn't just sit around and stress about Rebecca," Amanda says. "I mean, you've got to go on living, you know?"

That's pretty much what Molly just told herself up in her room. Still . . .

"I don't know," she says. "I've never gone out on a boat before."

"Oh, it's really fun. Lisa's brother will take us out. Will. Do you know him?"

"No."

"He's in college. He and his friends go out on the water almost every afternoon, and they usually don't mind if we tag along. It'll be really fun. It'll cheer you up. Maybe I'll call Ryan and see if he wants to go, too."

"Ryan?" Molly's spirits lift. She hasn't talked to him since she left his house Saturday night—not that she's spent much time dwelling on that. Still, now that Amanda's brought him up, she can't help wondering why she hasn't heard from him. He must know about Rebecca. He must know she's Rebecca's friend.

It's because you let him go too far and now he thinks you're a slut, Molly tells herself guiltily. *You shouldn't have done that.*

Yeah, but it wasn't as if they'd gone *that* far. They were just making out. True, she'd let him unfasten her bra and touch her, but only above the waist, and . . .

"Molly?" Amanda prods. "You there?"

"Yeah, I'm here. Okay, I'll come," she decides.

"Great."

"Are you going to call Ryan?"

"Sure, I'll call him right now," Amanda promises, and Molly feels a pinprick of happiness for the first time in what seems like ages.

She hears Rory's footsteps heading back down the stairs and

wonders briefly if she should tell her about the boating trip. Then she thinks better of it. She doesn't owe Rory any explanations about where she goes or what she does.

No. Like you said, you don't owe Rory a damned thing.

He's late for work this morning. Overslept, and no wonder. He spent all of last night tossing and turning, tormented by nightmares about Carleen.

Carleen, tossing that silky hair of hers and taunting him.

Carleen's tear-streaked face, accusing eyes.

Carleen pounding him with her fists, screaming, "How could you *do* this to me?"

Now he flips pages of his newspaper as he sits restlessly on the T, taking the Red Line as he does every weekday toward Cambridge. He has a car, and tried driving to campus the first few weeks he was living in the city, but soon discovered that it's just not worth it. Boston traffic is notoriously congested, and it's much more pleasant to take the T, where he can relax and catch up on the morning news.

Today he tries to focus on the paper, tries to think about something other than Carleen.

Kelly will be back later this afternoon from her weekend with her family in Washington. She'd flown home to look for wedding gowns and meet with the caterers her mother had hired to do the reception. She'd asked him to come, too, but he made some excuse about having too much work to catch up on.

In truth, he's been thinking for a while now that she's going a bit overboard on the wedding plans, but he hasn't thought of a way to say it without crushing her.

She'd called last night to say she'd hired a band instead of the pianist they'd agreed would provide simple, quiet background music at the reception. "They played at my sister's wedding, and they were just so wonderful," she'd told him. "I knew you wouldn't mind."

And her parents had talked her into a sit-down dinner instead of a buffet. "I know we said buffet, but they're paying for it and I didn't think it would matter so much to you."

She'd found her gown, and had to go back down for a fitting over the Fourth of July weekend.

"You understand, don't you?" she'd said, though they had plans to stroll around the Harborfest here the way they had last year, after hearing the annual reading of the Declaration of Independence over at the State House.

"Sure, honey," he'd said, quelling his misgivings. "I understand."

And he does. She's younger than he is; this is her first marriage; she can't help but want a big wedding with all the trimmings, no matter what she said when he finally proposed to her last year.

Oh, Kelly. You would have said yes to anything, just to get me to marry you, he thinks sadly. *You knew I had so many misgivings. You were too young, and you were my student, and I was trying to be so careful after everything that happened with Carleen—*

But then, Kelly doesn't know about that.

Nobody in his new life knows about that. For the most part, he has managed to virtually erase his past, as though he has simply always been this sophisticated, urbane Harvard professor, a fine, upstanding citizen.

The train pulls into a station. He glances up to see which one, having lost track of where he is. Charles. A few more stops to go.

He flips the page of his paper and scans the national news page distractedly.

More brush fires in California.

A recess in that racism trial in Texas.

Something catches his eye.

His heart skips a beat.

Two words jump out at him from the caption beneath a photo of a nondescript teenaged girl.

Lake Charlotte.

For a moment, he simply can't breathe.

He stares at the photo, belatedly recognizing the girl, and then at the caption, reading and rereading it.

Rebecca Wasner, 13, mysteriously vanished from her Lake Charlotte, NY, home this weekend.

Rebecca Wasner.

Molly's friend.

Trembling, he shifts his gaze to the article. He skims it until he gets to the paragraph about the uncanny coincidence that the girl turned up missing on the tenth anniversary of the first Lake Charlotte disappearance. It goes on to list the girls who had vanished that summer.

His gaze lingers on Carleen's name.

He forces himself to move past it, to keep reading, straight through to the end, where the author mentions that the strange disappearances of a decade ago were never solved, and police are working overtime to determine whether this new case can possibly be related. There's an eight hundred phone number listed for people to call if they have any relevant information about Rebecca Wasner, or any of the four girls who disappeared ten years ago.

"Maybe somebody out there knows something about one of them, something that they've been keeping a secret for all these years," a Lake Charlotte police detective is quoted as saying. "Something that seemed insignificant at the time, but might ultimately lead us to a suspect. We're not saying that whoever took those four girls is responsible for taking Rebecca, but we're not ruling it out, either."

The train pulls into a station. He glances absently out the window at the sign on the platform, then jumps up, realizing it's his destination. Harvard. He scurries through the doors just as they're starting to close, getting out in the nick of time.

Lost in thought, he begins walking slowly toward the steps as the train pulls past him, leaving the station.

Rory tilts the plastic pitcher to pour herself a glass of iced tea and spills most of it all over the counter.

"Damn," she says under her breath.

"Rory, please." Sister Theodosia looks up from her Bible.

"I'm sorry, Sister."

The nun gives a slight nod, tight-lipped, and goes back to her reading, the cup of tea she made earlier sitting untouched in front of her on the table.

Why don't you just go home? Rory asks her silently as she grabs a sponge and mops up the mess on the counter. *You're not doing anyone any good here. Mom is nuttier than ever.*

Earlier, her mother had babbled something about Rory running along outside to play hide-and-seek. "Carleen and Emily are already out there, hiding," she said. "I saw them."

Sister Theodosia hadn't seemed the least bit bothered by Maura's comment, nor had she allowed Rory to catch her eye.

With a sigh, Rory had said, "Okay, Mom, I'll go out later."

Rather than make repeated, futile attempts to bring her mother back to reality, Rory figures she might as well placate her, at least for now.

Meanwhile, there's Molly to worry about. She took off without telling Rory where she was going or when she'd be back.

Now Rory picks up her glass of iced tea and glances at Sister Theodosia sitting at the table, her lips moving as she pores over her Bible. With a sigh, Rory carries her drink into the living room and sits in her father's old chair, wishing, not for the first time, that he were here with her.

We need you, Daddy. We all need you so much. If you were still out there someplace. If only you could come back to rescue us.

She stares dismally out the window at the street, noting the police car still parked in front of the Wasners'. That poor family.

Poor Molly.

For a fleeting moment, when she told Molly she understood how she must be feeling, she thought she might have reached her. But no, Molly's stone wall was intact. She made it more than clear that she wants to be left alone, that she isn't going to let Rory comfort her.

Maybe that's just as well.

Rory sips her iced tea, her thoughts flitting back to what Barrett Maitland told her about Emily having a brother.

It's just so hard to believe that Emily kept such a deep, dark secret from Rory for so long, never letting on.

Then again, Rory, too, had kept a family secret. She had never told Emily the truth about Molly's birth—had never even considered it.

But I had to keep the secret. I didn't have a choice. I promised Daddy and Mom.

Maybe that's why Emily kept her secret. Maybe her father made her swear never to reveal it. Maybe having a mentally challenged child was as shameful to him as having a pregnant teenaged daughter was to Maura Connolly.

Rory wonders again about Emily's brother. Barrett said he's still living in that home down in Poughkeepsie.

St. Malachy's, wasn't it?

For some reason, that's been in the back of her mind ever since he told her.

That Emily's brother is there.

That, if she wanted to, she could actually go there. To Poughkeepsie. To see him.

But why would you want to?

Maybe because, she realizes, *if he really does exist, he's the only remaining link to Emily.*

Maybe because Rory desperately needs to put the past to rest so that she can begin to heal.

And maybe, she admits, because there's a chance that David Anghardt might hold some clue to what happened that summer. *After all, he must have been the mystery visitor Emily had mentioned. And if he was here . . .*

Could he have had something to do with the disappearances of those girls?

It isn't something she's even dared to think about until now, much less mention to Barrett Maitland.

For a moment, she considers asking him to come with her.

Then she thinks better of it. She still doesn't trust him.

No, she'll go alone.

She'll go tomorrow.

There's a thump overhead. Then another.

Frowning, Rory looks up at the ceiling. Maura must be up to something.

With a sigh, she puts down her glass of iced tea and goes up to the second floor. Her mother's bedroom door is open.

"Mom?"

No reply.

Another thump from overhead.

Sighing again, she heads up the second flight to the third floor, passing the closed door to her room and the one that had once belonged to Carleen. The last door, leading to the large, unfinished attic storage room, is cracked open.

As she walks toward it, Rory becomes aware of the slightest hint of perfume in the air.

Poison.

Carleen's perfume.

She stands absolutely still, sniffing. Yes, that's definitely what it is.

Can her mother be wearing it?

"Mom?" she calls, pushing the attic room door open and poking her head inside. But here, the air is close and smells only musty. There's no evidence of the perfume that lingered in the hallway.

"Mom? What are you doing?"

Her mother turns away from an old trunk open on the floor, and Rory sees that she's holding an armful of clothes. Old clothes Rory and Carleen used to use as little girls when they played dress-up.

"I need a costume," her mother says. "For the Halloween party at the church hall."

"It isn't Halloween, Mom," Rory tells her flatly.

Ignoring her, Maura turns back to the trunk, pulling out a long black feather boa that had belonged to her great-grandmother.

Rory remembers Carleen wrapping it around her neck and mincing around the dusty attic floor in a pair of Maura's old, too-big high heels, telling Rory, *"I'm the queen, and you're my subject, and you have to do whatever I say."*

"But that's not a good game. I don't want to play anymore."

"Come on, Rory, don't be a baby. Just a little while longer. Here, put this apron on. You can be my lady in waiting."

"What's a lady in waiting?"

"You know . . . like a maid."

"No way! I don't want to be your maid, Carleen."

"Oh, come on, Rory . . . it'll be fun."

She finds herself smiling slightly as those little-girl voices echo in her ears.

You were so bossy, Carleen. Such a typical big sister. What would you be like now? God, I wish you were here with me to laugh about those days.

Her mother is softly humming something.

Rory listens, recognizes the tune.

" 'I'll Be Seeing You.' "

It's an old song, really old, like from the forties. But her father'd had a record collection that contained a bunch of sappy old songs, and she and Carleen had once caught her parents dancing to that particular one in the kitchen, of all places, on a rainy afternoon.

They'd looked all embarrassed when she and Carleen had popped up unexpectedly, but they kept on dancing, with Mom giggling as Daddy twirled her around and around. It's one of the only memories Rory has of her parents laughing together. Happy. In love.

Until then, she'd never really believed that they'd loved each other.

And she'd forgotten all about it, until now, hearing that tune again. The words echo in her mind.

I'll be seeing you . . . in all the old, familiar places . . .

They loved each other. Yes. They really did. He really loved her. It must have killed him to see her drifting away from him, with all of her problems.

"Mom . . . are you all right?" she asks cautiously.

Her mother doesn't reply, humming, rummaging through the trunk.

Rory watches her for a moment. Then, feeling as though she's spying on an intensely private moment, just as she had that long-ago rainy day in the kitchen, she quietly slips away.

And in the hallway, she again becomes aware of the merest whiff of her sister's favorite perfume.

Frowning, Rory walks slowly toward Carleen's door. She opens it, poking her head into the room.

The scent is stronger here.

Her heart pounding, Rory closes the door and hurries down the stairs.

"There's no such thing as ghosts," she tells herself once she's back in the living room.

"What did you say, Rory?"

She looks up to see Sister Theodosia standing in the doorway.

None of your business what I said.

"Nothing," Rory tells her.

"Where's your mother? I'd like to do the rosary with her now."

"Mom is busy. I think she needs to be alone."

"It's time to do the rosary." The nun turns toward the stairs.

"Leave her alone right now, Sister," Rory says sharply.

Sister Theodosia turns back, her black eyes narrowing at Rory. "I don't appreciate that tone, Rory."

"Sister, maybe it would be better if you left. I think Mom and Molly and I need some time alone together. I mean, I do appreciate your coming here and everything, but maybe you should go."

"I plan to," the nun says, and adds, "in a day or two."

With that, she walks away.

A day or two.

Great.

Rolling her eyes, Rory picks up her iced tea again and sinks into her father's chair.

"John?"

"Shelly! How's it going?"

Her cousin's warm greeting takes Michelle by surprise. For some reason, she'd been expecting him to be as glum as her world suddenly seems. But John is his usual sunny self, thank God.

She contemplates mentioning the trip to the hospital yesterday, and decides against it. "I'm fine," she tells him instead. "How are you? How's Nancy and the kids?"

"Everyone's doing well. I heard about what happened over there, though. That's really a terrible shame."

He's talking about Rebecca's disappearance, she realizes. Not only is the news all over the local papers, but it seems to be causing a widespread stir. Lou called home at lunchtime to tell Michelle that the wire services had picked up the story and there was even a blurb about it in *USA Today.*

"But why?" Michelle had asked, bewildered.

"Because it's the anniversary of the disappearance of all those other girls, Michelle," Lou had said with exaggerated patience, as though a hormonal basket case like her wasn't capable of figuring out the connection. "That's either a morbid coincidence, or it means Rebecca's disappearance is linked to those cases."

"It *is* a shame," she echoes her cousin John's comment, propping the cordless phone between her ear and shoulder and walking absently to the living-room window. She parts the sheer curtains and peers out into the street. In addition to the squad car that's become a fixture at the curb in front of the Wasners' house, there are a few other unfamiliar vehicles now. Michelle suspects that they belong to the press.

"Listen, Shelly, it's funny that you called, because I was about to get in touch with you just now anyway. I was wondering if I could come over tonight to talk about that addition."

"I didn't think you could make it until later in the week."

"Actually, I forgot all about a conference I'm going to in New York. I'm leaving early Thursday morning, so—"

"Then our thing can wait, John. It's really no rush."

"No, it's not a problem. I just found out Nancy invited her mother over for supper. So I figured I'd work late tonight after all."

Michelle smiles, having met her cousin's mother-in-law a few times before. The woman made Iris look like an absolute dear.

"Okay, John, come on over," she says, grateful for the distraction. "I'll call Lou and tell him, to make sure he'll be here."

"Sounds good. What was that clicking sound? Did you hear it?"

"Just the baby monitor," she tells him. "Ozzie's upstairs napping and I've got it turned on. It messes with the cordless phone. Anyway, why don't you stay for supper? I made a meatloaf and I just finished mashing the potatoes."

"Meatloaf and mashed potatoes? Why all the fuss? Shouldn't you be sitting around with your feet up reading baby-name books right about now, Shelly?"

"I guess so. But for some reason I woke up in the mood to make like Martha Stewart."

"Uh-oh," John says with a chuckle. "When did you say you were due?"

"August. Why?"

"I was going to say you might be going into labor. The day she had Ashley, Nancy woke up and decided to bake a dozen fruitcakes. The night before she had Jason, she wallpapered the hall closet."

"Why?"

"God knows. She just went into this nesting frenzy. The doctor said it happens. Mother Nature's way of preparing you for motherhood—you know, feathering the nest and all that. Are you sure about that August due date?"

Michelle laughs. "Positive. I'll see you tonight, John," she says, and hangs up.

She returns to the kitchen and eyes the batch of chocolate chip cookie dough she was just whipping up.

She thinks about those contractions yesterday, then about John's comment, and laughs softly, shaking her head.

There's no way she's going into labor anytime soon. Dr. Kabir said her cervix hadn't started to dialate.

Still . . .

Nope.

No way.

She sticks her finger into the cookie dough, picks out a chocolate chip, and thoughtfully pops it into her mouth.

"So, like, you saw her the day before she disappeared?" Dana asks Molly, running a hand through her long, wavy, light-brown hair that's blowing back from her face as the boat picks up speed.

Molly nods, feeling weary, wondering how many times they're going to go over this. Ever since they got on the boat, Dana and Amanda and Lisa have been probing her about Rebecca, wanting to know every detail about her.

At first, Molly couldn't help liking the attention a little, especially when Lisa's brother Will and his friend Danny talked to her about it. They were both pretty cute, and it was fun to have them all interested in every word she had to say, although of course they're much too old for her. They're, like, Kevin's age. They're drinking beer. They offered it to the girls, and Molly took one, not wanting to be the only one not to. Will grinned, winking at her as he popped the cap off the cold green bottle and handed it to her, and she found herself wondering what the wink meant.

Does he like her? Wouldn't that be something?

No. He's too old.

Besides, she's not interested in anyone except Ryan, and, to her disappointment, she found when she met the others at the dock that he wasn't going boating with them.

"I couldn't get a hold of him," Amanda had said so casually

that Molly wondered if she'd even tried. Had she merely dropped Ryan's name to get Molly here?

Her sudden interest in being pals was no doubt due to Molly's connection to Rebecca. And she's beginning to find herself irritated that these girls who never paid any attention to Rebecca before are now so riveted by every detail about her life. It just seems so . . . sick.

I shouldn't be here, Molly thinks, looking back at the distant shore that marks the Curl jutting out into Lake Charlotte.

"Wow, I can't believe it, Molly," Lisa says. "First your own sister disappears. Now your best friend. It's just so creepy."

Startled, Molly can't think of anything to say. Nobody has ever brought up the subject of Carleen to her. At least, none of the kids from school have ever done it. It just happened so long ago, nobody her age seems to spend any time dwelling on it. They're too young to remember that summer.

But now, with Rebecca missing, and the newspapers making a big deal about the anniversary of the other girls' disappearances, the whole thing has apparently become relevant to everyone in Lake Charlotte. Molly feels sick to her stomach, and not just from the constant bump-bump-bump of the boat chopping over the water.

"I bet it's some psycho killer on the loose again," Amanda says. "I bet he killed those girls ten years ago, and he's going to start doing it again."

"None of us are safe," Lisa agrees solemnly. "Especially you, Molly. I mean, Rebecca was your friend. And your own sister was another one of the victims. And, God, you live right next door to the house where another victim lived. That girl Emily."

"Emma," Dana corrects her. "Yeah, Molly, I heard you even babysit over there. Is it scary?"

Molly thinks of the Randalls' house.

Of the footsteps she thought she heard yesterday.

"Not that scary," she lies to Lisa.

But she already knows that she'll absolutely, positively never be alone there again. Lisa's right.

No one is safe.

A shudder runs down her spine.

Especially not Molly.

CHAPTER
TWELVE

St. Malachy's Home turns out to be a sprawling stone mansion located on a steep bluff rising high above the Hudson River.

Rory guides Kevin's little red car through the open gates and up the winding drive to the home, noticing that the place has an air of neglect about it. The too-tall lawn is dotted with dandelions and the shrubs are overgrown, and the white paint on the sign at the front entrance is peeling.

How depressing, she thinks, looking up at the gloomy three-story building before walking up the wide, cracked concrete steps to the door. *Poor David Anghardt, locked away here for all these years, without even his own father coming to visit him.*

Then again, that was just Barrett Maitland's take on the situation. For all Rory knows, he's completely wrong. Or he could be making the whole thing up for some reason. Emily might never have had a twin brother.

Still, she'd been vaguely surprised when she called Information last night and discovered there really was a St. Malachy's in Poughkeepsie.

But that doesn't mean David Anghardt also exists.

You should have called here and asked about him before you drove all this way, she tells herself belatedly. *What if you made the trip for nothing?*

Who cares? At least it's a day away from Mom, and Molly, and Sister Theodosia, and Lake Charlotte. In fact, that's precisely why she didn't bother to call and check. She desperately needs an escape, if only for a few hours.

When she left, she didn't bother to tell any of them where she was going. She doubts Mom and Sister Theodosia will even miss her. And if Molly does, well, it'll be a taste of her own medicine. Let her see how it feels to wonder where someone is.

Molly didn't get home until well after midnight last night.

Rory, lying awake in her third-floor bedroom, heard her come in, not even trying to be quiet. It's as though she no longer cares what anyone thinks.

Just the way Carleen eventually acted.

Rory sighs and opens the door, stepping into what must once have been a grand foyer when this was a private home, as it must have been.

Now is a shabby reception area, with a tall counter tucked against the wall beside a sweeping, curved staircase. There's a middle-aged blond woman seated behind it, reading a hardcover Nora Roberts novel in a library's shiny plastic sleeve. She looks up at Rory, as though annoyed she has to interrupt her reading.

"Yes? Can I help you?"

"Yes. I'm here to visit a patient . . . David Anghardt?"

The woman's overly tweezed eyebrows disappear beneath her curled bangs. "David Anghardt?"

Rory nods, clenching her purse strap, not wanting to betray her overwhelming sense of anticipation.

"Are you a relative?" the woman asks at last, sounding incredulous.

So he does exist. And he is here.

"No," Rory tells the receptionist, "I'm just a friend."

"Your name?"

"Rory Connolly. But he won't know it," she adds quickly.

The woman's mouth purses. "Obviously not."

And Rory realizes from her expression that David Anghardt must be so severely handicapped that he can't be expected to recognize a name. Can he even speak? Should Rory have bothered to come at all?

The poor boy—*man*, Rory corrects herself. He'll be an adult now, her own age. And he's been locked away here for years, with no visitors. Even if he can't help her, maybe her visit will help *him*, somehow. It's the least she can do for Emily's brother.

"All right . . . please wait here for a moment." The receptionist sticks a straw wrapper into the page of her book and tosses it onto the counter, then strides away, disappearing behind a closed door.

Rory waits, looking around at the two uncomfortable-looking vinyl chairs separated by a low table covered in dated, dull-looking magazines—*Popular Science, Reader's Digest.* The walls are paneled in a rich, dark, ornately carved wainscot that must once have been highly polished. Now it's dull and dotted with ugly prints—birds, cats—in cheap metal frames. There's a large floor-to-ceiling window on one wall, the bottom half obscured by an oversized window air conditioner that must not be working very well, because the room feels close and warm.

Rory paces anxiously over and looks out the top half to see a wide lawn sweeping toward the bluff above the river. A chain-link fence runs along the back of the property. There are a few people out by a picnic table beneath a grove of tree-sized lilacs—some of them in wheelchairs, one in a white nurse's uniform.

"May I help you? I'm Lydia McGovern, the director of St. Malachy's."

She turns to see an older woman stepping into the room, the receptionist on her heels. She's as tall and angular as Sister Theodosia, her gray cardigan and black slacks baggy on her bony frame. But her face is softer than Sister Theodosia's, and her eyes, behind a pair of glasses perched low on her nose, are somehow both kind and wary as they focus on Rory.

"I'd like to see David Anghardt," Rory tells the woman, a fact she's certain she already knows.

The receptionist slips back behind her counter, but doesn't pick up her book again. She, too, is watching Rory with unveiled curiosity.

"You're a friend of the family?"

"I was. A long time ago. I was a friend of his sister."

"Emily." There's a flicker of sadness in the woman's eyes.

"You knew her?"

"No. I've only been here a few years. But Sister Margaret, the former director, told me what happened."

"She isn't here anymore?"

"No. Nobody's here, actually, from ten years ago. Almost everyone was laid off end the whole place nearly shut down at one point. David Anghardt was one of the few residents who stayed, probably because there was no place else to send him. Anyway, then we got our federal grant money, and Sister Margaret was able to bring me on board as her assistant director, and the two of us hired a new staff—"

"Where is Sister Margaret now?" Rory asks, impatient with the woman's painstaking history of the home and its financial woes.

"Oh, the poor dear had been suffering from glaucoma for years. She finally went completely blind. She's living at a retirement home in Kingston, but we still keep in touch."

"So she knew David's family?"

"Absolutely. She said that David adored his sister. And she felt the same about him. Such a terrible tragedy. Sister Margaret said that David was never the same since she vanished," Lydia says, shaking her head.

"No wonder," the receptionist puts in. "His own father—"

"Susan, please," Lydia McGovern says in a warning tone.

The receptionist picks up her book again.

The director turns back to Rory. "So you were Emily's friend? That would mean you must be from . . . ?"

"Lake Charlotte," Rory supplies. "It's north of Albany. Emily and her father lived next door to my family before she disappeared."

"You wouldn't, by any chance, have kept in touch with Mr. Anghardt?"

Rory senses that the woman is attempting to make the question casual. and keeps her reply on the same level. "No, I haven't," she says. "The last I knew, he moved away. Actually, I never saw him again after Emily disappeared."

"Neither did David," Lydia McGovern says. "In fact, Sister Margaret mentioned that she believed the father might very well have died soon after his daughter went missing. The loss must have devastated him. He lost his wife, you know, when she gave birth to the twins. She was from a wealthy family down South, and David's care is paid for by her trust fund."

"So that's how he's able to stay here. I thought maybe his father was sending money to pay for that."

"No. As I said, we've never heard from him again. That's why, when Susan said there was an old friend here to see David, I thought perhaps you would know."

"No," Rory says, "I wish I did."

She almost tells the woman that until a few days ago, she didn't even know David existed, but she thinks better of it. She wants to see him, and if she reveals that she's a total stranger to him, the director might not let her.

"Can I see him?" she asks, hoping she doesn't sound too eager.

Lydia McGovern eyes her cautiously again. Then, with a nod, she says, "I suppose so. It'll be nice for him to have a visitor. Nobody comes to see him except that nun."

Rory's stomach flips over. "Nun?" she echoes, frowning. "Which nun?"

"Sister Mary Frances. She's from a parish upstate, somewhere near Albany, I believe. She's been coming for years to visit all the patients here—"

"Oh."

Why did Rory speculate, for a moment, that it was Sister Theodosia coming to see David?

There are hundreds of thousands of nuns in the world, she reminds herself. *And the vast majority are wonderful people. The kind of people who, out of the goodness of their hearts, visit strangers in depressing places like this.*

She shoves aside a prickle of guilt for having come here for selfish reasons.

Even now that I know he won't shed any light on what happened, I'll spend more time with Emily's brother, and with the other patients, too, she promises herself.

"Anyway," the director goes on, "Sister Mary Frances seems to have taken a special liking to David, and he clearly feels the same way about her. He lights up whenever she's here. I wish she could get here more often, since it makes him so happy. But there are times when months go by without a sign of her."

"She just visited this past week," Susan pipes up, clearly not as absorbed in her book as she appeared to be.

"Oh? I didn't realize. It must have been on my day off. Well, that's good," Lydia says. "David needs a lift every now and then. Seeing you will be good for him, too," she tells Rory. "Come with me, I'll take you up to his room."

* * *

Molly wakes up, glances at the clock, and sees that it's past noon. She groans and rolls over onto her back, staring at the ceiling, thinking about last night. After docking the boat, she and Amanda and the others had gone to a party out at the Curl.

She slowly becomes aware that her head is pounding and her mouth feels strangely dry.

It must be a hangover, she realizes. *So this is what it feels like.*

Why had she drunk those beers? In part, because people kept handing them to her. She was treated like a celebrity by kids who never would have given her a second glance a week ago. And not just Amanda and her friends. The older kids who were there were all interested in her.

Well, not in me, she admits to herself.

They wanted to know all about Rebecca. About whether anyone was stalking her, and whether Molly had heard any screams the night she disappeared.

Disturbing questions, all of them.

God, why didn't you just leave? she asks herself guiltily. *Why did you humor those people? They could care less about Rebecca.*

Or about me.

But at the time, she couldn't seem to keep herself from talking to everyone. She'd even said that sure, Rebecca *could* have had a stalker without her knowing.

After all, anything was possible

And everyone seemed to pay more attention to her when she said things like that, instead of just, constantly, "I don't know."

Okay, she might have humored them with their nosy questions, but at least she hadn't said anything she'd regret, and she certainly hadn't *done* anything she'd regret, like Saturday night with Ryan . . . *had* she?

Her memories, especially of the end of the night, are a bit fuzzy.

But she's positive Ryan wasn't even there. *That,* she wouldn't forget.

Some of the other guys—older, high school guys—were flirting with her, but she hadn't been interested in any of them. All the questions about Rebecca upset her, reminding her that her best friend was missing, might even be—

God. The *last* thing she wanted to do was hook up with some guy she barely knew.

She just kept drinking beer, hoping to numb the pain, and looking around for Ryan, wishing he'd show up, disappointed when he didn't.

Disappointed enough about him, and upset enough about Rebecca, to drink more than she should have, and say things that she shouldn't have.

Okay, stop beating yourself up. It's over.

She forces herself to get up, feeling slightly dizzy, and, for a moment, like she's going to throw up. Then she slowly gets out of bed, and realizes that she has to get something to drink. Like, *now.*

Without bothering to get dressed, wash up, or brush her teeth, Molly makes her way downstairs, clinging tightly to the railing as she goes.

The house has a deserted feel to it. Where is everyone?

Who cares?

At least there's no one here to bug you.

In the kitchen, she pours a huge glass of iced tea and stands at the counter, drinking it down. She's never been so thirsty in her life.

She's pouring a second glass when the phone rings.

Maybe it's Ryan.

Or even Kevin.

She snatches it up and is bitterly disappointed when a male voice says, "Hello, is Rory there, please?"

"Nope," Molly says, without bothering to check. She's pretty sure no one's home, and, anyway, even if Rory is around someplace upstairs, Molly's not about to traipse all the way up there looking for her.

"Do you know when she'll be back?"

"Nope." *God, my head is pounding*, she thinks, wincing and rubbing her temples. *Does he have to talk so loud?*

"Can you please leave her a message?"

"I guess so," Molly says, in a tone that's meant to convey that she'd really rather not, so he'll say he'll just call back later instead.

No such luck.

"Thanks," he says. "My name is—"

"Hang on a minute while I get a pen," she says, opening a drawer and digging for a paper and pen, annoyed. "All right, go ahead."

"This is Barrett Maitland."

"Uh-huh." The name is totally unfamiliar, but she's sure she knows who it is. The guy Rory was talking to the morning Rebecca disappeared. The one who showed up here as Molly was leaving for the Randalls'. The one with the voice that seemed so familiar.

In fact, it still does.

"Do I know you?" she asks.

"We met briefly the other day on your front steps—"

"No, I mean from before. From, like, a long time ago."

There's a moment of silence. "No, I don't think so."

"Are you from Lake Charlotte?"

"No."

"Oh. Then I guess I don't know you. I just thought your voice sounded kind of familiar. Okay, go ahead . . . what's the message?"

"Just tell Rory I had to go out of town for a few days. I can't leave a number where I can be reached, but I'll call her when I get back."

"Fine," Molly says, jotting *left town, will be back* in messy handwriting Rory probably won't be able to read. Oh, well, too bad. *I'm not her freaking secretary*, Molly thinks grumpily, carelessly shoving the note under a magnet on the refrigerator door.

"Okay, thanks a lot. 'Bye," Barrett Maitland is saying, apparently in a hurry to hang up all of a sudden, which is fine with her.

Molly disconnects the call, and then, still holding the receiver, impulsively starts dialing Ryan's number.

"No!" she says aloud, hanging up.

She stands there, drinking more iced tea, considering it for a few seconds. Why not call him? She can mention casually that she was boating with Amanda, and out at the party at the Curl last night. Let him know that she's been hanging around with the in crowd, in case he hasn't called her because he thinks she's too much of a goober to hang out with.

Again, she feels a stab of guilt, thinking of Rebecca.

She tries to quell it. *Now that Rebecca's gone, I have to do something to take my mind off of it,* she justifies. *Besides, without Rebecca, it's like I have no friends.*

Christine, who used to eat lunch every day with her and Rebecca, is at camp for the summer, and Annie, another friend of theirs, is visiting her grandmother in Florida until after the Fourth of July.

No, there's no one else.

If Kevin were here, Molly thinks, *he'd hang around with me. He'd try to make me feel better about what's going on with Rebecca.*

Which is basically what Rory has been trying to do, she has to admit, to be fair. But she doesn't want Rory's help.

She dials Ryan's number again, and this time, she doesn't hang up.

"Hello?"

It's a girl's voice. Young. Bubbly-sounding. Ryan doesn't have a sister. She must have dialed the wrong number.

"Hello?" the voice says again, then giggles. "Baker residence."

So it is the right number. But who . . . ?

"Hey, come on, give me that, Jess," she hears Ryan say in the background, laughing. Then his voice comes on the line. "Hello?"

Molly hangs up.

So Jessica is over there with him.

She should have figured.

Amanda must have known. She probably hadn't even bothered to call Ryan about boating yesterday. She'd just used that as a ploy, as Molly had suspected.

Feeling desolate, she slowly walks out of the kitchen—then breaks into a run, dashing up the stairs and barely making it into the bathroom in time to throw up.

I've never been so miserable in my entire life, she thinks as dry heaves wrack her body. *And I really don't even care what happens to me. For all I care, the psycho killer can just come and get me.*

She knows, Barrett Maitland thinks, hanging up the old-fashioned black telephone in Mrs. Shilling's upstairs hall. He leans his head back against the cushion of the old-fashioned settee, closing his eyes.

Molly said she thought his voice sounded familiar.

He had never thought of the possibility that she'd remember.

He'd only seen her once. It had been at the playground at Point Cedar Park that day in July. Carleen was standing patiently beside one of those long, winding tunnel slides, trying to coax Molly to come the rest of the way down. Apparently, she had stopped halfway, with a toddler's stubborn, all-consuming interest in some bug she'd spotted there.

So Molly must remember his voice, talking to Carleen.

What had she heard him say?

Does she remember that specific incident? Is she connecting him to it? Or is her memory more vague, more speculative . . .

It has to be. She was so young . . . only three at the time. How could she possibly remember anything clearly enough to—

"Barrett? Are you all right?"

He jerks his head upright to find Mrs. Shilling standing before him, clutching an armload of dirty sheets. She must have been stripping the bed in one of the rooms. He hadn't realized anyone was up here. The last guest had left this morning, leaving him as the bed and breakfast's sole occupant, besides the hostess.

"I'm fine," he says quickly, wondering if she heard him on the phone. "I just made a call— Don't worry, it was local."

"I'm not worried. That phone is blocked from making long-distance calls," she says shrewdly, adding, "Not that I don't trust you, Barrett. But some of my guests . . ." She makes a tsk-tsk sound and shakes her head.

"I can imagine. Listen, Mrs. Shilling, I need to leave for a few days. I'll be back by the end of the week, maybe sooner. I'll pay to keep my room while I'm gone."

"Oh, you don't have to do that," she says, looking surprised. "It doesn't seem fair to charge you for it when you're not here."

"I really don't mind. I can keep my things there, rather than take them all with me."

"If you're sure," she says, looking pleased . . . and a bit curious.

He can see the wheels of her mind turning, wondering how, if he's just a writer, he can afford to be so free with his money.

"My publisher is paying some of my expenses," he says quickly. "So it's really no problem."

"Oh, I see." She still looks curious. "Where are you going?"

"Back to New York," he lies, irritated with her prying question. "I have some things to take care of there."

Does she believe him?

He can't tell.

One thing is certain. The woman is as nosy as they come. He can expect to have her look through whatever he leaves behind in his room while he's gone.

No matter. I'll just be careful not to leave anything that'll tip her off that this isn't the first summer I've spent in Lake Charlotte, he thinks, heading into his room to pack. *That's the last thing I need right now.*

"David? You have a visitor."

The man in the chair by the window appears not to have heard Lydia McGovern's words. He sits motionless, looking out through the glass, as though intent on something other than the leafy branches that obscure any other view.

Rory can only see the back of his head, but his short hair is the exact shade as his sister's, the rich, soft yellow of butter.

She glances at the woman beside her, and she urges Rory to go ahead, approach him.

Still, she hesitates, instead glancing around the room, taking in the stark furnishings—just a twin bed, a dresser that's bolted to the wall, and the one chair. There are no curtains at the window, and the carpet beneath her feet is strictly utilitarian, a dull, tightly woven gray, the kind of carpet you might find in a finished basement.

The room is fairly stark.

Still, on the wall there are a few framed prints, surprisingly of a much higher quality and more appealing style than those in the downstairs reception area. Both are watercolors, in thick, burnished gold frames that are obviously made of wood, not metal. One scene shows a sailboat riding blue waves, with a quaint harbor town in the distance, dotted with white picket fences, shops, and an old-fashioned drawbridge, half raised, across an inlet. The other is of a small boy in a sailor hat and a girl with a long blond braid, shown only from the back, holding hands and barefoot on a sandy beach.

There are some children's picture books on top of the dresser, and some crayons. The bed is covered in a bright patchwork quilt, and there are several stuffed animals tossed near the pillow. And,

Rory realizes, as she looks at them, and then at David Anghardt, that despite his age, he's apparently little more than a child. A lonely, abandoned child, trapped in a man's body.

She takes a step closer to him, calls his name.

No response.

"Stand in front of him, so that he can see you," the director suggests.

Rory moves closer, arrives in front of David Anghardt, looks down at his face. There is nothing of Emily here.

He has the classic features of one who is severely brain-damaged—the smallish, slanted eyes, the heavy, jutting brows, the lolling tongue, the malformed ears. He stares at her, or maybe through her. Rory shifts her weight, uncertain what to do

"Hello, David," she says.

And of course, there's no response. He just looks at her.

She turns to Lydia McGovern. "Can he talk?" she asks, half wishing she hadn't come, half glad she has.

"No, not in the true sense. He does make sounds. Sometimes a word or two can be discerned. But if you're not used to communicating with him, it's very difficult to tell what he's saying."

"Should I stay?"

"Certainly. I'll leave you two alone."

No! Rory wants to protest. *Don't leave me here alone with him. Help me. I don't know what to say, how to act.*

The woman walks briskly out of the room, and Rory is alone with Emily's twin brother, whose very existence was apparently so painful for his family that they didn't tell a soul he existed.

That might not be true, Rory reminds herself. *All you know is that Emily didn't tell you.*

For whatever reason, her friend had kept David a secret.

And maybe, Rory realizes now, that reason had nothing to do with her father being ashamed of him.

Maybe it was Emily who was ashamed. Maybe, being the new girl, she wanted so desperately to fit in that she decided not to mention David.

After all, you never know how people are going to react to something like that.

Rory looks down at the man-child in front of her, pain twisting her heart. "Hello, David," she says again.

Should she tell him that she's from Lake Charlotte? That she knew his sister?

No. He probably won't understand . . . and even if he does, why bring up Emily? He must be wondering what ever happened to her. I don't want to bring up painful memories for him. It's better to just keep things light.

"So, David," she says, crouching in front of him, her hand cupping her chin as though she's the most relaxed person in the world, "what kinds of things do you like to do?"

Great question, Rory. Nice going. What do you think he likes to do?

"Do you like to look out the window at the trees?" she asks, following his gaze. "Do you like to look for birdies?"

For Pete's sake, he isn't a little tiny kid. You don't have to talk to him like that.

Or do I?

She has no idea what to do, how to act.

So she just starts talking. About anything. About nothing, really.

"It sure is a nice day out there, David. It's warm and sunny. I had my car windows down the whole way. I like summertime, don't you? But I like the other seasons, too. Like fall, when the leaves come down. And winter, when there's snow . . . I miss snow," she adds thoughtfully, thinking again that it might be nice to come back to the northeast. At least for a while.

Not to settle down. No, she doesn't want to settle down yet. Maybe not ever.

For some reason, an image of Barrett Maitland flits into her mind.

It was nice, walking with him by the water the other night. They hadn't talked much, or held hands, or anything like that. Still, it had been pleasant. If she trusted him, she might even take the initiative to see him again.

But she doesn't trust him.

It's just instinctive.

So it's best to stay away.

David Anghardt makes a noise. A hissing sound, forced through his big lips, and she looks up to see him staring at her. This time, there's no mistaking that he sees her. His eyes are fastened on her, and he's trying to say something.

"What is it, David?" she asks, trying hard not to show that she's taken aback. "What are you telling me?"

He just makes that hissing noise again, this time more urgent.

Chilled, Rory wonders if she should go find Lydia McGovern. Or maybe she should just leave. After all, she's paid her visit. She's found out that Emily's twin brother really does exist—*and* that there's no way he's going to shed any light on Emily's disappearance.

But what about spending some time with him out of the goodness of your heart? What about visiting some of the other residents?

I will . . . just not today. Molly's at home. I didn't tell her where I was going. She might need me.

"I have to go now, David," she says hurriedly, standing and backing toward the door, waving and trying to sound cheerful. "You take care of yourself, okay? I'll . . . I'll come back and visit you again someday, okay?"

His only reply is that same urgent sound, as though he's trying desperately to communicate something to her.

"Ssss . . . Ssss . . ."

He's turned toward her, those brown eyes—their shade the same unusual amber-flecked color as Emily—following her, burning into her.

She tries to shut it out of her mind as she strides down the hall toward the stairs, eager to leave David Anghardt—and his depressing existence—behind.

Michelle scrubs at the grout between the tiles above the old claw-foot bathtub, knowing it's futile. The mildew stains are never going to come off. The house is old and falling apart, and she and Lou would be better off selling it now and cutting their losses, instead of putting any kind of money into renovations.

Too bad John didn't advise us to do just that last night, she thinks, remembering how much time her cousin had spent here, talking with Lou about the plans he was going to draw up for the new room.

While the two of them walked around the house, taking measurements upstairs and down, and talking about possibilities for other improvements, Michelle had busied herself ironing sheets—

something she has never done before in her life. She was just desperate for something to do, other than talk about the house.

"I'll start working on the plans right away, okay, guys?" John had promised when he left, carrying a plastic bag filled with chocolate chip cookies Michelle had given him to bring Ashley and Jason.

"You don't have to rush," Michelle had told him. "There's plenty of time."

"But Lou said you want to get started on the room as soon as possible, with the baby on the way."

"*Lou* wants to get started on the room. I'm not so certain it's a good idea," she'd said, not bothering to keep her voice down. Who cared if Lou, reading Ozzie his bedtime story in the living room, heard her?

And he obviously had. The moment she'd closed the door and walked back into the living room, Lou had asked what was wrong with her. "I knew you thought this house needed a lot of work, but I didn't realize you thought it was a lost cause," he'd said, setting Ozzie on the floor with his book and focusing his attention on Michelle. "What's changed your mind?"

What was she supposed to say to that?

It's just a bad feeling I'm getting around here lately.

And some weird things that have happened.

Like vanishing food.

And now I'm really starting to think the place is haunted, she thinks, spraying more Tilex onto the stained wall above the tub and scrubbing furiously.

She can just hear Lou echoing her, sarcasm dripping.

Haunted? Yeah, sure, Michelle.

Maybe if she tells him what Ozzie said tonight, as she was taking him out of the bathtub . . .

No.

That won't prove anything to Lou, other than that his pregnant wife has a grossly overactive imagination and it's probably rubbing off on their poor, innocent little boy.

"So what? So he said he's afraid to go to bed because of the lady in his room? I told you not to paint that gigantic mural on his wall. That life-sized Old Mother Hubbard is probably giving him nightmares"

That was exactly what Michelle had thought, when Ozzie had first mentioned the lady in his room—that he was referring to the picture of a bespectacled white-haired woman in an old-fashioned dress, holding a bone for her dog.

The only trouble was, when she'd brought Ozzie into the room after drying him off, and told him to show her the lady, he said he couldn't.

"She not here, Mommy," he said, looking around, his eyes wide with trepidation.

"Are you sure? Look at the wall above your crib . . . is she there?"

He'd glanced at the nursery rhyme characters, shaking his head. "Nope, not there."

"Then where is she, Ozzie?" Michelle had asked.

He couldn't tell her. He only shook his head, whimpering, then started screaming "No!" when she'd put him into his crib, even after she'd promised him she'd stay right upstairs here with him until he fell asleep. Finally, the screaming had stopped, but still, Michelle is keeping busy in the bathroom, her ears strained toward the hallway, in case Ozzie should wake up again and need her.

Meanwhile, Lou isn't yet home, and it's got to be well after nine. Darkness fell a while ago.

Where is he? she wonders, then realizes she might rather not know.

If Lou really is having an affair, or up to some other secretive activity, she can't handle it right now. Not with the baby in breech position, and Ozzie's mysterious lady, and everything else that's been going on lately.

She draws in a sharp breath as a contraction comes out of nowhere, painfully tightening her abdomen and causing her to double over.

It lasts at least thirty seconds, then passes.

Just more Braxton-Hicks, like Dr. Kabir said, she reassures herself. Funny. She just doesn't remember these early contractions starting so early in the pregnancy, or being this strong, with Ozzie.

Oh, well. Every pregnancy is different.

She'd better get used to this false labor.

After all, she still has more than a month to go before the real thing.

* * *

Grayson's Cove, North Carolina, is a small fishing village not far south of Roanoke Island, located on the Pamlico Sound separating the mainland from Cape Hatteras National Seashore.

At the airport, Barrett rented a car and made the long drive from Raleigh, arriving in the early evening, when the sun was still shimmering brightly on the vast stretch of dark-blue, whitecap-tipped water.

He had almost been expecting one of those built-up tourist towns that have sprung up along the Atlantic coast from Maine to Florida, but this is one place that seems to have escaped commercialization. The businesses along the main street are somewhat run down and strictly functional—banks, a grocery, a lunch counter, several Laundromats. No pricey boutiques or fancy cafes here, nor charming inns. Rory would probably be hard-pressed to find an espresso in these parts, he thinks with a smirk.

Barrett quickly finds a room at the only hotel in town—a motel, really; a somewhat dilapidated two-story structure with a long, outside balcony running the length of the place and affording the advertised water view—*if* you stand on one of the peeling metal chairs and crane your neck to see above the golden arches of the fast food restaurant on the next block.

After dumping his small bag on the sagging queen-sized bed and changing into shorts and a lightweight T-shirt, Barrett quickly makes his way back to the main drag, which is fairly deserted for this hour on a pleasant summer evening. Deciding to eat before anything else, Barrett eschews MacDonald's in favor of the luncheonette, which is, luckily, still open, and hopefully the kind of place where a newcomer can strike up a conversation with one of the locals bound to be sitting along the counter.

As soon as he walks in, Barrett sees that he made a good choice.

The few booths along the windows are empty, but the counter is occupied by several likely prospects. He surveys them, wondering who will be the most forthcoming and the least suspicious if he asks a few casual but probing questions.

The white-haired man in the slouchy fisherman's cap chatting the bored-looking counterman's ear off?

The friendly-looking black lady with the magazine propped open in front of her bowl of hominy grits?

The redneck type in the dirty T-shirt and Tarheels cap, munching on a sandwich and staring moodily into space?

The redneck, he decides, walking toward the empty stool beside the man.

The fisherman, though he's obviously the chatty type, has an empty glass of ice and a plate dotted with crumbs in front of him, which means he'll probably be leaving soon, since even Barrett knows that fishermen rise before the sun.

Meanwhile, the lady looks pleasantly absorbed in her magazine, and might not take kindly to being interrupted by questions from a stranger about the locals.

No, the redneck is a better bet. And if he doesn't give anything away, Barrett will try the counterman next, as soon as the fisherman leaves.

He sits and glances at the white specials board, with a couple of inscrutable phrases jotted in marker. He's starved, not having eaten since Mrs. Shilling's scrambled eggs and blackberry muffins early this morning, and a small bag of honey-roasted peanuts on the plane. Even the stale-looking glazed doughnuts under a rounded glass lid down at the end of the counter are making his mouth water.

"What'll you have?" the man stops mopping the counter to ask, interrupting the fisherman's nonstop conversation, which is apparently about someone named Maisie who recently had a gall bladder operation.

What Barrett really wants is a seltzer with a twist of lime, but this is no longer New York. He orders a Coke and asks for a menu. The vinyl cover is smeared with ketchup, and sticky, and the list contains your basic diner fare—BLTs, tuna salad—with the kind of heavy, down-home, full-fat-and-cholesterol cooking you only find in the South. Chicken-fried steak with cream gravy, collard greens simmered with bacon, pecan pie.

He sets the menu aside after glancing it over and noting the incredibly cheap prices, then turns to the redneck and says, "Excuse me, but I'm not from around here. Can you tell me what's good?"

"Everything's good," the man says, sounding mildly surprised, his eyes flitting over Barrett, but not in an overly curious way.

"Sausage gravy. Corn bread. Hush puppies. Fried chicken. You name it."

"I'll try the buttermilk biscuits with sausage gravy," he tells the counterman, who plunks his beverage down on the counter with a wrapped straw.

The redneck orders a cup of coffee and a slice of butterscotch pie with extra whipped cream. He's going to stay put for a little while. Good.

"My name's Barrett," he says.

"First, or last?"

"First," he tells him, offering his hand to the man, knowing the friendly gesture won't seem out of place or arouse the least bit of suspicion. Not here in the South, where the rental car agent offered him a stick of gum and the motel desk clerk called him *hon*.

"Jed," the redneck says, shaking hands. His are grubby.

Barrett does his best not to wince, and fights the urge to wipe his fingers on his napkin.

"Nice little town," he says instead, tilting his head toward the smudged plate-glass window, with its view of Main Street, and, beyond, the harbor dotted with sailboats. "I've never been here before."

"Yeah, it's all right. I just moved here myself, 'bout six months ago."

Barrett's spirits sink. He was hoping to talk to a native; someone who might be able to answer his questions. Still, you never know.

"What brings you to a little town like this?" he asks conversationally.

"Construction job. I'm workin' on repairs to the bridge across the inlet over there," he says, motioning toward the window, as Barrett did. He adds, stumbling a bit over the big words, "It's for one of them historical preservation things. That there's the oldest working drawbridge in the state of North Carolina," he adds proudly, as though he's personally responsible for restoring it.

"Interesting," Barrett comments, sipping his Coke and wondering how to change the subject. He decides just to come right out and ask, waiting until the counterman slaps a steaming, heaping plate of buttermilk biscuits and creamy white sausage gravy in front of him.

"I'm hoping to find a cousin of mine," he says to the redneck, as he picks up his fork and cuts off a small piece of sopping biscuit. He hopes the word *cousin* didn't come out too forced, making it sound like an obvious lie.

"Yeah? You mean, in these parts?"

He nods. "I did some searching over the Internet and found out he was living in this town." At least that part is true.

"Well, like I said, I'm new here. But Grayson's Cove's a tiny place. You don't have to be born and raised here to get to know everyone in town pretty damn fast. Who're you lookin' for?"

"His name's Anghardt. Russell Anghardt. Lived here for years, then moved away for a while, and came back about ten years ago. Ever heard of him?"

CHAPTER
THIRTEEN

"Where were you yesterday?" is Molly's greeting when Rory walks into the kitchen Wednesday morning.

And for just a moment—an inexplicable, precarious moment—Rory considers telling her the truth. For some reason, after a sleepless night and an acute uneasiness over coming face-to-face with Emily's brother, she needs to share the burden.

But not with Molly.

"I went down to Poughkeepsie to see a friend," she hedges, walking to the cupboard and taking out a box of Cap'n Crunch. She adds, truthfully, "And after that, I stopped in Albany to go shopping."

What she doesn't mention is that she'd wandered around the shopping mall for a few hours, trying to lose herself in something she had once found to be one of life's ultimate pleasures. She'd tried on a few outfits in a department-store dressing room, and found herself thinking of Barrett, wondering if she'd see a flicker of appreciation in his eyes if he saw her in the knee-skimming, pale-yellow halter sundress that complements her coloring. She hadn't bought it, had decided she wasn't going to buy anything—not if Barrett Maitland was going to be her subconscious inspiration.

Instead, she'd wandered into the Gap, and Express, and the Limited, and she'd looked at the hip, young clothes, and she'd tried to find something for Molly. Something that would look cute on her, and lift her spirits after everything that's happened. After all, she seemed to dress in mainly cut-off jeans and Kevin's cast off T-shirts.

Maybe, Rory had thought as she poked through a rack of midriff-baring tops, Molly's wardrobe can use a big sister's female influence.

God knew Mom certainly had been useless in that department.

Then again, Rory figured, it wasn't as if she herself is some fashion expert. She favors cut-offs and T-shirts, just as Molly does.

It was Carleen who'd had a real sense of style. She was always fooling around with a new look, wearing a drastic shade of lipstick, or curling and back-combing her straight, shiny hair until it was ratted and big in true eighties style. She used to try to make Rory over, too, but Rory never found it much fun to be teased and sprayed and plastered with goopy makeup, then forced into clothes that were uncomfortable and unflattering.

Besides, a new outfit isn't exactly going to ease the pain of Molly's discovery that she's Carleen's illegitimate daughter, or the gut-wrenching knowledge that her best friend might very well have met with a tragic, violent death.

"Well, you shouldn't just take off like that," Molly grumbles to her.

"Why? Did something happen around here that I should know about?"

"No, but if something had, no one would have known where to find you." Molly's tone is accusatory, but she isn't looking at Rory. She's sitting at the table, apparently reading the back of the cereal box as she munches.

"Okay," Rory says, sitting down across from her. "I'll make a deal with you. Next time, I'll tell you where I'm going and where I can be reached. And you do the same. That way, if we need each other, we can get in touch. That's fair, right?"

Molly shrugs.

"Kevin didn't call yesterday while I was gone, did he?"

"Kevin?" Molly's face lights up. "No, why? Were you expecting him to?"

"I just thought he might have gotten in touch by now. Then again, backpacking across Europe with his girlfriend, it's not like finding a pay phone and making an overseas call is going to be utmost on his mind."

"No, I guess not." Molly's expression is inscrutable.

"I see that Sister Theodosia is still here," Rory comments,

motioning toward the nearby window overlooking the driveway, where the big black car was still parked when she pulled in last night. "She didn't mention anything about leaving?"

"I haven't talked to her. Why'd you bother inviting her here if you're just so anxious for her to leave?"

"I didn't invite her. I—"

"What, she just happened to show up after you said you were going to call and ask her to come?"

"No, I did call her. But as soon as I talked to her and realized she's still the same, I changed my mind about inviting her."

"Why would you want to invite her in the first place?"

"Because . . . I don't know. Like I told you before, I thought she could help Mom."

"How? By praying over her? What did you think she could do? God, Rory, you don't know anything about anything that's gone on around here for years."

Rory is silent, pouring milk into her bowl of cereal. Molly's right. She hasn't been here. She doesn't know. All she has to do, really, is get through the summer, just until Kevin comes back. She doesn't have to make their lives right again.

She *can't* do that, anyway.

It's way more complicated than encouraging Mom to open up to an old friend, or giving Molly a fashion makeover. There are deep-rooted problems here, problems that might never be resolved.

The easiest thing to do is just get through the summer, and leave—go back to living her own life.

But is that the *right* thing to do?

Rory jabs her spoon into the bowl and shovels some cereal into her mouth, her appetite gone.

Michelle hates to use the television as a babysitter for Ozzie again this morning, but it's overcast outside, anyway, and he asked to watch a Berenstain Bears video. Now he's happily settled in the living room watching Brother Bear and Sister Bear work through some Bear Country crisis, while Michelle, doing her best to avoid her own sense of impending crisis, busies herself upstairs, cleaning the spare room that's going to be the baby's nursery.

They won't be needing it for a few months yet—they'll keep

the baby in a bassinet in their room, as they did with Ozzie, until he's sleeping through the night. That way, Michelle can pick him right up and do wee-hour feedings without even having to get out of bed.

Lou has already cleaned all the boxes and clutter out of the future nursery, but the room needs a good scrubbing before they even think about painting or carpet. There are cobwebs everywhere, and the hardwood floor is covered in dust bunnies, and the whole place needs to be aired out.

She opens the windows, then drags her big canister vacuum cleaner in from the hall closet. Ozzie absolutely hates when she uses it, covering his ears and crying about the noise the whole time.

It *is* loud, and maybe it's not such a good idea to use it, with him downstairs alone. She hesitates, holding the hose in one hand and an attachment in the other. If Ozzie called up to her from the living room, she wouldn't even be able to hear him.

Still, it'll only take a few minutes to do the dust and cobwebs. And she really wants it taken care of; she's filled with more energy than she's had in months, and this is the first chore on the ambitious To Do list she wrote this morning after breakfast.

Besides, what could happen? The doors are locked, and it's not like Ozzie is running around playing with matches or climbing out windows. She knows him well enough to realize that he'll be in front of the television set, mesmerized, until the video's closing credits, same as he always is.

She decisively snaps the attachment on the end of the hose, pushes the ON button with her bare foot, and starts vacuuming. God, it's ear-splitting. She stretches up on her tiptoes to run the attachment along the top of the window, then pokes it into the corner near the ceiling. A fine network of cobwebs, along with a small daddy longlegs, are promptly swallowed up without a trace.

Feeling better already, Michelle continues to work her way around the room, humming to herself, her own voice lost in the roar of the vacuum.

John Kline puts a fresh cup of coffee on his desk, sits in his chair, and adjusts the framed family photo on his desk, knocked askew by last night's cleaning crew, as always.

He loves this photo and is glad Nancy insisted that they have it taken at J.C. Penney right before Christmas, even though he'd grumbled about it at the time.

"Come on, John, it's not like I nag you about this constantly. You haven't had a picture taken since our wedding day," she'd pointed out, and it was the truth.

He glances at that particular photo—of himself, fifteen years younger, awkward in his tuxedo and sporting a full head of hair; and Nancy, slender and innocent in that white gown and veil. They're looking at each other in unabashed adoration.

Things sure have changed, he thinks, glancing at the recent family photo. Still, despite his receding hairline and Nancy's extra twenty pounds, they're still looking pretty contented. In this picture, they're joined by Jason, ducking those dark curls and wearing the embarrassed, forced smile one might expect of an adolescent boy forced to accompany his parents and sister to a shopping mall, wearing—gulp—a suit. Meanwhile, there's Ashley, blond, pretty in her velvet jumper, and flashing the camera one of those knowing, slightly exasperated expressions so typical of girls who are fifteen-going-on-twenty-one.

Looking at Ashley makes him think, again, of Rebecca Wasner's parents, and wonder how on earth they can possibly bear not knowing where she is, whether she's dead or alive. If anything ever happened to Ashley—or Jason—

But it won't, he reassures himself. Just because one girl happens to be missing doesn't mean someone's going to start kidnapping teenaged girls in Lake Charlotte again. No matter what the media is saying.

Needing a distraction, he reaches for the file filled with notes and measurements he made the other night over at Shelly and Lou's. When he started working on some preliminary sketches late last night, he made a startling discovery. It was too late to call them then, and so far, this morning has been too busy.

But now he'd better get in touch with them, before something else comes up. He's leaving to drive to New York for that conference before dawn tomorrow, and he won't be back until late Friday night.

He picks up the phone and dials the number, thinking, as he does, that he and Nancy really should invite the Randalls over for a barbecue some Sunday afternoon. They all live right here in town, but, somehow, they seem to get caught up in other things and never make time for each other. He has a brother and sister, and his parents are living in Florida, but Shelly has no family left. Such a shame that Aunt Joy died so young, he thinks, shaking his head.

Shelly was completely devastated by that loss. In fact, she's never entirely gone back to being her cheerful self.

The other night, she had seemed particularly stressed. In fact, she and Lou both had, he'd noticed at the tension-filled dinner table. Later, Lou had mentioned, as he and John were walking around the upstairs bedrooms while Shelly was ironing downstairs, that she's been moody lately, imagining things, worried about the baby, who's in a breech position. He'd said they'd spent all day Sunday at the hospital, enduring tests that had ultimately proven everything normal, aside from the baby's position.

Lou had also told John about his recent promotion at the law firm, and that he's in the midst of a difficult case at work, buried in research. Meanwhile, Ozzie's in the throes of the terrible twos, and they're trying to remodel the house.

Thinking back, John remembers the early days of his own marriage, when he'd been trying to get his architectural firm off the ground, and Nancy always seemed to be pregnant, or breastfeeding, and nagging him about something or other. He knows how challenging toddlers and infants can be, not to mention the frustration caused by a house that's falling apart even as you struggle to fix it up. He and Nance had completely gutted their own fixer-upper, bringing babies home to stripped wallpaper and bare beams and gaping holes in plaster.

We've come a long way, he thinks, looking back on that now-distant time of domestic discord.

Shelly and Lou need to know that everyone goes through times like this. We really should get together.

As the phone rings on the other end, he decides to ask his cousin right now to pick a Sunday so they can mark it on the calendar. If they don't reserve a day, it'll never happen. It'll be Christmas before they see each other again.

Then he remembers the baby. It isn't due until August, but she probably won't want to make plans for anything in the meantime.

After all, it might come early. Both Ashley and Jason did. And given those early labor pains—and the way she was bustling around the kitchen the other night . . .

The "nesting instinct"—that was what Nancy called it.

There's a click in his ear, and an answering machine picks up.

Hmm. Maybe she's in the hospital having the baby right now, he thinks, as he listens to his cousin's recorded voice.

"Hi, you've reached the Randalls. Michelle and Lou can't come to the phone right now, but if you'll leave a message at the sound of the tone, we'll be sure to get back to you as soon as we can. Thanks!"

There's a beep.

"Shelly, it's John. Listen, I was going over the measurements I took the other night, and I noticed something very interesting. I'll be out of town tomorrow, but I'll be back Friday night. Call me back as soon as you have a minute—*if* you aren't in the hospital in labor or anything," he adds with a laugh.

He hangs up the telephone and looks back at the folder, at the rows of numbers he'd jotted down the other night.

Unless he somehow managed to make several mistakes with the tape measure—which, is highly unlikely—there's quite a discrepancy in the dimensions of the inside and outside walls of the Randalls' home.

He's pretty sure he knows what that must mean. The place is a classic Victorian, built in the mid-1800's, when this area of northern New York State was a prime spot on the underground railroad route transporting slaves to Canada. John has seen quite a few houses built in Lake Charlotte during that era that have secret rooms, tunnels, even staircases, usually concealed behind false panels or bookcases.

Unless he's mistaken, the house at 52 Hayes Street is one of them.

Molly stands in front of the full-length mirror on the inside of Carleen's closet door, inspecting her reflection, comparing it to the sheet of photographs in her hand. They're wallet-sized senior portraits, and only one is missing, leaving an unevenly cut rectangular gap on one corner of the sheet.

Same color hair, Molly thinks, *but I wish mine was straight, like hers.*

Same complexion—not freckled, like Rory's and Kevin's. I have her pale skin, and her eyes, too.

But not her nose.

Whose nose do I have?

But she knows. In the mirror, she sees the inquisitive expression darken at the realization that it must be *his*.

The nameless, faceless someone who impregnated a thirteen-year-old girl, then obviously took off and abandoned her.

What kind of jerk would do such a thing?

Maybe he never knew, she speculates, needing, for some reason, to give him the benefit of the doubt. So he won't be a total jerk.

Maybe Carleen never told him about me.

But why wouldn't she? She was so young, Molly thinks, and she must have been freaked out. Why wouldn't she turn to the one other person who could share the responsibility for what had happened?

Downstairs, she hears a door slam. Must be Rory, going out. Mom and Sister Theodosia have already left for mass.

She never told Rory about the message from that guy, Barrett whatever-his-name-was, with the familiar voice. She had thought of it earlier, when they were both sitting in the kitchen eating breakfast. Rory's inquiry about Kevin calling had triggered her memory. She had been about to get up and take the message off the refrigerator door, where she realized Rory would never see it, when Rory had made that comment about Sister Theodosia still being here.

And then I just got sidetracked, Molly tells herself defensively. *I mean, it's not like I'm deliberately keeping messages from her, just to be a brat, just to get her back for . . .*

Well, for never being here.

Like missing one stupid phone message could ever be payback for *that*.

She frowns and turns away from Carleen's open closet door, putting the sheet of pictures back into the envelope in the dresser drawer where she'd found it.

I should really take this off, she thinks, looking down at the black lycra minidress she'd found hanging among her sister's—no, her *mother's*—things. She'd told herself that she was only trying it on because she wanted to see if she and Carleen were the same size—not because she wanted to feel close to her, or anything creepy like that.

The clingy dress, with its peekaboo cutouts in the sleeves and neckline, is so purely *eighties*, like the enormous hoop earrings she'd found in Carleen's jewelry box. She'd tried those on, too, and she tease-combed her hair and put a black lace hairband around it so that it looks like Madonna's did years ago, back when she was first getting famous.

The dress, and the earrings, and the hairdo have created an interesting kind of retro look. Molly tells herself she might be able to get away with wearing them in public. If she had someplace interesting to go, or someone interesting to go with.

Which you don't.

Ryan and Jessica are officially back together, according to Amanda, who reluctantly admitted as much when Molly called and confronted her last night. Amanda also asked if it was true that the police were combing the woods with bloodhounds, looking for Rebecca, and if Molly thought they were going to drag the lake.

Molly was so taken aback, so horrified by the very thought, that all she could do was stammer, "I . . . I don't know . . ."

Then Amanda asked if Molly wanted to come to a cookout with Lisa and Dana and Will and his friends.

She hadn't hesitated before saying no, making something up about having to help her mother around the house—such a typical excuse, something a normal person with a normal mother might say. But Amanda must not have thought anything of it, because she'd simply said that was too bad, adding a breezy "catch you later."

And now Molly's wondering if she should have gone last night, or if she should call Amanda and try to make plans for today. After all, she can't hang around this house by herself, dwelling on Carleen, and Rebecca, for the rest of her life.

Carleen is long gone, probably dead, and Rebecca—

Please, God, please let Rebecca be okay, Molly thinks, tears springing to her eyes. She can't take much more of this. She's seen the reporters and police coming and going from the Wasners' house, and she knows she should work up her courage and go down there, say something, anything, to Rebecca's parents.

But for some reason, she just can't. She can't, because what if Rebecca told them about the fight Molly had picked with her the night before she disappeared? What if they're somehow blaming everything on Molly?

Oh, God, oh God, what if it's somehow my fault?

Rory had said that it isn't.

But what does Rory know? She, of all people, doesn't have a clue about accepting responsibility for your mistakes.

That might not be quite fair, Molly amends, admitting to herself that Rory's done her best to pick up the pieces in Kevin's absence. But then again, her efforts are too little, too late, and Molly isn't going to forgive her, just like that, for taking off for so many years, and then for popping back up and dropping that bombshell about her being Carleen's illegitimate daughter.

For all I know, it isn't even true, she tells herself, idly toying with a snow globe on Carleen's dresser. *For all I know, Rory made the whole thing up, out of spite, just to hurt me, or to smudge Carleen's memory.*

But deep in her heart, she knows better.

Deep in her heart, she knows that her dark-haired big sister, whom Molly so closely resembles, was actually her mother.

That's why she's here, in this room, poking among Carleen's things as she has ever since she found out. That's why she's wearing her clothes, why she borrowed her makeup and some perfume before going out with Ryan and Amanda and their crowd.

As if maybe, some of Carleen's devil-may-care confidence might rub off on her, so she won't always have to feel so utterly lost and alone.

Barrett Maitland stands on the sidewalk, staring at the shabby bungalow on a shady side street a few blocks from Grayson's Cove's waterfront. Last night, after dark, the place had given off an air of abandonment, and foreboding.

Today, it isn't any less so.

He eyes the sagging front steps, the loose shutters, the over-grown patch of yard. The windows are all still covered by blinds, but there's a pickup truck in the driveway this morning, just as there was last night. Yet no one had answered his knock then, and no one answered it earlier, when he came by just after breakfast.

He'd gone to the local library after that, spent some time looking through old newspapers and records for information about Russell Anghardt. All he'd found was a reprint of the obituary of his wife, the same write-up that had originally appeared in a Raleigh paper, which he had already seen. It stated that Jane Anghardt had died in childbirth, leaving behind her loving husband and newborn twin son and daughter, as well as extended family in Raleigh. She was buried there, rather than here in Grayson's Cove.

Local real estate records showed that Russell and his wife had bought this house back in the seventies, in what would have been the year before the twins' birth and Jane's death. Barrett wonders why they moved up North for that short time, why Russell never sold the place, and whether it stood empty while they were gone.

He knows Russell Anghardt was originally from a small town in the Adirondacks, and figures maybe he was homesick for New York State. But then, after losing Emily, he must have been tormented by memories of her in Lake Charlotte, and decided to come back here, where he'd apparently lived quietly ever since. It makes sense.

"Looking for someone?"

He turns, startled, to see an elderly woman standing on the sidewalk, holding an oversized black poodle on a leash.

"Actually, I am," he says, pleased. He'd been about to either start knocking on neighbors' doors, asking whether anyone knows where he can find Russell, or to give up on the whole thing and go back to Lake Charlotte. And Rory.

"Who? Mr. Anghardt?"

"Exactly. This is his place, right?"

"Oh, that's it, all right." The woman wrinkles her nose slightly, glancing at the overgrown grass. "And his lawn sure could use a cutting. Ain't like him to let it go. He might not keep up with repairs around here, but it's hard to be fixin' things with that bum leg of his. Still, you always see him pushin' that lawn mower of his, limpin' along."

"He hurt his leg?"

"Years ago. While he was livin' in New York—"

Barrett decides to play dumb. "He lived in New York?"

"For a year, maybe more. Rented this place to a coupla no-good motorcycle riders. Kept poor Angel barking all night long."

Angel, presumably, is the dog. And this woman, like Mrs. Shilling of Lake Charlotte, appears to keep tabs on neighborhood happenings.

Barrett asks, "Did he have children?"

"A daughter—purty little thing. Emily. And there was a son, too. But he was mentally retarded. Bunch of older kids on the street used to tease him all the time. Throw rocks at him. Make fun of him. Rotten stuff like that. Used to make poor Emily cry. I think that's partly why they moved out of here for a while."

"What about when they came back?" Barrett resists the urge to nudge Angel, who's poking his clammy nose against Barrett's bare ankles.

"Only Mr. Anghardt came back. Must be seven or eight years ago now. I remember, it was the autumn after my mama passed away . . . Wait a minute, that was ten years ago. Ten years ago this coming autumn."

"What about his children?"

"Oh, that's the saddest thing," the woman says, shaking her head and pulling the poodle's leash so that it stops sniffing Barrett's ankles. "Poor man had already lost his wife. Never seemed to get over that. I always thought that was why he kept to himself. And then the kids—"

"What happened?"

"Both those kids were killed in a real bad car wreck up in New York State. Guess that's how he got his limp."

At first, Michelle thinks Ozzie poured his apple juice onto the kitchen floor while she wasn't looking. Why else would there be a yellowish puddle in the middle of the linoleum?

She puts the jar of peanut butter back into the cupboard, grabs the sponge, and bends over to clean it up, telling Ozzie, who's standing in front of the table, drinking from his sippy cup, "Get back into your booster seat, mister. Look at the mess you made on the floor with your juice."

Then she realizes that her legs are dripping wet.

Her shorts.

Her underpants.

It isn't apple juice.

Her water has broken.

"Oh, my God," Michelle murmurs, straightening and rubbing her forehead in disbelief. How can this be happening?

She's going to have the baby early after all.

Now.

She's going to have the baby now.

Not now, she corrects herself, fighting back panic. *Soon.*

"Mommy?" Ozzie asks, watching her, a tentative expression on his face.

"It's okay, sweetheart. Finish your juice. I have to call Daddy. And then the doctor."

Or should she call the doctor first?

She goes to the phone, careful not to slip in the puddle on the floor. She can't believe that her water has broken. With Ozzie, they had to break it during her labor, to help speed things along.

First she calls Dr. Kabir, who asks if she's having contractions, and orders her to go straight to the hospital.

"What about the baby's position?" she asks.

"We'll worry about that when we get there," the doctor says in his clipped middle-eastern accent. "Don't drive yourself, Michelle."

"I won't. My husband will come right home to get me."

What if Lou isn't there? The thought occurs to her as she's fumbling to dial the number of his office, noticing that the red message light is blinking on the answering machine as she walks away from it. Someone must have called while she was upstairs vacuuming, she thinks, distracted. Maybe it was Lou. Maybe he was saying he had to go to court this afternoon, or maybe making up some excuse for why she wouldn't be able to reach him at work.

But he's there. In his office. Where he should be. Picking up the phone, saying, "Michelle? What's wrong?"

"My water just broke."

"Oh, my God. Are you sure? It's so early."

The concern in his voice strikes her, makes her feel, at least for the time being, that everything is okay between them again.

"Well, I know I didn't pee my pants," she says, her voice

coming out in a high-pitched cross between amusement and hysteria. "I've been potty trained for years, Lou."

"I'll be right home."

"Hurry."

"Did you call the doctor?"

"I did. He said he'll meet us at the hospital. I'll go up and pack my bag. I hadn't done that yet. I thought we had time—"

"I know. What about Ozzie?"

"Ozzie!" Stricken, Michelle glances at her son, who's happily pouring apple juice all over the remains of his peanut butter sandwich, soaking it. "My God, I forgot all about him. I mean, he's right here, but . . . I'll have to call Molly," she realizes, remembering that his mother left this morning to go antiquing in Vermont through the weekend.

"Call her right away. I hope she can do it."

"I hope so, too," Michelle says, and hangs up. She thinks of Rebecca Wasner, and of Molly's drawn face on Sunday night.

"She'll help us out," she says aloud, dialing the Connollys' number "She *has* to."

"Hi, Mrs. Shilling," Rory says, when her neighbor's familiar face pokes through the screen door. "How have you been?"

"Not too bad, Rory." She opens the door, shoving her shoulder into the opening and asking, "How are you enjoying your visit home?"

"Fine, thanks." Suddenly, she wants to put off the real reason she came here. "Looks like rain, doesn't it?"

She glances up at the heavy gray sky, and Mrs. Shilling follows suit.

"It does," the woman says, then asks, nosy as ever, "Are you here to see Barrett Maitland?"

"I—why would you ask that?"

"Because I saw how the two of you looked at each other the other day. I figured maybe something was going on between you."

"Oh." Rory feels her cheeks grow hot. "Well, for the record, nothing's going on, Mrs. Shilling."

"I see," the woman says, wearing a slightly smug, *whatever you say* expression.

"I just wanted to talk to him about . . . something." She hadn't even known, as she walked out the door, that she was headed over here. She'd only been aware that she had to get out of that house, with its haunting memories and its awful, lonely silence.

But she had immediately realized, as she headed down Hayes Street, that she needs to talk to someone about yesterday's encounter with poor David Anghardt, and Barrett Maitland is the logical—no, the *only*—choice.

"I don't suppose you know where he went?" Mrs. Shilling is asking.

"Where he went?" Rory echoes.

"Didn't you get the message that he was leaving, Rory? I heard him— That is, I'm pretty certain he left a message with Molly, though I might be mistaken."

"You must be. I didn't get a message." Rory doesn't want to be thrown by the news that Barrett is no longer here, doesn't want disappointment to steal over her. After all, Barrett Maitland is just . . . what? Not a *friend*.

Just a writer who came to town and started poking his nose into things that were better left untouched.

"Where did he go?"

"I have no idea. That's why I asked you," Mrs. Shilling reminds her. "All I know is that he paid for his room yesterday morning and left some of his things behind, but nothing all that important."

"How do you know that?"

"I . . . Okay, Rory, I'll admit it. I checked. There was nothing there but some clothes, and shoes, and shampoo, stuff like that."

"Mrs. Shilling, I can't believe you snooped through his room," Rory says, feigning shock, even as her mind races, wondering why Barrett left town so suddenly

"It was the responsible thing to do, Rory," the woman quickly justifies. "In fact, I just got off the phone with Bucky down in Texas—he's a police officer now, you know," she adds proudly. "And he said it was the right thing to do. After all, poor Rebecca Wasner's gone missing right on this very block, and that Barrett Maitland is so secretive. For all I know, he could be a cold-blooded killer staying right here under my roof. Diana and Bucky were right. I never should have turned this place into a bed and breakfast. It's too dangerous for a defenseless woman my age."

Rory glances at Mrs. Shilling, whose robust figure is far from vulnerable, and fights back a momentary urge to smile. Instead, she asks, "I know what you're saying, Mrs. Shilling. For all we know, Barrett Maitland could be responsible for Rebecca's disappearance Saturday night. You wouldn't mind if I took a look up in his room myself, would you?"

The woman narrows her eyes.

"I'll confess," Rory says quickly, "that I really was romantically involved with him. I was hoping that the two of us had a future. You won't mind if I had a moment alone up there, just to come to terms with the fact that he left without saying good-bye?"

"Of course I wouldn't mind."

Rory can practically see the wheels turning in the woman's mind. Twenty minutes from now, she'll be on the phone telling her garden-club pals that poor Rory Connolly is broken-hearted about being jilted by that mysterious newcomer, Barrett Maitland.

"I'll be down here in the kitchen if you need me, Rory," Mrs. Shilling says, extracting an old-fashioned key from the ring in her pocket and handing it to Rory. "You just take your time. He was in the room at the head of the stairs—but then, you probably already know that," she adds with a wink that suggests Rory and Barrett might have been sneaking around the place after hours.

Shaking her head, Rory makes her way up to the second floor and unlocks the door.

The room is fairly small but has a high ceiling, very similar to the rooms in the Connolly house. But it's been painted and wallpapered and filled with period furniture to make for accommodations that are surprisingly tasteful, given Mrs. Shilling's tendency toward tacky behavior.

Feeling infinitely guilty, Rory opens the closet door and glances at the clothing hanging there, recognizing two of the shirts she'd seen on Barrett. The rest of his wardrobe is just as preppy—lots of khaki, and button-down shirts, and several pairs of loafers lined up neatly on the floor.

In the dresser drawers are more clothes: shorts, socks, underwear—boxers, Rory notes, blushing though she's alone. Of course he'd wear boxers. Everything about him says Brooks Brothers.

Which doesn't mean he isn't a serial killer.

Reluctant as she is to face her suspicions, she has to admit that

Mrs. Shilling is right. There's something secretive about Barrett Maitland, and he is, after all, interested in what happened to those girls ten years ago. Could he have been behind it?

But why would he come back?

If he'd gotten away scot-free for all these years, why not just stay away?

On top of the dresser, along with bottles of shampoo and mouthwash and some loose change in an ashtray, are a dictionary, and a neat stack of notebooks—all of them blank, Rory notices, rummaging through them. There are also pens, and several computer diskettes, leading Rory to believe that he has a laptop computer, and if so, must have taken it with him, since it doesn't appear to be here.

Precisely the kinds of trappings you'd expect to find in the room of a writer researching a book.

Or a serial killer taking pains to look like a writer researching a book, she thinks, toying with one of his pens, noticing it's a fountain pen, and an expensive one at that.

Barrett is perfectly aware of Mrs. Shilling's nosiness. He had to know she was going to snoop through his things the moment he left. Why would he leave behind anything that would give him away?

Rory goes to put the pen back on the dresser, drops it accidentally, and bends over to pick it up from the floor.

As she does, she notices something under the dresser . . . a small rectangle of plain white paper, looks like.

She picks it up, and it's stiff, like a business card, and the edges are uneven, as though someone cut them with scissors.

A photograph, she realizes, flipping it over.

A school photograph of Carleen at seventeen.

"How about some ice cream, Ozzie?" Molly asks, carrying the sobbing two-year-old back to the kitchen after his parents' car has disappeared from view of the front porch.

"No! I want Mommy!" Ozzie says, squirming.

"Mommy's going to the hospital to have the new baby, Ozzie, just like she said."

"No!"

Molly hugs him, her heart going out to the little boy. Poor

Michelle had been seized by a contraction, doubling over, clenching her huge stomach, just as she was saying good-bye; Lou had hustled her out to the car the moment it was over and she could speak again.

Ozzie—and Molly, too—had been startled by the sight of her in terrible pain.

"She'll be back in a few days, you'll see," Molly tells Ozzie now, nodding her head and feeling Carleen's huge earrings clanking. She hadn't had time to change out of this crazy get-up—Michelle had begged her to come straight over. Neither Michelle, nor Lou, when he dashed in from work, had seemed to notice her vintage eighties look. As soon as she gets a chance, she'll scrub off the makeup she'd been painstakingly applying in Carleen's mirror when Michelle's call interrupted.

"Your mommy's going to the hospital," Molly says again, "and guess what that means, Ozzie?"

"What?" he asks halfheartedly.

"You get to be a big brother. I have a big brother, and it's the most important job in the whole world."

Ozzie ponders that, then asks, still sniffling, "What do big brothers do?"

"All kinds of things. Mostly, they take care of their little brothers and sisters, making them feel safe, because when big brothers are around, nothing bad can happen."

And when they go off to Europe with their girlfriends without a second thought, all hell breaks loose.

"I want a big brother," Ozzie announces, on the verge of tears again, and looking around.

"I want Mommy, too. And Daddy."

Uh-oh. That backfired.

"I'll be your big brother while they're gone, Ozzie," Molly says, stroking his soft hair. "I'll keep you safe and make sure nothing bad happens. Okay?"

He looks dubious.

Is it that obvious that she's scared out of her mind at the prospect of being alone in this house again? But what else could she do when Michelle called but say, "I'll be right over"?

Michelle had said that they'd tried to reach her mother-in-law, Iris, in Vermont, to see if she could come back to stay for a few days. "If she calls, give her the number of the hospital," Michelle had said. "We'll tell her to come home right away."

And even if Iris didn't call and come rushing back, Lou would be home as soon as possible, so Molly won't have to spend the night alone in the house with Ozzie. But Molly can't help wondering how long it takes to have a baby. What if it doesn't come right away? It's early—Michelle wasn't due until August. What if there are complications?

If there are complications, she reminds herself, the last thing Lou needs to worry about is rushing home to a big baby of a babysitter.

Well, if they get hung up at the hospital, she can always call Rory to come over and stay—not that it's something she'd do unless she was out of her mind with fear. Nobody was home when she left, and she'd almost walked out the door without leaving a note, when she'd remembered what Rory had said this morning about letting each other know where they'd be when they went out.

Rory had done that, jotting only *Went for a walk, be back soon* on a scrap of paper and leaving it on the table.

So Molly had grudgingly turned it over and scribbled *Babysitting next door, be back????* before dashing out the door.

"Come on, Ozzie, let's have ice cream before your nap," she says again, brightly, forcing away her misgivings for his sake— and her own. "I'll see if there are any chocolate sprinkles left."

As she walks to the cupboard, she sees the red message light blinking on the answering machine. Somebody must have called while she and Ozzie were out on the front porch, waving good-bye.

She hesitates, wondering if she should listen to the message. Under normal circumstances she wouldn't, but what if it was Ozzie's grandmother Iris calling from Vermont?

After a moment, Molly presses the flashing button and hears the tape rewind.

"Shelly, it's John. Listen, I was going over the measurements I took the other night, and I noticed something very interesting. I'll be out of town tomorrow, but I'll be back Friday night. Call me back as soon as you have a minute—*if* you aren't in the hospital in labor or anything," the caller adds with a laugh, before hanging up.

Good guess, Molly thinks, looking around for something to write with. She finds a pen and a piece of notepaper and jots, *Michelle, call John when you have time.*

"Sorry, John," she says aloud, "I don't think that's going to be for a while."

Barrett is putting the last neatly folded polo shirt on top of the pile in his bag when there's a knock on the door.

Frowning, he glances over at it, wondering who on earth it can be. Must be somebody looking for a guest in another room, he thinks, deciding to wait a minute before bothering to answer.

He glances at the television set, where the Weather Channel meteorologist is talking about a series of strong storms due to move across the Great Lakes into northern New York State later today and tonight.

There's another knock.

Barrett clicks off the television set and walks swiftly across the threadbare motel carpet to open the door.

A uniformed police officer is standing there, with several others just behind him, looking poised to take action.

"Barrett Maitland?"

"Yes?" His heart is pounding.

The cop looks past him, taking in the open suitcase on the bed, the airline ticket ready on the desk by the door.

"We'd like to ask you a few questions," the cop says in a heavy North Carolina accent, his eyes coldly fastened to Barrett's face.

"Questions?"

Relax, he tells himself. *There must be some kind of mix-up. This can't possibly be about—*

"Questions about what, Officer?"

"Is it true you were snooping around Russell Anghardt's home over on Grove Street earlier today?"

"I wasn't snooping—"

"Neighbor of his said you were there, asking questions."

He raises an eyebrow. He'd never mentioned his name to that old woman with the poodle. How had they tracked him down?

Then again, it can't be too hard in a remote, tiny town like this, he realizes. There's only one motel, and he'd be willing to bet he's the only newcomer with a northern accent to show up here in the last twenty-four hours.

"After you left, Mrs. Knisley realized she hadn't seen Mr. Anghardt around lately, so she called us," the cop goes on, his eyes narrowed at Barrett, as though daring him to make a move or slip up, blurting something he shouldn't.

Barrett waits, holding his breath, thinking this can't be happening.

"We went right over there to investigate, Mr. Maitland. And when we did, we found Russell Anghardt's body, such a bloody mess that this sure as hell ain't no death by natural causes."

CHAPTER
FOURTEEN

Rory returns home just as it's getting dark outside, and sees that Sister Theodosia's car is no longer sitting in the driveway.

In the kitchen, on the table, she sees the note from Molly and is surprised that her sister actually did as she'd asked earlier and let Rory know where she'd gone. Maybe Molly's coming around.

"Mom?" she calls, walking to the foot of the stairs, turning on lights as she goes. "Are you up there?"

There's a faint, muffled reply.

Encouraged by it, Rory goes up, and taps lightly on her mother's closed bedroom door.

"Mom? It's me, Rory. Can I come in?"

"Come on."

She opens the door and sees Maura sitting in a chair by the window, her usual spot. Her hair is neatly combed and she's wearing a pair of lightweight summer slacks and a sleeveless blouse, dressed, for once, appropriately for the warm summer night.

"Where's Sister Theodosia?" Rory asks.

"She left."

"Where did she go?"

"Back to Buffalo, I guess."

At least her mother is lucid enough to know where her friend lives.

"Did she help you comb your hair and get dressed?"

Maura nods. "She said I would be too warm in a sweater."

Rory bites back the urge to say that she and Kevin, and probably Molly, too, had been telling her exactly that.

"When did she leave?"

"Right after we got back from the doctor."

"Doctor?" Rory repeats, startled. "What doctor?"

"I don't know . . . he gave me some medicine. Told me to keep taking it. Said it would help me to feel better. I didn't want to go, but Sister Theodosia brought me."

Well, hallelujah, Rory thinks in disbelief. She picks up an orange prescription bottle from her mother's nightstand, and glances at the label. The name of the medication isn't familiar, but she recognizes the doctor's name. Desiderio. It's the same psychiatrist that Daddy had taken Mom to years ago.

"Have you eaten anything, Mom?" Rory asks, smoothing the quilt on the bed and walking toward the doorway. "Do you want me to make you some soup or something?"

"I'm not hungry anymore. Kevin made me a sandwich earlier. I think I'll just go to sleep now."

Rory freezes in the doorway.

"Who made you a sandwich, Mom?"

"Kevin. Where is he now?"

"Mom, he's in Europe, remember?" She sighs. "Mom, did you take that medicine?"

"Not yet. I will, though. I'll take it later."

"You need to take it now, Mom. You keep imagining things. This isn't good. You go around seeing people who aren't here . . . Daddy, and Carleen, and Emily, and Kevin."

"Emily? Where is she, anyway? She was here before, but I haven't seen her in a while. You need friends, Rory. Someone to play with. You're so alone here."

Oh, Mom.

Touched, she says gently, "Mom, I'm not alone. I'm with you and Molly. I don't need friends. And Emily—"

"I know. She's gone," her mother says flatly. "Just like Carleen. And Daddy . . ."

"And Kevin. Good, Mom. I was worried that you didn't—"

"It's all right, Rory. I'm all right." She stands and turns away from the window. "I'm going to go to sleep now."

In the kitchen, Rory opens a can of tomato soup, pours it into a kettle, and turns on the burner. As she stands stirring it, she shoves aside disturbing thoughts about her mother and thinks instead about her long day at the big stone Lake Charlotte public library on Front Street.

Her misgivings had been eased somewhat when she'd found both of Barrett Maitland's books listed in the library's card catalogue. It had taken extensive searching through the paperback spinner racks to locate them, and when she did, she saw that it was indeed the man she knew smiling out from the photo on the back cover.

So Barrett Maitland really is an author.

That means he really could be writing about the Lake Charlotte disappearances . . . and probably *is*, Rory reminds herself.

Finding that photo of Carleen in his room means nothing. After all, he openly admitted that he's researching her disappearance— of course he's going to be interested in photos of her, and maybe have one in his possession. His other two books contain plenty of pictures, including ones of the victims.

But where did he get the picture of Carleen? Rory had recognized it as her senior portrait, the one that hangs above the staircase in the foyer.

Maybe one of her old friends had given it to him.

The thing was, Carleen didn't have a whole lot of friends left by the time she disappeared. She'd changed so much in the year they were in California, while she was pregnant, that when she came back she seemed to have no interest in picking up where she left off with her crowd. From what Rory knew, she ran around with older kids, mostly guys. Not the kind of people you'd go around exchanging senior portraits with.

Rory had glanced over Barrett Maitland's brief bio at the back of the book, seeing that he'd been raised in New Hampshire, gone to school at Bennington, and lived New York. Just as he'd told her.

That doesn't mean he wasn't lying, she thinks, stirring the tomato soup, pressing the lumps against the sides of the kettle to smooth the texture. He could have been lying about everything, even the book about the Lake Charlotte disappearances. Just because he's a writer doesn't mean he can't be a killer, too. After all, what kind of ghoul writes about such a gory subject?

Oh, come on. The fact that he writes about crime doesn't make him a killer, Rory reminds herself. *That's like saying all science fiction authors are likely to be aliens.*

The thought is so ludicrous that she has to chuckle aloud.

She finishes stirring the soup, pours it into a bowl, and carries it to the table. She sits down to eat, and then, remembering something, stands again and goes over to the phone.

After calling Information, she dials the number for St. Malachy's, wondering if it's too late to find Lydia McGovern there. But if she's not mistaken, it's the director herself who answers the phone.

"Hello, I'd like to speak to Lydia McGovern, please?" Rory asks.

"This is she. Who's calling, please?"

"I don't know if you remember me, Ms. McGovern—my name is Rory Connolly, and I was there yesterday, visiting David Anghardt?"

"Oh, yes, of course I remember you. You left so quickly."

"I'm sorry. I suddenly felt ill and I needed fresh air."

"Are you better now?" the woman asks, such genuine concern in her voice that Rory feels instant guilt over the white lie.

She assures her that yes, she's fine now.

"I'm glad. David was quite worked up after your visit. I think he was thrilled to have another visitor, someone other than Sister Mary Frances. After you left, he kept calling for her. 'Sister, Sister,' he kept shouting, and it took us quite some time to get him settled."

"Sister?" Rory echoes slowly. "That's what he was saying?"

"Yes, he just adores her. I think I told you—she's an occasional visitor to our home, but David is her favorite. She brings him a little gift every time—or, maybe I shouldn't say little. She does always remember to bring him those chocolate-covered raisins he likes so much, but she's also the one who gave him that beautiful quilt, and the lovely, framed watercolor prints on his walls. She understands how little money we have for the kinds of homey touches that mean so much to our residents."

"She sounds wonderful."

"Poor David misses her so terribly when she isn't here. In fact, I didn't realize she'd made a recent visit, as Susan said yesterday, but now it makes sense."

"What does?"

"That David ran away again on Saturday. He does that every once in a while . . . manages to sneak out of here, and get away. I think he's trying to find Sister Mary Frances, or maybe his father, poor thing. This time, he was missing for almost twenty-four hours before he was found Sunday morning wandering in the bus terminal in Albany."

"That's awful." Rory has chills just thinking about David Anghardt stumbling out into the world, where he'd be at the mercy of anyone ruthless who happened to get their kicks taunting someone like David. "How did he get all the way up there?"

"We're not sure. He must have taken a bus. The Adirondack Trailways line makes a daily stop at the gas station right across the road from our gate. Anyway, is there something I can help you with, Rory? I know you're calling long distance."

"Actually, Ms. McGovern, there is. I was wondering if you're familiar with someone named Barrett Maitland."

"Barrett Maitland? Should I be?"

"He's a true-crime writer, and he's here in Lake Charlotte researching the disappearance of Emily Anghardt and several other girls."

"Oh, the writer."

Rory doesn't have to see Lydia McGovern's face to know that it's wearing a disapproving look.

"You know him, then?"

"He's called here a few times. I spoke to him once or twice, and I told him that we don't release personal information from our residents' records under any circumstances."

"What did he want to know?"

"Where he could find David's family, for one thing. He needed an address. I pointed out that we don't even have one, but if we did, we certainly couldn't provide it to a total stranger."

"So he didn't say why he needed it?"

"Just that he needed to interview them for his book. He wanted to come here to talk to David, but I said absolutely not. I can't have him upsetting the poor boy."

Again, Rory feels a prickle of remorse for her own visit, hoping the woman doesn't realize that it stemmed more from curiosity and suspicion than a genuine desire to cheer up someone less fortunate than herself. She vows to go to St. Malachy's again this summer, and, next time, to bring David Anghardt some Raisinets, one of those huge boxes like they sell at movie theaters.

"Why are you curious about that writer, Rory? Has he been bothering you, too?"

"In a way," Rory admits. "But I wasn't sure whether to trust him."

"I wouldn't. These days, you just never know what strangers are up to."

"No," Rory agrees thoughtfully, "you certainly don't."

"Are you all right, hon?"

He blinks, sees that Kelly is staring at him across the table they managed to snag in the crowded Irish pub near Faneuil Hall. Concern is etched in her wide-set hazel eyes.

She's beautiful, he thinks—young, and beautiful, and excited about our future. She has no idea that I'm still hopelessly entrenched in my sordid past. What would she do if she knew the truth? Leave me? Would I blame her?

"I'm fine," he says, picking up his mug of Sam Adams and taking a long drink. "Just thinking about that research paper I'm working on. Who says professors get to take the summers off? I've spent every day in my office since the semester ended, and I'm not even teaching a course this session."

"You work too hard. Come with me to DC this weekend. It'll be fun. You can't come to my dress fitting, though—it's bad luck for the groom to see the bride in her gown before the wedding day."

"I was thinking . . . maybe we should think twice about having a Christmas wedding."

"What do you mean?"

"That time of year, with the weather so unpredictable, and so many people having to travel to get there . . ."

"We're the only ones who have to travel to get there," Kelly points out, her wineglass poised in front of her lips. "Everyone else lives in the Washington area, since you didn't want to invite anyone from here, or your family."

"I told you, I really don't have much family, and I'm not close to them."

"Whatever." She shrugs, watching him. "You're the one who wanted a Christmas wedding. You pointed out that you'll have all that time off for winter recess, and I'll hopefully have my thesis done by then."

"I know. I just never thought about the weather. That's all."

"So what are you saying? You want to move the wedding up?"

Actually, he'd been thinking of pushing it back. Way back. Waiting a while longer, just to make sure . . .

Make sure of what? he demands of himself.

That she really loves you?

That the past isn't going to explode in your face and destroy this whole new life it took so damn long to build?

"I don't know . . ." He sips more ale.

"Because we can always have an October wedding. The foliage is so beautiful then. Of course, you wouldn't have any extra time off, unless we could do it Columbus Day weekend—but my parents' country club is probably booked then."

"It's okay, Kelly. We'll just leave it at Christmas."

"Are you sure?" She's watching him closely, as though she's worried about him.

"I'm positive." He forces a smile.

"You'll see, honey." She reaches across the table and squeezes his hand. "Everything will work out perfectly. Trust me."

"I do trust you," he assures her.

The question is, Kelly, do you trust me? And if you do—you might be making the biggest mistake of your life.

"All right, Michelle," Dr. Kabir says, striding briskly back into the labor room, her chart in his hand. "The baby isn't necessarily premature—"

"But he wasn't due until August," Lou interrupts.

"We could have gotten the dates wrong, though he is on the small side—"

"How small?" Michelle asks, tense, still breathing her way through a contraction.

"Not dangerously so. Looks like he's in the safe zone, over six pounds, and, so far, everything looks okay, so—"

"But he's still breech?" Lou asks, standing by Michelle's head. He's been coaching her, doing his best, to his credit, to remember the breathing exercises they'd used two years ago when Ozzie was born.

"He's still breech," the doctor confirms, "But, given his size and the fact that labor is progressing normally, we're going to have you attempt a vaginal delivery."

"No surgery?" Michelle asks, half relieved, half intimidated by the prospect of the enormous, excruciating task ahead.

"Is that a good idea?" Lou asks warily.

"I've had twenty years of experience, Mr. Randall, and I've seen many patients through this type of delivery," Dr. Kabir says. "We'll monitor your wife and the baby very closely, and allow labor to proceed only as long as it progresses normally. Michelle will be transferred to an operating room at the end of the first stage, just in case a cesarean section is needed."

"When will that be?"

Lou asks the question that's on the tip of Michelle's tongue, as though he's read her mind. She can't speak anyway; another agonizing contraction is taking hold, squeezing the middle of her body from the inside out.

"The length of time depends, basically, on Michelle—on how long it takes her cervix to fully dilate. There's no way of predicting. When I examined her a few minutes ago, she was at three centimeters. She has to go to ten."

Michelle looks at Lou. "Ozzie," she bites out, her face clenched against the pain. "Molly . . ."

"She can take good care of him, Michelle," Lou says. "Don't worry. She was fine the other day."

"That wasn't overnight." She can't ignore a growing sense of trepidation—a distinct malaise that has nothing to do with labor and pain. She looks at the clock, sees that the hour hand has clicked its way past seven. It'll be dark soon.

And Rebecca Wasner's kidnapper—maybe killer—is still out there someplace.

She takes a deep breath, manages to speak over the contraction. "It's . . . owww . . . getting . . . late."

Dr. Kabir looks sternly at Michelle. "You need to focus on your labor, Michelle. That should be your main concern now. Don't use your energy to talk through the contractions; you're fighting a losing battle if you do. Try not to worry about other things—"

"My son!" she shouts, irritated. "He's alone."

"Molly's there."

"But she's afraid, Lou!"

She sees the glance that passes between her husband and the doctor.

"Our teenaged babysitter is staying with our son," Lou explains. "Michelle is worried about her being alone with him overnight."

"Women in labor can sometimes become irrational and paranoid," the doctor says in a low voice.

"I'm *not* paranoid!" Michelle practically screams, hating both of them.

"I'm sorry, Michelle," the doctor says, and turns to Lou. "Isn't there someone else you could call to go over and stay at your house so that she won't worry about this?"

"We're trying to reach my mother, but she's out of town. We left a message for her to get in touch and we'll ask her to come back."

"I'm sure your son and his sitter will be fine in the meantime," the doctor says in a calming voice, looking down at Michelle. He pats her hand, which is gripping the bed rail, and urges, "Try to relax. Don't fight the pain, try to breathe with it."

"No!"

"Michelle!" Lou says tersely. "He's the doctor. He knows what he's talking about."

She feels frantic, trapped in this bed, in this body, knowing only that Ozzie might be in danger and she's powerless to do anything about it. "Lou, you go . . . go home. I'll be fine."

"No way. I'm not leaving you now, Michelle."

"Your husband should be here, Michelle," the doctor agrees. "His job is to stay with you and coach you through labor. Both of you need to focus on that, now, okay? For the baby's sake, and your own."

"No," Michelle protests weakly, as the contraction eases and she allows her head to flop back onto the pillow.

"Keep her as calm as you can," Dr. Kabir tells Lou as he turns to leave.

"I'll try," Lou promises.

"No," Michelle says again, pleading with Lou. "Go . . . please. Before . . ."

But another contraction is building in a fierce, sudden, agonizing wave that sweeps her away before she can utter the rest.

Before it's too late.

Molly turns on the television set, idly flipping the remote control from channel to channel. Nothing good is on in the summer, she decides, considering turning it off. But then the house will be silent, and that would be much worse than watching some boring sitcom rerun.

She's still waiting for the phone to ring, for Ozzie's grandmother to say, "They're at the hospital? I'll hurry right back and be there in a few hours," or for Lou to say, "It's a boy! And I'll be home by midnight." Anything so Molly won't have to stay here alone all night.

She puts the remote control on the end table, next to the baby monitor, which is plugged in and turned on. Ozzie had cried miserably when she put him to bed, wailing that he was afraid of the lady in his room.

Molly figures he was talking about the painting of Old Mother Hubbard on the wall above his crib. Michelle had painted her smiling, but you never know with little kids. They're afraid of the strangest things.

At least, that's what Molly desperately wants to believe.

That Ozzie was terrified of a harmless, smiling mural of Old Mother Hubbard.

Because there's no such thing as ghosts, right?

"Don't worry, Ozzie," she had said soothingly, rubbing his trembling little body through his thin summer pajamas. "I'll be right downstairs. I won't let anything happen to you. I promise. I'll be right there if you need me."

She walks over to the window. It's dark out now, but she's reassured to see lights on in her own house next door. She can even make out her mother's silhouette in the upstairs bedroom window, behind the lace curtain. And Rory must be in the kitchen. A little while ago she heard the faint, reassuring sound of pots and pans clattering through the open screen.

It's nice to know that if anything happens, Molly can just scream and Rory will hear her and come running over.

What's going to happen? she asks herself suspiciously, turning away from the window. *What's going to make me scream for help?*

She can't help being on edge, thinking about Rebecca. There's still been no sign of her.

Did someone actually creep into the Wasners' house in the middle of the night and take her from her bed? Why didn't she scream for help?

She must have. But nobody heard.

How is that possible? Molly wonders uneasily.

Her parents and her brother were home, asleep in their beds. Besides, if anyone screamed in the middle of the night the whole block would hear. It's summertime. Everybody's windows are open; none of the big old houses in this neighborhood have central air-conditioning.

Whoever took Rebecca must not have given her time to scream.

Molly walks over to the couch and sits on the edge of the cushion, staring idly at the television screen, where Drew Carey is dancing against a backdrop of Cleveland.

I wonder what Rory's doing?

The thought has just crossed her mind when she hears it.

A loud, distinct thump, and then a scraping sound.

And it's coming over the baby monitor.

"I've changed my mind," Michelle says plaintively, standing, doubled over, in the middle of the hospital room.

Lou's hands are under her arms, supporting her as she waits out another vicious contraction.

"About getting the epidural?" he asks.

"No." She doesn't want a needle in her back. No way. Not even if it really does numb the agony of labor. "No, I changed my mind."

"About what?"

"About having another baby," she pants, sweat drenching her blue hospital gown. "I changed my mind."

Is Lou laughing?

Laughing at her?

She hates him.

Hates everyone.

"Leave me alone," she snaps, straightening, trying to walk, as the nurse suggested, saying it would speed the labor along.

Another contraction swoops in, taking her breath away, and she groans, clutching at Lou.

"Breathe with it Babe. Don't fight it."

"I can't."

"Breathe."

"I can't."

"Come on, Michelle."

"I want to go home. I want . . . Ozzie," she whimpers, needing desperately to see her beloved little boy, to know that he's all right. "He needs me."

"Ozzie's fine."

"No . . ."

"Come on, Michelle, this walking is crap. Get back into bed. I'll get the nurse. You can't take much more of this."

Lou hurries out of the room.

Rory slides a glass baking dish of brownies out of the oven, taking a deep whiff of the warm, chocolatey scent. Perfect. This is just what she had in mind.

A good, old-fashioned pig-out to take her mind off her troubles. Maybe Molly will come home soon and want to have some, too.

She remembers how she and Carleen used to bake brownies once in a while. They never came out very good, though—they were always too thin and too crisp.

Probably, Rory acknowledges, *because we ate most of the batter raw, and didn't have enough to pour into the baking dish. Carleen always hogged both of the beaters, too. She'd give me the bowl to lick, but there was never much of anything left in it by that time.*

Tonight she had gotten to lick the bowl, the spatula, and both beaters, savoring the rich, sugar-gritty chocolate batter and wishing, nonetheless, that Carleen was here to share it with her. Carleen, or Molly.

Well, she thinks now, as she carefully sets the hot brownies on top of the stove, *when Molly comes home I'll give her some. Or maybe I'll even run some next door, if she doesn't show up soon.*

That would be nice, she realizes. To pop over to the Randalls' with some brownies, just to make sure everything's all right. Molly had been so freaked out the other day when she was babysitting there.

But I won't put her on the defensive, Rory promises herself. *I won't let her know I'm checking up on her. I'll just say I thought she'd want some brownies. And that I've got nothing to do, so I thought maybe I could stay a while, and we could play cards, or something.*

Does Molly even play cards?

It astonishes her, sometimes, how little she knows about the girl who was raised as her own sister.

Carleen had played cards. She'd insisted that she and Rory play for each other's allowance. She'd won every time, of course. She'd been a major cheat.

If I play cards with Molly, it won't be for money, Rory decides. *And of course, I'd never cheat. I'll be the kind of big sister who's helpful and fun.*

She breaks off a corner from the sheet of rich, dark chocolate, pops it into her mouth, and promptly burns her tongue.

She grabs a knife then, and begins cutting the brownies into squares, even though they're still much too hot.

She's anxious, suddenly, to go next door to see her sister.

What do I do? Molly wonders frantically, leaping up from the couch, Carleen's enormous earrings jangling in her ears.

She stares at the baby monitor, now ominously silent.

Somebody—or something—is up there. In Ozzie's room.

Her first instinct is to get the hell out of here . . . just bolt for home as fast as she can.

But she can't leave little Ozzie behind.

She just can't.

Don't worry, Ozzie. I won't let anything happen to you. I promise. I'll be right there if you need me.

He's just a little kid, and he's scared, and he's counting on me. I can't leave him.

Maybe, she thinks wildly, nobody's up there. Maybe it was just Ozzie turning over in his crib. She knows from experience that the tiniest movement can sound deafening when magnified over the monitor.

But a little boy changing position on a mattress can't sound like thumping and scraping, can it?

Well, can it?

She hurries into the hallway, stops, torn between the staircase leading up into darkness, and the front door leading to safety.

Ozzie.

I can't leave him.

I'll just run up there, grab him out of his crib, and run out of here as fast as I can.

I'll run home.

Rory's there.

She'll know what to do.

Taking a deep breath, her heart pounding violently, Molly starts slowly up the stairs.

"Please, Lou, make it stop . . ." Michelle begs, her voice hoarse.

"I can't make it stop, Michelle. Isn't there something you can do?" he asks the nurse.

"Not at this point. It's too late for an epidural. She refused it when we offered it earlier, and now—"

"Well, isn't there something else? Some kind of drugs you can give her?"

Michelle sees the woman shaking her head as she places a Velcro blood pressure band around her upper arm. "It won't be long. She's almost fully dilated now."

"I need drugs," Michelle moans, feeling like an enormous fist is mercilessly squeezing her stomach. She's barely aware of the band tightening on her arm as the nurse takes her blood pressure. There's a whoosh as the pressure is released, and then the nurse is walking briskly out of the room.

"Lou," Michelle bites out, seized by yet another contraction.

They're coming in a fast and furious tide now, one excruciating wave of pain barely giving way before another washes over her. She's given up on the breathing, given up on any hope of getting through this torture without being ripped asunder by the pressure that's building relentlessly within.

"I'm sorry, babe," he says, holding her hand, stroking her fingers with his thumb. "It won't be long now."

"Ozzie . . ."

"Don't worry about him, Michelle. Not now. He's fine. We both know he's fine."

No, we both don't know that.

I don't know that, Lou.

"Owww ..." She sobs, clenched. "Make it stop, Lou."

"I can't, babe. God, I wish I could, but I can't."

In a fog of pain, she sees that there are tears in his eyes.

He loves me, she marvels, just before another contraction hits. *He really does love me.*

Rory puts the last brownie on the small Corell plate, deciding they do look better with powdered sugar sifted over them. She almost didn't bother.

Now she hunts through the drawers for a roll of plastic wrap, shoving aside loose measuring spoons and shish kebab skewers and almost cutting her fingers on the exposed blade of a butcher knife. She tells herself that she really should organize the kitchen one of these days—sort through the piles of junk in the drawers and cabinets. And what about painting, fixing up the place a little? She'd been so gung ho about it when she first arrived ... was it only a little over a week ago?

It seems like she's been here for months, so long that she's already exhausted by the prospect of redecorating the place.

And what about the people?

What about Mom and Molly?

Have I given up on them, too?

No, she tells herself firmly, finding a roll of foil and tearing off a sheet to put over the plate of brownies. *I'm going next door to see Molly, aren't I? I'm making an effort to build a relationship with her, aren't I?*

And Mom ...

Well, her mother is a different story. Her mother, while she allowed Sister Theodosia to drag her to the doctor today, has clearly lost her grip on reality—thinking Kevin was here earlier, making her a sandwich?

It's like she can't accept that people come and go, Rory muses, then amends, *No, she just can't accept that people go. Forever, like Daddy, or temporarily, like Kevin.*

Did she go around acting like I was here when I was living in Santa

Cruz, and Aspen, and Miami? Probably. She'd probably tell Kevin and Molly that I ate breakfast with her, or that I was next door playing with Emily.

Or maybe not.

Maybe her mother's descent into insanity had been much more recent.

Maybe something had triggered it.

Rory's coming home, perhaps?

Had that launched her into the past again, seeking other people who have been gone for years?

Rory tucks the foil around the bottom of the plate of brownies, picks it up, and starts for the door. She's almost there when the phone rings.

She hesitates, wondering whether to answer it.

There's no one she particularly wants to talk to. It's probably for Molly, anyway.

She continues toward the door.

Molly reaches the top of the stairs and stands absolutely still, listening.

There's not a sound but Ozzie's quiet, even breathing coming from the room a few feet away. The door is cracked, a shaft of nightlight spilling out into the dark hall.

Molly stares at it, wondering if she left it closed that much. Hadn't it been halfway open before? She could have sworn she left that cast-iron pig doorstop holding it open.

Is she losing it?

Or is someone here, prowling around the house.

Calm down.

At least Ozzie's okay.

She can tell by his breathing.

He's there, and he's okay.

All she has to do is tiptoe into the room, pick him up, and run right down the stairs and out the front door toward home.

So what if I look like an absolute fool? So what if Rory thinks I'm out of my mind? I can't help it.

I can't be alone in this house another minute.

* * *

"Hello?" Rory asks, snatching up the phone on second thought, just in case it's . . .

Who?

Barrett?

But it isn't. "Hey, Rory, is everything all right there?"

"*Kevin?*"

"How's it goin'? Can you hear me okay? I'm on a cell phone."

"Are you kidding? I can hear you just fine. Like you're right next door." She sets the brownies on the counter, leans against it, glad she came back to answer the phone. The sound of her brother's voice is reassuring.

"Good. Sorry I haven't called—it seems like every time I want to, I realize it's the wrong time there. I don't want to wake the whole house up in the middle of the night."

"Where are you?"

"Paris."

"Isn't it incredible?"

"Amazing."

"Have you gone up the Eiffel Tower?"

"Not yet," he says hurriedly. "Listen, this is going to cost me a fortune, so I'm not going to stay on long and tell you everything I've been doing. I just wanted to make sure everything is all right there. With Mom, and Molly."

"They're fine, Kev. Don't worry about them. Please. You've spent your whole life taking care of them."

And it wasn't fair, was it? For me to leave you alone with the burden. It's amazing you aren't bitter and full of resentment by now. Amazing you aren't totally screwed up, instead of being this totally great kid.

"I never minded taking care of them, Rory," he says.

"I know, but it's my turn now, Kev. You deserve to just enjoy Paris. Have a great time. And don't worry about us, because we're all fine."

"Okay, Rory, I'll try not to. Give Molly my love. Mom, too."

"I will."

Fighting the nearly overpowering instinct to turn and run, Molly approaches Ozzie's bedroom, pushes the door open gently, hearing the faint creak it makes as it swings toward the bookcase on the interior wall.

She steps inside, looks down at the sweetly sleeping face of the little boy. He's lying on his back, a stuffed Barney cradled in his arms. A rush of protectiveness sweeps over her, and she knows she could never have left him here alone.

Molly bends over, starts to slip one hand beneath his knees and the other beneath his shoulders to lift Ozzie carefully into her arms.

And then there's a sound.

The slightest sound, a mere whisper of a movement.

But in that instant, she senses with dread that she's not alone.

And she knows, even before she spins around to see the hauntingly familiar face staring at her with strange, hate-filled eyes, that she was right about somebody creeping around upstairs.

Only one coherent thought makes its way through Molly Connolly's mind before the intruder slams something into her head.

It's you. But that's impossible . . . What are you doing here?

CHAPTER
FIFTEEN

Rory knocks again, impatient, carefully balancing the plate of brownies in one hand.

There's no answer.

How can there be no answer?

She's been standing here for at least five minutes, knocking, calling Molly's name.

She knows there's someone inside. The lights are on, and she can hear the television set blaring through the screen.

An uneasy feeling has stolen over her.

What if something's happened to Molly and Ozzie?

She glances next door, at Rebecca Wasner's house, and feels sick inside. She should never have let Molly stay here alone all day and all night. The minute she came home and found that note about babysitting next door, she should have come right over and insisted on staying until the Randalls came home.

Maybe, she thinks hopefully, they've already come back from wherever they were, and Molly went out instead of coming straight home.

That would make sense, given the way she's been staying out until all hours with her friends this past week ... Except, if the Randalls were home, wouldn't they be answering Rory's knocks?

Well, maybe they came home, let Molly leave, and then took Ozzie and went somewhere, Rory thinks, grasping for any possible explanation.

And that one makes marginal sense.

Except that the television set is still on.

Wouldn't the Randalls have shut it off if they went out?

Something isn't right.

Still, Rory hesitates, uncertain what to do. If she goes home and calls the police and it turns out that there's a logical explanation for this—say, Michelle is here, but sleeping, or Molly is here, but in the bathroom or something—she's going to look like a complete idiot.

But if she goes home and does nothing, and something has happened to her sister, she will never forgive herself.

What do I do? What do I do?

Her gaze falls on the window overlooking the front porch. It's one of those old-fashioned types, with an expanding wooden screen you pop into the frame, instead of one of those built-in vinyl ones.

The same kind of screen the Connollys always had on their windows.

Once, when Carleen snuck out of the house and forgot her keys, she had climbed in a living-room window to get back in, bragging later to Rory about how easy it had been. Naturally, Rory had tattled to her father, who had been enraged that Carleen would pull what he had called "a stupid stunt. What are you trying to do, get yourself killed? If I happened to wake up and hear you crawling in a window in the middle of the night, I'd think you were a burglar, come downstairs with my baseball bat, and brain you."

Daddy never was one to mince words, Rory thinks wryly, even as she eyes the Randalls' screen, contemplating removing it and crawling through the window. If Lou Randall brains her with a baseball bat, she'll have only herself to blame.

Michelle is too far gone now to ask about Ozzie—she's fully dilated, lying on her back on the delivery table in the operating room, struggling to push the baby out.

It's not happening.

The tremendous pressure in her lower spine and rectum is becoming unbearable, and she's been trying to follow Dr. Kabir's instructions, bearing down and pushing in a desperate, futile effort to deliver the baby, whose position is just not conducive to birth. Every time she feels the potent, painful tension taking over she moans, "It's starting again," and then the nurse grabs one of her legs and Lou grabs the other, and they pull her knees up to her shoulders and they count to ten and the doctor shouts, "Push, Michelle, push. You can do it."

"I can't," she groans in despair, time and time again, as the tension subsides momentarily, only to build again. There's no relief, no end in sight to this torture.

"I can't do it, Lou," she gasps, as he puts an ice chip between her parched lips.

"How much more of this is she supposed to take?" she hears Lou bark at the doctor. "Can't you do something to help her? She can't do it."

"I *can't* do it. Oh, God . . . oh, God . . . here it comes again. Noooo . . ."

And they grab her legs, and the doctor tells her not to fight it, to push with it, and she hears savage, guttural sounds and she knows they're coming from her, and this isn't working, it isn't working, it isn't working.

"Help me," she begs the doctor, whose forced smile is beginning to show the strain of the situation.

"I am helping you, Michelle," he says soothingly, mopping his brow beneath his surgical cap.

"Here it is again . . . God, no, make it stop," she begs, besieged by another wave of torturous pressure.

"Doctor Kabir, can you please look at this?" she hears one of the nurses say.

"What? What is it?" Lou is asking, concerned.

"The baby's heart rate is dropping," Dr. Kabir announces sharply. "He's in distress."

Rory steps into the Randalls' living room, hurriedly yet carefully replacing the screen in the window, and telling herself all the while that she's really lost it. What does she think she's doing, breaking into the neighbors' house like this? They're going to have her arrested and thrown into jail.

But Molly's supposed to be here, and she might be in trouble, she rationalizes, and, realizing she's still holding the damned foil-wrapped plate of brownies, sets it aside on a nearby table.

She walks slowly across the room, glancing briefly at the television set, where *The Drew Carey Show* is in progress. Would Molly watch that show?

She has no idea.

She knows too little about her habits, what she likes to watch, what she likes to do . . .

I've got to get to know you better, kid, she thinks wistfully. *We can't let old hurts stand in our way forever. You're the only sister I've got.*

There's no sign of her.

There's a baby monitor sitting on the low table by the couch. Rory notices, with a start, that it's on. The red light is glowing. All is silent.

Is Ozzie sleeping upstairs in his crib? He must be. Why else would the monitor be on?

But where's Molly? Why isn't she here? She has to be here. She must be upstairs.

Rory moves slowly through the first floor, reluctant to go up to the second, afraid of what she'll find.

Is Molly up there . . . unconscious? Or worse?

There's no sign of anything amiss. Everything seems to be in order. On the kitchen counter is the one piece of evidence that Molly has been here recently—a message in her handwriting that reads, *Michelle, call John when you have time.*

From the kitchen, Rory goes up the back stairs to the second floor, finding them as narrow and steep as she remembers. The Anghardts had rarely used them, and it appears the Randalls don't, either. There are paint cans and tools stacked on the steps, a hazard to anyone trying to get up or down quickly.

On the second floor, Rory stands in the hallway, calls softly, "Molly?"

No reply.

She fumbles on the wall for a light switch, finds none.

Do you really want to walk along this dark hallway alone? she asks herself, hesitating, peering into the shadows, and then, *Do you have a choice?*

"Let's prep her for an emergency section," Dr. Kabir orders tersely, his soothing manner having evaporated with the announcement that the baby is in distress. There's a sudden storm of activity in the room, people bustling about, drawers opening, instruments clattering.

"What's going on?" Michelle gasps, looking from him to Lou, as the pressure on her lower torso intensifies again. "What's wrong with my baby?"

"Doctor Kabir?" Lou asks, squeezing her hand and looking at the doctor.

"We're going to have to do a cesarean section to save the baby," he says, quickly yet patiently. "I'm going to have to ask you to leave."

"Leave? I can't leave her," Lou protests.

"No, Lou, don't leave me," Michelle wails, seized by panic, knowing something is terribly wrong.

This is a nightmare, she thinks desperately. *It's got to be a nightmare, and I'm going to wake up.*

"She needs me here, Doctor."

"I'm sorry, Mr. Randall, but you'll have to step out. The nurse will come and get you as soon as possible."

"But—"

"Please, Mr. Randall. This is an emergency," Dr. Kabir says firmly.

Lou looks down at Michelle.

"Lou," she whispers, exhausted, wracked with pain, yet suddenly able to think with more clarity than in the last several hours. "Call to check on Ozzie."

"Michelle, don't—"

"Please, Lou."

"All right, I will," he promises, his face grim, as he turns and allows himself to be hustled out of the room.

"Molly?" Rory calls softly as she arrives in front of the last room, the one at the head of the stairs, the one that once belonged to Emily.

This is the little boy's bedroom, she knows. The door is closed. She reaches for the knob, turns it tentatively, wondering if he's there, asleep in his crib.

And if so, then where is Molly?

Has she vanished, just as Rebecca Wasner did on Saturday night?

Oh, God, please, no.

Rory opens the door with a quiet click, sees the glow of the Barney nightlight illuminating the small room. Her gaze flits over the window seat, the built-in bookcase, the crib.

The crib.

It's empty.

"All right now, Michelle," says the anesthesiologist, a pretty, efficient Asian woman with ice-cold hands. "I'm going to place this mask over your face, and you're going to start at ten and begin counting backward."

"And I'm going to ... be ... knocked out?" she asks, the sentence too long and exhausting, the pain too intense.

"You'll be unconscious for the surgery, yes," the woman says, amidst the flurry of preparations still taking place around them. "It won't take long. When you wake up, your baby will be here."

Yes, Michelle thinks, *my baby will be here.*

She feels the mask come down over her mouth and nose.

"All right, Michelle, let's start counting."

Ten ...

Nine ...

Eight ...

Ozzie! she thinks groggily, just before blackness claims her.

Lou feeds a quarter into the pay telephone in the small waiting room next to the delivery room, his hands trembling so violently that he can barely push the buttons to dial the phone.

All he can think is that his wife is about to go under the knife, and his baby is in trouble, and there must have been something he could have done, something along the way, to have changed the course of events leading up to this moment. He's utterly overpowered by guilt.

Guilt over the way he's treated Michelle lately, and the long hours he's been working. Sure, he was recently promoted, and of course the job is challenging. But mostly, he's been using the office as an escape from ...

Well, from home.

From his pregnant, moody wife and his rambunctious son and

the knowledge that they both need him, they need and depend on him so desperately.

And now there will be another baby, another person who will depend on him, and Lou is terrified that something's going to happen—that he's going to let them down, somehow, the way his father and his stepfathers let him and his mother down.

"I won't," he whispers, and turns, belatedly, to make sure he's alone in the waiting room. Yes, he's the only one here, the only one whose family's hanging in the balance, whose wife is even now risking her life to deliver their child.

You're being too dramatic. It'll be okay, he tells himself as the phone rings on the other end. *Women have C-sections all the time.*

But the baby is in distress.

He'd seen it himself, on the fetal monitor—the heart rate falling, the expressions of concern on the faces of the doctor and the nurses, the sudden rush to save his child's life.

He swallows hard, listening to the phone ring again, telling himself that he can't fall apart here, in the waiting room.

He never falls apart, period.

It's not allowed.

When he was growing up, Iris told him once, when she found him sobbing into his pillow because of a black eye he'd gotten on the playground, that boys don't cry. "Be strong, Louie," his mother had said. "Nobody wants a man who isn't strong. I know I sure don't. I've had my share of that."

So here he is. Strong. In control.

Wondering why the phone at his house is ringing again.

And now, again.

Where's Molly? he wonders, stricken by an added burst of panic. *And Ozzie? Where's my son?*

This can't be happening, he thinks, hanging up the phone and pacing across the room. *The whole time Michelle was freaking out over leaving Ozzie and Molly alone there tonight, I was positive she was just her usual paranoid, hormonal self. But now . . .*

What if she was right? What if some crazed kidnapper has my kid?

He has to get a grip. This is insane. There's got to be some logical explanation for Molly not answering the phone. After all, there was a perfectly good reason she didn't hear it the other day, when she and Ozzie were playing outside while he was trying to call.

But it's dark out. They can't be playing outside.

Okay, so maybe she's got Ozzie in the tub and can't get to the phone. Or maybe she chickened out about staying alone after what happened to her friend, and she brought him next door to her mother's house.

Yeah, that's probably it.

He can't go running home now. Not with Michelle in surgery. One thing at a time, he thinks shakily, sitting on the edge of a vinyl-upholstered couch and staring absently at the muted television set mounted on the wall, where *The Drew Carey Show* is just ending.

"Lake Charlotte Police."

"Hello. I need to report a missing person," Rory pants into the receiver, breathless from running down the stairs, out the Randalls' front door, and all the way home. "I mean, *two* missing persons."

"One moment . . ."

A click, a pause, another click.

"Ma'am?" a new voice says promptly. "Can I help you?"

"My sister is missing," she says, hearing her voice come out high and plaintive. "And the little boy she was babysitting, too."

"Are you sure?"

"I'm positive. I was just there. They were gone."

"Where are you now?"

"I'm home. I didn't want to stay there another second," she confesses, nausea reeling through her, along with disbelief. "I was afraid."

"Ma'am, please stay calm . . . where is 'home'?"

"Fifty-two Hayes Street."

"*Hayes Street?* And your name?"

"Rory Connolly."

"*Connolly?*" comes the predictable echo.

She can read the officer's thoughts. *Hayes Street . . . isn't that the street where Rebecca Wasner lived? Connolly . . . isn't that the same last name of one of those girls who disappeared from Lake Charlotte ten years ago?*

"All right, ma'am, please stay calm and stay right there. We're on our way."

She hangs up slowly and sinks into a chair, paralyzed with horror that this is happening again.

"Oh, Mama," she whimpers, feeling once again like a helpless, frightened little girl, needing her mommy. "Mama . . ."

"Rory?"

She looks up to see Maura in the doorway, her face ashen.

"Oh, God, Mom."

"Rory, what's going on? Is Molly—?"

"She's vanished, Mom," Rory wails, tears streaming down her face. "She's gone . . . just like Carleen."

CHAPTER
SIXTEEN

When he comes out of the shower on Thursday morning, he turns on the television set in his bedroom and flips to the *Today Show*, as he always does.

He likes Katie Couric, with her upturned nose and that Irish pixie look. His wife had looked a lot like Katie.

But he doesn't want to go there.

No, he doesn't want to start the day by dwelling on his miserable past once again. He has vowed, for Kelly's sake, to stop dwelling on it. What's done is done.

He pulls a plain white T-shirt over his head and hunts through his closet for a shirt to wear.

The show comes back from a margarine commercial. He glances over his shoulder at the screen and sees that Katie Couric's face is grim.

"This morning, police in Lake Charlotte, New York, a small town located north of Albany, in the Adirondack foothills, are looking into the mysterious disappearance of a teenaged babysitter and the small boy in her care. Molly Connolly, who vanished last evening from a quiet, residential neighborhood, is the second teenager to disappear this week from this tiny, peaceful town. We go now to NBC News correspondent Bryan Taylor in Lake Charlotte."

Molly . . .

It can't be.

He clutches the knob of the closet door, staring at the screen, hearing the reporter's voice, but not his words.

Molly's missing. She's missing. She's in trouble.

He knows what he has to do.

It's time to stop running from the past, time to face his responsibility—the one he selfishly turned his back on, walked away from. Face it head-on, no matter what the consequences.

I have to go there.

Now.

Back to Lake Charlotte.

"Katie, this peaceful town is the last place you'd ever expect to encounter something so sinister," says the reporter, standing on what looks like Main Street, USA, with a row of charming shops, flowering plants hanging from old-fashioned lampposts, a picturesque lake in the background. He's holding an umbrella; rain is pouring down, the sky and water melding in a foggy gray backdrop behind him.

Lydia McGovern sits in a doily-draped wingback chair in her living room, sipping her lukewarm tea, intent on the television screen. Only moments ago, she had set aside the tea and put her glasses back into the case in a nearby desk drawer, ready to find her raincoat and head out to St. Malachy's. But something the *Today Show* host had said captured her attention, made her stay and listen.

Lake Charlotte—that's where David Anchardt's family had lived when his sister Emily vanished.

And Katie Couric said the latest missing girl is named Molly Connolly. Can she possibly be any relation to Rory Connolly?

"But last night," the reporter goes on, "thirteen-year-old Molly Connolly mysteriously vanished from the house where she was babysitting, along with two-year-old Ozzie Randall, a child whose parents were at the local hospital, where his mother was giving birth to her second child. Just this past weekend, on Saturday night, Molly's closest friend, Rebecca Wasner, also thirteen, similarly vanished from the house directly next door to the Randalls'. Both girls are being described as responsible, wholesome teenagers, and foul play is suspected. Earlier I spoke to Betty Shilling, who runs a bed and breakfast on Hayes Street, where Molly Connolly, Rebecca Wasner, and Ozzie Randall live."

The scene switches to show a taped interview clip with a ruddy-faced woman standing on the porch of a large Victorian-style home. "I know both Molly and Rebecca very well," Betty Shilling comments, shaking her head sadly. "They're both fine young people, not the kind of girls who would run off without telling anybody where they were going." She adds darkly, "I just know somebody kidnapped them, just like what happened with Molly's sister years ago."

The reporter is back, saying somberly, "Molly Connolly's sister, Carleen Connolly, who was seventeen at the time, also vanished ten years ago this summer, along with three other young Lake Charlotte girls, Kristin Stafford, thirteen, Allison Myers, fifteen, and Emily Anghardt, thirteen."

Lydia leans forward as the scene of the reporter standing on the street is replaced by a close-up showing four photographs of pretty teenagers.

As she stares at the girls' faces, Lydia McGovern gasps in shock.

The bone-china teacup slips from her trembling hand, splashing tea on her ankles as it shatters on the parquet floor.

Michelle gradually becomes aware of the faint, fuzzy sound of voices.

Hushed voices, floating someplace above her head, she thinks vaguely as she fights her way from under the thick, gauzy shroud that doesn't seem to want to release her.

"No, she doesn't know yet, but I'm going to have to tell her as soon as she wakes up."

That was Lou's voice, she realizes groggily.

What is he talking about?

Who doesn't know what?

Confused, she tries to get her bearings. She feels battered, raw . . . her stomach is sore, so very sore.

What happened?

The baby!

Reality comes rushing back to her, and she fights to open her eyes.

"Lou!" she calls, letting her lids flutter closed again against the bright light in the room. She must be in the hospital.

Lou's still talking in that whisper, ignoring her.

She realizes her attempt to get his attention must not have been audible. She's so tired . . . so tired.

"Lou!" she calls again, and this time she hears herself, her voice a rasping croak.

"Michelle?"

She opens her eyes and sees him standing above her, his face drawn, deep trenches under his red-rimmed eyes.

Has Lou been *crying?*

"Lou . . . the baby . . ."

"It's okay, Michelle, take it easy. The baby's in the ICU nursery—"

"What's wrong with him?"

"*Her*, Michelle. It was a girl."

"A girl?" Dazed, she tries to grasp that astonishing news. "But . . ."

"I know. The ultrasound was wrong. Doctor Kabir said that happens sometimes. He said the technicians shouldn't venture a guess about the baby's sex unless they're pretty positive."

"A daughter," Michelle says, stunned.

"And she's going to be okay. They're keeping a close eye on her, but she's already doing much better than she was last night."

"Last night? It's morning?"

Lou nods.

"The baby's okay?" she says again, just to be sure.

"The baby's going to be fine."

She gropes her clouded mind, aware that there's still something . . .

No, she doesn't know yet, but I'm going to have to tell her as soon as she wakes up.

What had Lou been talking about?

Another face appears beside her husband's. An unfamiliar one, belonging to a nurse.

"Hello, Mrs. Randall, I'm Patty, and I just came on the morning shift. I'll be taking care of you. How are you feeling?"

"Hurts," she manages, trying to shift her weight in the bed.

"I'll get you some more pain medicine. You've been through quite an ordeal. We've had you pretty doped up. You're going to feel kind of out of it for a while."

"Lou," Michelle says, uneasy, ignoring the nurse, "Where's Ozzie?"

And then she knows, from the look in her husband's eyes, that something is wrong.

Terribly wrong.

Rory offers her mother a steaming mug of tea. "Here, Mom, try to drink some of this."

There's no reply. Maura just sits there at the kitchen table, staring off into space, as she has been since last night, when Rory told her the crushing news.

Rory sets the mug in front of her, slides the sugar bowl toward it, and walks back to the sink. She busies herself putting away the dishes in the draining rack, dishes that have been sitting here all night. The bowl she'd mixed the brownies in, the beaters she'd licked, the spatula . . .

It seems like so long ago that she was standing at the counter, baking brownies, thinking of bringing some next door to Molly.

Why had she waited so long?

Why had she bothered to stop and wash all the dishes before putting the brownies on the plate?

Why hadn't she just let the phone ring when Kevin called?

He would have called back. For all she knows, those few minutes she'd spent talking to her brother could have been the crucial moments when Molly and Ozzie were being kidnapped right out from under her nose.

Why, though, hadn't she seen or heard anything?

The windows were open.

People were around, too, on the street.

The police told her that there had been two newspaper reporters sitting in a car right out at the curb between the Randalls' house and the Wasners' house until about nine o'clock, staking it out in case one of Rebecca's parents emerged and would agree to talk to them. They'd been avoiding the press.

Even after the reporters gave up for the night and drove away, several neighbors had told the police that they were walking their dogs, or roller-blading by, and no one had seen anything suspicious.

Of course, the intruder could have come through the back-yard—could have been hiding in the woods along the back of the property, could have stolen in one of the back windows after dark, just yards away from this very kitchen window where Rory was washing her supper dishes and baking utensils.

She glances out the window now. Rain is streaming down the pane, pattering against the wooden steps outside. The storm had blown in around midnight, right around the time that Detective Mullen had reluctantly left for the hospital, to find Lou Randall in the ICU nursery and tell him that his little boy was missing.

Rory doesn't want to think about what that must have been like.

She had talked to Lou later, when he called sometime around three in the morning. His voice had sounded flat but controlled, and he had told her tersely that the baby was all right, but Michelle was still unconscious, and he was going to stay there with her, at the hospital, until she woke up.

"I've already had reporters trying to get up here to talk to me," he said, sounding disgusted. "The hospital has tightened security. But I don't want somebody else getting through, telling Michelle what happened before I get a chance to. She needs to hear it from me."

And Rory had said, her heart wrenching for those poor people, "If there's anything I can do—"

"No," he'd cut her off, not unkindly, "there's nothing. I just thought I should call you, because . . . I don't know why I called."

"I'm glad you did," Rory had told him quickly, feeling some kind of tragic bond with the neighbor she'd never even met.

Reporters had been sniffing around here, too—even daring to ring the doorbell in the middle of the night. Detective Mullen, who had returned by then, had answered it, and sent them packing. But earlier, Rory saw camera crews out on the street, gathered along the sidewalk in front of all three houses—the Connollys', the Randalls', and the Wasners'. The police had made them leave, though—had blocked off both ends of Hayes Street so that only residents could come and go.

Rory turns away from the sink, knowing she should face the phone calls she has to make. She needs to try to find Kevin in Paris, though she has no idea where to start. And she should really call Sister Theodosia, too.

The house has quieted now, everyone but Detective Mullen having left when a call came in that there'd been a bad accident on the Northway just outside of town—a tractor-trailer and several cars.

Earlier, it had seemed like cops were everywhere, even in Molly's room, going through her things, ostensibly looking for some clue that might identify the person who had abducted her and Ozzie.

Detective Mullen had asked Rory repeatedly whether there's anyone, anyone at all, who would be a likely suspect.

Barrett Maitland.

She hadn't said it at first. No, because when it came right down to it, she couldn't believe that he could be guilty of anything more than snooping into the painful past, and only because of the book he was researching.

But finally, grimly, she had spoken his name to the detective, who scribbled it down, and immediately made some phone calls, launching an investigation into Barrett Maitland.

If he isn't behind this, then who can it be?

It has to be a stranger—some psycho stranger who preys on young girls. And Ozzie—well, he had simply been taken because he was there, with Molly.

Poor Lou and Michelle Randall.

Poor Mom, Rory adds, turning to look at her mother, still sitting, vacant-eyed, at the table. She doesn't even look up when the phone rings.

Rory lets Detective Mullen answer it, as he's been doing all morning. He's wearing his coat, apparently getting ready to head out to the accident scene, as he'd mentioned. The tiny Lake Charlotte police force is apparently feeling the strain today, the few officers doing their best to be everywhere at once.

A moment later, the detective is handing her the phone, saying, "Rory, it's for you. Somebody named Lydia McGovern. She said she needs to talk to you right away."

Molly blinks into the complete darkness, hearing Ozzie crying someplace nearby, calling his mommy in a plaintive tone.

"Shh, Ozzie, it's okay," she calls softly to him.

He continues to cry, his sobs desolate.

Molly wants to cry, too. But she doesn't dare. If she does, she'll just lose it. And she has to stay in control. Something tells her that her only chance of making it out of here alive is to keep her wits about her.

She doesn't even know where *here* is.

All she knows is that she blacked out in Ozzie's bedroom, and when she came to, she was in this pitch black, musty-smelling place, her arms stretched up over her head, with hard metal bands around her wrists that are attached to a cold, clammy wall behind her. There are bands around her ankles, too, and heavy chains clink every time she tries to move her legs.

It's some kind of dank, damp cell or dungeon, and she and Ozzie are trapped here. She can't see him, but she knows he's nearby, someplace on the floor. His sobs are pitiful; it was better before, when she'd first awakened and he was silent, apparently asleep, and she thought she was alone here in the dark.

Now, in addition to Ozzie's cries, her ears pick up another sound. Not far from her head.

A clanking sound, like a chain scraping against rock, and then a low moan.

Somebody else is here with them.

"Who's there?" Molly asks, trembling.

"Molly?" The voice is barely more than a hoarse whisper, yet it's chillingly familiar.

"Oh, my God," Molly breathes, incredulous, relieved. "Rebecca?"

"Barrett?"

"Jack! Thank God. I thought you'd never get here." Barrett stands and moves quickly across the tiny cell, clutching the iron bars, grateful at the sight of his father's old friend and their family attorney, looking crisp and official in his black Armani suit. "They wouldn't let me call you until last night, and I was praying you'd get the message."

"I didn't get home until after midnight. I flew out first thing this morning. I almost didn't make it out of JFK—there were all kinds of delays because of the storm up there. Barrett, what the hell is going on?"

"Jack, I swear I'm innocent."

"You're being held on suspicion of murder, Barrett."

"I swear I didn't do it."

"What are you doing down here in the first place? And who is this guy, Russell Anghardt?"

"I'm researching a book. I got tangled up in this murder case somehow. I came down here looking for the Anghardt guy to interview him as part of my research. I had no idea he was dead. And apparently, the body had been there for a while—it happened at least a week ago. I wasn't even here then, and I can prove it. I was in Lake Charlotte—"

"Lake Charlotte, New York?" the lawyer echoes thoughtfully. "Listen, Barrett, let me have them get you out of here and into a meeting room where we can sit down and talk about this from the beginning."

"Ms. McGovern?" Rory asks, after taking the receiver from Detective Mullen, who mouths *I'll be back* and waves at her before striding purposefully out the back door.

"Hello, Rory. I've been watching television. That girl who vanished up there in Lake Charlotte—is she . . .?"

"My sister. Molly."

"Oh, Rory, I'm so sorry . . . how dreadful. Are you all right?"

"I'm hanging in there," Rory says, feeling vaguely impatient. It's nice of the woman to call, yet there's nothing anyone can do or say to make things easier right now.

She glances at her mother, who has risen from the table and is walking, zombie-like, into the front hall.

"I'm so sorry to bother you at a time like this," Lydia McGovern goes on, as though she's read Rory's mind.

And Rory realizes the woman isn't just calling to offer her sympathy or prayers because Molly is missing.

"What is it, Ms. McGovern?"

Maura's footsteps creak slowly up the front stairs to the second floor.

"I just . . . I thought I should tell someone. But maybe I shouldn't be bothering you with this right now. It just seemed so strange—"

"What, Ms. McGovern? What do you have to tell me?" Rory asks, clutching the phone, sensing that the woman is distressed.

"I was watching television—the *Today Show.* And they showed photographs of the girls who disappeared from Lake Charlotte ten years ago. There was one picture—"

"Which one?"

"I don't know which girl it was. I couldn't read the names beneath them without my glasses. But the face—even though it was blurry, I recognized that face. Rory, I'm absolutely certain it was Sister Mary Frances, that nun who has been visiting David Anghardt."

The bookcase swings closed again with a quiet click, shutting out the gray light spilling through the rain-splattered windows of the baby's room.

It was dangerous to sneak down to the kitchen for something to eat. But when a person is getting weak from hunger, what choice is there?

Besides, the house is obviously empty. The police left hours ago. And it had only taken seconds to dash down the back stairs, grab some bananas from the basket on the counter, and back up again. Which was supposed to be the whole point of the mission last night, before everything fell apart.

The voices are back, arguing with each other, deafening.

It was a mistake to think you could sneak out of here with her right down there in the living room. What's wrong with you?

I was starving. And I was planning to be so quiet, and I was going to go down the back stairs. How was I supposed to think of everything? I forgot that damned baby monitor would be broadcasting every move I made.

Well, you've really done it now. The only smart thing you did was grab that doorstop and slam it over her head when she turned around and saw you. Did you see the look in her eyes? She knew it was you. She was horrified.

And so were you, when you saw who she was.

So now there's two of them, shackled in that horrible little room, almost like before. And that little kid whining nonstop for his mother. If he doesn't shut up, you know what you're going to have to do.

This is all Rory's fault. That much is obvious. If she had been there for me when she should have, none of this would have happened. I tried to tell her. I didn't come right out and say it, of course, but I couldn't. I just couldn't. You'd think she would have been smart enough to realize, though.

But no. Miss Selfish thinks only of one person. Herself.

Never mind that now. What you need to do is get the hell out of here; leave this house and get out of town before somebody sees you.

But how?

It won't be safe to sneak out of here until late. After dark. And even then, how do you know Rory won't come prowling around here again?

Maybe the best thing to do will be to get rid of Rory, once and for all. That's what she deserves, after the way she failed you.

To die a slow, horrible death.

"Russell Anghardt was brutally beaten with a blunt instrument," Jack Berkman tells Barrett. "So brutally that his body was unrecognizable."

"Are they even sure it's him?"

"Pretty sure. The tests aren't completed yet for a positive ID, but no one else lived in that house, and he hasn't been heard from since he stopped at the local market to buy milk and some lottery tickets about ten days ago."

"Jack, like I've been telling you, ten days ago, I was in Lake Charlotte—"

"And the Grayson Cove police are checking out your alibi as we speak, Barrett. But I've got to warn you, this could get complicated anyway."

"I know. Now that two girls have disappeared there again, and I just happened to be in town this summer—"

"Again."

"Again," Barrett echoes, looking his lawyer in the eye. "But I swear, Jack, it was just like I said. A coincidence. Last time, and this time."

The lawyer eyes him intently. "And you're sure nobody knows about you and Carleen Connolly?"

"I'm positive. She told me she hadn't told anyone about us."

"You're sure? You don't think a seventeen year-old girl would go bragging to her friends about sleeping with a rich guy, a college graduate spending the summer at his parents' estate?"

"I'm positive she wouldn't have done that. For one thing, she didn't have girlfriends—not the way most teenagers seem to. She was more of a loner. And she went out with a lot of older guys. Maybe not rich, but the money didn't mean much to her. It was more a power trip thing with her. She liked the excitement. And she was a classic rebel. Snuck around behind her parents' backs. Her father, mostly—she was always talking about how strict he was, how he would kill me if he ever found us together."

"Nice," Jack comments, steepling his fingers.

"The only one who might have ever seen us together would be her younger sister, Molly. She was there once, on the playground, when I went to talk to Carleen. But she was so little, I doubt she'd remember . . ." He thinks about what Molly Connolly had said on the phone the other day, though. She had asked him if she knew him, saying he sounded familiar.

"And now Molly's missing," Jack reminds him. "What if she did remember? What if she had told someone that she thought she knew you from someplace? They're going to try to link you to her disappearance."

"I know, I've been thinking about that ever since you told me what had happened to her. But look, Jack, I'm obviously innocent. I wasn't even in town last night when Molly disappeared. I was sitting here under lock and key in this godforsaken North Carolina jail cell. Somebody else is behind this, probably the same person who kidnapped Carleen and the others ten years ago."

"Possibly. But I wish you had stayed out of it, Barrett. If anyone recognizes you from hanging around town that summer—"

"I didn't hang around town much. You know where my parents' place is, way the hell up in the foothills, totally out of the way. I was working on a mystery novel that summer, my first one. It sucked," he adds ruefully, wrinkling his nose at the memory. "The only time I ever really came to town that summer was to meet Carleen, and that was always after dark. She'd sneak down through the woods in her backyard to the road by the lake, and I'd pick her up there, and we'd go back up to my parents' place. That was the summer they were in Europe; there was no one around except me."

"And you left immediately when you heard what had happened to Carleen?"

"Exactly."

"Why?"

"Because I was afraid. I'd been sneaking around with this girl, and she was underage, and it was like a witch-hunt around there

at that point—people just going nuts, suspicious of everyone.
And ...."

"And?"

"Because the night she vanished, she was supposed to meet
me. I was waiting in my car on Lakeshore Road. She never showed
up. So I finally went home. I couldn't call her. And the next
morning, I heard on the radio that she was missing. So I left."

"Jesus, Barrett. Do you think she had told anyone she was
meeting you that night?"

"I told you, I'm pretty positive she didn't."

Jack sighs. "What did you do when you left Lake Charlotte?"

"I went straight to New York to stay with my brother, found
a job in publishing right afterward, and that was that. My parents
sold their place that fall and bought the villa in Tuscany, and that
was the last time I ever set foot in the Adirondacks."

"Until this summer."

"Until this summer," Barrett repeats, nodding.

"Why did you decide to write this particular book?"

"Guilt, like I said." He shrugs. "I guess I never forgave myself
for running away like a coward that summer. Hell, or for sneaking
around with Carleen, when I knew she was young and screwed
up. I should have known better than to get involved with her,
and when she disappeared, I shouldn't have run scared, thinking
that somebody was going to think I did it."

"That very well could have happened, Barrett," Jack says with
a shrug. "I can see why you'd want to get out of there. You were
just a kid. But to go back to Lake Charlotte now, when it's been
behind you for ten years ...."

"I don't know why I did it, exactly, Jack. When I proposed the
book to my agent, it was just, you know, an idea that had been
eating away at me for a while. And my agent happened to mention
it to my editor, and the next thing I knew, they wanted to see a
proposal, and wham! I had a book deal."

"You could have said no. God knows you don't need the
money," Jack says. He, of all people, is well versed in the Maitland
family's financial status. The bottom line, of course, is that Barrett
will never have to worry about money, thanks to the trust fund
courtesy of his great-great-grandfather's vast New England bank-
ing fortune.

"You're right, Jack. I could have said no to the deal," Barrett agrees. "But I guess, in a way, it's like I told Rory—that I was hoping to find something in my research, some clue that would point to the person who abducted all those girls. And even if I don't solve the mystery, I feel like writing this book is a way of doing something, somehow, for Carleen. In her memory. Because I really think she's dead, Jack. I really do. And I wish to God that I could find out what the hell happened to her."

Tears stream down Michelle's cheeks as she stares at the miniature red face of her newborn daughter in Lou's arms. He stands next to the bed, handling her with utmost gentle care now that she's been released from the ICU nursery.

"Can I hold her?" Michelle asks, looking from her husband to the nurse, Patty.

"It would be difficult with your incision," the woman says hesitantly.

"Please." Michelle desperately needs to hold that tiny bundle close.

"All right," the nurse says, coming closer to the bed and pressing a button to raise the mattress, bringing Michelle's head and shoulders a bit more upright. "Put her up near Michelle's shoulders," she instructs Lou. "Careful not to touch anywhere near her stomach."

Lou obeys, gingerly laying the blanket-wrapped bundle across Michelle's chest just below her neck. He stands there, holding the baby steady, and her daughter's eyes blink, staring into Michelle's from mere inches away. They're puffy from the drops placed in them after birth, and the slate-blue color Ozzie's were for months after he was born.

Michelle sobs, thinking of her son, and clings to this child she battled to bring into the world, trying somehow to draw strength from her very existence, needing to believe that another miracle— *just one more miracle, please, God*—is possible.

Rory drums her fingertips on the kitchen table, still clutching the telephone receiver.

Lydia McGovern's words ring in her ears, chilling her to the bone.

Sister Mary Frances, David Anghardt's mysterious visitor, is actually one of the girls who disappeared?

Which girl is it; which girl is still alive?

Which girl has become a nun, and is visiting St. Malachy's?

"It has to be Emily," Rory murmurs aloud, pacing across the kitchen floor. That's the only thing that makes the slightest bit of sense. She had barely known Kristin Stafford and Allison Myers, but she dismisses the notion that one of them would have any connection to David Anghardt. Carleen, either.

But Emily—*she* would need to keep visiting her twin brother, bringing him little gifts: chocolate-covered raisins, and the quilt and paintings for his room.

But why would Emily have become a nun? And why wouldn't she tell anyone at the home who she was? Surely someone would have recognized her—

Rory suddenly remembers something else Lydia McGovern had said. That the entire staff had been replaced not long after Emily vanished, and that the former director of the home, Sister Margaret, had been suffering from glaucoma and eventually went blind. It stood to reason that her eyesight would have been failing long before her retirement. So she probably wouldn't have been able to recognize Emily even if Emily came face-to-face with her, if Emily didn't tell her who she was. Only David would have known that the nun was his sister.

But again, why, if Emily's still alive, would she have faked her disappearance?

What possible reason could she have had to vanish, abandoning her poor widowed father, whom she loved so much?

It doesn't make sense.

But then, Rory obviously hadn't known her best friend as well as she'd thought. Emily hadn't trusted her enough to tell her about David, or about the shoplifting arrest—

Rory stops pacing and frowns.

Emily had been caught shoplifting a ring.

Rory had already concluded that she must have shoplifted most or all of the things she had claimed her father had given her. What she couldn't figure out was why.

Now she wonders, not for the first time, if Emily was desperate to convince herself that her father loved her ... because maybe he didn't. Maybe he blamed Emily for his wife's death. After all, Emily's mother had died giving birth to her and David.

It makes perfect sense, Rory realizes.

Maybe that was why Mr. Anghardt had shut David away in that home, and why he was always so gruff and distant with Emily.

Maybe he resented his own children's very existence.

And maybe Emily took advantage of what was happening in Lake Charlotte that summer, with the missing girls. Maybe she simply faked her disappearance and ran away to some convent.

Hadn't she suggested to Rory that Carleen might have done that very thing? Not the convent part, of course, but Rory clearly remembers Emily saying that Carleen must have run away, trying to reassure her that Carleen was alive, and that she'd turn up again someplace, someday.

Only Carleen never did.

But . . .

What if the person visiting David Anghardt at St. Malachy's isn't Emily, but Carleen? It seems unlikely, but . . .

There's always a chance.

Rory feels a twinge of exhilaration at the prospect that her sister might still be alive. It's quickly replaced by doubt.

It doesn't make sense that Carleen would be out there somewhere, dressing up as a nun and visiting David Anghardt in Poughkeepsie. As far as Rory knows, Carleen hadn't been aware of his existence, either.

No, it has to be Emily.

But even if Emily faked her disappearance and is still alive, where is Carleen?

Where are the others? This strange discovery about Emily doesn't explain what happened to the rest of them.

Or to Molly, Rory thinks desolately, swallowing hard over the lump in her throat.

I've got to find Emily Anghardt, if she's still alive. I've got to find out where her church is. Lydia McGovern said it was someplace near Albany.

Then, suddenly, it occurs to her that Emily might not actually be a nun. That the habit might be a disguise.

But why?

A disguise would make sense if she didn't want anyone to know she was still alive, but a *nun*? Sister Mary Frances.

"Sister, sister . . ."

David Anghardt's urgent cries echo in Rory's ears, and she's sure she gets why Emily would choose to disguise herself as a nun. Because she knew David would recognize her anyway, and if she didn't want anyone else to know who she really was, it would be okay if he called her Sister. Nobody would suspect that she was really Emily, his lost sister.

So, most likely, she isn't really Sister Mary Frances living near Albany.

Where are you, Emily?

And why did you run away?

Rory realizes it doesn't matter. Not now. When this is all over, and Molly is home where she belongs, maybe she'll look for Emily, and find out what happened.

But right now, she has to concentrate on finding Molly.

What if it's already too late? she wonders, staring out the window at the rain pouring down.

Finally, he's made it, after hours stuck in traffic—first on the clogged Mass Pike leading west out of Boston, then on the Northway, where a horrendous accident had closed the road just short of the exit for his destination.

Now he's here, driving through the downpour battering the town of Lake Charlotte, following the familiar route to Hayes Street.

Along the way he passes several familiar landmarks—the big stone library, the brick post office with white-paned windows, Talucci's Pizza Parlor. Amazing how some things look exactly the same.

But not everything. There's a new, trendy-looking cafe where the Rainbow Palace used to be, and McShane's Hardware has closed down, along with the old A&P supermarket on Front Street. And the entire town seems to have had a facelift—there are quaint, hand-painted shingles hanging from brackets above some shops, and hanging flowers dangling from the lampposts, and far fewer potholes than he remembers.

It's comforting, in a way, to see that the little town he'd once called home has lived up to the potential he always sensed. And yet the changes leave him with a hollow feeling—the knowledge that if he hadn't been forced to flee years ago, he might have enjoyed spending the rest of his life right here in this picturesque town after all.

You weren't forced to flee, he reminds himself. *You made your choices. You knew the risks. And you paid the price.*

He slows the car on the wet brick pavement, approaching the corner of Hayes Street.

"What the . . . ?"

There's a roadblock, and a cop in a bright orange raincoat is standing beside it, talking to people in a white van marked *Eyewitness News.*

He pulls to a stop and watches as the van turns around and drives away.

The cop spots his car, and glances at the Massachusetts plates. He walks over to the window.

He rolls it down and tries to sound casual as he says, "Good morning, Officer."

"Can I help you, sir?"

"Yes, I have to get down Hayes Street."

"You don't live there."

"No," he admits. "But I need to visit someone."

The officer looks dubious. "They expecting you?"

"No."

"Which house?"

"Number 52."

The officer raises his brows. "The Connolly place? You know—"

"That Molly Connolly is missing. Yes. I know."

"You're a reporter, right?"

"No."

"Oh, come on."

"I'm not. Really."

"Yeah?" the officer smirks. "But you urgently need to get over there, right?"

"Exactly."

"Mind if I ask why? I'm assuming you're not selling Mary Kay cosmetics." He laughs at his own joke.

"No, I'm not." He forces a chuckle, then hesitates.

"Well?" The cop is waiting, an expectant look on his face. "Why are you going to the Connollys' place this morning?"

Here goes.

He takes a deep breath, looks the officer in the eye, and says, "Because I'm Molly's father."

CHAPTER
SEVENTEEN

The phone rings as Rory is sitting on her mother's bed, watching Maura just lying there, staring at the ceiling. She hasn't spoken a word all day. It's frightening.

"I have to go down and answer that, Mom," Rory says, getting up and hurrying to the door. "But I'll be right back."

No reply.

Rory tells herself that after she takes this phone call, she'll have to get in touch with Dr. Desiderio. She doesn't want to bring Mom to his office—she can't take the chance of leaving home in case the police need to get in touch with her. But maybe the doctor will make a house call under the circumstances.

She dashes down the steps and into the kitchen, wondering if it's Detective Mullen. He had called a while ago, back at police headquarters from the accident scene. He'd asked Rory more questions about Barrett Maitland, and said he'd be in touch again shortly.

Or it could be Sister Theodosia, Rory figures, reaching for the phone. She'd left a message for her at the rectory in Buffalo.

She hadn't had any luck in tracking Kevin down. She'd realized belatedly that she should have asked him for a number where he could be reached when he'd called last night. She just hadn't thought of it at the time And even if she had, she might have decided against it. She had been so adamant that Kevin deserved to cut the ties that for so many years had bound him to home in a stranglehold. She had wanted him to get away for once, carefree, the way she had done when she was his age.

Maybe it's better he doesn't know what's going on with Molly, she tells herself now. *He'd want to come rushing home. And maybe he won't have to. Maybe she'll turn up, safe and sound. In fact, maybe this was all just some crazy misunderstanding, and maybe this is her calling now.*

She snatches up the telephone receiver and says, "Hello?" even as she realizes that it can't possibly be Molly, that it isn't just a misunderstanding, that this is real.

Molly is missing, and Rory has to face the truth: Molly, like Carleen, is most likely gone forever.

"Rory?"

She freezes, clutching the phone against her ear.

That's Molly's voice.

On the phone.

It's Molly.

It's Molly.

She's alive.

"Oh, my God," Rory breaks down, sobbing. "Where are you, Molly? Are you okay?"

"I need you, Rory. Please, please come." Her sister's voice is trembling, high-pitched and unnatural. She sounds out of her mind with fear.

"Where are you, Molly? Where are you?" Rory is frantic.

There's a pause. "You can't tell anyone. Don't get the police, Rory. You can't bring the police. You have to sneak in."

"I won't, I swear. The police are gone. There's no one here but me, Molly." *And Mom, but she's catatonic.* "Hurry, tell me—*where are you?*"

"I'm next door," her sister says in a strangled whisper. "At the Randalls'."

"What?"

"I'm being held prisoner in this secret room, Rory. With Ozzie. And Rebecca. And we need you. Hurry, Rory. Come now—"

"But how do I find you?"

"The room's behind Ozzie's bookcase. Come, Rory, please—"

"I'll be right there," she blurts, hanging up and dashing toward the back door.

Halfway there, she pauses, and scurries back to yank open one of the cluttered kitchen drawers. With violently shaking hands, she rummages through the measuring spoons and shish kebab skewers until she finds what she needs.

Then she bolts out the back door into the pouring rain.

"We have to name her, Lou," Michelle says suddenly, turning her head away from the window beside her bed. The rain is coming down in sheets, driven by strong gusts of wind, and all she's been able to think is that her precious Ozzie is out there someplace, terrified, wanting his mommy.

And she's helpless to do anything about it.

If she thinks any more about that she'll go crazy, so she's trying to focus on the baby, her tiny daughter, who is curled up, asleep, in the see-through isolette at the foot of the bed.

"I know we have to name her," Lou replies from the chair by the window. He, too, has been staring desolately out at the storm.

"We should really do it soon."

"I know. The nurse asked about it earlier, and I told her we just couldn't deal with it right now But . . . we should."

Michelle sighs heavily, wincing as her stomach muscles painfully strain her incision.

Ozzie is frightened and alone. Ozzie needs her. Where is he? Or is he even alive?

A sob escapes her throat.

"Do you have any ideas?" Lou asks, looking at her, telling her with his eyes that she can't lose it now. She has to hang in there. For the baby's sake.

"Ideas?" she echoes morosely, struggling to focus. "For names?"

"For names." He nods, obviously as distracted as she is.

"No. No, I don't have any ideas." Numb, she remembers how they had laughed over the process of naming Ozzie.

"How about Rainbow, Michelle?

"Nah. Sounds too . . ."

"Feminine?"

"Yeah, and . . ."

"Flower-childish?"

"Exactly."

How long ago those giddy days of her first pregnancy seem.

"Why don't you just name her, Lou," Michelle says, turning

her head on the pillow so he won't see the tears streaming down her cheeks.

"Actually, I have a name picked out. I think you'll like it."

"What is it?" she asks hollowly, staring at the empty bed next to her, not caring.

"Joy," he says.

"Joy?"

Her mother's name.

Touched, despite her grief over Ozzie, she turns toward her husband. "It's perfect, Lou."

He nods.

"Joy," she says tentatively, looking toward her sleeping newborn daughter.

Joy . . .

Something Michelle is convinced she'll never experience again.

Russell Anghardt's steel-toed boots make a clumping sound on the steep old wooden steps leading down two flights to the secret basement room that had once been used to conceal slaves.

Very clever, the way the bookcase swings open to reveal the hidden panel hiding the entrance.

Very convenient, the way the room is outfitted with shackles, a common fixture in rooms used for the underground railroad. If anyone ever approached the secret room, the fugitive slaves would hurriedly slip into the shackles, and the people hiding them would escape hanging by claiming to have captured the runaway slaves and imprisoning them with the intent of returning them to their southern owners.

The girl illuminated in the flashlight's beam is poking along the second flight of stairs, taking much too long.

"Get down there."

She flinches at the harsh order. "I'm going. There's no railing, and I don't want to fall," she whimpers, clinging to the stone wall as she takes another step down.

"Oh, please. Do you know how many times I've had to lug things up and down these stairs? Heavy things. Like *you*. And I've never fallen. Get movin'. That sister of yours is gonna be here any second."

Might as well poke her in the back with your gun for effect, even though you have no intention of shooting her. That wouldn't be any fun. Too neat, and over too fast.

But the girl doesn't know that. All you had to do was point that gun at her, and she'd been willing to do anything you asked. Even call her sister from the upstairs phone and repeat everything you told her to say, word for word.

"Please, I'm going. Please don't shoot me."

Finally, they've reached the heavy, rough-hewn wooden door leading to the long, narrow dungeonlike room that runs along one side of the old house's foundation.

"Get inside."

"What are you going to do to Rory?"

"Shut up. Get your hands back into those shackles, Carleen."

"But I'm not—"

"Shut your mouth! Hurry up."

"Please don't hurt Rory."

"Shut up!"

The girl's jaw clamps closed and she allows herself to be securely locked into the wrist and ankle cuffs once again. But that damn bratty little kid has woken up again and is crying for his mother.

No time to silence him now.

No, I have to hurry back upstairs for our little reunion. Rory will be here any second . . . and will she ever be surprised to see me!

Rory turns the knob on the back door of the Randall house and finds it unlocked.

Strange.

Her heart is pounding as she steps into the kitchen and, after pausing only briefly, pulls the door closed behind her. Instantly, the roar of the summer storm is muffled.

The house is silent.

Rory is about to call her sister's name when she realizes that wouldn't be wise. Whoever is holding Molly prisoner might be here.

But she managed to call me.

If she could do that, get to a phone and call, why couldn't she just escape and run home?

It doesn't make sense.

But Rory can't stop to dwell on that. All she knows is that her sister had sounded petrified, and that she'd begged Rory to come.

She clutches the handle of the butcher knife in the folds of her untucked button-down shirt, moving tentatively across the kitchen floor.

Molly had said she was being held in a secret room behind Ozzie's bookcase.

That means it's in Emily's old room.

Rory opts again for the back stairs located just off the kitchen, moving up them as quietly as possible. Every time a floorboard creaks, she freezes, listening.

There's never any sound.

Whoever is holding Molly prisoner must have left the house, she tries to reassure herself. And there must be a good reason Molly could make a phone call, but not escape. Maybe she's tied up.

Then how did she dial?

Maybe just her legs are bound.

Then how did she get to a phone?

It doesn't make sense.

None of this makes sense.

But Rory can't stop to ponder the situation.

Molly needs me.

She arrives at the top of the stairs. The shadowy hallway looks empty.

She makes her way along it toward the open door to the room at the head of the stairs, knowing even as she does that this is crazy. She should have told someone where she was going. She should have told the police.

But Molly said not to bring the police. She must be worried that they'd show up with sirens wailing and storm the house. That means her captor must be nearby.

Panic builds inside her as she steps across the threshold of the little boy's bedroom. It's dimly lit by the Barney nightlight and the shaft of dismal gray light falling through the rain-splatter window.

Poised, she looks around, seeing seemingly sinister expressions on the faces of the nursery rhyme characters on the wall, finding an eeriness in the nightlight's violet glow, sensing foreboding in the bookcase with its rows of benign children's classics.

She moves toward the bookcase, noticing that it's slightly askew. Yes, one end is bumped out on an angle from the wall. With trembling hands, Rory reaches toward it and gives a tug. There's a faint scraping noise as it swings toward her to reveal a flat panel fitted into the wall.

She hesitates, staring at it, wondering why the bookcase wasn't left closed, making it impossible for someone to know about the hidden panel. It's as though someone deliberately left it ajar, wanting the secret room to be easily accessed.

Who had done it?

It must have been Molly. She would have had to come out to use the telephone, wouldn't she? *Surely there's no extension in whatever room is concealed beyond the bookcase*, Rory tells herself, finding the notion ridiculous.

And yet, this whole scenario is bizarre.

Why, if Molly had been able to come out to use the phone, would she have gone back into the room? Why wouldn't she have made a run for home?

Befuddled, Rory has no idea what to expect as she reaches out and tugs on a slightly raised edge of the panel. It comes loose, and she is able to pull the rectangular piece right out of the wall, revealing a narrow opening.

"My God," she breathes softly, staring into the blackness on the other side.

A musty smell has spilled into the room. Musty, and damp.

I should have stopped to grab a flashlight, she thinks, clutching the handle of her knife as she bends forward to stick her head into the hole.

It takes a moment for her eyes to focus. The dim light from the room behind her spills in so that she can just make out a steep, narrow staircase leading downward, shrouded in dust and cobwebs. Someplace overhead the rain beats a relentless staccato, and the wind gusts outside, rustling the trees.

I'm out of my mind, Rory realizes as she stoops and steps into the opening, then stares at the steps leading downward, disappearing into the shadows.

I can't do this. I should go back, get to a phone, call the police.

But Molly told me not to bring the police.
Molly begged me to hurry.
Her life is in danger.
She needs me, and I can't let her down.

Her breath catching in her throat, Rory begins the long, slow journey down into blackness.

"Barrett?"

He looks up from the hard cot with its stained mattress, where he's been sitting, brooding, since his lawyer left hours ago.

Now Jack is back, still looking unrumpled and crisp in his Armani suit, in marked contrast to the guard in his sweat-wilted uniform.

"Jack!" Barrett leaps up from the cot to hurry over to the bars. "Can you bail me out now?"

"Not just yet, Barrett," the lawyer says, and his spirits sink. "You're still being denied bail."

"This is ridiculous! Can't they check out my alibi? I didn't kill the guy!"

"They're looking into your alibi," Jack says in a calming tone. "But try and be patient, Barrett. This is going to be a long process. Right now, you're their prime suspect."

"Just because I asked a few questions about the guy?"

"This is a small southern town, Barrett. You're an outsider. A well-dressed Yankee comes snooping around, asking nosy questions about one of the locals, and people are going to be suspicious . . . especially when the person in question turns up brutally murdered."

"I know all that," Barrett says impatiently. "But I swear I didn't kill the guy. Besides, you said they weren't even sure it was him."

"I just came from the medical examiner's office. They've made a positive ID. That body definitely belongs to Russell Anghardt. And there's something else I found out . . ."

John Kline sighs in relief as he makes a right-hand turn off Broadway into the hotel's congested parking lot.

It's taken him over six hours to make what should have been a three- or four-hour drive to New York City from Lake Charlotte.

It's the weather, responsible for a number of accidents along the thruway, and hopelessly snarling traffic as he drew closer and closer to the city.

He's missed the morning session of the conference, he thinks, glancing at the clock on the dashboard as he reaches down to eject the cassette tape from the stereo console. But at least he finished that Michael Crichton book on tape that Nancy had bought him last Christmas. He's been trying to get through it for months, but hasn't had the opportunity to make a long drive. Normally he prefers to listen to news radio on a car trip, but Nancy had convinced him to try this instead.

"You never read anymore, John," she'd said when she handed him the box of cassette tapes on his way out the door at dawn. "Here, take this. It'll relax you."

Sure, he thinks wryly, *I'm as relaxed as a person can be after a six-hour drive on jammed, rain-slicked roads.*

He steps out of the car, grateful for the awning overhead that keeps him from getting soaked.

"Is this rain *ever* going to let up?" he asks the valet, handing over the keys.

"Doesn't look like it, sir."

John goes around to the trunk to grab his trenchcoat, briefcase, and overnight bag. If he hurries, he'll have time before the next session to check into his room and make a quick call home to tell Nancy he made it in one piece.

Molly hears the footsteps slowly approaching, one creaky step at a time.

It's Rory. She knows it's Rory.

She's walking right into the trap.

Oh, Rory, why did you have to listen to me? Couldn't you tell I was being forced to say those things? You had to know it was dangerous to come over here alone. Why would you risk your own life to do what I asked?

Molly turns her head, glances at Rebecca chained to the wall beside her, her face clearly visible in the ghostly glow of a flickering lantern. That's not all that's visible. But Molly's trying not to look at the macabre spectacle on the floor, only inches from her feet. Or at the other two occupants of the cell.

Rebecca's eyes are wide behind her glasses, filled with terror. She and Molly exchange a glance.

Don't do it, Rebecca's warns.

Believe me, I won't, Molly's assures.

They both know what will happen if Molly cries out to warn her sister.

Sick with fear, she shifts her gaze to their wild-eyed captor, and the gun being held to a whimpering Ozzie's white-blond curls.

"She's hungry," Patty, the nurse, says, carefully lifting the sobbing baby from her isolette. She turns to Michelle. "Do you want to try nursing her?"

Michelle hesitates.

"It's all right," the nurse says. "We can take her down to the nursery and they'll give her another bottle. Sometimes it's hard for a C-section patient to breast feed."

What she doesn't say is that it isn't just last night's surgery that's crippling Joy's mother, making her unable to do more than lie here staring into space.

It isn't fair to her, Michelle realizes, her baby's cries causing something to twist in her gut. Poor little thing. She's so new, and so tiny, and she needs her mommy.

She glances at Lou, still sitting in the chair by the window.

He nods at her, silently telling her that it's okay, she doesn't have to feel guilty if she allows the nurse to take the fussy baby away.

She remembers how she'd kept Ozzie with her every possible moment after he was born, gladly waking to put him to her breast every time he made the slightest whimper.

She looks at the baby again, her little face bright red with fury.

"I'll nurse her," she tells the nurse, holding out her achingly empty arms.

Rory has reached the bottom of the stairs, two treacherous, endless flights down into the depths of the house, only to reach a dead end.

There's nothing but a wall in front of her, she realizes as she runs her hands over the rough, clammy wood. Then her fingers catch on something—a cold metal ring. It isn't a wall, she realizes, pulling on the ring. It's a door.

She steps back, pulling it slowly open, her heart seeming to thunder in her ears so that she can't hear her own ragged breathing.

A spooky, flickering light spills through the opening.

It's a candle, or a lantern or something, and this is a room.

Rory peers warily inside, standing her ground, petrified of what will happen if she steps over the threshold. But she can see nothing from here, nothing but a stone wall a few feet away.

Molly.

I have to get to Molly.

It's the only thing that spurs her forward; the certain, chilling knowledge that her sister is in trouble.

She takes a step forward, and then another.

She turns her head.

"Molly?"

She gapes in horror at the sight before her.

Her sister, arms and legs shackled, chained to the stone wall in a grotesque contortion.

And beside her, Rebecca Wasner, in an identical pose . . .

She starts toward them, sobbing, "My God, who—"

"Hello, Rory. So glad you could join us."

She stops short, paralyzed at the sound of that voice.

It slams into her and instantly erases the ten years since she last heard it.

"Surprised, Rory?"

She turns then, slowly, to look into the demented eyes of Emily Anghardt.

Michelle strokes her baby's soft black fuzz, marveling at how small her head is, how perfect her features are, how hungrily she suckles at her mother's breast. There's a strange feeling of contentment stealing over her despite her anxiety over Ozzie; an age-old bond being established between mother and newborn.

She looks up to see Lou in his chair, watching her, tears in his eyes.

"I'm sorry, Michelle," he says unexpectedly. "I'm so sorry for the way I've treated you lately."

"Oh, Lou . . ."

"I've been stressed about work, and the house, and the baby coming, and I took it out on you, and I'm sorry." The words come in a rush.

Stunned, Michelle looks at her husband's agonized face and says, "My God, Lou, I thought you were having an affair . . . or worse."

"An affair?" He makes a choking sound, a laugh or a sob, and shakes his head. "Why would I have an affair?"

"I don't know, maybe because I've been driving you crazy lately, complaining about everything. God, I didn't know I had nothing to complain about then. Nothing that mattered." She's crying now, great heaving shudders that rock the baby in her arms but don't interrupt her hungry gulps.

"It's okay," Lou says, coming to stand by her, putting his hands on her shoulders. "We'll pull through this, Michelle. No matter what."

No matter what.

She knows what that means. No matter if Ozzie comes back to them safely, or if he's—

The phone on the bedside table rings.

She and Lou look at each other.

"Answer it," she tells him, filled with dread. "It might be the police. Maybe they've found him."

"Maybe," Lou says, but there's little evidence of hope in his tone or expression as he wearily picks up the receiver.

So.

According to Jack, Russell Anghardt had been arrested over a decade ago by the Grayson Cove police, for molesting his children's fourteen-year-old babysitter.

Barrett should have suspected that it would have taken something like that to drive him out of town, moving back up North with his two kids. Of course, it's been his dirty little secret all these years. Jack managed to uncover that detail by bribing some retired cop he'd run into down at the luncheonette.

It seemed that Jane Anghardt's wealthy family in Raleigh had managed to keep the news out of the papers, and had hired an expensive lawyer to get him acquitted through a legal loophole.

Russell had been estranged from his wife's family ever since her death, when Jane's parents tried to gain custody of the twins.

It seemed they were convinced that he was some kind of lowlife, and their daughter had gotten entangled with him as a form of rebellion against the polite southern society in which she'd been raised.

"They were probably right about him being a lowlife," Jack had said. "Child molester, too. But he managed to stay out of trouble after leaving North Carolina."

"Yeah, or he just didn't get caught," Barrett had said.

He and Jack had quickly pieced together the rest of the story.

How, after his acquittal, Russell Anghardt must have beat a hasty retreat out of town, taking Emily and David up North, settling in Lake Charlotte, near his hometown, where he'd been raised in a run-down orphanage. He had placed David in a home, probably to avoid the kind of conspicuous, relentless teasing the boy had endured in Grayson's Cove, and he had warned Emily not to tell any of her new friends he existed.

"Who knows what kind of abuse that poor girl suffered at the hands of her father," Jack had speculated, shaking his head sadly.

"Obviously, he's a likely candidate for chief suspect as the sick monster who kidnapped the other three girls in Lake Charlotte that summer," Barrett had said. "We've got to tell the police there what we've found out, Jack."

"I'm going to do just that."

And that's where the lawyer is, presumably, right now, while Barrett restlessly paces back and forth in his tiny cell, puzzling over the rest of the mystery. It makes sense that Russell Anghardt, an accused child molester who happened to live right on Hayes Street, would be responsible for the disappearances of those four girls ten years ago.

His own daughter—well, he must have been abusing her and just snapped, killed her, destroyed the body.

And the others . . .

Kristin Stafford had been riding her bike on the bike path along Lakeshore Road. According to her father, her tires had needed air. What if she'd gotten a flat, and decided to hike, with her bike, up the path through the woods that Barrett had realized just last week leads directly to the backyard of 54 Hayes Street? She must have fallen right into Russell Anghardt's lap.

And Allison Myers had vanished from a July Fourth picnic at Point Cedar Park, a park Barrett himself knows well. There's an entrance to the park on one end of Hayes Street; it's the park that has the playground where Carleen used to take Molly. Had Allison Myers wandered away from the crowd at the picnic? Had Russell Anghardt been lying in wait?

And what about Carleen? She used to cut through the woods on her way to meet Barrett on Lakeshore Road. He knows now she must have gone through the backyard of the house next door to get to that path. Through Russell Anghardt's yard. In the middle of the night. When she was supposed to be asleep in her bed.

Carleen Connolly hadn't vanished from her bed, as her mother had assumed. She was supposed to meet Barrett that night.

She must have been abducted by Russell Anghardt from his own backyard.

If she weren't trying to meet me, she wouldn't have disappeared, Barrett tells himself, wincing against a barrage of guilt. Guilt he's grown accustomed to. Because somewhere deep down, he has always known that Carleen hadn't vanished from her bed, and that if he hadn't run scared like a coward, he could have gone to the police with that information. Maybe it wouldn't have solved the mystery, but he should have gone.

He'll have to live with that knowledge for the rest of his life.

The one chance he has of easing the guilt even the slightest bit is to help find Molly, and Ozzie, and Rebecca. Rory must be beside herself, and the Randalls, and the Wasners.

But Barrett has no clue what could have happened to the three missing children. Russell Anghardt is dead, and, according to the medical examiner, has been for over a week.

So he couldn't have kidnapped Molly, Ozzie, and Rebecca.

Who did?

Barrett frowns, wracking his brain, desperately trying to come up with a likely suspect and drawing a blank.

I was right.

It's the first thought that flits into Rory's head as she gapes into the unmistakable face of the girl who had once been her best friend.

Emily is still alive.

And . . .

Her mother was right, too. Her mother might be fading into insanity, but she still has her lucid moments.

When she told me she saw Emily, she wasn't hallucinating. Oh, God, Mom . . . I'm sorry. I'm sorry I dismissed you so flippantly.

You were right, Mom.

Emily is really here.

But . . .

Emily?

Emily's the one who's responsible for this?

And gradually, as she stares at her, and time seems to have dragged to a halt, Rory vaguely notes details. Peculiar, garish details.

Like the oversized plaid flannel shirt she's wearing in the heat summer.

The tweedy cap, the old-fashioned kind with the visor and ear flaps, a few strands of long blond hair escaping it.

And, on her feet, a big pair of men's work boots.

The kind of boots her father always wore. And that hat, and the shirt . . .

"Emily?" She finally finds her voice, staring at her friend with a potent mix of apprehension and utter confusion.

"Emily's dead" comes the reply, barked in an unnaturally low, gruff tone.

Bewildered, Rory can only stare, now taking in the gun in Emily's hand, and the terrified little boy she's aiming at.

Ozzie Randall, his face dirty and tear-streaked, is huddled on the dirt floor at Emily's feet, clad in pajamas, his little arms and legs bound with rope. He's the picture of misery, his body wracked with silent shudders, what little sound that escapes his throat sounding hoarse, as though from hours of crying.

Her gaze moves past Ozzie, back to Molly, and she realizes, with a start, that Molly is wearing a black minidress that had once belonged to Carleen, and one of Carleen's old headbands around her black curls, and a pair of big, dangling earrings.

Molly looks just like Carleen, she realizes. *What is she doing in Carleen's clothes?*

And what is Emily doing dressed up like her father?

None of this makes sense.

She turns back to Emily, acutely aware of the gun in her hand, the gun that's pointing at the frightened two-year-old. She knows she has to do something, fast, before something tragic happens. Her hand tightens around the handle of the knife still concealed in the folds of her shirt.

"What are you doing here?" she asks Emily.

"One guess," Emily says with a brittle laugh. "I was homesick, so I came back to Lake Charlotte."

"When?"

"Oh, a couple of weeks ago, I guess."

"You've been hiding in this house all that time, Emily?"

"I told you, I'm not Emily!"

"I'm sorry . . . Mr. Anghardt," she adds tentatively, and sees a satisfied expression on Emily's face.

"Are you ready to die, now, Rory?"

Chilled, she struggles not to betray her horror at those words, spoken so casually.

"Die? Why do you want me to die, Mr. Anghardt?"

"For Emily's sake. Because she tried to tell you . . . she tried to make you see what was happenin' to her. And you ignored it."

"What, though? What did I ignore?"

Just keep her talking, Rory tells herself. *Wait for a moment to catch her off guard, and then make your move with the knife. Go for her eyes. Gouge out her eyes.*

Oh, God.

Can I do this?

She glances at Ozzie, at Rebecca, and finally at Molly. Their lives are hanging in the balance. She *has* to do it.

"You ignored the clues!" Emily barks. "You ignored Emily's clues. She knew for sure that you'd figure it out."

"Figure *what* out?" Rory's hand tightens around the knife handle.

"What I was doin' to her. All the time. Whenever I felt like it."

"Oh, God." Rory stares at Emily's face in horror.

"I made her my own little sex slave," Emily says with a bitter laugh. "And then, she wasn't enough for me. Started fightin' me. Threatened to tell someone. So I found others. I kept them right down here, chained to that very wall, and no one ever knew. Not even Emily. This door is soundproof. Nobody ever even heard them screamin'."

Rory struggles to digest what Emily is saying, her mind racing, her knife poised.

She's talking about Carleen, Rory realizes. Carleen, and Kristin Stafford, and Allison Myers. Russell Anghardt abducted them, kept them in this dungeon, made them . . .

She feels weak. Like she's going to pass out.

I can't. I have to stay strong. Steady. Wait for the right moment.

"So Emily never knew?" she forces herself to ask, as though this is the most ordinary of conversations. Two old friends catching up.

She doesn't dare look at Molly, or anywhere but Emily's face. She's afraid that the moment she breaks the connection, Emily will stop talking.

And kill me.

"No, Emily didn't know. Not for a long time. Not until one night, when I got careless sneakin' into her room—the bookcase is in her room, you know. But she never knew about the secret door. I never told her . . . not until she woke up and found me openin' it that night. That's when I told her the whole story. How I stumbled across it accidentally, not long after I bought the house. Who knew this fallin'-down old house was hiding such a treasure? I bought it so cheap, Rory, from that old lady . . ."

Mrs. Prendergrast.

". . . and when I found this room, I knew it was a sign. I knew what I had to do, because it was so obvious, so perfectly obvious. A man has needs. A man can only fight his needs for so long. That's what I told Emily. I had needs, Rory. And she should understand. It was her duty to fulfill them, because if it wasn't for her, her mother would have been there to do it instead. But Emily killed her mother, Rory. Emily and her brother did it, just by bein' born. It wasn't my fault that Jane was gone, and I had to find other ways to fulfill my needs."

This is insane, Rory tells herself. *She's insane. She's taken on her father's personality.*

It sounds eerily as if Russell Anghardt is actually talking. Emily's voice is deep, and has that same faint southern twang she remembers hearing on the few occasions when Emily's father would speak more than a word or two.

He'd seemed so quiet. So insignificant. How could Rory never have realized that he was such a monster? How could she never have known of the danger that Emily was in?

And now she's going to make me pay the ultimate price for being so blind, she realizes with sickening certainty.

"What happened when you showed Emily the room, Mr. Anghardt?"

"Oh, she was all worked up. She knew those girls, you know . . . my beautiful slaves. One of 'em was already dead, though. I had to kill her, to shut her up. She was a screamer, that one. The first one. Kept cryin' for her mommy. So I shut her up good."

Thirteen year-old Kristin Stafford.

"Emily begged me to let the other ones go, though. She even tried to attack me—picked up a sledgehammer I kept down here, just in case somebody got out of control, and she hit me with it. Hit me in the leg. And when I tried to come after her, she took off. Just took off, just like that."

"Where did she go?"

"She wandered around from place to place. Did what she had to do, to make enough money to survive. It wasn't any different from what I used to make her do, 'cept now it was with strangers. And she wasn't a bad person, Rory. She never lost touch with that brother of hers, even though I used to tell her not to bother with him. If it wasn't for appearance' sake, I'd 'a never even bothered to take him out of that home for a visit."

"So Emily visited David over the years?"

"Sure. She'd dress up like a nun, so no one would ever know. It was her little joke. David always called her 'sister' anyway."

Rory keeps her expression neutral despite her startled realization that she'd guessed right about Emily's motive for disguising herself as a nun to visit St. Malachy's.

"And Emily never visited you for all those years, Mr. Anghardt?"

"Nah. But I knew she knew where I was. Back home, in North Carolina. I figured she'd eventually come look for me there. Because I was her daddy, no matter what happened between us. I knew she'd come back."

"And she did?"

"Sure did. Just a few weeks ago. Showed up on my doorstep out of the blue. First thing she noticed was that I had a limp from where she hit me. And you know what? I think that made her feel good."

Rory nods, willing Emily to break the relentless gaze she's focused on Rory, to look away, even for a second. Just long enough for Rory to attack her.

"At first, you know, when she showed up on my door, Emily acted like she was there for a friendly visit. But then I realized that wasn't it at all. You see, for all these years, Emily's been mad at me. Gettin' madder and madder. Rememberin' what went on between us. What I did to those other girls. Guess she decided she wanted to get me back."

There's a faraway gaze in Emily's eyes now, but they're still focused on Rory's face. If she makes the slightest move, Emily will notice.

"What did she do?"

"Attacked me. Tried to kill me." The voice is indignant now. "But I won. I wasn't goin' to let her get me. No, sir."

"So you left North Carolina, then? And came here?"

"Yup. It was easy to sneak back into this house. Those old screens . . . you just climb right in. And those people who live here now, they don't know about the bookcase. Nobody ever knew, but me and Emily. And, of course, those girls. But that don't matter now."

"Why not?" Rory asks, filled with dread, knowing the answer even before Russell Anghardt points.

She follows the direction of her gaze, and sees the three grotesque corpses crumpled on the ground not far from Molly and Rebecca's feet. And she knows, without being told, who they belong to.

Kristin Stafford.

Allison Myers.

And Carleen.

A wave of dizziness sweeps over her, and she senses she's going to faint.

But she can't let that happen.

If she faints, she'll never wake up.

This is my chance—she's looking away!

The sudden realization stuns her momentarily, and then, knowing that it's now or never, she leaps on Emily Anghardt.

"No!" the woman screams.

Knock the gun out of her hand! Rory commands herself, and does it with ease, taking advantage of the moment Emily let her guard down.

Then they're rolling on the floor, scuffling, Rory struggling to hold on to the knife, to position it for attack.

"No!" Emily shrieks again, and then there's a blinding pain as she raises her knee into Rory's stomach.

Blinding pain.

Utter shock at the severity of the pain.

And in that moment, with a savage tug, Emily wrenches the knife from Rory's fingers and wields it above her head.

In his North Carolina jail cell, Barrett waits, pacing, for Jack's return.

He can't stop thinking about the Connolly family.

About Rory, in particular.

How much pain can one person endure?

First she lost one sister . . .

Now another?

And it's all my fault, Rory, Barrett says silently. *If I had gone to the police, told them what I knew about Carleen's whereabouts that night, they might have figured it out.*

He stops to rub his exhausted eyes, struggling to grasp any possible clue to the identity of the person who kidnapped Molly and Ozzie and Rebecca.

It can't be Russell Anghardt.

Russell Anghardt is dead.

But who killed him . . . and why?

Barrett slams his hand into the unforgiving stone wall of the cell in sheer frustration, utterly baffled.

* * *

"You shouldn't 'a done that, Rory."

Her head is jerked back painfully by her hair, and she stares into the crazed eyes of Emily Anghardt. Then she feels the cool blade of the butcher knife pressing against her throat. If she moves, if she swallows, if she breathes, the blade will slice into her skin.

Please let it be quick, she prays.

She can hear Molly sobbing from somewhere nearby, and Rebecca, and Ozzie, too. The cell is filled with terrified cries, and all Rory can think is that they're going to have to watch this, watch Emily slit her throat right in front of them. And then what will happen? Who will be next?

"Say good-bye to little Ozzie, Rory," Emily says, laughing, pressing the knife, ever so slightly, into her skin.

Rory feels a stinging pain; still she holds her breath.

The knife is dull, she remembers. It had probably been in that drawer for years, with nobody using it. Maybe it isn't sharp enough to—

"Say good-bye to Rebecca."

More pressure from the knife.

More pain.

Rory remembers how she'd cut her hand only last night on the blade, how she'd bled.

She braces herself.

Closes her eyes.

Begins praying the Hail Mary.

"Say good-bye to Carleen."

Rory's eyes fly open.

Carleen?

What's Emily talking about?

"Where's Carleen?" she asks, trying not to move as she speaks, even as she realizes what Emily is talking about.

"What do you mean, where is she?" Emily sounds irritated.

Rory's ears catch a faint, distant sound.

"Are you *blind*? Carleen's right over there," Emily says. "You know, I thought for sure she was dead for all these years. When I caught her sneakin' across our yard in the dead of night all those years ago, I knew she'd have to pay. Trespassin' isn't right, is it? So I brought her inside, and I kept her there for a while, with the others. Then I thought Í killed her—I left her here to die, you know, with the rest of 'em, when I moved out of this house. But she didn't die. How do you figure she got away? I almost fell over when I saw her come through that bedroom door last night—"

Emily turns her head toward Molly, shackled to the wall, looking exactly like Carleen in that dress, those earrings, that hairband.

This time, Rory doesn't hesitate.

She writhes out of Emily's grasp, and, once again, they're scuffling on the floor, fighting for the knife, each one's hands wrapped around the handle, vying for control.

As she struggles with Emily, she's vaguely aware of noises overhead.

"Help! Help!"

It's Molly, shrieking.

Rebecca joins in.

"Help! We're down here! Hurry!"

In a haze, Rory remembers that she'd left the bookcase ajar. Maybe somebody is in the house, and noticed it.

Yes!

She hears pounding footsteps.

"You bitch!" Emily is on top of her, suddenly, and has the knife against Rory's throat again.

Rory's hand is closed over Emily's on the handle, and she's using every bit of might to keep Emily from pressing that dull blade into her neck again, and she knows she can't hold on much longer.

Just as her strength is giving out, the footsteps burst into the room.

A moment later there's a sharp, deafening explosion of sound.

She feels Emily collapse on top of her, erupting into agonized shrieks; she tastes the unmistakable, tinny salt of blood in her mouth.

It takes her a few moments to realize, amidst the commotion in the room, that it's Emily's blood; that the sound was a gunshot; that the police have stormed the room.

Emily is pulled off of Rory, still screaming "I've been shot! My God, I've been shot."

Dazed, Rory allows Detective Mullen to help her sit up, hears him asking if she's all right, but can't muster a reply.

She sees Ozzie, sobbing, cradled in one officer's arms as another works to release Rebecca from the cuffs around her wrists.

Molly is waiting her turn, watching Ozzie with concern, and then her worried gaze shifts to Rory.

"Let me help you up. Can you stand?" Detective Mullen asks above Emily's distraught shrieks and Ozzie's frightened cries.

Still Rory can't find her voice.

Her eyes are locked on Molly's as the detective gently pulls her to her feet, asking if she's been injured.

She shakes her head, numb.

"Rory, your neck," Molly says, tears glistening in her blue eyes. "You're bleeding. She cut you."

"Hmm?" She looks down, sees her own blood staining the open collar of her shirt, dripping onto the locket she's never taken off.

"It doesn't look like a deep cut. Paramedics are on the way," Detective Mullen tells her. "They'll take care of you, Rory. And I'll need to talk to you, of course . . . but it can wait until later."

"How . . . how did you know where to find us?"

"Because of Michelle Randall's cousin, John. He's an architect. He had taken measurements of the house recently, and knew there must be a hidden room. He thought nothing of it at the time, just left a message for Michelle to call him."

Rory nods, remembering the phone message in Molly's handwriting on the kitchen counter.

"Anyway," Detective Mullen goes on, "John was in New York on business today and didn't find out what was going on here until a little while ago. When he called his wife and she told him about Molly and Ozzie disappearing from this house, he realized what might be going on and called Michelle and Lou at the hospital right away. Lou knew exactly where the opening would be—he'd noticed one day recently that the bookcase in Ozzie's room seemed askew, but had been too busy to take a look at it. And Michelle had been hearing strange noises coming from her son's room."

"Thank God . . . thank God you got here in time," Rory tells the detective.

He smiles and touches her arm. "Are you sure you're okay, Rory?"

She nods, takes a step as he turns away, then stops, her knees wobbling.

"Molly," she asks her sister, "are you all right?"

"I'm fine. Just shaken up. Rory, if you hadn't come, she would have—"

"I know." She heaves a shuddering breath as more footsteps pound down the stairs.

"Ozzie? My God, Ozzie?"

Lou Randall bursts into the room, glances around wildly, spots the little boy, and sobs, "Oh, God, thank God!" He takes his son from the officer's outstretched arms, holding him close, saying his name over and over again, as Ozzie whimpers, "Daddy! Daddy!"

Feeling like she's watching a surreal scene from a movie, Rory looks back at Molly, but her sister is obscured behind the officers who are now working to free her from her bonds.

Across the room, Detective Mullen is winding a makeshift tourniquet around Emily's bleeding arm, and someone else is reciting the Miranda.

Tears are stinging Rory's eyes now. She takes a tentative step, and then another, toward the skeletal remains on the floor, pushing past the detectives crouched beside them, knowing what she'll see even before she spots it.

There.

It's clearly visible around the neck of one corpse.

A locket, identical to her own.

Her father's voice echoes in her ears.

Never take them off. They will remind you that you're sisters, a part of each other forever. Someday, you'll be best friends. You're lucky to have each other.

One of the officers puts a hand on her arm, pulls her back, murmurs something about not disturbing the bodies.

Tears stream down her cheeks, enormous sobs wracking her body as she absorbs the terrible, undeniable truth. The loss is crippling; somehow sudden, yet long delayed.

And now she knows.

After so many years of wondering, and praying, and hoping.

Now she knows.

Carleen is dead.

You're sisters, a part of each other forever . . .

"Rory?"

She turns at the sound of her name.

Molly's standing there, freed from her shackles, looking pale and unnerved . . . and small. And alone.

"Rory?" Her voice is quaking. "I'm so sorry I made you come here. She made me—"

"I know, Molly. God, I know." She opens her arms, and her little sister steps into them, and then they're both sobbing, and clinging to each other, and Molly is thanking her, over and over.

"Let's get out of here," Molly says at last, pulling back and looking around with a shudder.

"Okay," Rory agrees, squeezing her hand. "Let's go home."

EPILOGUE

"**M**olly? Are you almost ready?"

"God, Rory, cut me a break! I'll be right down, okay?"

Rory's eyes meet Barrett's, and they both smile.

"Thirteen-year-old sisters," she informs him, "can be a real pain in the—"

"Relax, Rory. She's making herself beautiful. Can you blame her? We're going to the fanciest restaurant in town."

"I still think we should have chosen someplace less . . ."

"Expensive," Barrett asks, reading her mind. "I know you do. After all, you're a real starving artist now," he adds, with a glance at the easel Rory set up in the living room, her unofficial "studio."

"But I told you, Rory, it'll be my treat."

"And money is no object for you. Do you have to rub it in?" Rory asks with a grin. "Must be nice to be filthy rich."

"Oh, believe me, it is." Barrett raises an eyebrow at her. "Maybe someday you'll find out."

Her stomach flutters at the suggestive look on his face, even though she knows it's soon . . . much too soon to be thinking about settling down with him.

Then again, she's already made the decision to stay here in Lake Charlotte . . . at least for a while.

And so has Barrett, having spent the rest of the summer and all of September staying in a house he rented in town, working on his book.

It's October now.

Out on Hayes Street, the leaves are dazzling reds and pinks and oranges and golds, and there's a perpetual hint of woodsmoke in the crisp air. Mrs. Shilling has temporarily closed down her bed and breakfast and gone to visit her son Bucky down in Austin. Cheryl Wasner's chrysanthemums are in full bloom, and there's an artful display of pumpkins and cornstalks on their porch. And out on the sidewalk in front of the Randalls' house, every night after supper, Ozzie has been learning to ride his new red tricycle with his father's help, as Michelle and his baby sister, Joy, look on from the front steps.

"Rory? Does this look all right?"

She looks up to see her mother walking slowly down the stairs.

"Mom! You changed your mind! You're coming with us?"

"If it's not too late to invite myself along," Maura says, clinging tightly to the bannister as she descends. "And if you think I look presentable."

Her mother's hair is neatly combed, and there's even a touch of lipstick and mascara to enhance her striking features. She's wearing the simply cut navy wool dress and matching pumps that Rory bought her on a recent, memorable shopping trip, with a disapproving Sister Theodosia in tow.

"You look beautiful, Mom," Rory says truthfully. "Did you remember to take your medication?"

Maura nods.

She usually does remember, lately—no longer needing to hide in the fog of her mental illness. She still has bad days, though they're fewer and farther between as time goes on: days when she forgets, for a while, that Rory lives here now, and Kevin has moved into a place of his own in Saratoga, and Carleen . . .

Carleen is never coming home.

Rory spared her mother the vile details of Carleen's imprisonment and death, not wanting her to be tortured by knowing how her beloved firstborn had suffered. Rory still can't quite grasp that Carleen had been so close to home the whole time—left to die a slow, agonizing death, abandoned by Russell Anghardt in the dungeon beneath the house next door.

Carleen was laid to rest at last after the medical examiner released her remains to the family in July. Her grave is in the cemetery behind Holy Father Church, beside the simple stone marker where Patrick Connolly is buried.

And somehow, seeing her father and sister united in death,

Rory had felt the sense of closure that enabled her long-delayed healing process to begin.

Visiting David Anghardt again had helped, too. This time, she had brought him some chocolate-covered raisins, and she had spent the entire day with him. She'd helped him string big wooden beads and sung songs, and had talked to him, rewarded when he smiled at the end of the day and tried to say her name. Choked up, she had promised him she'd be back soon. She hadn't mentioned his sister; Lydia McGovern had said that she'd decided it would be better if she didn't.

"He's really going to miss seeing her," the director had said sadly. "It's hard to believe that someone who loved her brother as much as she did could have been capable of such heinous crimes."

"She was her father's first victim," Rory pointed out. "It doesn't make what she did any more tolerable, but I can understand how she got lost in her own tragic world."

After so many years of living under horrific circumstances— first in her father's house, then on the streets—Emily must have just snapped. When she went to confront her father, she flew into a rage and killed him. Then, aghast at what she had done, she had gone over the edge into madness.

"But why on earth was she wearing her father's clothes, thinking she was him?" she'd wondered aloud to Barrett, bewildered, knowing she'd never shake the haunting memory of Emily's creepy portrayal of Russell Anghardt.

"It was her response to the overwhelming realization that she'd killed him. An escape, maybe, or a way of keeping him alive. Didn't you ever see *Psycho*, with kooky Norman Bates impersonating his dead mother?" Barrett had asked, and Rory had shuddered.

Now Emily is in a federal prison on kidnapping charges, and her lawyers are trying to prove her mentally unfit to stand trial. Either way, she'll never be free again.

And Rory has vowed to keep visiting David Anghardt.

"Are Kevin and Katherine meeting us there?" Barrett asks, checking his watch.

Rory nods. "They're probably waiting already. Come on, Molly, move it!"

"All right, already. I'm coming!"

A door bangs open upstairs, and, moments later, Molly appears at the head of the stairs. She's wearing a red dress that shows off curves Rory didn't realize she has, and teetering in a pair of too-high heels.

"Careful," Rory and her mother say simultaneously, then look at each other and smile.

Molly rolls her eyes.

Barrett says, "Are you ready? Because Kevin and Katherine are waiting. And Travis will be there, too, by now."

"I'm ready," Molly says, walking down the stairs on wobbly feet, clinging to the railing.

Rory wants to tell her to go change into a pair of flats, but she holds her tongue. She knows how she would have reacted if Carleen had said something like that, in that annoying, superior, big-sister tone of hers.

She waits for Molly to descend the stairs as Barrett and her mother start out to the car.

"Are you nervous?" she asks her sister in a low voice when Molly reaches the bottom step.

Tonight's meeting with Travis is all Molly's talked about for days. She's finally ready to meet her father—the man who has spent the last thirteen years living in Boston, wondering about her, so concerned that he'd hired a private detective to keep tabs on her, to make sure she was all right.

It had taken awhile for Molly to agree to see him.

After all, it hadn't been easy for her, for any of them, to accept that he had been much older than Carleen, and married, when they became involved. Travis was an instructor at a nearby college, and, as he'd told Rory, his marriage was already in trouble when he met Carleen, who passed herself off as twenty-one with no problem. It wasn't until she came to him and told him she was pregnant that he'd discovered the truth.

Stunned and horrified, he'd asked her if she was sure the baby was his—and she'd flown off the handle. Stormed away, refusing to speak to him, though he tried to get in touch with her afterward, wanting to own up to his responsibility.

The next thing he knew, she'd moved to California with her family, and his marriage was falling apart. So he'd gone to Boston to make a fresh start, and managed to pull his life together over the years. He's teaching at Harvard, he told Rory, and is getting married again over the holidays.

"But I want to be a part of Molly's life," he'd said earnestly. "If she'll let me."

For a while, Rory hadn't thought Molly would.

With a stubborn streak that would have done her mother proud, Molly had refused to see him when he turned up in town the day of her rescue—but then, she was still shell-shocked from the trauma of what she'd been through.

Gradually, though, as summer turned to fall, Molly had shown a growing interest in the letters and gifts Travis had been sending to her.

And now, finally, she's agreed to let him come back to Lake Charlotte on Columbus Day weekend. In just a short while, she'll meet him face to face.

"Am I nervous?" she echoes Rory's question. "No! God, why would I be— Whoops!"

Molly's ankle turns on the step and she starts to fall forward.

Rory reaches out and catches her, holding her steady.

"You okay?"

"Yeah . . . thanks," Molly adds, looking sheepish. "You saved me."

Rory shrugs. "What are sisters for?"

And together, they walk out into the night.